SIGN of the
SLAYER

SIGN of the SLAYER

SHARINA HARRIS

Entangled Publishing, LLC
644 Shrewsbury Commons Ave., STE 181
Shrewsbury, PA 17361
rights@entangledpublishing.com

Entangled Teen is an imprint of Entangled Publishing, LLC.

Visit our website at www.entangledpublishing.com.

Edited by Liz Pelletier and Lydia Sharp
Cover illustration and design by Elizabeth Turner Stokes
and LJ Anderson, Mayhem Cover Creations
Stock art by MagicPics/gettyimages
Interior design by Toni Kerr

ISBN 978-1-64937-331-1
Ebook ISBN 978-1-64937-338-0

Manufactured in the United States of America

First Edition August 2023

10 9 8 7 6 5 4 3 2 1

To those who feel like their dreams are ridiculous and out of reach…they aren't. Let this be your confirmation to keep going. Don't let anyone dim your light.

At Entangled, we want our readers to be well-informed. If you would like to know if this book contains any elements that might be of concern for you, please check the back of the book for details.

The Baddest Band in All the Land
Raven

C an a human take part in photosynthesis?

I mean, I *am* an organism, standing still at attention, grass beneath my feet. The sun's gone down, but the bright stadium lights burn through the darkness of the football stadium. And with all that light and my sweat dripping to the ground, then yeah… I'd say I'm an unwilling part of photosynthesis. Not to mention there's fifty-three of us band members, so I'm pretty sure our collective buckets of sweat are quenching this dull green grass' thirst.

The crowd is rowdy—a deafening blend of claps, chants, and taunts—but today it seems like a crowd of giants clapping with supersize hands, roaring in booming voices. It's like the ground has opened, and I'm flailing in a sea of noise. I pull in a breath through my nose, release out my mouth, and count to ten.

Saxophone tucked in the crook of my arm, I cradle my Yamaha like it's a newborn baby. Tonight, my instrument feels as heavy as Plymouth Rock. My forearm shakes under the strain.

Get it together, girl.

I don't get it together. I can't. My body doesn't feel like it's my own. It's like I've been spread out and rolled over with a rolling pin.

My skin tingles and twitches at the slightest ruffle from the starched band suit. Even the neck strap feels like rope burn as it twists, rubs, and digs into my skin.

Still, I don't break the line.

If I move, I might as well be dead.

Okay, so I've been told I'm a drama queen. To my knowledge, no one's ever died from a band director's baton, although Dr. Jeffries, the band director, is infamous for tossing his conducting wand like a ninja star when someone doesn't know the music. No, any potential death would be out of embarrassment, because breaking the line would be due to a mistake.

My mistake.

And I never ever make mistakes in public. If I do, I lose my cool, and if I lose my cool, *again*, well... I can't imagine what the State will do to an eighteen-year-old Black girl. They already proved what they could do to a twelve-year-old with a short fuse.

The football players sprint past the band, running much more enthusiastically than they were five minutes ago, when they fumbled the ball and allowed the other team to score.

"Get off the field with ya tired asses," someone yells from the stands.

The fans clap, slow and frustrated. Our football team, well... sucks.

Our band, however, does not.

We won the competitions and gained national recognition despite our small-but-mighty band, which is why we have brand spanking new uniforms and a charter bus (not that we use it on the regular—but since we're playing our rivals, we have no choice but to stunt on them). No one gives a damn about the football players or the fifty-year-old rivalry between the Alpine Rattlesnakes and the Texan Wildcats.

For the first time since the game started, I smirk, though no one can see it under the shiny black top hat. My smile drops when I hear the announcer's voice echo over the PA system.

You know the famous guy who does the epic voice-overs for movie trailers in Hollywood? Well, the announcers for small towns in Texas, with way too much time on their hands, are a mixture of that guy plus a choir director who's trying to outdo the lead singer. You know Kirk Franklin's name but not one vocalist, right?

"Ladies and gentlemen! We know what you've been waiting for. You're here to see the baddest band in the entire state of Texas. No, the entire *world*. There is no equal! Don't believe me? Tap your neighbor. Ask ya mama and feast your eyes on the incredible…the splendid…the excellent…and the resplendent Harbor View High School Marching Rattlesnakes!"

While our announcer hypes up the crowd for the half-time show, our two drum majors, with batons in hand, march toward the middle of the field.

The head drum major whistles a long-short sequence followed by four short whistles.

The whistle is just what I need to snap out of my funk and focus. Our drummers slap the snares, setting the rhythm of our marching cadence.

I alternate each knee in a high step and march until I reach the middle of the field. As the section leader, I train, drill, and lead the sax players. Our section isn't what gets the crowd hyped—that would be the drum line or the trumpets—yet I feel someone's stare.

Girl, no one's staring at you.

I give a hard eye roll to my paranoia but check my peripheral anyway and roll my eyes again when I discover the culprit. All that heat is coming from Kendall, the dethroned, disgruntled *former* section leader.

He wants me to trip, to fail, to have a slight imperfection in my lines and placements. I had surprised him, along with many others, when I beat out the two-years-running section leader for first chair during summer camp.

The drummers speed up the tempo, and we transform our

slow, dramatic steps into a sprint until we reach our marks. I pivot on my heels, doing an about-face, and stand at attention—waiting for the rest of my section, as well as the other horns, to follow suit.

That jerk Kendall is a foot off his mark. He's too close to me, and he knows it. Thoughts of kicking him in his polyester-clad ass tempt me, but I lift my sax to my mouth, blaring the first notes to "Crazy in Love." When the drummers drop the beat, I crisscross my legs and dip into a hip roll.

The crowd cheers when they recognize the song. Ever since Beyoncé's *Homecoming* performance at Coachella, everybody and their mamas have been doing some offshoot of the routine. Ours is the best rendition, of course.

The Dancing Dolls, in their skintight gold-and-blue leotards, slink sexily past me and my frumpy-ass black, blue, and gold suit. With their long legs encased in shiny brown-gold stockings, they kick high in the air and form a U-shape around the drum majors. As gorgeous as they are, the Dancing Dolls are not the main attraction. The drum majors are, and they do not disappoint as they eat up the dance routine with their gold staffs, bending over backward until their tall hats brush the ground. Then they pop up, throw their batons into the air, catch them, and shimmy low to the ground.

We finally end the show with an original song Dr. Jeffries composed. It's giving old-school Earth, Wind & Fire vibes as we high-step off the field. We keep marching until we reach the edge of the rubber track that surrounds the football field.

Once the coast is clear, I slump my shoulders forward, pull off the mouthpiece from my sax, and slide it inside the horn so I won't crack my reed again.

"Kendall!" I yell at his back. He turns and pulls off his hat.

"What now, Raven?"

"You know you were standing too close to me." I grind my teeth, preparing for the lecture—no, the curse words Dr. Jeffries will shout once he watches the film. It doesn't matter if Kendall screwed up; as the section leader, all mistakes by my crew fall on me.

Our saxophone squad forms a tight circle around us, moving us away from the track. We're a team, and even now, as the top two players argue, they try to keep our business in-house. Usually, I ignore Kendall's crap, but this is the third time he's done this to me, so I can't let that shit slide. Despite our tight circle, Deidra, my best friend and a piccolo player, pushes into the center.

"Who invited the white girl?" Jonathan, one of the sax players, says from behind me.

"Hush, Jonathan." I shush him.

Deidra is one of two white band members. We're always tied at the hip. And when Grandma Lou took us on a rare road trip to see Prairie View A&M University perform at the Battle of the Bands in Atlanta, I knew I wanted to march in the band when I go to college next year. I've practiced my ass off to prepare for the scholarship tryouts next February. I assumed Deidra would PWI it, aka go to a predominantly white college. She was like, nah. She's applied to Prairie View, and if she gets accepted, I know she'll ace band tryouts.

"What are you doing here, Mouse?" Kendall taunts. A few of the players chuckle as Deidra's face blushes beet red. She earned the nickname because occasionally her second-hand piccolo squeaks like a mouse. That stupid name bothers her because her family can't afford a better model.

When I inch closer to Kendall, Deidra pulls me back by my shoulder. "What happened?"

"Kendall happened. Twice during the routine, he was off his mark."

Cam, a junior saxophone player, lets out a groan. "Aww, c'mon, man. You know Dr. Jeffries will chew out the whole damn section." He slaps Kendall's chest with the back of his hand. "You gotta stop doing this, my man."

Kendall rolls his eyes. "You buggin'. You know I hit all my spots. On and off the field."

Gross.

"First of all, lying is a sin, and you're doing it on both accounts." I point my finger at him. "Besides, we'll all see it next week when we review the performance."

He shrugs, hugging his saxophone to his chest. "Maybe I wasn't off my marker. Maybe *you* were standing too close to me, Boonies. Did you think about that? Anyway, we'll see what Dr. J. says."

Cam shakes his head. "He'll see the truth, my man."

"You serious right now?" Kendall's voice kicks high. "You're so far up Raven's ass, you'll agree to anything she says."

I sigh. I should've known my summer fling with Cam would bite me in the aforementioned body part. He's taller than me, and at five foot eight, it's slim pickings to find a tall, good-looking dude with a decent personality and top-notch breath. The breath is a nonnegotiable for me.

Anyway, the thing with Cam started because I was kinda...I don't know, depressed over the summer. Like I was missing someone, which is ridiculous. Deidra thinks it's because I'm mourning my mom and grandfather, but they died long ago. How can I miss people I don't even remember?

Cam looks me up and down, and I know he remembers that one night. Thank God for the ugly hat and fugly uniform—otherwise, he could see the full-body blush, even with my dark brown skin.

Cam flexes his jaw, clenches his fist, and I can tell he wants to punch Kendall for bringing up the past. "Raven and I are friends, man."

"Yeah, and you want to be more than friends, but your girl got all stuck up once she became section leader." Kendall strokes his mustache, his stringy and patchy pride and joy. "Shit like that didn't happen when I was section leader."

"Sorry, my man. You ain't got the lips or the hips," Cam says, and the rest of the section chuckles.

"No, but I was a good leader." Kendall looks me up and down. "Dr. J will see through you, sooner or later."

I usually don't get mad so easily, but heat gathers in the pit of my stomach, slowly rising to my head. And when the heat of my anger hits my face, it's a wrap—for me and for him—so I've got to shut this down before my anger explodes.

He's not worth the stares or the trouble. I raise my hand and put it in front of Kendall's face like it's a stop sign. "Whatever. Do you. Being mediocre is on brand for you, anyway." I stomp away, back toward the bus.

Deidra, I assume, follows close on my heels. I'm halfway across the field when she grabs my wrist, and I spin around, ready to blow. She knows not to touch me when I'm mad.

But it isn't her. It's Kendall. My skin boils, and I can feel the heat rising from my skin.

"What?" I snap.

"One of my homeboys warned me about you."

I bite my lip. Kendall moved to our little gem of a town in Harbor Hills, Texas, freshman year, so he wasn't around to witness my fall from grace. Still, we live in a small town where people— especially boys and old ladies—love to gossip. No, not a surprise at all that he would have heard about it—more so that he *just* brought it up.

Still, my legs shake.

"Told you what?" My voice is as shaky as my legs.

"That you've got a bad temper and you got locked up at a detention center. You out here frontin' like you didn't go all crazy on that dude."

"She crazy. She crazy. Just like her grandma!"

"Check you out, gossipin' like a biddy." My voice freezes the atmosphere. Darkness gathers in my vision. I try to blink it back, but it rolls in like quick-moving clouds before a storm.

"Don't get too close to her... You know she lost her mind."

I grab his suspenders, get close, and whisper, "Figures that you tell tales like an old lady... You already march like one."

"What the hell is up with you?" Kendall tries to peel my hands off his uniform. My hold is so tight, the stitches stretch and nearly rip apart.

A smell wafts between us, a potent combination of urine and days-old roadkill. It's like... It's like I can smell his fear.

"What's wrong?" I taunt. "Afraid the rumors are true? That I'll—"

"Raven." Deidra grabs my hand and tugs on my elbow. "Let's go. He's so not worth it."

Her words roll the darkness away. I release him, shaking my hands and my head of the strange scent.

A few others from my section jog over. "Damn." I look at Deidra, worried they witnessed my slip-up.

She seems to understand my silent anxiety. She shakes her head and mouths, "You're good."

I exhale, long and slow. I'm glad they didn't notice when I nearly lost control. Usually, when anyone stepped to me, I'd crack a joke and embarrass the hell out of them. Not today. Kendall had exposed a nerve—something I'd hidden for six years—and he hadn't just plucked it, he'd sawed at it with razor blades.

Kendall stares at me, just like how the other kids used to do in middle school. My heart drops. No.

No.

I worked too hard to create a new me. I pressed my emotions down so hard and tight, it's like I stuffed all my real feelings in a vacuum-sealed bag. I'm not going to let this fool undo all of that.

I look at Deidra. "Let's go get our snacks from the bus," I

say, then glance at Kendall. "Sorry I scared you." I put a hard emphasis on the word *scared* as I stare at him, daring him to voice his fears.

"Ain't nobody scared of you, Boonies." Kendall waves his hands like he's brushing away trash. Still, I notice his trembling fingers. "You better be glad you're a female. I ain't tryin' to catch a case." When he licks his lips, the tip of his tongue touches his lopsided mustache. With his supersize round brown face and short legs, he's a dead ringer for Mr. Potato Head.

Deidra puts her hands on her hips and cocks it better than a mama yelling for her kid when the streetlights turn on. "My girl here is basically a black belt."

"Y'all have dojos in the boonies?" Kendall snorts. Deidra and I only live ten miles outside of town, but he and his buddies loved to call us "country."

"No, we don't. Her grandmother taught her. And she's like... seriously awesome."

Heat crawls up my neck. "Geez, Deidra." And just like that, my section-leader cred (and yes, it's a thing—ritual and everything) is blazing in flames.

The entire section cracks up. They wouldn't be laughing if they witnessed Grandma Lou in action—full-on splits, throat punches, and everything. Then, after the 'ritis, aka arthritis, set in, she adopted an older version of her favorite problematic action star, Steven Seagal—a twist of the wrist and a well-placed throat chop, but Granny ain't lifting a leg.

When she first taught me how to fight, back when I was just five years old, it started as basic throws and self-defense tactics. Grandma said the world is cruel, so she refused to send her baby out ill-prepared and unable to protect herself. Her training got a lot more intense over the last twelve years, but that doesn't mean I want the section to know about it.

By the time Deidra drags me away from the small crowd, my

so-called friends are still laughing.

I roll my eyes at her.

"What'd I say?"

"Stop telling folks that Grandma Lou taught me how to fight. You know how ridiculous that sounds?"

"Would you have rather I let Kendall blab about you losing your cool?" she whispers.

"That didn't happen," I snap, and I'll admit my tone is kinda bitchy.

She winces.

Okay, maybe I'm full-on bitchy. I don't mean to be mean, but I don't need her throwing the past in my face.

"Seriously… I'm sorry, Raven." She sighs and slumps and frowns. "I… I just want to make sure you're okay. You've been off all day."

I swallow down the harsh truth. All day, I've been stomping around and snapping at people. I even got into an argument with my grandma when she asked me about a test I was stressing over. "Yeah, I know. I… I don't know why. Something just doesn't feel right."

"Then you tell me about it. Don't stuff it down. Otherwise, you're gonna explode."

"That's why I have you. You're my little bomb diffuser." I laugh without much enthusiasm.

"You don't need me to calm you down. You've got this. Don't let these stupid hicks make you feel unworthy."

I laugh for real this time. She really has my back. I glance at her, knowing I'll find her chewing her lips from pale to pink. "You know you're stuck with me, right?"

She nudges my shoulder with her own. "I've accepted my fate," she jokes, but her voice shakes. "Besides, it's more like *you're* stuck with *me*. You aren't exactly a people person."

She's more than right. In fact, we're friends because Deidra never stopped trying. Back in middle school, after *the incident*, no one wanted to befriend the weird girl with the murdered mom and grandfather.

Until Deidra.

Back then, she sat with me at lunch when I made it more than clear that I did not want to be bothered, communicated by my impressive fort of books, lunch trays, and milk cartons. But she sat with me, mindlessly chattering on and on about books and TV, and the next thing I know, she's coming over to my house and Grandma Lou wants to meet "her people."

Still, I'm not as bad as I was back then. I've even made friends with a few of my fellow band peeps.

Our charter bus is parked near the back of a paved parking lot near a swath of tall, pea-green trees. It's quiet. Dark. The lighting poles surrounding the parking lot are off—the opposing team probably killed the lights on purpose so they can jump us.

A sharp *snap* from the woods slices into the silence.

"What was that?" Deidra whispers.

"Sounds like someone stepped on a stick." I stop in my tracks, staring into the forest. A flurry of leaves shakes from the top of a tree. I take one step, two.

A pair of glowing yellow-gold eyes stare back at me.

"What the…" Sweat beads across my forehead, my lips, and my pits. It's not stone-cold fear that rattles me. My blood sprints, pumping through my veins and heart, heating my feet and hands. And something inside of me unfolds like a flower—a feeling of certainty, something telling me to go, go go.

Not away.

Toward it.

I take a step closer.

"Ummm…Raven, where are you going? Get back here." Deidra's words snap me out of my haze.

It's peak irony that my white bestie is warning me to stay put.

But…she's right. I pick up my feet and drag myself *away* from the edge of the parking lot. I had no idea I'd even walked that far—I'm not normally a check-the-noise-in-the-woods type of girl.

"You're doing that thing again."

"Huh?"

"Staring off into space, in a trance, tracing the air and muttering scientific nonsense."

I close my fist tight, forming a barricade around my index finger. I hadn't even known I was doing it. It's been happening infrequently for a while now, so I don't think anyone but Deidra has seen it, but someday this tendency is going to get me in trouble. Deidra thinks I should go to a doctor or counselor—but honestly, I'm not sure what to tell them. *Sometimes I black out a bit and look like I'm trying to do some mad science when I'm stressed or overstimulated.*

It's like my brain needs to reboot and my body powers down. It's been happening a lot this past year.

No, I absolutely cannot ask for help. Besides that, counselors are just waiting on me to have another "violent episode," as they called it. I can't trust anyone but Deidra at this point, and I don't want to worry Grandma Lou.

"What were you drawing this time?" Deidra asks quietly. "Looked like a lopsided boat."

Moon. A crescent moon. Something about mercury. Whenever I do the embarrassing muttering thing, I never recall what I say or trace with my fingers, but this time…this time, I remember.

My vision blurs like there's water in my eyes, and everything stops.

Deidra's quiet and still—it's like I've pressed a pause button. All is quiet—nature, even the yells from the crowd back at the football stadium.

I shut my eyes.

This moment, this newly unlocked freaky talent, forces me

to stop and think and feel.

It feels like a humid-hot Texas summer—invasive, oppressive, omnipresent with the taste of castor oil. Something is changing inside of me. And listen, I'm way past puberty, so I know it's not something as simple as bigger boobs.

The fuzz obscuring my sight rolls away. When I open my eyes, I find Deidra's attention on me, waiting for her question to be answered.

I shrug. "Who knows what I was doing?"

A bulky shadow slips past my periphery. I snap my head, focusing on the darkness in the woods as I search for those creepy eyes.

"Did you see that?" I whisper.

"See what?" Deidra asks at full volume.

I stand still, waiting for the thing to show up, but nothing happens.

"Nothing. Let's hurry." We don't have time to gab. Rule number one in the horror films—don't stand around and get killed.

I grab Deidra's hand and pull her close. We rush inside, dash to the back of the bus, and raid our snack stash. After we grab our few bags of chips, we run away from the bus until the stadium lights soak our faces. We look at each other and sigh—part relief, part breathlessness, part embarrassment for freaking out.

Deidra points at the timer on the scoreboard. "We've only got five minutes until the third quarter starts."

Before we make it back to the stands, Dr. Jeffries and his two assistants speed-walk past us like a group of fanny-packed grandmas at the mall, the rest of the band trailing behind them. Dr. Jeffries never speed-walks. If he needs something done, he usually yells through his megaphone for someone else to do it.

"What happened?" Deidra asks one of her piccolo friends.

"The other band tried to fight us," she whispers to Deidra. "Dr.

J wants us to leave ASAP."

After everyone hustles back to the parking lot, I count off my section members as they climb into the bus to make sure they're all accounted for—even Kendall. I scan the bus again, visually checking for a second time. Between the glowing eyes and the noise from the woods, and now our sudden departure, I'm on edge. "All right. My section is here." I hand the clipboard to the assistant director and move to the back to sit with Deidra.

"God, I'm still hungry." She pats her stomach as if she didn't just wolf down a bag of chips. "Do you think Dr. Jeffries will stop somewhere on the way back?"

I shake my head. "I mean, they just tried to fight us, so I'm guessing no." Doesn't matter we're three hours away from home— Dr. Jeffries wouldn't risk our buses getting rocked by a mob of angry townies. Again.

"You can have my peanut butter and crackers." I point under her seat, and she dives for my stash.

"Bless you."

The doors to the bus squeak as they close, and the rumbling vehicle takes off with a lurch.

A drummer hits his sticks on the back of the seat in front of him while one of the cymbal players drums a beat over his instrument. After a few seconds, I recognize the beat to an old Migos song, "Stir Fry," that was popular when we were in middle school, I think. The rest of the bus yells "aye"s and "hey"s, and some of them dance and rap along to the song. That is until Dr. Jeffries yells *shut up*.

Everyone groans, but I'm honestly glad he did. I need peace and calm to soothe me out of my crappy mood. I grab my AirPods and slip them in my ears, then tap Deidra's shoulder. "Wake me up when we get there."

She nods. But before I press play on my phone, I hear a growl from outside the bus that turns my blood cold.

"Did you hear that?"

"Hear what?" Deidra asks at full volume.

"That…that screech or whatever."

"No." Deidra shrugs. "Must be a jackal or a bear or something."

"I don't think so." Sure, there are jackals and bears in Texas, but a jackal sounds like a big dog, and a bear's roar is much throatier. The growl from outside was pitched higher, a combination between a hiss and a shriek.

Heat flares in my hands. I look down and find them red, as if I'd pressed them against the burner of a stove.

My heart pumps a one-two punch against my chest. I flex my hands. Something's not right.

"What's up?" Deidra nudges my shoulder.

I shake my hands, my head, and swallow the urge to voice my chaotic thoughts.

"Nothing. Absolutely nothing."

That Ain't No Jackal
Raven

I'm jarred awake as my head slams against the back of the seat in front of me. The felt material that scrapes my forehead feels like steel, and I know I'll have a carpet burn.

Instrument cases fall like raindrops and crash like thunder from the racks above our heads. I duck and dodge the raining horns and flutes and clarinets.

Deidra screams beside me, and my head snaps toward the sound of a *crack*. She grabs her bleeding forehead and looks down at her hands. Her fingers shake with blood.

Deidra whimpers. Her mouth moves soundlessly. Strings of saliva drip from between her lips.

"Shit." I grab her head, holding her together. "We had an accident. I'll get help."

She grabs my wrist, holding me in place.

"Okay. I'll just…" I look around. The bus has stopped, and people are standing and scrambling—struggling to get out of any open window.

A high-pitched scream fills the air. No, not *a* scream. Screams near the front of the bus.

"R-raven?" Tears roll down Deidra's cheek.

Someone must've died.

A low growl from outside curls around my bones as something rams against the side of the bus and knocks it clean off its axis. It teeters and totters and finally rights itself, but not before my mouth fills with blood. My tongue throbs.

The growling grows louder, nastier. *Closer.*

The screams bouncing around inside the battered steel grow scarier.

I peer out the window. Stare at the hulking shadow moving along the side of the bus.

A bear? No, that's impossible.

"Raven?" The pain in Deidra's voice grabs my attention. Even in the dim light, her eyes look unfocused, as if she is about to pass out. I press harder on the wound. "You'll be okay," I say, desperate to help her, to take her pain away, to focus only on her…when the *thing* from outside suddenly fills the front of the bus.

My hands fall from Dee's head. How did *It* get inside?

Air clogs my throat. I blink once, twice, not believing my eyes.

This is no animal—not a bear, not a jackal. It looks like a man. Skin as pale as the moon highlights ruby lips. The irises of his brown eyes are tainted crimson, while the surrounding whites transform to obsidian. Like a snake making room for larger prey, his jaw unhinges as his fangs, dripping with thick, yellow saliva, lengthen.

Holy crap. That's not… It's not what I think it is. It can't be.

I lean closer to Deidra and press my palm against her forehead. I pull her close when I feel her shivering.

Dr. Jeffries pushes himself from the seat.

"Kids, go out the back exit. Now." His voice is calm in the storm, and he snaps his command as if we're running drills at practice.

Everyone scrambles, but I'm rooted to my seat, one arm around Deidra's shoulder, one hand against her forehead. Her sticky blood seeps between my fingers.

Dr. Jeffries shoots the thing a hard glare, and for a split second, I think maybe, just maybe, he can reason with it. "You need to—"

His words are cut off.

The thing, the monster, grips its gnarled fingers around Dr. Jeffries' throat. His extended fangs sink into his neck. He sucks down Dr. Jeffries' blood, grunting like a wild hog.

"Oh, my God," I whisper while everyone screams. "A v-vampire?"

God, how can this be real?

Deidra grabs my fingers and whimpers, and I squeeze back as cold realization hits me. We're sitting ducks packed in a tin can.

For a few heartbeats, silence fills the air. And then pandemonium breaks.

Cam, who sits behind me, bangs against the window, but it's jammed.

"Do something, gal." I hear Grandma Lou's voice urging me to fight.

I can't. The screams from my bandmates lock my muscles. The vampire is a mere forty feet away.

"You gonna let me take you down? You ain't ready for the world." In my mind, I see Grandma Lou standing over me, cane pointed at my neck.

I struggle to stand. I feel another tug from Deidra, but I shake off her hand. Shake off my fear.

"D-don't go." She shakes her head. "Don't leave me."

I hear another howl from outside the bus.

"There's another monster out there. Get under the seat!" I yell.

The whites of her eyes stretch, but she slumps down.

I take a step forward as the monster tosses Mr. Jeffries' body through the shattered front window.

A few people stand between me and Deidra and the monster. The others have managed to climb out through the windows, and from the skin-rippling screams, I guess they didn't make it far.

They're picking us off.

"Do like I taught you!" a voice inside me orders.

The monster's attention swings to me. I hold my breath, back away, but he advances. I try to yell. "S-stop!"

He doesn't stop. He rushes me, swings his fist, and lands a punch on my face. The sheer force of his blow sends my body soaring through the air until my back slams against the exit door.

Somehow, I stand, groaning. Everything hurts.

Tiny explosions detonate inside my skull. The headache from hell doubles my vision, tripling my pain so much that it seizes my muscles.

Lava incinerates my veins. I claw at my wrists. They burn and itch as if something foreign is invading my body.

The pain drops me to my knees. "W-what…what's happening to me?"

Liters of sweat soak through my T-shirt. All I can do is breathe—breathe through *their* screams, *my* pain, and *our* fear.

After what feels like hours but must be only a few seconds, the pain finally cedes.

The monster stares at me, licking his bloodied mouth. An eerie, Pennywise-the-killer-clown smile stretches his lips. He takes one step and then another, slowly stalking me, eyes glued to me like I'm the snake and he's the mongoose. I swallow what feels like a cotton ball clogging my throat. He's deliberately taking his time to amp up my fear.

And sweet baby Jesus, it's working.

But Deidra needs my help. Gotta save me, save my friends.

My mind clears, and my heart pumps with purpose.

"He's here!" someone with a deep, guttural voice yells. The vampire, now only ten feet away, snaps his overlarge teeth at me in a silent threat that freezes my heart. With a growl, he whirls, then, in a blur of motion, is off the bus.

My head droops like a wilted flower as I close my eyes, grateful for the reprieve but dreading what comes next. I inhale and instantly regret it when the smell of copper—the smell of blood—fills my nose.

I open my eyes slowly and find the glassy eyes of Cam staring back at me. I look away. An hour ago, those eyes were like a puppy dog seeking my attention, wanting…more from me. The regret that pooled in my stomach for months now turns into lead.

Another explosion rocks my entire body, and a blindingly bright light fills my vision. I kneel as my muscles twist around my bones—compressing and stretching, like they're trying to fit into another mold.

A thousand sharp, burning needles jab into the flesh of my palms. It feels like a hot poker emblazons my skin. Circles appear on my palms in real time, as if someone is etching them in my hands, and I scream, high and loud.

"Raven!" Deidra shouts, but it sounds like I'm underwater.

"I…" I pant. "S-something's happening to me."

She crawls to my side. "You're glowing." She grabs my hand and waves it in front of my face.

The light dims, but it's the shit on my hand that doubles the knots in my stomach. I stroke the intricate design—two inverted triangles, surrounded by a hexagon, two large circles, and three smaller nodes.

"What the hell is this?" I ask, though right after my question, the answer rushes me with clarity.

Deidra points to the nodes. "That's mercury, sulfur, and salt."

I nod and swallow—science nerd to the rescue. "It looks like some witch shit."

She shakes her head. I wince when I notice the blood caked at her temples. "It's a circle, not a pentagram. But I think it has something to do with that demon. That's what it was, right?"

Something in my head, my heart, whispers *vampire*.

I flex my hand and stand. "I think I need to go. Stay here and don't move."

"I don't think I can." Her eyes are misty. "Don't leave. Don't get yourself—"

I point to the dent in the back door. "I did that. I can handle it, but I can't handle you getting hurt. So please stay here and let me go."

We have a stare-off. A long howl from outside jolts my resolve, but I'm not as afraid as I was five minutes ago.

"Fine." Deidra slumps to the ground, like her worry for me was giving her strength to sit upright. I wait until she's wedged herself between the two seats in front and behind her.

I dash outside and find three figures fighting in the middle of the road. A highway light flickers overhead, casting a chilling spotlight. Two vampires attack another guy who's built like a football player. But he's not dressed like one—he's wearing a navy-blue suit with a blazer, pocket square and everything. And the wildest thing is, the guy doesn't seem to break a sweat. With the swipe of his fingers, he launches one monster across the pavement. The other one flies, like Superman or something, rushing him midair. The guy in the suit narrows his eyes, and it looks as if an invisible force is lifting the vampire into the sky. Then, the vampire's body flies up and slams down like a mallet to a whack-a-mole against the pavement.

He's literally beating their asses with his mind.

While the suit repeatedly slams the vampire, the other one creeps behind him.

The one who attacked the bus and killed my friends.

A rash of red fills my vision, and suddenly all my tension shifts outward. I sprint before he can make his sneak attack and slam my body into his, keeping my balance so I don't fall with him.

The vampire topples over with a loud *thud* onto the ground and rolls hard over the asphalt. He lifts his arms in the air, taking inventory of the road rash along his limbs, with pebbles and bloody gash marks.

But just as quickly as it was cut open, his skin knits back together.

Like, it's legit healing.

He shakes out his arms, jumps to his feet, and crouches low. "Slayer."

Slayer? I scrunch my forehead.

Oh. Him.

I look at the guy in the suit, clocking how his eyes widen when he sees me. "Why are you out here?" He says in a Caribbean accent that my bumpkin ass can't place.

"Because I can help." I tell him the truth.

"It's too dangerous. Return to the bus immediately."

Um, excuse you. I just tackled a whole-ass vampire. "I seem to be doing okay."

He shakes his head as if he's trying to add sense to the situation. I mean, he's the one who's kicking vampire ass with his mind. In a suit.

"Get behind me. Vampires from the Saqqara clans are tricky."

"Who?"

"The flying one."

"Oh. Superman with fangs."

"Yes. Him. Stay out of the way." His rough and rumbly voice reminds me of a monster truck, with monster tires, that just rolls and crushes over anything in its way. Not that his voice sucks, but there's something about it that plucks at my nerves. Something that offends me.

My attention snags on the scarred tissue around his neck, the only slight imperfection in his Pretty Boy image. It looks like someone ripped his throat open, threw some hydrogen peroxide on it, and was like, *"You good, bro."*

I clear my throat. "I think you meant to say thank you."

"You surprised him—that's all. But you won't have the element of surprise next time." He jerks his thumb behind him.

I quickly do what he asks—clearly, he knows what he's doing—but I don't cower. I move into a fighting stance, feet spread, arms up, eyes alert. The two vampires close in on us, their eyes on the biggest threat—him.

"You'll never be king," the one with brown scraggly hair taunts.

"You'll never *see* me take the throne," Pretty Boy vows.

The vampire yells and flies toward him. Pretty Boy moves to the side, grabs his arm, and throws him across the other side of the road.

The vampire in front of me takes advantage of Pretty Boy's opening and swings out his claws, nearly clipping his ribs.

Nearly. I step in and do the same move and toss him away like yesterday's garbage. Except, instead of tossing him a few feet away, he's landed a few *hundred* feet away.

That's not what I expected or what I'd meant to do. I look down at my hands, then at the vampire, then my hands again.

Who am I? Did I eat or drink something that made me stronger? I had a PB&J, popcorn, Coke. Nothing outside of the usual.

I don't do drugs—not even weed. Okay, I had that edible brownie a few months ago, but that should be out of my system. Besides, edibles don't turn you into Wonder Woman.

A voice whispers in my head: *The better question is* what *am I?*

I'm strong. Like, really, really strong. Simple as that, for now.

A *thud* from the bus catches my attention. What is Deidra doing over there?

My focus drifts back to the vampire I'd thrown.

He looks at the bus, sniffs, and then looks at me. He's standing near the back of the bus—near Deidra.

"No." I stare at him, probably with a wild look in my eyes. In seconds, I sprint to the bus. He leaps and lands in front of me, grabs my arm and tosses me like a frisbee, just as I'd done to him. Then, he runs toward the bus.

I scramble to stand, to get to him, to Deidra.

Her screams propel me to pump my legs, my arms. With the

wind slapping at my face, I jump over the three steps on the bus. But by the time I arrive, the vampire has disappeared.

Grabbing the top of the bus seats, I hopscotch over bodies and scattered limbs to get to the exit door. There are so many bodies, I don't see her. "Where are—?" The question dies on my tongue when I find her wedged between Cam and Malia.

Slowly, carefully, I ease the bodies away and grab my friend. Deidra's chest shudders hard like an overstuffed washing machine, while her legs, bent at an angle, remain motionless. One hand grips her flute, wielding it like a weapon.

Her wide eyes stare at mine. No impish grin, just crinkled grooves around her lips and between her eyes. Blood spurts from her red-stained mouth. I look down at her throat, and it looks just like Pretty Boy's clawed-through neck. No bite marks, just claws.

With firm hands, I place my palms on either side of her throat. Red rivers gush through my fingers, and it's hard to keep a grip— the blood makes it too slippery.

"It's not bad. It's not bad at all." Salty tears settle on my lips. My hands shimmer, a metallic silver on my right and gold on my left, but I don't let go of her to figure out what the hell is going on. I can't. I'm the only thing that's holding Deidra together.

Her eyes lock on mine, asking me all sorts of silent questions I don't know how to answer. The blood, the slashed throat, the wide-eyed fear feels familiar—like I've seen this before.

I shake my head. I can't wallow in my strange déjà vu. Not when she's…

"Hurts." Tears gather in her eyes, slip down her cheeks.

"It's not bad. I'm gonna fix it. I-I promise."

I fix everything for her. If someone gave her shit, I always had her back. I won't stop now.

"Friends forever?" she asks, as she's done time and again.

She releases her last breath. In the span of seconds, I see our past—the girl who kicked the boy in the nuts when he called me

Wreck-it Raven during art class. The girl who made me a *Boys Suck* playlist when Deon broke my heart.

The girl who tried but failed to sneak me out of the house to see an R-rated movie. But really, her goal was to sleep over. Something Grandma never allowed.

I see our future sailing away. Double dates in college. Marathon movie nights in our dorm rooms.

Darkness edges my vision. I can't see her. I can't see anything. Just like that time before. I'm losing it. I'm losing control, and for once, I don't want to stop it.

"Forever and ever," I vow.

Let it Burn
Raven

Deidra's head slumps forward. Her skin cools, her eyes forever closed.

She's gone. She's… She's dead.

I'm not hot anymore. I'm shivering, cold; everything hurts. Even my tears are ice-cold as I fall onto the blood-soaked floor. Balling my hands, I pound the ground with my fists, screaming, wailing. A chaotic beat raps against my head, like drumsticks to my skull.

I can't see anything in front of me — it feels like a black cyclone is spinning me around, dragging me by my ankles into a deep abyss.

My body fights to move, to push my head above the water, but nothing can stop my descension.

I'm drowning.

But somehow, I'm breathing. I drag in a breath, stop struggling for control, and embrace the dark.

The chaos.

There's clarity in the chaos. My mission is clear: *kill him*. The one who killed Deidra.

The dark cyclone blurs my vision, but I don't need my sight to find the vampire — I feel him, the evil beat of his dark heart. Smell the dregs of blood and vomit and something rotten to the core — maybe his soul.

Pain throttles me through the shattered window, off the bus, but I don't have to run too far. A white mass appears in front of me. That's it. That's him.

I let out a scream, a wail. I charge. When I move, the ground shakes, the concrete splitting beneath my feet and indenting like footprints in the sand. My hands wrap around something flesh-like but cold. There's a rush of blood thumping beneath the surface. His throat. The darkness I felt earlier twists around my hand, spurring me to squeeze harder, to end him.

Bones crunch beneath my hand. But he hits me with a swift uppercut, and I lose my grip, regain my vision. When the darkness recedes, I suck in air.

The cyclone shifts and travels inside of me. I feel it, still strong and ruthless and powerful.

As he stumbles back, clutching his throat, he rasps, "What are you?" His voice is deep and rough, as wicked as the nine circles of Hell.

What am I? Who am I? That question echoes in my head again. *Strong* was my answer, earlier. Now… Now, I'm a band geek. Just a furious band geek. And I want to kill this monster before he can kill anyone else.

"I…"

He doesn't stick around to hear my answer. He jets off so fast, he's a streak against the night sky.

When I turn around, Pretty Boy is impaling the other vampire on the broken bottom half of a streetlamp.

I squeeze my eyes shut, reopen them, and find dancing dust particles floating in the air.

"Hey," Pretty Boy says as he jogs over to me. He looks me over. "Good. They didn't hurt you." He gentles that rough voice of his, and it doesn't grate my nerves this time. Besides that, I like… I like that he's soft with me.

"N-no. Just…just everyone else I couldn't save…" I snap my jaw shut, as if I can shut out the truth.

His eyes are dark and broody, and though I can't read everything in their depths, I get the strong sense that he knows this feeling. There's something there that lets me know he understands my pain.

He lifts his hand, reaching out to me.

I flinch. I... I don't think he'll hurt me, but I just can't.

He makes a fist and lowers it slowly, as if lowering a weapon. "Sorry. I won't touch you." He stuffs his hands into the pocket of his fancy-ass slacks, then jerks his head toward the open road. "I need to find him—the one who got away. He needs to die for what he did tonight."

He killed my entire band, my friends... Deidra, Cam, Kendall, Anderson. Misery pools in my stomach when I think about Deidra's excitement about her date with Anderson. They never got their chance to kiss at Norma's Diner.

I clutch my stomach and crouch until my knees hit the ground. "T-they're gone." My voice cracks.

I crack.

And when I do, coldness seeps into my bones. Deep inside, I know that I'll never feel the warmth of the sun again. Not like before.

I stare at my left hand. The glowing stopped after the monster ran off, but there's something else here.

Inside of the two circles inked in the middle of my palm is a hexagon. Inside of that, there are a blue crescent moon and a golden sun that looks like it's being eclipsed. Three large stars flank the moon, and three golden rays jut out from the sun.

"What does this even mean?" I flex my hand and then shake it, hoping whatever this is will disappear, especially before I see Grandma Lou. The woman is super religious. She'd cross herself if she came across anything that looked remotely devious—something tells me an arcane palm tattoo won't be received well.

Which, yes, is such a small thing to be worried about right now.

But I'm not sure I'm ready to deal with anything else quite yet.

"Hey." He kneels and then drapes his jacket across my shoulders. Staring at my feet, I wrap the jacket tight around my body.

"Look at me. Please."

I do as he asks, and I find him searching my face. As he does, I finally take him in. With his blemish-free mahogany skin, down to the detail of his low-cut fade with short, springy twists, "Pretty Boy" doesn't do him justice. He's beautiful. And with him standing at six foot two or three, he's what Grandma Lou would call tall, dark, and handsome.

"I'm sorry about your friends. I know what you're going through."

"Vampires killed your best friend, too?"

"No. Just ruined my life," he whispers, but his voice isn't soft; it's heavy, like those bright brown eyes. And I can see his pain and memories play out like a movie. He lost someone. I squeeze my own eyes shut, uncomfortable with viewing his pain. Those eyes, man. They're gossiping bitches.

"You should stay away from them," he says.

"Stay away from who?"

"Vampires."

"It's safe to say that I hate all vampires."

But I can't promise this beautiful stranger that I'll stay away. I clench my fists. Not while whatever the hell is pumping in my veins gives me the strength to fight. Until today, I did not know monsters existed. But they do—no denying what I saw, and no denying that whatever weirdness is going on with me is connected to them.

"Yeah. It's a safe bet to hate them." He pushes himself up from the ground. "I'll give you a few minutes to yourself, but we need to get out of here soon."

I nod. "I'm ready."

Pretty Boy leans in closer to me and then pauses. Shaking his head, he backs away from me and stuffs his hands into his pockets…again. "Before we leave, I've got to…take care of a few loose ends. I'm sorry for that, too."

He strides away into the darkened night before I can ask him to explain his apology. There are no lights except the ones on the bus, but somehow, I can see him walking toward a luxury car.

I don't know how long I've been sitting as my mind races—as I try to grapple with the scene in front of me. Vampires exist. I can only imagine Grandma Lou's reaction. Knowing her, she'll shake her head and claim that she knew about it because one of her old neighbors or cousin so-and-so is a vampire. Nothing surprises Granny Lou.

All I want right now is to be safe in her arms.

When Pretty Boy returns, I realize I don't even know his name.

I look up. "I'd offer you my hand, but it's bloody. I'm Raven."

He nods and goes about unscrewing a cap. A cap on a gasoline can.

I frown. "Are you not going to share your name?"

"No. Hopefully, you'll never remember this night."

"Highly unlikely."

He gives me a don't-believe-me-just-watch look.

Sigh. He must be some sort of government-agent type, but for hunting vampires. "Do you have a phone?" I clear my tight throat. "I need to call mine to find it and then call my grandma."

"No."

"What do you mean, no? You don't have a phone?"

He points to the tattoo on my hand. "Looks like you're a slayer now, which means the life you knew is gone. I'll take you somewhere safe, and I'll get someone to call your people."

"I don't know what that means, and I don't care. But I need…" I take a deep breath. "I need to speak to my grandmother. *She's* my people, and she'll worry." In another hour, she'll pull into the school parking lot and wonder why we haven't arrived.

"Being a slayer means you fight these monsters. The world can't know about them."

"I'm a slayer...like Buffy?"

"Who?"

"You know, that show—*Buffy the Vampire Slayer*." They play the reruns all the time on television.

"Haven't seen it." He lifts the red gas can. "We have to burn the bodies before they turn. Your cleanup crew can handle the rest."

"Cleanup crew?" I repeat as I jump up from the ground. "Those are my friends, not an oil spill on the highway."

"Those aren't your friends anymore. And with those symbols on your hand, with the power you bear, you're a target. If you run home to your grandmother, you might as well sign her death certificate."

"T-they can find me?"

"Yes. Without the proper blocks, you're like a 'Krispy Kreme Hot Now' sign. But don't worry—where you're going, they'll teach you how to find and fight vampires."

I nod. If Grandma Lou were in danger because of me, I couldn't live with myself. But nothing he says will stop me from letting her know that I'm alive.

"Go to my car. I'll handle the rest," he instructs.

"You mean burn my friends' bodies."

He nods.

"Because they'll come back alive."

"*Alive* is an optimistic word. They'll be Ticks."

"Ticks?"

"Mindless vampires. All they can think about is feeding. It's not a happy existence."

"Like the Reapers from *Blade II*?"

He gives me another dull look. I think he's tired of my movie references, but honestly, how in the hell else can I wrap my mind around this mess?

"Haven't seen it."

But maybe they aren't like the Reapers. Maybe they can acclimate to their new nature. No way could Deidra eat another human being. She's vegan, for God's sake. "Maybe—"

"Do you really want your friends to taint their souls? To take more lives? Better yet, do you want to have to kill them?"

I swallow. "There must be another way. Are you telling me that there's never been a Tick who couldn't get it together?"

"Sure, yes."

"Aha!"

"But it takes years of training to get their hunger under control. They must be under constant supervision from a Royal, their maker, which they can no longer do."

"Why?"

"Their maker is dead—I killed him."

"But my friend, Deidra. Her throat was slashed, so—"

"If her throat was slashed and he didn't drink her blood, then she's dead. She's not coming back as a Tick."

The finality of his statement wraps around my chest and squeezes my heart. I could've tried to help Deidra as a vampire. Deep down, I knew she wouldn't harm another human being.

"Don't do this to them."

I bite my lip, attempting to hold back my tears. "Fine. I'll go."

"Door's unlocked."

I don't reply, just drag my feet and head to the car—a dark-blue BMW. Weird how I can decipher the color in total darkness.

Another superpower I'll have to catalogue. And when I settle, I'll make a list. I love making lists—even more so, I love breaking down the meaning and analyzing things within an inch of their lives. And this list will be the best one yet, because I'll use it to figure out a way to kill those assholes, lots of them, so that what happened to me never happens to anyone else.

I settle into the seat, wincing when I notice that I'm leaving bloodstains on the floor mats. The vehicle has a new-car smell. If it's a rental, he's not getting his deposit back.

A minute later, a loud *boom* rocks the car and orange light brightens the sky.

Tears cloud my vision. My lips tremble. And I cry.

I cry for my friends.

I cry for Deidra.

I cry for Grandma Lou, who lost yet another person in her life. She might retreat into her shell. As it is now, she only leaves the house for church and necessities in town.

Pretty Boy returns to the car. Before he presses the ignition button, he rubs a silver chain that dangles from the rearview mirror. Hanging from it, a charm in the shape of a broken wing gleams. It doesn't look like his style—more feminine and a little cheap, to be honest—but it seems like he treasures it.

"Nice necklace," I say, stealing a glance at him.

He doesn't say a word, just shifts the car into gear, grinds his jaw under his nearly smooth-shaven face, and punches the gas.

I slide my body closer to the passenger-side door, wiping my tears with the back of my hand. "Where are we going?"

"A motel near the Houston airport."

"I've got questions."

He doesn't invite me to ask, but he doesn't tell me to shut up, either, so I ask.

"Are you a vampire slayer?"

He laughs and spares me a glance. "No," he answers. He tightens his grip around the steering wheel.

"Do you work for the government?"

"No."

"Are you a mutant?"

"Like from the X-Men?"

I'm surprised he referenced something from pop culture. "Yeah, exactly that."

"No." He tilts his head as if considering my question more deeply. "Well...maybe. I don't know." He rubs one of his hands along his twists.

"How long have you been able to do the mind thingy?"

"Long enough," he says, then turns on the radio. "We've got two hours ahead of us. You should try to get some sleep."

"Fine, Pretty Boy."

The car swerves. "Pretty Boy?"

I don't repeat my response. If I do, he'll know that I think he's cute.

But I don't want to sleep. I need conversation. I need chatter to help me process, help me forget. If I close my eyes and fall asleep, I just know I'll find Deidra's lifeless body waiting for me in my dreams.

Or if I let my guard down, that thing—the darkness that slithers around me even now—will take over. It's always been there, but tonight... Tonight, it spread like wildfire.

And if I let it take over, do I run the risk of becoming something worse than those vampires?

Despite my fears, I drift off.

The sounds of airplanes startle me. My eyes fly open and close just as quickly when the fluorescent lights blind me.

Where am I?

I open my eyes just enough to scan the area. I'm in a parking lot. The car faces a one-story structure that looks like it's held together with toothpicks.

I'm alone. Pretty Boy isn't here.

The silver chain hanging from the mirror glints in the moonlight, and I don't know why, but I want to hold it, touch it. There's a story behind this necklace. A little pin pricks my heart because I know it belongs to someone he loves.

I grab the chain and stuff it in his jacket pocket—the jacket I'm still wearing. Then, I snoop around the car, looking for clues to his existence. Surely, he has an identity. No one in a fancy car and suit doesn't roll with ID or something. I lift the middle console, find an envelope, and flip it open. Inside is a folded rental car agreement. I scan the document and zero in on the customer's name.

Khamari St. John. I trace his name. My fingers tingle.

"Khamari." I whisper his name, and it's as if silk feathers brush my skin.

I like his name. I like it a lot. Now, I want to find the beautiful boy with the beautiful name. I stuff the agreement inside the envelope, pull the blazer tight, and open the car door, releasing a breath when the car alarm doesn't blare.

A few feet ahead, I spot a dingy green door with peeling paint and the word Registration stenciled on it.

I hurry inside and find Pretty Boy. "Just one night—" He turns around and frowns when he sees me. "You should've stayed in the car."

The older lady he's speaking to has thinning blond hair and dull eyes. But when she takes me in, her eyes brighten. "Ma'am! Are you okay? Are you in trouble?"

"I'm fine." There's a mirror behind the desk, and I catch my reflection. Yikes on bikes.

My skin bears a dark-red tint, as if I'd showered in blood. Not to mention my helmet hair—blood and sweat and fear further poofed my thick strands.

"I'm calling the police." She picks up the landline on her desk.

"No," I urge, waving my hands. "It's not what you think."

"Sheila." He speaks to her like she's a little girl.

"Yes?" she asks as her eyes dim to a faded blue.

"Put down the phone."

"B-but she's hurt."

"It's okay. This is my girlfriend. It's our anniversary, and we'd like a room."

"Ohhh," she whimpers in a childlike voice. "Happy anniversary." She gives a wide smile that creeps me right the hell out.

"Thank you. Two years going strong. Saw her playing music on the football field, and I knew she was the one for me."

It sounds so real, I can imagine him staring at me while I practiced with my section before the football players took over the field for practice.

"That's so nice. I was in love once. Long time…long time ago." She sighs.

"That's great, Sheila. She's fine. We're fine, and we'd very much like our room now."

"Okay, then. I'll give you the honeymoon suite." She turns around and pulls the keys from the rack behind her.

"Oh, and here are some goodies. Earplugs for the airplanes. We only give them to special guests." She does the weird, creepy smile thing again. "Mints and chocolates."

"Oh, he loves chocolates!" I add to this weird-ass conversation.

He spears me with a look, and I shrug.

I can play along, too. Besides, she's being nice to us.

"Me, too!" Sheila claps. "Oh, and here. Have the anniversary bear."

"The what?"

She bends over and grabs a miniature teddy bear with a heart and red ribbon around its neck. "For our special guests," she explains, handing the bear to him.

He gives her a quick, awkward thanks and takes the bear. Then, he swipes the keys from Sheila and grabs my hand. He pulls me all the way around the corner and up the outdoor stairs to a room on the third floor. He doesn't let go, not even when he jams the key into the lock and twists.

I look at the heart-shaped bed that even from here looks hard as a brick. But I won't complain. My limbs are heavy. So are my eyes. And during my little cat nap, images of Cam and Deidra tortured me.

I flop on the edge of the bed, not even caring that the mattress lifts from my weight. He tosses the stuffed bear onto the bed, chocolates and earplugs landing near the pillows.

"Do you want to shower or sleep?"

I shake my head. "I just need to sit here for a bit."

He doesn't respond but goes into the bathroom. I hear the running water. I guess he plans to shower.

But he's not showering, because he returns quickly with a wet cloth. He lowers himself in front of me and lifts a white cloth in front of my face, silently asking for my permission.

"I don't think Sheila's going to believe our story tomorrow if we have blood on these washcloths."

He tucks a thick strand of my hair behind my ear as his eyes scan my body and then return to my face. "We'll both be gone by then."

I moisten my lips.

His pupils dilate. He releases a shaky breath and rubs my cheek. The warm, rough cloth scrapes my skin. Quick and efficient, he gently wipes the blood and sweat and even fear from my face. He goes to the bathroom and returns with another clean cloth, which he uses to clean my arms.

I close my eyes, and I swear it feels like I hear a melody. It sounds like gospel at first, but then the song opens and changes pace, more like rhythm and blues and melancholy.

"Raven." His rough voice and accent roll over me. I feel hot all over. And oh, God, the way he says my name, *Ray-van*, makes me feel like the fourth of July—he's the firecracker and I'm the sky.

His fingers brush my temple.

"Yes?"

"About tonight."

Tonight. Tonight. Deidra and Cam and vampires.

And death and death and death.

My body shakes. I hear a high-pitched whine and realize it's mine. But how can something like that escape my lips? The pain of my thoughts stops.

He's doing something to me.

Something soothing, like lavender, blankets my thoughts.

"Raven. Listen to me. Everything is okay," he whispers. "I can make you forget what happened to your friends."

I grab his wrists. "Stop."

"Stop?"

"Don't," I say as I shake my head, shake away his influence. "Don't make me forget." My voice strains against his magic, his power, whatever this is.

I don't want to forget this night. In my gut, I know the pain anchors me. I don't want to forget Deidra or Cam or even Kendall.

I don't want to forget...*him.*

"Okay."

"Okay?"

He nods and stands. "I'm going to grab my bag from the trunk and take a shower. I think I have something you can change into."

"Okay but...but hurry." I hate how weak my voice sounds, but I can't help it.

"I won't leave you for long."

True to his word, he returns soon and offers me a clean white tee and basketball shorts.

While he's showering, I quickly change my clothes. Then, I curl into the bed and pull the anniversary bear close to my chest. The earplugs roll on the bed. I push them into my ears and pretend to sleep. I have a feeling that Pretty Boy, aka Khamari, will try to use his cheap parlor tricks on me, and I don't want someone messing with my head.

Pretty Boy runs a quick shower, and minutes later, he's back. The warmth from the shower pours into the room when he opens the door.

When I crack my eyes open, I see he's fully clothed. He pulls the chair near the desk out, sits, and crosses his arms and feet.

We stare at each other for a bit. I don't look away—I seem to be hypnotized by the contrast of his bright brown eyes against his mahogany skin. But it's not just his looks—his presence gives me a sense of comfort. Deep down, I just know that if another vampire rolls through, he's got my back. I turn onto my side and slip out one of the earplugs.

Not that I need his help. I grimace as I close my fist under the covers.

There's softness in his eyes. Brown eyes, whiskey eyes. A lightning bolt charges my heart.

"Do you like what you see, or are you in shock?" His question hacks away at my dreamy thoughts.

"I... What?" I stutter out the words, stunned by his sudden mood shift.

"You're staring."

"So are you."

He looks away and lets out a long sigh. "I don't have time for this."

"Then leave," I say with much more bravado than I feel.

"I'm not leaving you."

Thank God. "You're a little moody, huh?"

"Hungry."

"Then grab a Snickers and lose the attitude," I tell him as I pull the covers over my head. That way I won't embarrass myself by staring at his profile or whatever. I put the plug back in my ear.

Though silence and darkness surround me, sleep doesn't come, and for once, I'm thankful.

Because if I'd been sleeping, I wouldn't have noticed him

creeping around the room or felt the weight of his stare. The pretending-to-sleep-jig is up when I feel the mattress move. I lower the sheets from my head and find him kneeling beside the bed. The red and green lights from the vacancy sign cast stripes of light across his face. He smiles and mouths something. That's right. I put those courtesy earplugs in—just in case he used the same sexy command-y voice he used on Sheila at the registration desk. She's probably still thinking about her long-lost love and the cute couple she put in the honeymoon suite. I sit up and swing my feet to the drab, worn carpet. Pretty Boy kneels in front of me, positioning himself between my legs.

He swallows and mutters, "Lada mercy," I think, and it takes everything in me not to smirk at his slip in control.

It feels like I'm dreaming—a small reprieve from tonight's nightmare. But I'm not. I am very much awake and…he's real, and how *I'm* feeling—is real… ridiculous. I fully accept that I'm a moth and he's a red-hot flame. And honestly, I don't get why my heart clangs against my chest and why my blood rushes through my veins. And there's this melody that's playing softly in my mind. It's too low to hear, but there's a piano melody I can just make out. It's haunting, aching, hopeful. It makes me want to hold on.

I zero in on his mouth to read his lips and recognize him saying my name. He says it so slow and deliberate I wish I could hear the sweet way he says it—even if it is to erase my memories.

He's speaking again. When he pauses, I blink and nod like Sheila downstairs did.

He cups my cheeks and leans so close our mouths are insanely close. The air is weightless, and it takes every fiber in me to weigh myself down before I float an inch closer to him. I wonder how it'll be if we kiss. Soft and reverent? No. The look in his eyes is pure hunger.

A guy that starved can't be gentle. He would take, and I would let him.

He leans near my ear and whispers something I can't hear, and it annoys me that I can't make it out. Then he moves back into my line of vision.

As he hesitates, his eyebrows lower and draw together like there's a magnet in the dead center. Deep grooves rise like mountains on his forehead, and I can tell he's no stranger to frowning.

I... I don't want him to leave. Trembling and with a mind of their own, my fingers bridge the short distance between us. My forefinger lands just below his hairline.

His eyes are gold. I don't think he's breathing right now.

Neither am I.

What am I doing? I should know better, but I don't just let my touch linger. Being the moth that I am, I drag my finger along the grooves of his frown, the curve of his nose, down to his most excellent lips. I don't stop—yes, *truly* I should know better, because now I'm tracing the scar along his neck.

Before I can finish my exploration, he grabs my hand and squeezes my fingers together. His golden eyes liquefy into a molten fire. "You can't," he mouths.

Can't what? Like him? Touch him? I can't ask him. I'll never know. Despite the facade, a tear wells in my eye.

I focus on his lips again.

"Sleep, Raven. You're safe now."

When he stands and closes the door, I let the tears fall. I pluck out the earplugs and tuck the teddy close to my face. The horrors of what happened today overwhelm me. Luckily, Anniversary Bear's cheap fur is better than Kleenex.

After a much-needed cry session, I roll out of my blanket burrito.

He left me. He thinks he just erased my memories and left me alone in some weird-ass motel room.

"Jerk." I grab a towel folded on the nightstand and stomp to the shower. The hot water is just what I need to get my head right, to convince myself it's okay that he left. It's not like he owes me anything. He saved my life. He did more than enough, more than what he wanted my memory to give him credit for.

I pat myself dry and open the bathroom door. As I dress, the doorknob rattles.

Someone's trying to break in.

Don't Come for Me, Unless I Send for You
Raven

The doorknob rattles again. I freeze, but the tattoos on my hands tingle.

"Knock, knock. You can open the door because it's almost sunrise," a female voice singsongs from the other side of the door. "It's us. The"—she lowers her voice—"vampire slayers."

"For God's sake, just bust down the door. She might be dead already," a male voice mutters.

I hear a *tsk* followed by, "Don't say that. Besides, I can feel her energy. Can't you?"

"I'm coming in now, unless you want to open the door."

What? Now? "I… I'm naked!" I call, scrambling to grab the T-shirt I left on the bed.

"Oh, well. One minute, then. Unless naked is really a code for danger?" Her voice is calm and cautious.

"No, no danger! I just got out of the shower. Please don't come in."

I hear someone sniff. "I do smell soap. Okay, then. I believe you. I'll be just outside." I can't tell if Ms. Cheery is handing me a warning or providing comfort, but I rush to put on the clothes Pretty Boy gave me.

I'm finished, but I can't seem to find the courage to open the door. Something tells me that opening the door means my life will change.

But they take the decision out of my hand when the doorknob

twists. I back toward the nightstand, clutching the teddy bear to my chest. Despite her cheery voice, if I learned anything tonight, it's that a monster can look human.

The door pops open, along with the latch that secures it.

"Hey there!" A girl about my age waves from the doorway. A guy looms behind her.

I frown. "Get the hell out of my room." With my free hand, I reach for the lamp on the nightstand, ready to use it as a weapon.

"No, wait, please. We mean you no harm." She holds her arms up, palms facing me. When I notice the symbols on her hand, I relax my grip from around the lamp.

"I'm Charlotte." When she smiles, dimples appear on her glowing umber cheeks. Her thick locs are piled atop her head into a high bun. Her hairstyle showcases her high cheekbones. And to top off her gorgeousness, a beauty mark sits just below one of her dimples.

"We're here to help you," the perfectly calm stranger who broke into my motel says in a reassuring voice.

"Help me by leaving."

"We can't—you need our help, even if you don't know it yet."

I stand there with my heart racing, my mind urging me to flee, my tattoos tempting me to fight.

"Oh, dear." Charlotte bites her lips as she takes me in. Her hazel doe eyes are heavy on the sympathy side. I hate it.

The guy steps inside the room, too, and inspects me. But instead of the sympathy that Charlotte has shown, his striking eyes, which are different shades of blue, reflect annoyance. "A teddy bear. How old are you?" he asks, all rude and shit. "I swear they're getting younger and younger." He runs a hand over his low-cut, curly black hair.

"Eighteen," I enunciate. I toss the bear on the bed, but the damage is done.

"It smells like blood. And you look like hell." He whispers the last part, but I can hear it, and he knows it.

"Richmond, please." Charlotte shoots him a frown.

He just shakes his head, and I can instantly tell we will never be friends—a nice face but a nasty attitude. The rest of him is nothing else to call home about, either, especially with all that arrogance.

Charlotte walks closer to me. "We're with the Slayer Society." She reaches out, palm up, and asks, "May I…check your hand?"

"Oh, you mean that tattoo thingy that appeared last night?" I look at my hand and study the tattoo. Maybe this girl will tell me what the hell is going on. I need to know, especially if someone tries to hurt my grandmother.

Palm up, I let her inspect. Her warm fingers brush my skin.

"It's on the left? And it has her guild outlined and…and it has color." Charlotte's voice is sharp, and her hold on my hand tightens.

"Yeah, so?"

"Most slayers have it on the right hand, without the guild and color." She sighs. "Let's just say it's unique. But you know"—she looks at me, ratcheting up her smile—"I think it's a good thing."

"It's an omen," Richmond says, his voice husky.

She shushes him. "We don't know that."

"Tell that to Tennessee." Rich sneers his lips like he's an Elvis impersonator.

"What about it?" I ask.

"Not it. Him, a slayer. Had color early on, couldn't control his powers. The kid was pure chaos."

"He had problems even before he became a slayer." Charlotte squeezes my hand.

"You have problems, girl?" Richmond asks, all up in my business like we didn't just meet five minutes ago.

I open my mouth to answer, but then I freeze. Flashes from a few hours ago and from five years ago mix like a fruit smoothie in a blender. My heart squeezes like someone determined to wring all the juice out of a lemon. I swallow a few times, forcing moisture to release the trapped answer in my throat. "Don't we all?" I croak.

"Ain't that the truth," Charlotte says with a nod. "And, umm, congrats are in order! You're a Distorter."

"A what?"

"Distorter."

"That sounds horrible."

She pats my hand before she releases me. "Oh, no. Distorters are lots of fun. Excellent fighters, highly creative—quick thinkers, too. The Architect already knows what he wants you to do. We'll just have to discover it."

"Who the heck is an architect?"

"*The* Architect is a supreme being who created the Alchemist Order and Slayer Society. He gives us our powers, sweetie." She bats her long lashes.

"So… The Architect is like God."

She shrugs. "There are many gods. You may continue to serve the god you prefer because we don't worship The Architect. They just give us the means to protect humanity. It's plain ol' good versus evil, though not all vampires are bad."

Richmond and I both snort.

"Anyway, we were in New Orleans when we got an anonymous tip about you. Do you know who called it in? The person distorted their voice."

Pretty Boy aka Khamari. He refused to give his name, erased ol' girl's memory down in the lobby. The jerk tried to erase mine, too.

Irritation cloaks my skin like sweat, and just like that, it feels like I need another shower. I rub an arm and shake my head. "I know someone helped me—a guy, I think—but I didn't see his face. He mentioned that I'm a slayer. After that…I blacked out."

Charlotte tuts. "That happens a lot. The surge of power is overwhelming."

Richmond tilts his head from right to left, as if he's weighing the truth of my answer.

He opens his mouth to speak, but Charlotte cuts in.

"We'll see what we can do to find out who helped. We can't let the world know of our existence. That would defeat the purpose of us being a secret society and all." She claps her hands as if to change the subject. "Regardless, we are here to take you to your new home."

"Umm… No, ma'am. I have a home. Now, I know that guy said I had to kill vampires, and I don't mind that part. I just don't want my grandmother to think I'm dead."

Charlotte winces and walks toward the bed. "Maybe you should sit down. Actually…don't sit. There're probably bedbugs on the mattress." If my life wasn't falling apart, I'd laugh at her obvious disdain at the state of this room. She rubs her arms, as if to ward away the cooties.

"I'm Raven, by the way. And you can give me the bad news," I invite.

She nibbles her lips. "Well, there's a lot to discuss, and this area isn't secure. We're about half an hour until sunrise, but you never know. How about we talk in the car? I promise we won't hold you against your will. Come to our headquarters, hear us out, then decide. If you don't want to be a slayer, you can leave anytime."

I cross my arms. "Has anyone left before?"

Richmond snorts. "Yeah, but they come crawling back when they realize they're basically live targets for vampires. They know how to find us by smell."

Pretty Boy mentioned vampires knew about slayers and were attracted to us, but he said there was a way to block them. No harm in asking. "Isn't there a way to hide my scent?"

Richmond rolls his eyes. "Right. But why would we give away the serum?"

"Hush, Richmond." Charlotte swats him.

"It's Rich," he corrects her.

She sighs and looks back at me. "There's a difference between surviving and thriving. We'll give you the tools to thrive, and I promise you, if you don't want to stay, we will make sure you don't remember and give you as much protection as we can extend. Which…admittedly, isn't much. I'm sorry, but I can't say more until we leave here."

With the dark early-morning sky behind him, Rich leans against the doorjamb and snaps his fingers. "Grab your teddy and let's go, kid."

"My name's not kid."

"Uh-huh," he says, but his eyes sharpen suddenly and he puts a finger up and presses it against his lips. "We've got company," he mouths.

We all go quiet, and I snatch the lamp from the outlet. Rich rolls his eyes to the sky, shakes his head, and then disappears from the doorway.

A few tense seconds later, I hear them—couple of mouth-breathers for sure, and one of them…I think I hear two…lets out a nasal hiss.

But most importantly, I smell them. One smells like a rainstorm; the other, like candy—the nasty cheap and stale kind that sticks to the roof of your mouth.

I tap my nose and look at Charlotte. "I can hear them and smell them… How?"

"Heightened senses. Perks of being a slayer." She steps outside the door. "Stay here." Charlotte runs out of the room, leaving it open, and jumps off the balcony into the parking lot. I don't listen. I follow and jump right behind her. There's a trio of vamps, but Rich seems to handle them with ease. He flips one over his back and front-kicks the other. When the third vampire punches him in the gut, Rich bends over and grunts.

"Don't worry," he says, his voice strained. "I've got it, babe."

"All right." Charlotte waves and leans against a car.

She looks down at her hand and adjusts her rings and bracelets.

"No need to help," he yells, taking another punch to his face.

"That's what you get for being mean to our recruit." She wags her finger at him.

"What the hell are you doing?" I jog past her. I mean, he's a jerk, for sure, but he needs help.

"He's the Maximus—the strongest of us slayers. He's just playing around, being a big baby." Her eyes flash with irritation. "Wrap it up, honey bun."

He slices his hand with a blade and chants something in Latin, I think. Light glows from his hand and then blasts up into the sky, and blue mist forms around his body. Once it clears, I notice metal plates wrapping around his arms. He clangs the steel together, forming an *X* with his metal forearms. Two long, silver blades extend near his hands.

Wow. The guy looks like a civilized version of Wolverine.

"Minimum damage today, gentlemen." Rich twists his torso and executes a hammer punch to the vampire's face, lobbing off his head in one swift motion.

Before I can process a head rolling across the parking lot, a lanky vampire with dingy brown hair materializes in front of me. It's him. The one who got away—the one who killed Deidra.

He smells dank and dark—like death.

I slug him across the jaw and smile when I hear a crack. Might be his head that knocks against the concrete, might be his jaw.

"Wait! He's a Royal." Charlotte finally looks alarmed. "The Ankh clan." She points at his arm, and I notice a tattoo. It looks like a cross, but instead of a straight line, there's a large loop on top. I'd seen this symbol branded on some guys around campus.

Charlotte rubs her bracelet across her wrist, slicing the skin open and letting the blood drip like water from a leaking pipe.

She moves her hands like she's dancing with water and blasts the vampire away with a gust of wind. He lands just an inch away from a car across the parking lot.

I mean, her powers are cool, but I'm pissed that she stopped me from slugging him again. "Why'd you do that?"

"We can't kill him. He's under the king's protection," Charlotte warns.

We don't have kings in this country...

I take a step back, but the vampire straightens and speeds toward me, forcing me to decide. Cranking back my fists—fists once slick with Deidra's blood—I ram my hands through his chest and rip out his heart.

"Holy shit," Richmond whispers from behind me.

"What?" I ask, but then I look down at the chunks of guts on my hands and forearms. The blood splatters on the ground and soaks through my white tee. The vampire is somehow still alive, and his eyes roll back. I step away and squeeze the heart in my hand.

"Forever and ever," I vow before I smash his heart against the pavement and stomp.

His skin sizzles, and the stench of burning flesh fills the air. His body becomes more and more sunken and gaunt as mere seconds pass. His graying flesh disappears, giving way to muscle and bone. Then the vampire turns to ash, sprinkling softly on the ground near my shoes.

What. Just. Happened?

It feels like I'm an oversize balloon, brimming with helium. And as soon as I killed the vampire, the balloon pops. My body slumps forward, and I suck in all the air I just lost.

It was me who grabbed the vampire's heart and yanked it out of his chest. But at the same time, it wasn't me. It was like...like something is puppeteering my body—my emotions, too. Because I most definitely wanted to kill him. I *enjoyed* it.

"What the hell was that?" Rich asks.

I lift myself up and take another deep breath. "That was me killing the piece of shit who killed my best friend."

"I had him."

"But I wanted *him*."

"Oh, my goodness." Charlotte grabs my arm and wipes it down with a towel. "Are you okay, Raven?" I nod, but I don't make a sound. There's a low buzzing in my ear.

"Can I… Can I take a shower?"

"You just took one," Rich whines.

I gesture at my blood-covered arm. "That was before I ripped out someone's heart."

He snorts. "Next time, stab them with silver."

"I thought that was for werewolves?" Besides, it's not like I can make silver armor like he can.

"The Architect alchemizes silver, making it purified and perfect, which makes vampires allergic to it."

"The sun's rising." Charlotte waves at me. "Go on. We'll be here waiting."

I jog to the outdoor staircase, but with my heightened senses, I can hear Rich whisper to Charlotte, "Just what in the hell was that?"

"We'll talk to her when she returns. We need to give her time to process."

"No, we need to understand who and what she is before she gets into this car."

I falter in my steps, their conversation reminding me of the one my grandmother had with the social worker who tried to take me away.

I'll figure out what's wrong with me and piece myself back together. Like always.

They continue arguing, but I ignore them, along with my thoughts, as I head for the room to shower.

Mediocre White Men
Raven

When I finish, there's lotion, clothes, and deodorant waiting for me on the bed, and I know it's from Charlotte. In less than thirty minutes, I'm back downstairs. Charlotte leans against the car door and opens it for me. The sun rises just above the horizon, pink and purple clouds drifting in the sky. The pretty combination soothes me. In the last few hours, all I've seen is black and red.

"Your aura went completely black when you fought that vampire," Charlotte informs me, jumping straight into the conversation and breaking my trance.

"Y-you saw darkness in me. Is that normal?"

"I didn't see it, but I felt it." She leans over and buckles my seat belt, then clears her throat. "To answer your question, no, it's not normal and you're not... You're more powerful than a new slayer. That's for sure."

"Yeah, I'm strong. I felt it come over me when they attacked."

Charlotte settles into the passenger seat before she says, "All slayers have a dormant gene, and it only activates when a vampire triggers their powers, usually through an attack." She nods. "But this is different."

Rich pushes the ignition button and then looks back at me. "What happened back there?"

Charlotte frowns at him. "I should ask you the same thing. Since when does it take you so long to kill vampires? And made ones at that."

"We were out in the open. I had to be careful. Good thing no one was in the parking lot." He frowns and looks down at his tattooed palm, then shakes it like it's defective or something.

"I suppose, though you know I was looking out for eyes and ears. Not to mention I have enough serum to dose a dozen humans, and you very well know that."

I remember him slicing his hands and somehow creating a weapon from blue mist. "Will I be able to create weapons like you?"

"Maybe, just not as efficiently. I'm the Maximus."

"Congratulations?" I frown, shaking my head.

"Oh, he's just the most powerful slayer in the world. Which is why I didn't help." Charlotte waves at him dismissively without looking at him. "Now, back to you. How are you so powerful?"

I shrug. "I've had training."

"Oh, yeah? Got your yellow belt from the YMCA?" Rich laughs at his own joke.

I roll my eyes. Grandma didn't do belts unless she was threatening to whoop my ass, but she never laid a finger on me outside of training. "No formal system."

He snorts. "Well, they'll give you what you need."

"Who is 'they'?"

"American Slayer Society."

I repeat the name under my breath and chuckle. "ASS?"

"Hmm?"

"The acronym is ASS. What does ASS do?"

"We save the world." A proud smile spreads across Charlotte's face that matches the pride shining in her eyes.

"'We.' There is no 'we,' yet. Besides, I'm too young, remember?" I shoot daggers at the back of Rich's head.

"We don't get to choose when we're given the powers. The Architect has chosen you," Charlotte gently explains.

"Why?"

Rich yawns. "All of this is in orientation."

"We've got a long drive." Charlotte shrugs. "Might as well get her acclimated."

"We aren't flying?"

"No. You'd be a flag in the system that we can't yet explain. Especially since we don't know your decision yet. We'll have to lie low for now. But the good thing is that during the drive, I can answer all your questions. You'll be the most prepared recruit ever by the time we reach Atlanta."

"Atlanta!"

"Yes. Well, our headquarters are about thirty miles south of the city, but we have slayers located all over the world. Since I'm the second in command, I'm no longer a field agent." She bends over, then pulls out a water bottle from under her seat and passes it to me.

"Thanks." I take a long gulp. After I satisfy my parched throat, I ask, "When did you become a slayer?"

"In sixty-four."

"1964?" I squeak. She looks my age.

"No. *1864.*"

I swallow. "You're like…one hundred and sixty."

"Excuse you," she snaps. "One hundred and fifty-nine."

"Shut. Up," I yell.

"That's exactly what I want you to do," Rich mutters.

"I ain't lying," Charlotte says in a voice that reminds me of Grandma Lou. I mean, shoot, she's older than my grandma. Way older.

"I have so many questions."

Then a thought occurs to me. "Wait a minute!" I push myself to the edge of my seat and lean over the middle console between Charlotte and Rich. "Y'all don't die?"

"Oh, no. Get that out of your head," Rich says in a dry,

humorless tone. "We can die, and we do. Most don't last past ten, maybe twenty years. Take my advice: Don't get attached to anyone."

"What's the secret to your success, oh great and mighty Maximillian?"

"It's Maximus. I'm the chosen one." He grins and gives me a look. A look that says *bow down, bitches*. But honestly, those two vampires were wailing on his ass before he used his li'l powers, so I'm not all that impressed. Of course the chosen one is a mediocre white man.

"What makes you the chosen one?"

He opens his hand and waves it. "See that jewel?"

I look at the twinkling stone, can practically feel the energy and power oozing from his hand.

"The Philosopher's Stone gives me unparalleled power, the strength of four or five Royals," he says as if that means something to me.

"What if someone takes away your bling?"

"You can't." He smirks. "Many have tried—all have died."

You should put that on a T-shirt. I mentally roll my eyes. Even Charlotte looks low-key annoyed.

"So why did it take you so long to kill off two vampires?"

I toss Charlotte a look, and she chuckles behind her hand. I didn't even see him handle the other one—I was too busy killing the other vamp.

Rich snaps his hand shut. "Do you even know what a Royal is?"

"Nope, but apparently I know how to kill one with my bare hands." *And without the bling.*

Charlotte clears her throat, and I recognize she's gearing back up for professor lecture mode even before she says, "Royals are a small percentage of vampires sired by the father of vampires, Alexander the Great. Through his bite, they gained special powers, all of which he bears. There are three separate clans, each with a specialized power: the Ankh clan are masters at mind control, the Hekau clan specializes in many forms of energy manipulation, and the Saqqara have gravity-defying powers. They're able to fly and teleport. Alexander the Great mastered all powers."

I nod along and then stop. "Hold up," I say, raising my hand.

"Do you want me to repeat what I just said? Oh, yes, you probably want to understand how the clans are organized."

"No. I want to talk about Alexander the Great. *The* Alexander the Great is a vampire?"

"Yep." Rich pops the *P*. "The very first. History lessons are also a part of the curriculum, so ask your History of Alchemy Magister. Any more questions?"

"Yeah, how long until I'm—"

"Good." He cranks up the radio, and Charlotte smacks his hand.

"Listen, why don't you get some shut-eye," she negotiates. "We can resume our chat when you wake up."

"I am tired," I agree.

But secretly, I'm reeling. Her answers only make me more confused about this slayer mess. For now, I will allow them to take me to this ASS society. I figure I have two options: either learn how to properly kick some vampire ass or call Grandma Lou to bust me out.

I cross my arms and close my eyes. My mind turns over the outlandish info Rich begrudgingly shared. Though Rich seems like an asshole, there's one thing he said that I agree with—don't get attached to anyone.

"We're in cow country now," Charlotte says when we arrive at headquarters on the outskirts of Atlanta, about fifteen hours later.

Much to Richmond's pleasure, we didn't talk about vampires and slayers. I slept most of the way, Charlotte sang, and Richmond drove—not because Charlotte didn't offer but because he didn't want anyone else to drive.

"Welcome to our headquarters. Home of the American Slayer Society and Tria Prima Academy. Your new home," Charlotte trills.

"Maybe." I still might pop a pill to erase my memories. Wait, do they have a pill for that? Because if so, sign me up. But if I *do* take something to erase my memories, that will require them also dosing Grandma Lou, because she would have questions about school and the massacre, and, I don't know…why my friend of a decade is missing. Either way, my life is screwed.

"You're going to love it here once you get settled," Charlotte says. "Atlanta is the perfect, unassuming town where slayers can train and lie low. Despite it being a large city, it has one of the lowest vampire populations per capita."

"Really? Why is that?"

"Too sunny. Too muggy. Too far south."

"Yeah, but the vamps like to vacation here and sample the locals, so don't get too comfortable." Rich turns down a paved road that leads to an open wrought iron gate. "And I'm hearing rumors that a clan just moved here."

"Yes… I'm sorting that out. But trust me. It's not as bad as D.C. or New York."

I snort at the normalcy of the comment. That's what everyone says about other cities they don't live in. I've heard folks in Houston and Dallas say the exact same thing about Atlanta.

While Rich and Charlotte argue about vampire populations, I roll down the windows and let the warmth of the sun hit my face.

The Tria Prima Academy looks like a fancy corporation, nestled in the middle of nowhere, with a man-made lake in the front.

The dome-shaped building is stark white. Etched in the building are three circles that give me Olympics vibes, but there are symbols within the rings. Charlotte told me the three primes stood for mercury, salt, and sulfur—the same chemicals Deidra pointed out on my palm.

At the top of the roof are a series of metallic spikes shaped like stakes, because some cheeseball probably thinks it's cute. The wraparound horizontal windows bear a dark tint. No one can see the inside from out here, and I wonder if we can see the outside when we're in. Rich pulls us into an underground garage and parks the car.

"This doesn't look like a school," I mutter as I unsnap my seat belt.

"That's because it's a combination of the school and headquarters. The west wing is for the school and dorm rooms. The east wing is for headquarters and business aspects of the Slayer Society and Alchemist Order," Rich answers, surprisingly.

Charlotte grabs the keys. "I'll call the car service and let them pick up the rental."

Just before we enter the building, I pause at the door. Something rolls and tumbles in my stomach.

I want to go home. I imagine Grandma Lou's weathered brown face. I see the worry lines that crisscross her skin.

"Me being here is a mistake. I don't belong here."

"I'll let you deal with the emotional thing, Charlotte." Rich slaps her shoulder and goes in without us.

"Nice," I hiss.

Charlotte shakes her head. "He comes off as an—"

"Asshole?" I helpfully supply.

She nods. "But he's saved a lot of lives. He has a good heart."

No, he does not, and I hope sis isn't in too deep with him. But it's not my place, and better yet, I don't want to be in *this* place.

"Do you like superhero movies?" she asks me.

I shrug. "Yeah. They're okay."

"Think of this moment in time as your origin story. And one day, many years from now, you'll have distance from this moment. And between today and then, you will have saved countless lives and made an impact that is too complex to define. If you need to grieve, then grieve. If you need to yell, then yell."

"What if I just need revenge?"

"Against whom?"

"Vampires."

"Which ones?"

All of them. "Does it matter?"

"Yes. Did you not hear the part where I told you not all vampires are evil?"

I shrug, but inside, I burn. Just last night, my friends got ripped apart by those monsters. Next time I see a vampire, it's on sight. We are fighting to the death, okay? I'm not sticking around to give it a "how nice are you" quiz.

"Whatever your motivation, take the next step. And the next step is opening the door and walking toward your destiny."

I swallow the fear building in my throat, then say, "Fine. Let's go."

We veer off to a side entrance. Charlotte leans over to a square black screen next to the door, and something that looks a lot like a blue laser scans her eyes.

"Welcome, Charlotte," the mechanical male voice greets her. A green light shines, and a happy beep chirps from the system.

"Thank you, Albert. I have a recruit with me. Please scan her eyes and take her pulse and vitals as well."

"Yes. My pleasure. Recruit, please lower your head and keep your eyes open."

I do as he says.

The door swooshes open, revealing a tall steel panel.

"Please, place your hand on the scanner," Albert instructs.

"Sure, why not?" I follow its instructions. The scanner heats beneath my hand, and Albert asks me to scan my other hand, too.

"We're doing all of this to check your pulse and body temperature," Charlotte says. "Vampires are not allowed on the premises."

"Oh?" I lift an eyebrow. "Not even the good ones?"

Charlotte snorts. "Got a smart aleck, I see."

"You may enter. Welcome to Tria Prima Academy."

"Happy to be here." I give the faceless AI a two-finger salute.

When we step into the headquarters, my mouth drops. It's stunning and intimidating and over-freaking-whelming.

"What is this place?"

"Your new home. Let me give you a quick tour." She points to the tapestries that hang from the vaulted high ceilings and drape over the polished floor like runners. The blue, silver-and-gold, and green banners connect with one another at the center of the room in the shape of a triangle. "The three tapestries represent the different houses in the Alchemist Order and Slayer Society: Internists, Distorters, and Evokers."

"Very, um…stately."

"I know, right? They're new. We got them after we hosted the Slayer Olympic games in ninety-six."

"As in 1996?"

"Yes."

"I wasn't even born then."

"Oh, yeah. Something else you'll get used to. Time is a man-made construct."

Ironically, large clocks hang on the opposite wall of the entrance, showcasing different times in various cities around the world.

"We're in the west wing, which houses the academy and living quarters for the students. In the east wing are headquarters and living quarters for teachers and slayers in the field."

When we round the corner, I notice a life-size limestone statue of a man dressed as an ancient Greek warrior with bronze shin guards, or whatever the heck they wore in battle back then, and a plume stuck atop his helmet.

"Is that…Alexander?"

"Yes. We had the statue made after we eliminated him. The statue is a keepsake that will rotate every few hundred years. He'll go to our Asian division in fifty years or so."

We briefly stop walking, and I take in the father of vampires. The former warrior's face is a mix of classically beautiful and crude features. A square chin bevels his sharp, angular jawline. Curly hair falls just below his tree-trunk neck. Wide, symmetrical lips soften his blunt, crooked nose. But his eyes are the creepiest. Made of ivory, they're shiny—one eye brown and the other blue.

The statue is enclosed in a thick glass case and sits on a raised platform. The black-and-gold platform has something etched on it, but before I can read it, Charlotte takes off again, chittering away about the food hall. My stomach grumbles.

"Let's get you something to eat, okay?" she says sympathetically. "After that, we can register you for classes and a uniform. What's your size? You look like a small or medium."

"I'm, um…a medium, I guess."

"Great! I'll get you a laptop, a phone, and a whole new identity should you decide to stay with us. Oh! And then I can introduce you to your roommate."

"I have a roommate?" In a house this big, we should each have our own suite.

"Yes. It's great because you can learn from each other, and now you'll have another friend. Well, besides me."

Friends. My stomach hollows. *I only want Deidra.*

"We'll also need to get your blood drawn. You killed a Royal last night."

"So?"

"So, we'll just need to prove that you are new and innocent to all of this. And that you had no choice but to eliminate him."

"You mean I'll be on trial?"

"In a manner of speaking. The king or prince will taste your blood, which allows them to view what happened. I think you'll have a solid case, seeing as he attacked us first. He attacked you twice."

My blood boils, burns, bubbles. I shake my head slowly. No way. No way on God's green earth am I allowing some freaking vampire to slurp my blood like a Costco sample.

"I don't think so."

"It's protocol, sweetie. Out of my hands, and if you don't comply, it'll go all the way up to The Architect."

The Architect sounds like the Wizard of Oz, or maybe Santa Claus, but I won't be here long enough to bust up this lovely cult they've got going.

"Oh, they may also help us figure out who helped you during the initial attack." She lowers her voice. "I know it's difficult to think about, so the blood sharing would be good in this case. It's important for both slayers and vampires to keep our secrets. I hope it wasn't a regular human."

The way Khamari beat those vampires with his mind, he damn sure wasn't a regular-shmegular dude. But he went to great lengths to make sure I didn't remember him. A teeny-weeny pang of guilt hits me, knowing that his business will now be in the vampire streets, thanks to my snooping.

Will he regret helping me once I blow his identity?

Charlotte gives me a kind smile. "It'll be quick and painless—I promise. You won't even have to be around them. And truly, we have no choice here."

"But what if they disagree? What if they think I'm a stone-cold killer?"

"Oh…well…" She shrugs. "They may make a motion to kill you."

"Say what?" WTF is up with me and death? Like dang, give me a break.

"But don't worry. That hasn't happened in a long time—at least several decades, I think." She waves away my valid question.

According to Little Miss *time is a man-made construct*, that could've happened last year for all I know.

"If they kill me, I'm haunting all of you. Including those vampires."

"Sure, maybe. Haven't heard of a ghost vampire slayer, but that sounds like a blast. Don't worry, though. I'm sure they won't kill you. If they do, we'll just go to war." She shrugs like it's no big deal, and I don't know her well enough to understand if she's joking or serious.

Regardless of the answer, no way in hell did I survive last night just to let a bunch of old vampires kill me.

They can keep their war, and their cult leader can keep these powers.

Just as soon as I can, I'm going back home to Texas.

Life is But a Dream
Khamari

I lean back in the chair in front of Dr. Persing's desk, staring at her. She takes off her glasses and rubs her eyes. The hum of the machines in the lab cuts into the silence.

The freshly printed papers are warm, but the results leave me cold. Nothing has changed. "Dr. Persing, I thought you said the results from the injections were promising?"

The other doctors avoid my gaze. There are four of them—two in internal medicine, one in infectious diseases, and Dr. Persing, a hematologist. She's been with me for the past year. The others are *volunteers*. That's what we planted in their minds, anyway. And these volunteers had one job, a big job—cure vampirism.

If we discover the cure, we can save my brother.

Vampirism at its core is a disease. Porphyria. A defective hemoglobin that makes us sensitive to light. The result causes our skin to burn and makes us experience extreme nausea—not the garden-variety nausea, but a deadly kind that makes you puke blood out of orifices until you die. It's like the vampire Ebola. And the only known way to counteract the illness is to ingest blood.

When I realized this, I formed a dream team of doctors under the guise of saving my brother. But the dream team is quickly turning into a nightmare—Khaven's illness has only gotten worse, and the doctors seem to be losing their shit under our mind alterations.

"The results *seemed* promising," Dr. Persing finally responds.

"The patient's red blood count hit eight thousand, and he was energetic."

"He's not *the patient*; he's Khaven."

My brother.

"My apologies, Prince Khamari," Dr. Persing says through a tight smile. "The red blood count plummeted, and he… *Khaven* fell ill again. We just can't quite get ahead of how Khaven's blood reacts to Porphyria. He's just…like most of the half-breeds that are on the lower scale for strength."

"But that wasn't the case a year ago. He was as strong as me."

Dr. Persing nods. "I understand, and if he had any other blood type, we could try transfusion to stem the regression."

I don't respond, just stare at the numbers that won't give me the answers I desire.

Dr. Persing scratches the back of her neck. "His Golden Blood type is one in a million," she mutters to herself. "But just think of what we can do once we find a cure. He could…could be the key to curing others." Her voice, rarely animated, snaps my attention.

There's only forty other people in the world known to have the Golden Blood type, which lacks the antigens to fight disease and means he can't receive transfusions from other common blood types. Ironically, his blood is universal to anyone with any other blood type. He's a medical anomaly—and his uniqueness is killing him. But the goal has always been to cure Khaven, not just treat his symptoms, and from there, the doctor can keep the results from her work to use on *others*—not my brother.

"The goal is to save him, not to farm out his blood. Don't forget it."

"O-of course, Prince Khamari. I would never."

I throw the crinkled paper into the bin near the sterilized chrome table. The bin topples from the force. "We've been at this for three months with no progress." I stare at the other doctors.

"You're supposed to be the most brilliant minds in the world. Why in the hell can't you figure this out?"

Why can't you cure my brother?

Dr. Hayes, the one I *recruited*—yes, that's what I'll call it—from the CDC and the reason I convinced my grandfather, the Ankh King, to move to Atlanta, grabs her forehead.

"I-I don't know." She drags her hand through her cropped afro.

The doctor beside her, Dr. Jonsberg, jerks his head from side to side. "I. Don't. Know." He parrots Dr. Hayes.

"I don't know. I don't know. I don't know," the others shriek.

Dr. Persing's shaky hand twirls the beads on her necklace. "What's happening?" she whispers. If it weren't for my heightened hearing, I wouldn't have heard her over the doctors parroting one another.

They circle the room like mindless puppets.

That's what they are—puppets. And we need a puppet master. Ransome's and Rider's job is to ease their minds, erase their memories. The humans are probably in agony. If not controlled, the memories will rush through and break them. Humans—their minds and bodies—are incredibly fragile.

"Where are Ransome and Rider?" I snap.

Dr. Persing takes a deep breath. "I couldn't get a hold of Rider. Ransome says he's…busy."

My gut spasms. I have a feeling why he didn't show.

It's a strong possibility that Ethan, the vampire who attacked the slayer girl and the marching band in Texas, told Ransome about the attack. He's a loose end I need to capture, kill, and then burn all evidence of.

For once, I didn't think with my head. By the time I got on the road, the trail was cold and the sun was rising, because I'd stayed behind with a beautiful girl in my arms.

The only thing that can possibly save me is that, if Ethan brings it up to the council, he's as good as dead. He attacked humans, unprovoked, and he partnered with a made vampire to do it. But if he rats me out, I'll need a solid reason and an alibi.

No one can know the truth.

And now Rider's not answering our calls. Maybe Ethan won't tell the Elders, but he'll sure as hell tell his friend whose distant-cousin-slash-uncle, Garin, is on the Elder Council.

The muscles in my stomach damn near turn from solid to liquid at the thought of them finding out the truth behind my visit. I don't need yet another reason for them to doubt me. Not right now.

Ever since Julius announced his plans to step down as the Ankh King and let me succeed him on the throne, Ransome and Rider have been a collective pain in my ass. Julius chalks it up to youth, though the brothers are centuries old. I'm Julius' grandson, I'm powerful, and the king himself chose me, his blood relative. Just how much longer do they need to learn to respect the decision for the throne?

I refocus on Dr. Persing. "Where's Khaven?"

"Khaven left when he realized the doctors' minds weren't altered. He said it was a matter of time before their minds snapped, and he didn't want to stick around." She nibbles her lips, darting glances all around at the parroting doctors. "Looks like he's right."

A lick of anger zips through my spine. My irises have turned silver, if Dr. Persing's slow step backward is any sign. But it's not her fault Ransome and Rider are fuckups.

I stride over to the cabinet, unlock it, and pull syringes from the case.

Needles in hand, I speed through the room and dose the docs. With their human eyes, they don't see me; they can only feel wind flutter their clothes and goosebumps plump their flesh—a human's low-level response to a predator.

Seconds later, the drug-induced doctors sway side to side from the effects of the drugs. Dr. Persing scrambles to cradle the head of one of them before he falls onto the tile floor. I easily catch the others and break their falls one by one.

"They should rest for a few hours. Let Dominic know I want them in the guest bedrooms for now. No one is to enter, and make sure he locks the doors from the inside, yeah?"

Dr. Persing, still fingering her necklace, nods.

"That should buy us enough time to get the brothers back here."

"Shall I call Hilda?" She reaches for the cell phone on her desk.

Hilda, like me, is another Royal with the power to manipulate and erase memories. Her powers are good but not great. My mind manipulation powers haven't matured just yet. But for now, for Khaven, I can't rely on potential, because somewhere locked away in the doctors' minds are the keys to a cure. Unfortunately, the brothers' mind-manipulation powers are exceptional.

"You can call Hilda, but I prefer Ransome and Rider."

Dr. Persing's thumbs move across the screen. "She's not the best, but we can still get the doctors to cooperate, and that's the most important part." She slides her phone back on the desk and rubs her hands together. "I know you're frustrated. I get it. We're so close, but there's a missing piece. We aren't dealing with a typical vampire or human subject—we're dealing with a vampire-human hybrid with a Royal father and human mother. And nothing from this monitor"—she points at the screen that gives real-time updates on Khaven's condition—"is helping. Honestly…I'm a bit out of my element."

"It doesn't matter." My voice hardens. "We'll keep trying. If you can't keep up, leave."

"Of course, Kham—Prince Khamari." She looks away, pretending to stare at the computer on her desk. She isn't used to the new title. Neither am I.

My phone dings with an email.

There's been a major attack on a group of students in Texas, involving Royals and Made vampires. As a result, we eliminated one of your protected clansmen. We have the blood sample from the slayer. Can you convene with the Society today at 2 p.m.?

I smile at the message. A daytime meeting means Julius can't attend and I can intercept the blood and her memories. The others don't need to discover I traveled to another state without their knowledge and permission. And then maybe, finally, they'll want to talk through my partnership proposal.

"Khamari," Julius calls from the door to the lab. "What happened to them?" He points at the pool of doctors on the floor. "You got hungry?" A sly smile reveals a hint of fang.

I grimace, unable to return the smile. "No. The doctors were losing it. Ransome and Rider—"

"Need to be taught a lesson." The warm smile slips from his face. His accent, a combination of British and Caribbean, is more pronounced when he's angry. "Remember, respect is earned, but fear pushes it forward."

"Understood." Rider and Ransome and the rest of the clan who hate me because of my impure bloodline won't respect me until I make them. Looks like I need to bust a few heads.

"Trust me," I say. "I'll deal with them. But I've got a meeting with the Slayer Society. There's been an attack on a group of humans. I'm happy to drink the sample and piece things together for us."

Julius nods. "Idiotic Made vampires. First line of duty when you become king—figure out a way to get those old bastards from the other clans to agree on limiting the Made vampires. We aren't ready to announce our existence. We don't have the numbers for Royals."

And we never will. The only way to create a Royal is to have a human directly bitten by Alexander, who is now dead.

I snort. "How am I supposed to convince the Elders when you can't?"

Royals love getting the Mades to do their dirty work. They view them as expendable. And besides, the Elders Aldercy, Garin, and Maab will never agree to that mandate. Especially Garin. He was one of the vampires who opposed me leading the Ankh clan, and he's especially set in the old ways, including the use of Mades.

"I'll be on the Elder Council, and I can tip the scales for votes." Julius pats his chest.

The Elders are some of the oldest vampires. Some are past kings and queens from the Saqqara, Hekau, and our clan, the Ankh. The Saqqara and the Hekau both have local Elder Councils. Our clan, the Ankh, is the most powerful, due to sheer numbers and its current leader, my grandfather. He's not ruthless and bloodthirsty like the other kings and queens. He's a forward thinker—he invests in technology and has a great relationship with the Alchemist Order and Slayer Society, at least on the surface. He hates them, but he knows how to play the game, and playing the game means doing away with archaic practices that needlessly slaughter humans or threaten to reveal our existence.

There's a lot to admire about my grandfather—a lot I want to carry over into my own reign.

"I'll handle the doctors. I'll handle Ransome and Rider, too." Julius claps my shoulders, and his voice goes from doting grandfather to fearsome vampire king. Never mind that he doesn't look a day over forty.

"No, King Julius, it's my responsibility."

After his announcement that I will soon replace him as king and rule the clan, we both agreed I'd call him King Julius in public, and he'd call me Prince Khamari. Calling him grandfather, in his opinion, makes us look weak.

Julius' eyes train on the only human standing. "Dr. Persing, please see yourself out," he says in that disparaging voice he reserves for humans.

After Dr. Persing rushes past us to leave without saying

goodbye, Grandfather levels his attention to me.

"I'm practically retired. I've got the time. Go on and meet with the Society. We don't need them breathing down our necks—not now, as we transition power."

"Why does it matter if they know I'll become king? I thought you wanted me to get closer to the Slayer Society and Alchemist Order." In fact, he'd proposed a program where I would work more closely with the Slayer Society, under the guise that we rid ourselves of the Made vampire problem. The mindless, bloodthirsty vampires who rarely control their bloodlust are the ones who threaten our secrecy. Yet, Royals are the ones who make them.

"They'll want to test you, and they'll have their little spies around. They don't need to know we're permanently based in Atlanta just yet. And not to mention the other clans will try to snipe you, too, so no more sneaking on your little day trips to check out your old life. That's over now. It's best they think you're dead and gone."

"How'd you know?"

Had he read my mind? The first thing he taught me—hell, I taught myself—is to keep my thoughts in check.

"Relax. I didn't read your mind. Another reason I chose you is because your mind is a tight maze." He taps his temple. "Can't have a king who can't control his thoughts. But that doesn't mean I don't know what's going on. I know *everything*, Khamari. Just like it'll be your responsibility to know what your clansmen are doing. Otherwise, you'll get a knife to the back. Got it?"

"Good as done." I cross my arms and nod.

"You look just like your father when you do that." He swallows hard and looks away. "Damn shame you didn't get to spend more time with him. I can't prove it, but I know someone from the Hekau clan murdered him. He had entrance and exit burns all over his body. They won't admit they did it, though.

Jealous bastards. Our powers have always intimidated them. And your father, he…"

Julius clears his throat. "Get going. I'll find the brothers and get them to do their damn jobs." He taps his fist against his chest and tilts his neck to the left. To any observer, it would look like a greeting from a king to another Royal, but for us, it's a signal—a request to grant him access to use his telepathic powers. There are ears and eyes everywhere.

I release the invisible shield around my mind.

"Don't worry. I'll make them bleed." Julius' voice echoes in my head.

"Are you sure? I can handle it."

"I'll leave them in good enough shape so you can mete out your own punishment. You know the old ones only respect violence."

I nod.

Grandfather gives me that warm smile again. The one that reminds me of my father's, at least from what I've seen in photos.

"You're doing great, son. You've got it all—charisma, charm, and most importantly strength."

I know that when he says *strength*, he really means my powers. Most Royals only have one power, but I have three—mind-manipulation, of course, and then my specialties, dreamwalking and telekinesis. Julius thinks I'll be a powerful king, with three powers under my command. Will I be powerful? Yes. In time, more powerful than any vampire in all three clans. But I wasn't sure they'd let me ascend to power. Not without a fight. Lots of fights.

"They'll fall in line soon." His voice drops to a chill. "They'll have no choice."

"Thanks. I'll let you know what I discuss with the Slayer Society when you wake up tomorrow night." I pat his shoulder and rush out of the lab. On my way out of the house, I find my brother in the sitting room with a pile of gadgets surrounding him.

"Khamari?" Khaven is sitting in his wheelchair with a mini screwdriver in hand. A blanket with my alma mater covers his legs. He gets a kick out of the fact that his long-lost younger brother played football.

Though he's only twenty-three years old, illness has diminished his frame. And with the tangled curls that border his face, he looks like a cherub. He rubs at the insert on his forearm that monitors his health.

I remember the day I met him. Khaven wasn't as sick back then. In fact, he was walking, albeit slowly. Months later, he walked with a cane. He met me near the stairwell of the plane, waiting for me to descend. As soon as my feet were planted on the ground, he pulled me into a hug and whispered, *"Welcome home, little brother."*

"Hey." I nod toward the hallway, letting him know we would have to move and talk. "What are you working on?" I point at a watch in his hand.

"Modifying an Apple Watch for Julius. He wants one like mine."

Khaven beefed up his watch to monitor his health and the progression of his disease. He's a wiz with technology and even created some spy gadgets for my meetings with the slayers and vampire council—none of which I've used. I didn't want to explain why I tracked their movements or recorded conversations. There is no need for that...yet.

Khaven's electric wheelchair hums beside me as I walk toward the garage.

"Why does Julius need one?"

"I convinced him," he replies cryptically.

I shake my head. My brother and grandfather's relationship is declining faster than Khaven's health. There's something deeper going on, something that started before I came to live with the clan. Grandfather claims it's because Khaven is no longer next in line for the throne. But in the time that I've gotten to know my brother, I've become certain he'd much rather spend his time on tech, not vampire politics.

Khaven says Julius is up to something and he's determined to out him.

I grunt, but I don't dig any further. I'm still pissed that Khaven left his therapy session. "Why weren't you there with Dr. Persing and the others?" I ask.

"The doctors, you mean. Human beings with spouses and kids and a full life."

When I look at him, I notice the guilt in his golden eyes.

"Nothing's going to change," he says. "And now the clan is questioning you, ever since you convinced Julius to move us all the way down south...just to save me."

"I don't care. I'll be king soon. What I say, goes." We make it to the garage door. But before I can open it, Khaven closes his eyes and opens the door with telekinesis.

"Don't use your powers." I step through the entryway.

"I want to—otherwise, I'll get rusty. Where are you off to?"

"Doing some errands. Then later, I'm meeting with the Slayer Society."

"How much later?"

"Daytime."

He stares at me, a smile curving across his lips. "You think they'll say yes?"

Khaven is all for my plan. In fact, he's the mastermind behind us having the Society invest in synthesized blood.

I nod. "I don't see why not. It's a win-win."

"Good. Remember, you aren't the pawn. You'll be the king."

I chuckle. "Still not the most important piece."

"Important enough." His liquid eyes go hard.

I walk to the door and open it, waiting for Khaven to go back up the ramp. "Be sure to go to the lab. Dr. Persing will be back soon."

"Got it." He coughs into his fist, his bony shoulders shaking. When he lowers his hand, blood-streaked mucus stains his palm.

The taste of terror, thick and foul, clogs my throat. *No time. No time at all.* And I only just discovered that I have a family a year ago. Khaven welcomed me wholeheartedly, and every night we talked for hours about my time living as a human. When the other vampires sneered at my existence, he was my staunch advocate. He was the brother I'd always wanted but never had growing up as a poor foster-care kid in Jamaica, where I was passed around from foster parent to foster parent.

All the anger from the day recedes as fear rises. Fear suffocates. Fear clouds judgment.

Fear has no place here. But the highs and lows, the hope for a miracle, knowing there's none granted for the damned, all feel like pinpricks to my lungs.

"Hey, listen, Mari." His voice is weak. "If I don't make —"

"Quiet," I snap, then repeat our mantra. "No fear. No doubt. You know this."

"But —"

"You will beat this. No matter the cost, understand?" Not just money, but my life, my soul. What good is an immortal life if you can't save those you love?

"Yeah. I think I do understand," he says as if he can read my thoughts.

"Good." I place my hand on his shoulder. I want to grab him, hug tight, but if I do, I might hurt him.

The little smile on his face disappears, as if he can read my fears.

"Go to the lab and find Dr. Persing," I tell him. "We've both got work to do."

He needs to stay alive. And I need to con the vampire clans and the Slayer Society.

No New Friends
Raven

From atop the nightstand, my alarm blares, startling me awake. "Shit." I try to smack my palm against the clock like it's a bug on the move.

But when I try lifting my hand, it just won't budge.

"Get up, girl," I mutter to myself and roly-poly over, pushing to sit up in bed. The act alone takes eleven hundred years. Starched cotton sheets tangle around my ankles.

"Morning, Raven."

I clutch my heart at the welcome. "Oh, hey," I greet the girl, my new roommate.

When I met her two days ago, I wanted to burst into tears. With her curly brown hair, freckles, and green eyes, she looks so much like Deidra that seeing her felt like a kick to the gut.

But she isn't my Deidra—she's Dakota. And unlike my bestie, she's painfully shy and speaks in whispers. If my hearing wasn't on hound-dog settings, I wouldn't be able to catch her soft replies. But she isn't so bad. She didn't tell me to shut up when I woke up screaming from nightmares. She simply handed me a bottle of water and sleeping pills.

I close my eyes and drop my head back against the headboard. *Why do I feel like hell?* Charlotte told me that slayers rarely get sick.

"You were screaming again last night."

"Sorry." This time, I whisper. That's right. I can't get a good night's rest.

"It's okay. I've got my noise-canceling headphones, but the others can probably hear. I'm thinking that maybe we can soundproof our room?"

I grab my elbows and hug myself tight. "If we ask, then the teachers will know."

"We can order a kit online and have it delivered. Believe it or not, they uphold our privacy." She takes a deep breath and adjusts her oversize glasses. "You aren't the only person who has nightmares."

"You have them, too?"

"It's been two years, but yeah." She chews her lips. "I'll never forget what happened to my family."

The urge to ask her what happened hops to the tip of my tongue, but I swallow my curiosity. If she shares, then I'll have to share, too, and then…no. No, I'm not ready for all of that. "Thanks for the tip. I'll…let you know if I need it because, ya know…might not be here."

"Oh." She says it in a voice pitched low and exceedingly sad, like someone's died and she's very, very sorry for it. Her eyes are as sad as her voice.

I'm taking the week before I make my decision on whether I'll stay. Even though Charlotte promised that if I'm not feeling it, I can leave, if I take her up on that, I won't have protection and my memories will go *poof*.

Which is why Dakota's looking at me like I'm ten steps away from my grave.

"I'm not going to run away into the night, you know." I'm sure I'm not the first reluctant slayer. I mean, who in their right mind would want to fight monsters like it's their nine-to-five?

Not to mention I'll never see Grandma Lou again. Part of my recurring nightmares is hearing her soul-wringing cries over my bodyless grave. My nightmares are so vivid, I smell the salt of her tears. Her pain suffocates me. Drowns me.

So, I'll play this maybe-I'll-stick-around game. Make some "friends," borrow someone's cell phone, and then either send a signal or ring the alarm to Grandma Lou.

I've got to see her or at least speak to her, give her the proper goodbye she didn't get with my mom and grandfather.

"Random question," I say, "but...do you have a phone?"

"Of course."

Ha! This'll be a cakewalk, baby. Cake. Walk.

"But...if you're making a call to a loved one, you're wasting your time."

"Huh?"

"Yeah. They like to 'take away temptation.'" She adds air quotes. "By now, they've finagled a way to change the person's phone number, email, and social media accounts." She gives me a what-can-you-do shrug.

Grandma Lou only has a landline, no social accounts. Still, that's super shady. "I know you're lying."

"Afraid not. It's like the witness protection program, but in reverse. And we have the means to alter their memories. So, even if you see them, they won't know you."

It feels like a sumo wrestler does somersaults in my stomach. Is she for real? "W-what if I go back for a visit?" My voice shakes.

"You can try, but we all have trackers."

"I don't." *Do I?*

"You will. That is, if you want to be in the field. But, hey. The silver lining is you have someone out there who loves you. Someone who survived. A lot of us lost our family and friends in our...transition. Be grateful for that." She lifts her quivering chin as she says, "Be grateful that you can protect them, even if they don't know it...or you."

I lost my friends, but I'm not in the mood to share or correct her. I don't want to remember. The memories already robbed my nights.

I lift my lips into what I hope is a passable smile. "Right. Silver lining."

Change of plans. Go to class, snoop around the academy, find an exit or two, get some of that vampire repellent or whatever it is that blocks my slayer smell—lots of it. There's gotta be a recipe. It's not like it's available on Amazon.

When Dakota smiles, I smile back, throwing her the deuces in my mind.

She then turns to make up her bed. I copy her movements just in case there's some sort of inspection. Charlotte assures me we have *loose* ties to the government, but I still don't know what to expect.

After I straighten my sheets, I quiz Dakota. "What's on the agenda today?"

She sits on the chair near the small coffee table. "You're in the Tyro class, which means you're a beginner, so you'll learn various fighting techniques and the basics in alchemy."

I nod, not understanding what the hell Tyro means. I think back to the shocked look on Charlotte's face when I ripped out that vamp's heart. Or Pretty Boy's expression when I stood my ground.

"Can Tyros kill vampires?"

"What do you mean?" Dakota tilts her head.

"I mean, can I go out there and fight vampires? Like, go on missions and stuff."

And then go AWOL.

"Oh." She laughs. "I mean, yeah, but you're a new Tyro, so it's gonna take some time. Like six months to a year. And usually, it's just scoping out vampires with a senior slayer in the field."

"That long?"

"Trust me, it'll feel like it's not long enough. But once you get into the field, you get to choose a cool code name that's either a city, state, or country."

"Ah. Thus, Charlotte, Richmond, and Dakota."

"Yes, exactly. Anyway, there's a lot to learn. It's difficult to kill vampires." Her cheeks go red as she pushes a curly strand of hair behind her ear. "I might as well tell you." She closes her hands into tight, small fists. "I got a failing grade on my first mission. Actually…a few missions."

"They give out grades. Like school?"

She nods. "Exactly like school, but much more important, because the things you learn are a matter of life and death. Do you know what I did before I became a slayer?"

"No." How could I? I just met the chick.

"I'd just graduated high school and joined the Peace Corps. I built houses and ditches, those types of things. I rescued animals and found good homes or sanctuaries for them. I would never, ever want to harm another living creature."

"Eh, vampires are kinda already dead."

Two red dots stain her cheeks. She looks like a Raggedy Ann doll. "But are they really? They have a heartbeat. They have a brain. They have feelings. I've seen the fear in their eyes when they're about to die at the hands of a slayer, and I just…can't do it."

I shrug. "I can understand that. If that's not who you are, you shouldn't feel forced to change your nature. Hell, none of us should. Having these powers isn't a gift—it's a curse."

"Exactly! Charlotte says it's a mental block, but maybe…maybe The Architect made a mistake with me. I'm not a good slayer."

Dakota rolls her shoulders slowly, as if she's uncomfortable in her skin. "I work with Charlotte and Paris. I'm their assistant. A role usually meant for a trusted human, but the last one died, and here I am."

It's on the tip of my tongue to say, "Lucky you," but she might get offended by my slightly morbid sense of humor.

She finally looks at me. "So now you know my big secret. Well, it's not a secret, and no one ever lets me forget it, but I'm going to change. I'm going to prove that I can be tough."

"Now you're going to kill vampires?" I cross my arms. "That

doesn't seem right."

"No. Charlotte says I don't have to kill vampires, but I should learn basic skills to defend myself and properly use my powers if I decide to do a rescue mission. But I can't help if I become a liability in the field."

"I can respect that."

She smiles, and her dreary expression brightens. Her moss-green eyes glitter with determination. "Thank you." She looks at her phone. "You should probably get ready. I'll lay out your uniform for you."

I nod and head to the bathroom. When I return, I find a pair of black leggings and a gold tank top with a moon and sun embroidered on the top left side. By the time I get myself together, we're late for the Tyros Fighting 101 class. But it doesn't matter, though, because the teacher walks in thirty minutes after the start time.

We pass the ten-foot-tall mesh cage that encloses the arena and slip off our sneakers, careful not to dirty the sturdy blue mat.

The training area is half martial arts studio and half gym. Sparring equipment, including headgear, target mitts, and gloves, are tucked neatly along the cage wall.

Sweat and funk that even Febreze can't freshen cling like dew on grass. I breathe in deep. *Not so bad.* Blood and burning flesh smell worse.

Students jab the punching bags, and a symphony of grunts, heavy breathing, and curse words echo throughout the training area. The loudest noise is from a guy who's curling 250-pound dumbbells in each hand.

"No." One of the older students patiently speaks to a young boy who can't be older than thirteen. She points at the gash on her callused hand. "Go deep until you feel a connection with The Source. Only then will you be able to close my wound. Go on." She smiles.

"That's Charleston," Dakota says to me as we pass. "She's super talented."

The young boy that Charleston instructs nods and squeezes his eyes shut. A blue mist swirls from his hands to hers. Her skin stitches back together within seconds. A blood smear is the only evidence left behind.

Charleston jumps and squeals. "You did it, Jay!" Then she pushes up her sleeves and jabs herself with a small knife, this time on her shoulder and much deeper. "Again."

"That's the Internist Guild. Internists focus on healing."

"I'm a Distorter." I lower my voice. "Internist seems like a bleh power to me. Give me the power to kick someone's ass over healing any day."

"That's, um, interesting that you know your guild. Usually, you would have to do an aptitude test, plus the unveiling ceremony. The Maestros can usually tell based on personality and fighting skills, but The Architect makes the final decision during the ceremony. Once you take the oath, it'll appear on your palm, here." She points to my hand and then frowns. "Huh."

"Huh? What, huh?" I stare at my hand.

"Do you see the sun and moon? Your tattoo has color."

"Yeah, and?" Charlotte already noticed that when she met me.

"It takes years, like ten or fifteen, to get color in your tattoo."

"Huh," I repeat, because I'm not really sure what to say to that. It's not like I chose how my tattoo looks.

I guess she has nothing to say to that, either, because she opens her palm and reveals a symbol of an eye. "This is the Eye of Ra."

"Sorry, which guild is that again?"

She bites her lips and gives me a strained smile. "Internist."

Ahh, crap. "My bad. Did I say bleh? I meant that's cool. Like Wolverine or something!"

"I guess." She's embarrassed and unsure, and I feel like a jackass.

"No, it's true. Someone chops off your arm, and it grows right back? How cool is that?"

"It doesn't really work like that. You have to go within, meditate, and use your life force. So, if you're fighting a vampire, you can't exactly sit down and do breathing exercises in real time."

I wince. "For real?"

She nods. "With time, you can tap more quickly into your power. Some masters can do it in five seconds. But they are, like, seriously old."

"Yeah, right? Forgot that we don't do the whole aging thing."

Another little gift from the cult master supreme being or whatever. Forever young until they're done with you.

"Ah, man, Maestro Cali is teaching us today," I hear someone moan from the back of the cardio area.

"Where's Maestro Kansas?" someone else whispers.

A woman with spiky black hair strides across the room. Maestro Cali, I assume. "Shut it with the complaints," she sings as she stands before us. "And be grateful I've agreed to train you. Maybe, just maybe, you all won't die within a year. Tyros, get in formation," Maestro Cali barks.

The slayers spring into action, tucking away their equipment and neatly reracking the weights. All but two fall into line. Dakota and me. We're both the new recruits—well, kinda.

I chance a glance at Dakota, who looks at Maestro Cali as if she's the devil. And the Maestro is looking at Dakota like she's a misbehaving imp. Maestro Cali narrows her eyes, and I can imagine what she's thinking. Instead of wearing the ill-fitted pantsuit she had on when I first met her, Dakota's sporting an oversize blue T-shirt with an Eye of Ra on the center. I wince again when I think of my careless comment. Just because I don't want friends doesn't mean I want enemies. And so far, she isn't so bad.

Maestro Cali grabs Dakota's elbow and hustles her to the

other side of the room, near the weights. I follow them, making sure that… Shoot. I don't know. Making sure my non-friend is okay, I guess.

Arms crossed, I lean against the weight rack. A steel barbell jabs into my back, but I don't move. I swing my head from side to side. From what I can see, there are no exits besides the door we entered. No phones or computers are in sight. I'll probably have more luck in an actual classroom. Besides, this room with a million and one weapons is not the place to plan an escape.

Digging my heels into the spongy mat, I stare on, curious and quiet and ready to take flight like a fly on the wall.

"What are you doing here?" Maestro Cali hisses. Her dyed black hair, spiked and sticking in various directions like a porcupine, is as sharp as her words.

Dakota wraps an arm around her waist, checking over her shoulder to see if the other kids are listening. A few students are stretching their arms and legs and *ears*. Some of them whisper behind their hands. A trio of guys break formation and openly stare like we're the stars in a horror show.

"Paris says it's time for me to resume my training. And I want to learn, too."

Maestro Cali snorts, looks back at me, then at Dakota. "You've got a bodyguard now?"

"She's my friend."

Eh. I don't want someone else to die in front of me. But I don't want to embarrass her, so I clamp my mouth shut and give the Maestro lady a tight smile and a quick wave.

She lifts her thread-thin eyebrow that's starkly dark against her pale skin. "Heard she ripped a vampire's heart out, so you could do worse."

Dakota gasps and throws an accusing glance my way.

I snort. "Charlotte's been talking, huh?"

"No. Blame Bitch Rich."

"Who?" I push off the rack and walk over to them.

She rubs her ruby red–painted lips together before she scowls. "Bitch Rich. The Maximus. Movie-star looks, shitty personality. Thinks he's God's gift to the world, and maybe he is, but why brag about it, right?"

"Right." I'm not gassing her up. I totally agree.

She returns her attention to Dakota. "Is Paris pressuring you? Because last time we trained, you weren't exactly up to it, Miss Peace Corps. Not to mention you're scared of the fuckers."

Dakota balls her fists. "The Architect gave me powers for a reason, so I need to use them."

There's something lurking in her eyes—steel. Resilience.

The Maestro looks up at the ceiling and groans. "Whatever. I'm not going easy on you."

Dakota's face instantly brightens.

Now that that's settled, Maestro Cali turns and tosses me a look. "Let's go." She stops her march and grabs my hand. I jerk it back.

What is up with people grabbing me without my permission?

"I want to see your palm," she says.

I open my hand. "Bitch Rich has been talking again?"

"Don't call him Bitch Rich. Only adults can say that."

Girl, please.

She examines my hand. "And no, this is all Charlotte. She says you're a Distorter like me. Though spiritual ink with your guild rarely pops up for weeks, maybe even a few months."

"Oh, yeah… Y'all do the sorting-ceremony thingy, right?"

"Yeah, except that it's not a dusty magical hat. It's a directive from—"

"The all-knowing Architect, right?" I roll my eyes.

Cali's lips wrestle with a smile. "Got a good feeling about you." She drops my hand. "Hope you don't die anytime soon."

"Yeah, same."

Dakota shoots me a smile and a thumbs-up. I guess her

wanting me not to die is a good thing.

As we march back to the other side of the room, I pay closer attention to my new non-friend. Even with the enormous shirt, I can tell she's emaciated. Her hair hangs lifelessly around her shoulders. Her back is ramrod straight, and her clavicles stand out under her alabaster skin.

"What is she doing here?" another student asks. As the students chatter, Dakota's head droops.

I step beside her and nudge her shoulder. "Don't worry about them," I tell her.

"You all probably know Dakota as Paris' assistant." The Maestro raises her voice above the fray, but the students quiet down quickly. "She's a Tyro, like you. Unlike some of you, she already has her field name, but, trust me, she's earned it working directly with our Commander."

Dakota swings her big doe eyes up to stare at Maestro Cali. She looks surprised by the praise.

"She doesn't look like a Dakota. She looks like a drowned mouse."

Mouse. The name strikes me like a dagger to the heart.

The guy who made the comment is not quite six feet tall, with brown hair and hard brown eyes. He's good-looking in that all-American-quarterback kind of way. He gets a few nervous snickers from the group.

"Now, we can't all have a rich mommy and daddy to baby-wipe our faces when the vamps come a-callin', can we, Andreas?" our teacher roasts him.

Andreas' face, along with his neck and arms and ears, turns fire-engine red.

Maestro Cali points to Andreas. "And don't laugh at his stupid jokes." Her attention moves around the room but settles on the trio that flanks him. "He's a privileged child of high-ranking Magisters. He makes no difference to your survival rate."

Well, dang. Now, I want to know his story. He's obviously in a different guild, from his green T-shirt and the 3D-looking cube design on it, and I wonder what he can do. I promise myself to get the tea from Dakota after class. But for now, I need to focus on the firecracker teacher in front of me.

"Listen up, Tyros. Three miles. One hundred push-ups, one hundred pull-ups. Rock climbing." She points to the wall behind me.

My mouth drops. I've never scaled a rock wall.

"Ten thousand feet under one hour, with no harness and no rope."

"But we've never climbed the wall without them," someone whines.

"Do you really think you'll have time to hook onto something, scale a wall, and chase a vampire?"

I mean, no, but still. Let me work up to it.

No one answers.

"The wall is timed. And trust me, you do not want to come in last." She looks at me and Dakota.

"What happens if you're last?" I ask.

"You don't pass, you don't go into the field."

"Ugh." I'm literally between a rock and a hard place. If I refuse to climb the wall, I won't get out of here anytime soon. That is, unless I can escape. But can I really duck and dodge people who can scale thousands of feet without a rope?

"I've got to do this," I tell myself. Sure, I haven't climbed a rock wall before, but I've overcome a million difficult things already. This stupid wall won't stop me from living my life.

Latin is for Lovers
Raven

Apparently, slayer powers do not give you the ability to scale walls like Spider-Man. I fall not one, not two, but four times. Luckily, one student showed me how it's done. I mimicked her movement, using my legs to push up and swing for momentum. Oh, and per her snooty tip: "Toes on the holes, dumbass."

Everything in my body, especially my behind, screams at me to quit. I'm second to last, but I finish. Everyone does except for Dakota.

"Get down from the wall. Time to move on," Maestro Cali yells as the rest of us hydrate and wait for the next set of insane instructions.

Dakota tumbles off the wall and jogs up beside me. The class is in some formation, but I'm not sure where I fit in, so I edge just beyond their straight lines. The section leader in me is unimpressed with my performance, but hey, not my fault if I'm not given my mark.

The Maestro turns around and addresses the rest of the group. "Today, everyone will do a five-minute simulation on The Beast. We'll observe as a group and critique what went wrong, what went well, and what you can adjust. If you fail, you'll need to provide me with an analysis and alternate strategy. Each week, we'll add five minutes. Until you're ready to go out in the field, I will drive you, I will stretch you, and I will push you until you expect the unexpected and nothing on God's green earth is new to you. Understood?"

"Yes, Maestro Cali." They speak in unison. I mutter a few beats behind the group.

"Now, I'm going to sweeten the deal. Whoever can kill a vamp inside The Beast simulation can join me on my next assignment over the weekend."

"Don't get too excited," the Maestro warns over the excited chatter from the Tyros. "It's a boring monitoring mission, but I promise to teach you all my tricks. And during missions, I'll treat you like an equal."

"A field mission? Like, outside, with equipment and stuff?" I squeak.

"Affirmative," the Maestro confirms.

"That's awesome!" someone else says.

Excitement buzzes around the room. No one likes Maestro Cali, but it seems they still want to learn from her.

"I'm choosing only one winner."

"What if multiple people win?" one of the girls asks.

She snorts. "It won't happen."

"But what if it happens?" she asks again.

"I'm only bringing one of you. Pick a random number and deal with it."

I tuck my hands against the small of my back. My heart thunders in my chest. It's not that I'm afraid of a simulation, but I am nervous. On one hand, I'm great at performing music. But I don't love the idea of being critiqued by others. Not only that, but I'm also not sure how to use my powers just yet. The only thing I have going for myself is strength. And though my strength saved me from the vamps, when I used it, Pretty Boy, Charlotte, and Bitch Rich stared at me like I'm a ticking time bomb. And honestly, I really don't want to be known as Wreck-It Raven at Tria Prima.

Might be worth it if it gives me the opportunity to get the

hell out of here, though.

"Who wants to go first?" Maestro Cali challenges the group.

No one volunteers; we just silently stare at one another, waiting for a brave soul to raise a hand.

A big part of me wants to win, so I can run away equipped with vampire blocker and weapons. But do I really have a shot at this? Not only that, but I have to do the simulation in a way that doesn't make me look incompetent. Maybe I can watch the others, copy their movements?

"Why don't we see what Mouse can do?" Andreas not-so-helpfully offers.

Dakota wipes the sweat on her baggy gray jogging pants and stretches. Her dim brown eyes focus on the wall behind us. Andreas is an ass, but she really does resemble a scared mouse.

Whenever he says *Mouse*, I see Deidra again, grinning and marching and playing that squeaky piccolo. The squeaks annoyed our band director so much that he gave her a loaner to use during the games. Deidra paid it no mind. Her mother had scrimped and scraped to buy her that secondhand instrument.

My stomach knots. I clench my fist. "Stay here," I whisper harshly to myself.

"Quiet, Andreas." Maestro Cali's sharp words jerk me back to the present. "Who wants to go first?"

A girl with white-blond hair and big blue eyes raises her hand. On her palm is a tattoo of the half moon and half sun that represent my guild, the Distorters. Her tat has no color, so I wonder back to Dakota's comment about color representing strength.

Does that mean I'm stronger than her? Doesn't seem logical, considering I just started training, but nothing about this entire thing seems logical or real.

Maestro Cali turns away, moving toward the boxy black machine in front of us. "Simulations are randomized, so don't give me shit about giving someone preferential treatment." She stops walking. "I don't much care for any of you, but I really don't care for funerals. Got it?"

"Yes, Maestro Cali."

"All right, Barbie. You're up first." The Maestro jerks her head toward the luminescent bio-dome.

"It's Santa Barbara," she mutters.

Maestro Cali points to the stack of black suits behind her. "Suit up and step into the arena."

Barbie shimmies into the silicon-like material. Little white dots cover the entire suit.

I wince at the thought of shrugging my hips into the unrelenting suit. "Is that our uniform?" I ask Dakota.

"No, it's just something the geniuses in the Alchemist Order cooked up."

"Right, the Alchemist Order. Who the hell are alchemists?"

Dakota smiles at my confusion. "They're the scientists and techies that help us with our gear. They teach us chants and prayers to summon powers. Hey, are you any good at Latin?"

I shrug. "I can get by." I mostly learned Latin in freshman and sophomore year because I *thought* I wanted to be a doctor.

"Then you are way ahead of the class," Dakota says. "The hardest part is learning Latin and remembering the chants and prayers."

"Well, that's a relief." It really is. I'm ready to kick ass—as soon as possible.

"I never could pass the simulations, either." Dakota sighs. "I've got a lot to learn, but I'm glad I can do it with you." She looks at me all hopeful-like.

"I'm not…" I catch myself.

"You're not what?" Her eyes look worried.

Not trying to make new friends.

But how can I say that to her with her Bambi eyes and wobbly

Bambi legs and every other innocent thing she has going on?

"Nothing." I grit my teeth. I'm sure once she gets to know my lovely grumpy self, that'll make her back away.

Once Barbie enters the ring, the Maestro hands her a pair of headphones and adjustable headgear to cover her eyes and ears.

"Ready?"

Barbie gives a thumbs-up and steps through the nearly invisible bubble that forms a dome over the arena.

The Maestro flips the start button, then steps back with the rest of us slayers to observe. A large projector shows an aerial view of Barbie, but we can also watch the action without the projector, as we're all standing just outside of the bubble.

Barbie stands in a wide-open space the size of a football field. The night sky, littered with stars, blazes bright. From the air that puffs from her lips, it's cold. She doesn't shiver as she scopes out the area. Her attention snaps to the old barn that stands about a hundred feet away. Near the barn is a red-clay-colored building with a dome-shaped roof. A pitchfork and large, round bales of hay sit propped against the building.

The setting isn't that creative, but apparently, what they lack in scenery, they make up for in violence. Seconds later, a vampire materializes and slashes at her. Barbie darts away. The vampire disappears and then materializes again, this time on the roof of the barn.

"A Saqqara," one of the Tyros whispers. "Tough match-up."

"Saqqara vamps attack and disappear, tiring and frustrating their opponents, so she'll have to be patient." Dakota gives me a pointed look. "Distorters are notoriously impatient."

"Okay, and?"

"You don't seem like the patient type."

I snort. "Listen, I'm different." I shift my focus back to the screen.

Barbie clicks her index finger against a spiked ring. Blood

trickles to her hands, oozing past the transmutation circle tattooed on her palm.

It's the same thing the Maximus did in the motel parking lot. A blood sacrifice of some sort to activate his power.

Barbie slaps her hands together, kneels, and slams her hands against the ground. With bloody fingers, she speed-writes symbols on the dirt. It looks like some sort of math formula, but instead of numbers, there are shapes and symbols that kinda remind me of the tats on our hands.

A silver orb bursts forth from the ground. She grabs it and then flattens the energy ball between her palms, clasps her hands, and stretches it into a lasso. She wraps the rope around her right forearm and bicep.

The vampire appears again, this time a few inches to her left. Barbie yanks a blade from her belt and slices his chest. The vampire staggers back and disappears into thin air. He teleports a few more times. Barbie slashes and feints, but she hasn't yet used the alchemy weapon wrapped around her arm.

Right before he appears, the wind picks up, blowing her hair ever so slightly.

Is that his "tell"?

The vamp vanishes again. Barbie whirls the rope in the air. It glows an iridescent silver. The rope snaps to the left and wraps around nothing. But then the vampire appears, struggling against the tightening lasso.

She jerks the squirming creature to the ground, dragging him until he lies beneath her booted heel. A grin stretches across her face as she grinds her foot into his neck. The vampire snarls and snaps, struggling against the electric bond.

My heart is pounding. This shit looks so real. So real that my mind drifts to the memory of my own nightmarish experience.

But when she slaps her hands together, I come back. Barbie removes a blade from her sheathe, mutters some sort of Latin-chant thing, and then thrusts the blade into its heart.

The screen flashes black. I glance at the clock. She has a minute and a half to spare.

"Well, would you look at that." Maestro Cali gives a slow clap, and the rest of us join her. "Looks like we have a winner for the stakeout, unless someone else can defeat The Beast."

The class breaks out into excited chatter as Barbie unhooks herself from the simulation system. Maestro Cali waves at her to stand beside her and face the group.

"You did well." The Maestro clears her throat. "Talk us through what happened, step by step."

Barbie nods and squares her shoulders before explaining, "After the second time he teleported, I noticed a slight stirring in the air, like a gust of wind from the direction he'd come from."

So my hunch was correct.

"I used the electrified lasso to stun him," she continues, "then brought him closer so I could stake him."

The Maestro nods. "If you noticed the pattern a second time around, why did you let him repeat it five times?"

Barbie clears her throat. "I wanted to be sure I was right. Didn't want to show my hand too early."

"Nope," the Maestro says, shaking her head. "Next time, do it when you first notice a pattern. That was a *simulation* of a Royal. Not a real one. And you can't afford to give Royals more time. We're stronger than Ticks—Made vampires—but we are not physically stronger than the Royals." She looks at the rest of us. "Follow your instincts. Some of you are still thinking like regular humans and second-guessing yourselves. We are hunters. We must use the strength of our enhanced senses that go beyond taste, touch, smell, sound, and sight."

"You're right." Barbie's squared shoulders lose some of their starchiness. "Sorry."

"Don't be sorry, just be better. Learn from this and use the

knowledge to your advantage. Always take the advantage." The
Maestro slaps Barbie's shoulder and points to the line, effectively
dismissing her. "Who's next?"

The rest of the group is less than extraordinary. Maestro Cali
yells at them for not knowing how to do the basics, like forming
a defensive barrier. I somehow get her to do a quick demo, or
rather, she forces one of the other Tyros to show me.

Following Barbie, the only other Tyro who survives is Andreas.
During his performance, Dakota tells me that he's an Evoker, a
nature manipulator, so he uses the earth and rains bullets on the
vampire and strangles him with vines. He also surfs around the
arena on some sort of water-slash-ice-scooter he'd created from
a puddle of water, looking like a fake-ass Avatar.

Honestly, he could've quickly decapitated the vamp with the
vines, but I could tell he was showing off for his friends. After
he wins, he brags that he's a descendant of Albertus Magnus, an
alchemist and saint.

It's a real shame sainthood isn't genetic.

The only ones left to go now are me and Dakota.

"Okay, I guess since we have only two winners—"

I raise my hand. "I want to try."

Maestro Cali shakes her head. "No, this isn't happening."

"Why not?" I grit out.

"After all the...dispiriting performances, I realize you're too
new. You don't even know the phrases to conjure weapons."

"I'm a quick study." In high school, all I did was study. Studying
kept me busy—kept the probing eyes of teachers and principals
off my back. Most importantly, it made Grandma Lou proud. It
made her forget about that one time that I nearly lost it.

Maestro Cali marches to where I'm standing and towers over
me. She shoves a hand through her hair. "Look, we all have horror
stories. This group"—she jerks her head toward the others—
"some of them have been around for a year or more. You don't

understand the elemental breakdowns and—"

"Decapitate the head or fatally stab the heart. Those are the two primary organs any creature needs to live."

"Fine. You get a gold star. But it still doesn't make you ready."

"I don't care. I'm built different." My insides are a squirmy mess, but on the outside I just shrug. She needs to get out of my way so I can win. To prove to myself I'm not a hopeless weirdo who can't keep it together.

The pensive look on the Maestro's face drops. "All right. Your fake funeral."

I pump my fist and look at Dakota. "Wish me luck."

She tugs at the stray wild curl that droops from her ponytail. "Good luck with everything."

I smile, plan in place. Watching the other Distorters gave me ideas, and it's especially helpful when Maestro Cali breaks down their moves and explains how to better leverage our powers. Distorters can alchemize an object or material into something else. I saw one Tyro use the material of a wheelbarrow, turning it into a gun.

I hop into the simulation suit, wriggling the sticky silicon over my perspiring skin. The Maestro hands me the headgear and headphones.

"Good luck," she says in a voice that conveys she doesn't expect much.

I mean, didn't she just compliment me on ripping out a vampire's heart?

I narrow my eyes and mutter, "Thanks."

She puts her hand on my shoulder. "It's not enough to be strong or angry or brave. We need alchemy because we aren't as physically strong as the Royals, and learning that will take some time. Maybe less time for someone like you, but it won't be quick and easy. You've got to learn the alchemical formulas, for one."

"What do you mean by 'learn'?"

"As in memorize them and then chant." She snorts. "It's not like the formulas appear out of thin air."

My heart tumbles and thunders in my chest. "T-they don't?" I most definitely saw the formulas when we were attacked a few days ago. Is that not what it was like for the people I watched in the simulation just now?

Maestro Cali crosses her arms. "No," she says slowly. Her eyes narrow. "That's the biggest gap. That's why you should sit this one out."

Okay, so that's another weird thing that I can do and others can't. I'll obsess over it later.

I shrug off her hand and advice. "Let's go."

The simulation flips on, and everything goes dark.

A Pain in My Ass
Raven

Like the others before me, I see the same barnyard and farmhouse. But what I couldn't imagine before is the feeling. Just a few seconds ago, the suit was hot and sticky against my skin—now I'm shivering from the cold. Ah. So that's the reason for the small white dots. It must be some sensory-simulation thing.

The vampire appears, but he's not flying. His body illuminates with blue light. Bolts of electricity seem to orbit his body. His hair is long and blond, and he's stocky and stacked like Thor from the movies, but he has an iron suit, and a helmet partially covers his head.

I laugh at fake Thor until the bastard zaps me with electricity.

First off, *oww*. Those sensory things are disrespectfully sensitive.

Also, what the hell is up with this simulation? This one is different from the other ones. My heart beats fast as I tuck and roll away from the sparks of fire the vamp shoots at me. I run inside the open barn as I mentally review the vampire's stats: Power clan vamp. Hekau or whatever the hell. Energy-based powers. In summary, this asshole shoots electricity.

Electricity, huh? I need an insulator for protection, and I have zero idea how to create a suit.

"Wood. I need dry wood." But I don't exactly have an axe, nor am I Groot.

What did the others do? Sliced their hands, did a chant or

prayer thingy, and asked The Architect, who I'm starting to think is as real as the Easter Bunny, for what they wanted. Oh yeah, and they drew symbols on the ground. That, I cannot do. Hopefully the formulas pop up again; otherwise, I'm getting fried.

I look around and find a spade propped on the table. I reach for it and nearly get zapped by Robo Thor.

I grab it quickly and sprint out of the barn, into an open field. My feet catch on a water hose, and I fall to my knees. He's still near the barn, but Robo Thor zaps me in my ass.

"Shhii—" I can't even finish my curse. My body seizes, making me shake.

I can't move. Cold pools in my stomach and spreads all over my body. My muscles spasm, but I force myself to roll away from the next bolt. My hip bangs against the sprinkler line.

The sprinklers!

The spade is too far away, and I can't move my legs yet. Curling myself into a ball, I dig my fingernails into my left palm. The blood drips from my hand onto the ground.

"Um… Hey, Architect dude. Can you give me water, I mean, aqua? Not sure why I have to ask you in Latin and draw a bunch of symbols, but yeah."

Nothing happens from The Architect, but Robo Thor is close. I can't run, and honestly, I'm screwed.

And now you're going to prove Maestro Cali right.

"No. Forget that." I slam my bloody hand to the ground. "Aqua! Please!"

In my mind's eye, I see a symbol outlined in white—a triangle pointing downward. I quickly draw the shape on the ground.

My hand lights up, heat sears my palms, and it feels like they're magnetized to the ground. My hands shake from the surge of pressure. This thing inside of me—I don't know if it's the slayer power or the darkness—takes and takes and takes. Sweat trickles from my forehead. Blood drips from my nose. I can't wipe. I can't move. The only thing that I *can* do is let the power surge. The glow from my palm shoots into the sky, and water shoots from the ground.

Robo Thor jerks, and the currents that orbit his body short out. After he falls to the ground like a sack of potatoes, the electricity immediately vanishes.

I'm breathing hard, but I can finally feel the muscles in my body loosen. I skip-hop to the spade and then stab the vampire in the heart. But the water doesn't stop. It's spurting now in all directions. The ground turns soggy.

"Umm. You can stop now!" I yell at no one in particular as I circle the field. The water rises at an alarming speed. Just a few seconds ago, the water soaked my shoes. Now it's around my calves. Robo Thor's body floats over to me. I kick him away, but he doesn't just roll away. I kick him so hard his body flies across the field and splats against the sky. Well, I guess it isn't a sky but a dome. He's stuck on the top of the dome for a second before his body crashes into the water. Water that's now at my knees.

"Okay, I'm done now." I wade through the water, waving my hands, hoping that signals the Maestro to shut it down.

The simulation goes black. The water and field and Robo Thor are gone. I toss off my headset and shrug out of my suit to get my body back to normal temperatures.

Finally, I turn around to find open mouths and whispers greeting me.

Oh. Right. There are other people here—witnesses to my calamities. My butt tingles with pain and embarrassment. My muscles are heavy from exhaustion, not from the water but from the power that projectile vomited out of me. I want to fall on the floor, or bend at the waist, and sleep for a million years. Instead, I place my hands on my hips and try to pace my breathing from broken pants to measured breaths.

"Hell yes, New Chick!" someone yells and whistles. The entire class breaks out into a round of applause.

I smile, surprised by the cheers. I guess weirdness is accepted at schools that train you to kill monsters.

Maestro Cali nods and waves at me to go to the front. "What the hell was that? You broke The Beast."

I look over her shoulder. Sure enough, the black board with nobs sizzles with a plume of smoke.

The adrenaline from my win vanishes. My smile drops. "You've got insurance, right?" Okay, so maybe I went too far. I always do. I scramble for the most logical excuse: find it, grab it, use it. "The water must have shorted it."

She narrows her eyes. "You did a lot of things wrong. A. Lot."

"I killed it."

"Sheer luck."

I shrug. "Doesn't matter." I clear my throat, clear away my nervousness. "He's dead."

She narrows her eyes. "And how in the hell did you know how to draw the alchemy symbol for water?"

"I—" I pause, thinking through my answer. Do I really want to tell her I can see things in my mind? The very thing she said we cannot do? I mean, they think I'm weird enough with the colorful tattoo and the Wonder Woman strength.

I'll ask Dakota about it.

"Dakota taught me."

Maestro Cali studies my face for a moment. I tense under her gaze.

Eventually, she shakes her head. "Well, next time, you may not be lucky enough to have water around."

"There's water everywhere. Even in your body."

She snorts. "Everyone's a genius until a vampire zaps you in the ass…or you nearly drown yourself."

I'm exhausted, embarrassed, but I stuff the feelings down and try like hell to erase any stitch of emotion from my face.

She stares at me for a while before she shakes her head again. "I'm watching you." She doesn't say it in a threatening way, but in a voice that sounds like she's low-key fascinated.

Maestro Cali faces the class. "Looks like we have three winners. But only one of you can join me tomorrow night. Andreas, Santa Barbara, come up to the front."

Andreas pushes people out of the way while Barbie marches all proud to the front.

"We'll do a random number selection," Maestro Cali says. "I'm thinking of a number between one and one thousand."

"Five hundred and two," Andreas says quickly.

"One." Santa Barbara puts up her finger.

"One hundred," I guess.

"Santa Barbara, you're in," Maestro Cali says with fake enthusiasm.

I cross my arms. "What was the number?"

"Not yours."

I can hear the lie in her voice.

"Class dismissed. Remember, I want those essays—an analysis of why you sucked today."

The students rush out of the room, but I don't. I follow Maestro Cali, but she doesn't turn around. She just strides across the gym. "Get gone, Tyro."

"Why did you do that? I want to...to get better. To get out in the field. Vampires murdered my friends."

"Relax. You just got here five minutes ago." She opens a door—to her office, I presume. I spot a laptop and a cell phone. My fingers tingle from the temptation of technology. I don't step inside, though.

"You want revenge? Train hard and study harder. Your mind and imagination are your greatest weapons." She taps her temple. "Go to the library, check out the audiobooks. Eat, sleep, and breathe the material. And most of all, learn to control all that power. Because if you don't, it'll kill you...or you'll end up hurting someone you didn't mean to."

My stomach drops at the last piece of advice. I know very well what happens when you lose control. People get hurt, not just physically but emotionally, too. I'll never forget the way Grandma Lou looked at me—she feared me. She didn't know what to do with me. But I know she loves me.

"It umm... It won't happen again. I won't lose control."

"You're here to learn, so there's no need to beat yourself up about it." Maestro Cali reaches into a drawer and pulls out a flask and downs whatever is in it. The smell of pine stings my nose. Damn these overpowering senses.

She lifts an eyebrow while I stare at her. "What? You gonna tattle?"

"No. Do you." I shrug. It's five o'clock *somewhere*—however, on the East Coast, it's ten a.m.

She takes another swallow and then re-twists the cap. "You've gotta figure out how to best optimize your guild."

"You mean our guild, right? We build weapons or whatever."

She nods. "It's deeper than that." She lifts her hand and traces her tattoo. "The sun represents gold, the perfection of creation. We are masters at breaking down elemental components and rebuilding, like engineers. The moon represents silver. It represents making weapons with silver to ward off evil."

"Vampires," I whisper.

"Among other things. There's lots of evil in the world, and not just supernatural creatures." She closes her fist and then waves me away. "All right. See you later. Talk to people. People other than me."

"The other students..." I bite my lips.

"Don't worry, you'll make friends." She brushes off my concern.

"I don't want to make friends. I want to learn and...and..."

"Kill. That's what we're teaching you. How to be a killer." She looks me dead in the eye, challenging me to look away.

I don't. Instead, I lift my wobbly chin and nod. "Then so be it."

She harrumphs and stands. "If you have any questions, ask an instructor. Most of the teachers here are alchemists, the keepers of our history and the geniuses that make up the curriculum and blueprints for weapons. They are part of the guilds, too. You'll see the symbol stitched on their blazers, cardigans, and shirts. They help us master our abilities, since many of us slayers are out in the field. Anyway, they'll fill in the rest of the gaps. Got it? Good." She slaps my shoulder on her way out of the door.

"And what about—"

"I've gotta go, Tyro. Do as I say, and you'll get what you need."

Pretty Brown Eyes
Raven

Taking Maestro Cali's advice to heart, the next few days, I practically sleep in the library.

But it's the alchemy classes that jumpstart my understanding.

The training and courses alternate every other day, from theory to practice. On Mondays, Wednesdays, and Fridays, we practice various forms of fighting skills, with and without conjured weapons.

On Tuesdays and Thursdays and a half day on Saturdays (yeah, ridiculous, I know), we study the meaning behind alchemy. The courses are:

1st Period - Alchemy History & Philosophies
2nd Period - Egyptian Alchemy 101
3rd Period - Signs & Symbols
Lunch Break
4th Period - European Alchemy
5th Period - Medical Alchemy
Open/Study Period

The learning pace is brutal, but I enjoy reading and writing and learning so much that I don't have enough time to think about Deidra, Grandma Lou—you know, life before my powers. Not only that, but I'm not half terrible at memorizing the symbols and applying it to practice.

I hate fifth-period medicines class… 0/10, do not recommend.

For one, Magister Corrine Magnus doesn't teach—she just

points her long, auntie-red painted fingernails at the PowerPoint slides and reads line by line. When I try to ask clarifying questions, she rolls her eyes and challenges me to "discover the solution on my own."

Like, girl, if you don't want to be here, then just say it.

My favorite courses are the histories of Egyptian and European Alchemy. Dakota said that all Tyros had already taken the European Alchemy course, so I had to take it as an elective class to play catch-up. Dakota elected to take the class again, since she's been out of the classroom to help the commander and Charlotte with admin work.

Those classes are fascinating—a kick-ass blend of history, science, philosophy, and even religion. Back then, a lot of people got down with alchemy—kings and popes and people who made household tools. But then, over time, people associated alchemy with mysticism, which challenged their religion. And listen, folks still go to war for their beliefs, so it became a big red flag to dabble in the "occult," but really it deals with science.

So yeah, learning all the history is awesome. But while there were many pros to alchemy classes, there are cons, too.

Said con, Magister Dieter Magnus aka Andreas' dad, is giving me the stink-eye when Dakota and I walk into his class. Unfortunately, he teaches two of my classes.

Dakota whispers, "Why is he staring at you like that?"

I shrug. Who knows, other than the man doesn't like me. So maybe we didn't start off on the right foot when he mentioned the greatest minds in alchemy came from Europe and I, of course, challenged this, because historians document alchemy to originate in ancient Egypt.

"How can we argue the greatest minds came from Europe when the entire basis of alchemy was to keep it a secret? I mean, why would the Egyptians write everything they knew down when they wanted to keep it on the low?"

Apparently, debate wasn't encouraged, and he simply listed a bunch of dead people who made contributions—one of them being an ancestor, Albertus Magnus.

I ignore his stare and settle into my seat in the middle row. Five rows of seats lead down to the lecture pit. The class is big, with a little over forty students. Each Tyro wears a similar outfit during our Alchemist Class schedule: black cardigans or blazers with our guild emblem stitched on the right pocket. Every student could wear khakis or black pants and skirts.

My roomie is babbling a theory that she wants to run by Magister Dieter about the location of the Emerald Tablet. I don't think the physical tablet exists, because we've got everything we need inside of us, but now's not the time to start this debate back up again.

"Please turn your pages to seventy-five. I assigned you all to read one hundred pages after our last class. Whether you read this will be apparent in our class discussion. This, naturally, is graded." Magister Dieter waits one point two seconds before he launches into the lesson.

"Alchemists, even in the early days, stressed testing and learning. They combined the spiritual aspects of alchemy, as explored by Aristotle, and the establishment of modern science. But as chemistry rose in prominence from the likes of Robert Boyle and Isaac Newton—both of whom were alchemists, by the way—the popularity of alchemy waned. But we, the Alchemist Order, understood the importance of transformation, which is why Eduard Magnus, descendant of Albert Magnus, discovered a way to make the Philosopher's Stone even more powerful." He pauses for a moment, adjusting his glasses, and squints at the class.

"Someone...tell us what happened during the fourteenth century?"

Dakota, who has the quickest hand in all the land, raises and waves her arm.

"Yes, Ms. Dakota?"

"Humanity refers to it as the bubonic plague or Black Death, which is the bite of an infected flea. However, the true cause of the plague came from the bite of a *Tick*, or what we refer to as Made vampires. It's thanks to The Architect that we eliminated the plague."

I shake my head. I still can't believe vampires nearly decimated humanity. And what's even more wild is that humanity covered up what truly happened.

The Magister beams. I'd never seen his mouth stretch out on full display. I don't know him like that, but in my few interactions, I've noticed his thin lips pursed in an *O* shape or pressed in a line.

I steal a glance at Dakota, who struggles to hide her smile. She's a Grade-A suck-up, but I respect it. Honestly, she's a genius at the alchemist stuff, and I'm tempted to tell her to switch tracks. But she doesn't need anyone else to tell her what to do with her life.

The Magister continues. "Alexander, in his arrogance, allowed his progeny to create offspring who are far inferior vampires in intelligence and in controlling their blood thirst. Those poor, mindless souls overran Western Eurasia and North Africa, causing the death of two hundred million people and nearly depleting the European and African Slayer Societies."

Pretty Boy's sharp words ring in my mind. *"Do you really want your friends to taint their souls? To take more lives? Better yet, do you want to have to kill them?"*

I swallow the rising lump in my throat. Pretty Boy was right. I didn't see it then, but I wouldn't want that for my friends. Deidra would have rather stayed dead than destroy humanity. Even still... I don't think I would've been able to destroy her body.

Dakota bumps my shoulder. "Are you okay?"

I nod, smile, and return my attention to the lesson, though she's still staring at me. Maybe she's finally piecing together the reasons for my screams at night.

"It was Eduard who understood we needed far more power to fight, and thus he resolved to infuse the power of our strongest slayers. It was…the ultimate sacrifice of these brave souls to give their power. Power they could no longer use or take back. And with their powers combined, the stone selected its first and only bearer, Richmond."

I mentally calculate because math is so not my subject. But homeboy is like six hundred…wait, more like seven hundred years old.

Since Dakota is staring at me with sad eyes, I lean over to crack a joke. "No wonder he's so cranky."

Dakota whispers back, "You haven't heard the stories, but trust me, his name is well-deserved."

"Ugh. Tell that to Charlotte."

Dakota snorts, grabbing the attention of our equally cranky Magister.

Magister Dieter stops his pacing and stares at me. "Why don't you share what is so funny with the class?"

I clear my throat. "We were just discussing how much we appreciate Rich's service to humanity and how he's able to keep such a *pleasant* bedside manner."

The rest of the class laughs. Okay, so Rich truly is a bitch to everyone and not just me.

"Is that sarcasm, Ms. Raven?"

"No way, Magister Dieter."

"Unless you've got an actual question or would like to contribute to the classroom, I suggest you remain quiet."

I mime zipping my lips. He continues.

"Now, Eduard, along with the one hundred powers from our slayers and allies, gave us the advantage to win. But it is The Architect who gave us knowledge and power. Much like man was given fire and the ability to speak — "

I raise a hand but don't wait for him to call on me before asking, "Does he really exist?"

"Who?"

"The Architect. I haven't seen anything about him online. All the documents I've found say that the most ancient power who gave knowledge of alchemy to humans is the god Thoth, who supposedly gave us the Emerald Tablet that maybe was given to the Atlanteans, so…just wondering if he's an actual entity and if the tablet truly exists?"

Need gold? There's a formula for that. Need the key to eternal life? Check line twelve, row twenty. Okay, I wasn't sure what it looked like other than the color, and that was the entire point. We've seen the Philosopher's Stone, we have our powers, but no one I've asked so far has met this Architect or has seen this green tablet.

The room goes oddly still. No one speaks or breathes, and *maybe* I went a smidge too far, but seeing as I want to make sure I'm not joining a cult and all, I feel my questions are valid.

"I mean, no disrespect." I hold up both hands. "I'm just trying to understand…" My voice peters out when I notice Magister Dieter turns fifty shades of red.

"For this class," Magister Dieter says in a dangerously soft voice, "the Internet is *not* your friend. Any text or experiment or written history about alchemy that's worth anything is within the walls of Tria Prima Academy or on the pages we Magisters have painstakingly created. Not wild conspiracy theories."

I close my textbook, check the cover, and find his name in all caps, bold, and in white.

Right.

"We must learn from the greatest minds in alchemy." He closes his eyes, and I think he's counting to a hundred before he opens them.

"Now, I will assume your recent arrival is the reason you are so woefully ignorant."

Yee-ouch.

I don't speak a word, just sort of drift amongst the sea of snickers.

Dakota with the quick hands waves one in the air. "Magister Dieter?"

"Yes."

"Why do you think we haven't had access to the Emerald Tablet since ancient times?" She gives me a quick glance and licks her lips. "B-because T-the Architect could have easily given this to us in theory, right? Like he gave us the stone."

I give her a thumbs-up under my desk. That had been my argument. Why couldn't this entity give us the Emerald Tablet and be like Oprah, where "You get a car" and "You get a car," but you know, for Philosopher's Stones? Then we wouldn't have to depend on Rich aka fake Jesus to be the chosen one. We could all make our own.

The Magister doesn't scoff or blush tomato red. He just stares off into space, and I wonder what's with the scary lip quiver.

Finally, he speaks. "I think The Architect knows the tablet could get into the wrong hands. Because we are human, after all. Not everyone could or should handle such power."

The bell rings, and as class ends, his scary look disappears.

Before the students leave, Magister Dieter announces a five-page essay on the history of the Emerald Tablet. Everyone groans and stares at Dakota.

I jump from my seat, needing to hustle back to my room to pick up my lab coat for alchemy experiments next period after lunch.

"Wait up." Dakota runs until she reaches my side before she says, "This isn't the way to the cafeteria, FYI."

"I know. I'm going back to the room to grab my books and lab coat. I'll grab a sandwich before my next class. You need anything from the room?"

Dakota shakes her head. "Hey, I hope it was okay to bring up our debate. I don't think he knows what you think."

"Nah, I appreciate it. He seems to like you." Still, I'm kinda annoyed. I mean, what did I ever do to him?

She lets out a true sigh of relief that tells me she was nervous about the whole thing. "Good. Cool. See you at the library after class?"

"Yep."

I grab my things and I'm heading back to the classrooms when I hear a familiar voice shout, "Hey, New Chick!"

I turn. Andreas waves. I sigh, not in the mood to chat with yet another descendent of Albertus and Eduard Magnus.

He's leaning against the wall, and I can tell he thinks he's cute by the way he's squinting his eyes and smiling, like there's a camera two feet away from him. He pushes off the wall and walks over slow and dramatic, like he's marching on a low-speed treadmill.

"What are you up to tonight?" he asks.

Sweaty nightmares are the first thing that come to mind, but I shrug. "Sleep. Study, I guess."

He snorts. "It's Thursday."

"Oh, is it?" I ask without an ounce of sarcasm. Time means nothing to me right about now.

"Yeah, and on Thursdays we usually go out to this really cool club. Caters to people" — he looks around and leans in closer — "like us."

"What do you mean, like us?"

"People who like a little fun. You were in high school, right? I'm sure you went to parties."

My ears perk up. Go out, as in leave this place? Maybe even figure out my plan for escape? *Hell, yes.*

I don't have to force a smile for the first time in days. "We can go out and have fun?"

He smiles. "We have to be reasonable and keep a low profile, of course."

"Who all's gonna be there?" asked every Black person ever. In my case, I also need the details because I don't want to hang out with Andreas alone.

"It's a bunch of us from class. We're going to take a few cars into the city."

"Sounds good. I'm eighteen... That a problem?"

"You don't have a fake?"

"Nope. Must've forgotten to grab it when that one vampire slaughtered my friends."

He raises a hand. "Sheesh. No need to get sensitive. Anyway, where we're going, you don't need an ID. And don't worry, the Society will hook you up with a fake later. You'll need it to frequent the shitty bars the Rogues like to go to."

"The who?"

"Rogues are unsanctioned vampires—the ones not officially registered to a clan, usually because they're loners who like to kill without question."

"Ah, okay. Cool. I'll let Dakota know about the plans. Where should we meet you?"

He kinda grimaces when I mention Dakota's name, and I honestly don't give a damn. In this universe where monsters exist, I'm no longer the odd girl people avoid. But that doesn't mean I'll ever forget that most humans are basically assholes to people they deem *outsiders*.

"Time? Place?"

He dips his chin. "Fine. Ten p.m. Meet us in the garage."

"Cool."

After class, I rush to the library and find Dakota at an otherwise empty study table.

"Guess who's going to a party tonight?"

Her smile drops. "Who?"

"We are."

"Eh. Rather not." She shakes her head and returns her attention to the open book in front of her.

"Why not?"

"I'm not a party girl. Plus, all the others think I'll rat them out, since I still work for Paris and Charlotte part-time."

"Oh…will you?"

"No, of course not. But I don't feel like hanging with people who'll walk on eggshells around me. So go out and have fun. I'll just be…*here*."

The way she said "here" reminds me of that sad tuba song when people guessed the wrong answer on *The Price is Right*. Grandma Lou loves that show. I shake my head, swallow quickly, and try to block out memories of my favorite person in the whole wide world.

"Are you sure?"

She nods. "Very. I'll just stream some shows."

"Okay." I nod. "And by chance, do you have anything I can borrow to wear?" The Society provided me with the uniforms but nothing fun, and the clothes I bought online with my Society allowance won't get here until the weekend.

She winces. "No, but I'm sure Charlotte has something."

"Oh, I bet." Charlotte always slays. As Grandma Lou would say, she's dressed to the nines and tens.

"She's probably in her office now. Do you want me to show you where she is?"

"Yeah, that'd be great."

Dakota takes me to the west wing, where the higher-ups' offices reside. Ten minutes later, we stop in front of Charlotte's office.

"I'm going to head back to the room," Dakota says. "See you later."

"Bye."

I turn to face Charlotte's office. An interlocking cube, a symbol that represents Charlotte's guild, the Evokers, is carved in the middle of her door. I knock twice, and the door snaps open.

The smell of pumpkin spice wafts from her office. Her sofa is stuffed to the brim with an army of burnt orange and cream pillows. A whole-ass pumpkin sits on the windowsill. Some papier-mâché-embossed painting that looks like leaves glued onto a wooden plank hangs proudly (I guess) above her desk on the back wall.

All in all, it looks like autumn projectile vomited in her office.

"Good morning, Raven." The beauty mark below her dimple lifts when she smiles.

As usual, she's dressed well in a scoop-neck cream blouse, peach silk pants, and blue spiked heels. Pinned on her shirt is a blue-and-white cube that represents the Evokers.

"Mornin'." I toss a few pillows to the other side of the couch and sink into the comfy cushions. "How come you don't wear a uniform like the other students and teachers?"

"Because I'm a boss."

"Fair enough."

Charlotte strikes a match and lights the wick of a pumpkin-scented candle.

The pumpkin in the corner is already overkill to my nose. I gag. "The smell doesn't bother you?"

I recently discovered that I can't do candles or perfumes. Because of a slayer's heightened senses, it's hard to take in too much of anything.

Charlotte blows out the match. "No. If you meditate and get a hold of your senses, you can control it."

"What if I lose my edge?" Vamps have a distinct smell—they smell like an experience. A beach, rainstorms, burning forest. And I need every advantage over those things.

"I'm not in the field anymore, so I suppose I don't need to be as sharp."

"You like doing this secretary, peace-on-earth stuff?"

I've heard from Dakota that Charlotte largely negotiates with vampires and governments on human and vampire peace-building policies.

"Mhmm. Best decision I've ever made."

ASS is one of many slayer organizations around the world. Seems like we have plenty of soldiers, but we need leaders like Paris and Charlotte to smooth over alliances, keep tabs on the Royals and Rogues, inform our government of important information, and maintain the relationship with diva alchemists. Despite Charlotte coming off as a pacifist, since Evokers are really into balance and nature, Dakota claims she is a master at combat.

She blows out the candle. "There. No loud smells, my sensitive little lamb."

"Your sensitive lamb passed The Beast simulator the other day."

"More like destroyed it." She wags her finger at me, though she gives me a concerned-parent look. "But sure, congratulations."

"Yeah, well. Maestro Cali didn't choose me to go on the stakeout with her."

Charlotte smiles. "Are you still having bad dreams?"

"W-what?" My heart ba-dumps. "Who told you? Dakota?"

"No, calm down. But I can hear you, sweetie. I'm just two doors down from your room. Since Dakota is an admin, we have her in the teachers' suite. You didn't notice your room is in the east wing?"

"Oh, so…the other kids can't hear me?"

"No. Teachers can. And honey… You need to focus on healing. I don't feel any blackness in your aura today, but it was there. I know it. And it can come back, stronger than ever. You need to address something like that. You never know how things will manifest."

I roll my eyes. "I'm working on it," I mutter.

"We have group counseling." She leans forward, propping her elbows on her desk. "I'm leading a session tonight—"

"No, thanks. I have plans. And speaking of, I wanted to see if you have any nice clothes I can borrow."

"Oh, the students are going out tonight?" She nods. "It's good you're making friends."

"Mmm. So, you got anything?"

"Honey, I've got plenty. Come on."

Andreas lets out a low whistle when I enter the garage. "You clean up nice."

I twirl a bit because he's right. Charlotte hooked me up with a royal-blue bodycon dress that crisscrosses my back. The hem hits just below my ass. We had a minor argument about the shoes. At first, she offered me strappy silver shoes that I had to admit really set it off, but when I tried walking, I looked like a toddler learning to walk in stripper heels. I mean, to be fair, I didn't really have time to strut my stuff when I mostly wore cushioned old-lady shoes for marching band.

Finally, Charlotte helped me alchemize the perfect pair of blue suede shoes with thick platform wedges, making it much easier to walk.

There are ten students—four of us ride with Andreas, and thankfully the Black girl who crushed rock climbing comes in his car, too, so I'm not the only Black person. We give each other the "look," and she introduces herself.

"I'm Lexington, but call me Lex."

"Raven."

She nods. "You've been doing pretty awesome in fighting classes. You'll get your code name soon."

"Thanks, Lex."

We hop into the SUV that Andreas is driving and ride for about forty minutes until we hit downtown Atlanta. Or at least I think it is with all the tall buildings, restaurants, and bright lights.

"What's the name of this area of ATL?" I ask.

Lex snorts. "No one from ATL says ATL."

"It's West Midtown," Andreas yells from the front seat. "Used to be a shitshow, but they've done a lot of work. Now it's lively. Great restaurants, bars, clubs, you name it. But this place we're going to is toward the older side of it."

Lex and I give each other the "look" again, and I relax my tense muscles. We know what the code word "a lot of work" really means. West Midtown probably has been gentrified within an inch of its life, driving up property value and driving out the folks who lived there. Grandma Lou went off regularly about this, especially when it happened a few towns over.

Our destination stands on the older side of the road from where we're parked. The white brick building looks like an abandoned car shop, with a double-wide garage in the middle of the structure. Old wood-plank pallets, trash, and paint buckets litter the entrance.

There's an enormous sign that reads CLOSED in orange letters hanging on the door.

"All right, ladies. Spray time."

"What does—?"

I don't have time to finish my question, because Andreas leans over the driver's seat and sprays me down with an unknown substance, like we're at a picnic with a million mosquitos.

I cough from the spray. "What the hell is this?"

"Scent blocker. Special batch from my mom and dad." He sprays himself with another canister.

Hell, yes. This is just what I want. I smile at my boon and swipe the nearly empty can and stuff it into my bag. "You say your parents know how to make it?"

Maybe Magisters Dieter and Corrine could be more than pains in my ass after all.

He snorts. "Yeah. So do I."

Even better. I hide my grin. "Can you share the ingredients?"

He squints his eyes at me. "You're looking to get into some trouble? Sneak out?"

"S-neak?"

"Don't worry. I got you. We all like to party, so as long as you're with me, I'll get you what you need."

B-I-N-G-O.

He shoots me an oily smile, and I smile back. For real this time. If I know what it takes to make the blocker, I can leave here immediately.

"So anyway," I say with a huge grin stamped on my face. "Why do we need to block our scents?"

"This *may* be a supes club." He gives me that signature oily grin again. Like seriously, I've never seen a smile that greasy.

"A soup club?"

"Supes," Lex helpfully supplies, like saying it again provides clarity. "The *supernatural*. Run by a group of vampires. We get werewolves here and there, but rarely. They hate vamps about as much as we do."

"Wait a minute. This is a vampire club?" I squeak. "And werewolves? They exist?"

"Yes, and yes." Lex nods.

"Nope." I shake my head and cross my arms.

I'm already not in the mood to back it up on vampires. But werewolves? I mean, have they seen the movies? The fangs and fur and chewing of bones?

"I'll just stay out here until you're ready." I look at my watch. It's a quarter till eleven, and Charlotte told me we have a two-a.m. curfew. I can wait or make one of them call me a cab to take me halfway back to headquarters.

"Sure. If you want to stay outside and wait for a vampire…or a werewolf to sniff around the car and wonder why you're here." Andreas shrugs.

"They can't smell me," I say, pointing to the canister.

"Yeah, but they can hear you and see you. And then they'll wonder if you're a spy or something. Up to you." He opens the car door and hops out.

Lex looks at me. "It's not so bad."

"Have you ever been caught?"

"Once or twice."

"And?"

She opens her door. "We killed them." She smiles before she jumps out.

Shit, son of a sucker. *Argggggh!* I open the door and slam it shut.

I march over to Andreas, who's grinning ear to ear as he's speaking to another Tyro. Of course the son of Magisters Corinne and Dieter is an asshole. It's firmly in that gene pool.

I point my finger at his chest and poke it. "You know what?"

"Careful. We're at a place with heightened abilities. The car is blocked. Outside"—he waves—"is not."

I clasp my hands and step back. I don't need words. I give him the "look." Not the Black-people-consensus look that I gave Lex and will no longer give her—she's dead to me now.

No, I give him the Black Mama look. One that Grandma Lou gave me many times over the years. The one when you're a kid in public and you show your ass. You do it because you know Mama's not gonna try you in front of these strangers…not in the age of social media and well-meaning-but-nosy citizens who love to call the cops about absolutely nothing. Nope. You just wait until you get home.

Just. Wait.

Andreas, here, doesn't know about the look, and he doesn't have to. He will feel my wrath. I point two fingers to my eyes and then point them toward his eyes. "Just wait until we get back."

He slides something into his mouth and then grins, revealing a pair of fake pearly white fangs. "Let's go." Andreas points to the door. The same one with the CLOSED sign.

Andreas knocks on the door, and it swings open. The smell of burning pine hits my nose, which reminds me how strong vampires' distinct smells can be. Standing in front of the entrance is a behemoth of a vampire with a purple Mohawk. Tatts crisscross his forearms, chest, and biceps. His overworked pecs are packed into a fishnet tank top.

Andreas lifts his mouth and hisses and sprouts his fake fangs. "Me and...my pets."

Yeah. Imma beat Andreas' ass.

We step into the club, and I scan our surroundings. Although the outside looks like a dumpster-fire hot mess, the inside is a goth's wet dream. Lots of black leather couches, lace curtains over blackout windows, and a huge red teardrop chandelier with red lights. Bright Pop Art pictures hang throughout the club. A few catch my eye, like the bottle-blond Alexander the Great with his piercing and freaky eyes. There are a dozen photos of him with different expressions: fierce, smiling, seductive, and a duck face. I've never met him, and I never will, but I'm damn sure he's never made a duck face.

When Andreas hooks his arms around my neck, I dig my fingers into his forearms.

He winces. "Damn, girl."

"Just a sample of what I can do." I smile and sink my fingers in deeper.

"Don't make me bleed," he whispers.

I let go. "I'm going upstairs."

"But you're a human. A regular one." He lowers his mouth

to my ear. "I sprayed myself down with a scent that makes me smell like a vampire."

I lean over, sniff, smell, and gag. He smells like garbage on a beach. "You really are a jerk." He literally reduced us to his vampire groupies.

"They won't mess with you if I'm around."

That spray blocked my slayer scent, not my humanity. I roll my eyes and tamp down my urge to punch his face. "I think I can handle myself." I pivot on my feet and stomp upstairs. A large body blocks my path.

"Hey, move it. I mean…excuse me." I sigh.

When the guy in the nice suit turns around and I recognize those brown eyes, my mouth drops.

"P-pretty Boy?"

Call Me by My Name
Khamari

Her sexy, husky voice that's been on a loop in my dreams calls out to me like a siren's song, just before my stomach drops. *She remembers me.*

I forget the house music thumping in the background. Fangs and claws are out, and blood trickles from the necks of humans and vampires and supes onto the black marble floor. El Diente is something of a haven—a place where supes who aren't so hyped up on sticking with one species can commune and drink and hook up.

Raven's standing there on the dance floor as sweat-slicked bodies grind against one another. I scan her face. Her lips twist, and her eyes shine—she isn't scared or lost; she's pissed.

What's more, I wonder why and how she found her way into this den of demons.

I may be a dreamwalker, but seeing her appear in front of me, I worry that someone's messing with *my* mind. I pretended to drink her blood and walk her dreams and reported back to the council that Ethan, the vampire she'd killed back in Texas, acted impulsively and had obsessed over one of the humans he'd scented. That happened often enough—bloodlust. And it could transform a perfectly reasonable law-abiding Royal into a lawless Rogue.

Just as I suspected, the Elders want to figure out a way to take advantage of the Slayer Society's rare slipup in one of their own killing a Royal. The slayers infamously adhere to protocol, so the favor they will owe us is a boon. Not to mention getting rid of Ethan. He was a live wire, and Julius feared he would burn us down.

Now, the Elders want me to sink deeper into the Society. Speaking of which… "What the hell are you doing here?"

And how do you remember who I am?

She tilts her head back, looks at the ceiling, and exhales like she's releasing helium from a balloon. "I'm just trying to figure out a way to escape this *place*." She says "place" like it isn't the club she's trying to escape, but maybe her life. Which is a question I've tried to figure out for the past year, too.

"Come with me." I slide to the right of the stairwell, blocking photos of me at my newly inherited club. I grab her hand, and she squeezes mine.

"Your hands are warm, at least."

"Why wouldn't they be? It's hot in here." I drag her to the top of the stairs and wave off a clansman before he can bow. It isn't outside of the norm for me to buck tradition, so thankfully he doesn't look alarmed.

I move her to my favorite spot in the club—high, secluded, secure. I guide her to the leather couch across from me. "Take a seat."

I nod at the guard, my signal for him to leave, and flip on the music to give us some privacy. Instead of the house music that thumps the speakers and shakes the walls, I put on something smooth and low and slow. Something I hope she'll like.

When the instrumentals for Lucky Daye's "Roll Some Mo" play through the overhead speakers and she rolls her shoulders to the beat, I know I've hit the jackpot.

"You want a drink? Lemonade? Tea?" I offer.

"Dirty Sprite."

"You aren't old enough."

"And how would you know?"

I know more than she'd feel comfortable with me knowing. It's the only way I can cope with leaving her behind—to secure every detail of her life yet do absolutely nothing about it.

"I have my ways."

She snorts. "You don't even remember my name."

I smile, determined not to confirm. Her name dances on the tip of my tongue. I dreamed of that name. I did a lot of things to her name.

Yeah…I'm keeping all *that* to myself.

I wave toward the bottle services on the long black table. "We don't have Sprite, but how about cranberry juice?"

"With vodka? Sure." She crosses her arms and gives me a dangerous look to accompany her dangerous curves. And where in the hell did she get that dress? It's a shock to see the little band geek with the black coveralls as the sexy girl in front of me.

"You need to keep your wits here." Still, I pour her cranberry juice with a splash of Ketel One. Once I'm done, I place her drink on a cocktail napkin.

"Tell me. How do you remember me?" I say it lightly, but inside my heart is jamming against my chest. I can't afford for my powers to be jacked.

"I have my ways," she throws back at me.

"Which are…?" I ask simply, trying like hell to remove the command that naturally weighs my voice.

"Earplugs. Compliments of Sheila, along with the honeymoon suite."

"So, you couldn't—"

"And why are you here? This is a supes club, so what are you?"

What am I? I'm not ready for that conversation. Not ready to see the interested look in her eyes fade to black. "Just a man with a dream."

"And that is?"

"Peace on Earth." I tell her the truth even though I know the truth isn't possible.

She mutters under her breath as she reaches for the drink. Her eyebrows furrow, and her fingers hover just above the stout glass. I know she's thinking about the possibility of it being drugged. Good. She needs to question everything in both the human and supernatural worlds.

I lean over to the table between us. When I pick up the glass, our fingers brush. Sparks of electricity ignite at our touch. I almost flinch but pretend not to notice the energy. I drink a sip from her cup, lifting my eyebrows in a silent challenge, and then lower the glass back to the table.

"You're warm, so you aren't a vampire." She leans over and grabs the drink, taking a small sip.

"Ah, yeah. They are cold bastards." Inside and out.

"You're a werewolf, then." She leans back as if afraid of my answer.

I shudder. "They aren't the best at concealing their identities."

She nods. "Are they killers, though? Like in the movies?"

"Just like humans, there are good ones and bad ones. Just depends on the temperament. That's why we have slayers."

"But we only slay vampires."

"That's how slayers started, and yes, it's your specialty. But you do a lot more. Well, some of you, I hear."

She sighs, and her chest lifts with the motion. "Lots to learn."

"Yeah. The more you learn, the better your odds of survival."

"Why'd you leave me?" she asks suddenly. "Just a teddy bear tucked under me. And you tried to erase my memories!"

"You had a lot happen to you that night, and I... I only tried to erase my part in it. I'm not worth remembering."

"Is this where you expect me to say, no, you're the most important part?" She rolls her eyes. Then, she smiles.

Jesus.

I know if anyone could hear my thoughts, they'd call me a simp, but her smile feels like a sunrise. Slow-moving, steadily warming up, but worth the wait.

"Some vampires found me at the motel, but the slayers found me in time."

I stand from my seat, then sit beside her. "I heard."

She takes in a sharp breath, but she doesn't move.

"I'm sorry." I thought I covered my tracks, my scent. *My chain.*

"I…must have left something behind," I reply, trying to remember every move I made at the hotel to figure out where I messed up. "Something with my scent that made it easy to find me."

"Oh!" Her eyes go wide. "Yeah. You must've." She tosses back her drink, and I refill it before I respond.

"Did you take my chain? The one with the wings?"

"No." She shakes her head slowly.

She's not a convincing liar.

"I'll need that back, Slayer." I hold out my hand.

"I don't… I don't have it on me. Where would I put it?"

I scan her body, and yeah, nothing else can fit in that skintight dress. "Why would you steal it?"

"I-I don't know. I saw it, and I liked it." She shrugs. "I don't have sticky fingers…usually." Her eyes look semi-apologetic. "My bad."

"I will need it back."

"Who did it belong to?"

This time, I'm the one to move away.

"Someone special?" she asks. "It's delicate. It doesn't seem like your style, but…"

"But what?" I dare her to finish her statement. She has the grace to look away.

"Does it belong to you?" she asks.

"It does now."

She taps her chin. "But it didn't before?"

I lean back, trying to pull in my anger, and ask, "Why are you pushing me on this?"

"You said you lost something special, too, to vampires. I just… It makes me feel less lonely. Like I'm not the only unlucky person on Earth. And it makes me feel good that I'm not the only one who hates them with every fiber of my being. And you give me hope because you're doing all that you can to fight them." She shrugs. "I bet you're on some James Bond–type shit. Like a secret mission, right?"

"Something like that," I mutter.

"The things you and I can do mean someone else out there won't end up like us."

My heart incinerates at her declaration. "Yet you're here. You and your…friends. The people who come here are looking for danger. They're looking to get burned."

"What about you?"

I swallow, looking straight in her eyes. "Right now, I'm burning."

She looks down at her hands clasped around her drink. She lifts it to her mouth and pauses. "I get the impression that you don't burn easily."

"You'd be right. But how do you know?"

"Your eyes."

I force myself not to blink. "What about them?"

"You look like you're surviving. Each day is just like eating a dry piece of chicken."

I pour myself a shot. "Choking it down, huh? Sounds pathetic. Sad."

"You look sad, but your eyes light up when I ruffle your Pretty Boy feathers."

"I don't have feathers." I have fangs—sharp ones. With her delectable cocoa scent, it's a constant struggle to pull them back.

But there's something slightly different, muted.

Human. Smart—she's protecting herself, at least. Humans either smell of artificial sprays like cologne, deodorant, and lotion, or an earthy scent—like oddly sweet-smelling dirt.

I chuckle. I have a feeling Raven would balk at the idea of smelling like sweet dirt.

I switch to safe topics like music. We talk like this, probing and somber and fun, but each of us never revealing much. It's a dance. An unsatisfying dance, because I want much more. I want to know this person in front of me.

"Hey. I know this sounds weird but…do you mind if…?"

"Anything," I promise. *Shit.* I shouldn't promise anything. "Within reason."

"Can I borrow your phone?"

"My phone?"

"Yeah. I want to umm, check the time."

"You want to call your grandmother."

She nods. "You remember."

"Of course."

"Of course you remember, or of course I can borrow your phone?"

I reach inside my pocket, select the one that I know for sure isn't tracked, and hand it over. "Here."

She stares at my phone and holds it like it's a winning lotto ticket. "Thank you. You have no idea how much—"

"I do know." I stare at her. "But are you sure this is something you should do?"

She twists her mouth into a small pout. "Wouldn't you want your loved one to know you're alive?"

"Not if it risked their life."

She shakes her head and squeezes my phone so hard I swear it's about to snap. "You don't understand. They're going to erase her memories and then she'll forget all about me!"

"I do understand—more than you know. I made the same mistake you're about to do. I risked her life, and I lost her."

"Lost her? The...the girl with the chain?"

I nod, look her deep in the eyes, lower my guard, and empty my words of half truths and lies. "There's not enough soap in the world to wash away your slayer scent. We are everywhere. You need to train, learn how your enemy operates, and then, when you know what you're doing...maybe you can see your grandmother. But if you make that call and she remembers you and wants you home, your heart will break."

"But—"

"And, if they do her the favor of blanking her memories, your heart will still break." I hold her stare, hoping she understands the futility of her decision. "In every scenario, *you* lose. But your grandmother won't. She will have her life. She won't have to look over her shoulder or die a violent death."

Her head lowers like someone's got a string attached to her forehead and slowly tugs her down.

I grab her hand, her free hand, still leaving her to make a choice. An option I never really had.

My thoughts launch at high speed, turning and churning, lightning fast. I'm selfish. I want her to make the same choice I made. I want to justify my actions.

Eyes down, she slides the phone on the table, returning it to me. She wipes at tears on her face. "I'm sorry," I say quietly.

"You're right." She looks at me, a lone tear sliding down the rounded apple of her cheek. "I'm not the only person who's lost someone." She gives me a small, sad smile as she says, "Guess we're members of the same club now."

More than you know.

She looks away, then down at her watch. "It's close to curfew. They're probably looking for me."

I nod. "I'll walk you downstairs."

"You don't have to."

"I'll do it anyway."

We walk down the stairs side by side. I want to hold her hand, but showing affection to a human will get tongues wagging. And I do not need that because it'll go straight to Julius.

Julius hates humans.

I can hear and smell the rain from outside. I signal to the bartender, and he hands me an umbrella. As we step outside, I follow close behind her, protecting her from the soft, warm rain.

"You see them?"

"Yep." She points to the group of kids near black SUVs.

"You should tell them not to come back here."

Once they leave, I'll make damn sure to put them on the blacklist.

"I'll relay the message. But either way, I won't be coming back. Don't you worry."

"I can walk you to your—"

"No." She shakes her head. "Too many questions I can't answer. Like your name."

I wrap my arm around her waist before she can walk away. Her head nestles under my chin, her butt against my front. I lower my mouth to her ear. I can hear the song of her blood, the rhythm of her pulse, the pounding beat of her heart. Everything about her calls to me.

"Do me a favor?"

"What is it?"

"Be smart. Stay safe."

"I don't plan on dying. Got a lot of living to do. Got a lot of vampires to kill."

My heart freezes. "Yeah. You do."

"Don't worry about me, Pretty Boy. And I'll return those angel wings one day." She turns to face me. Her lips are close. I want a taste…a bite.

"We'll see each other again, won't we?"

I hope not. It was hard enough to drown out the knowledge that she was somewhere in my city. But seeing her tonight makes it harder to pretend.

I have to stay away. She can't find out that I'm the monster that haunts her nightmares.

"Goodbye, Raven."

"You remember?" She smiles, but then she frowns. "You never told me your name."

"Doesn't matter."

You've already got a piece of me. The wings. And I want them back. Before I can demand that she meet me and return my chain, I turn away and go back to the club, to my dark existence.

It's better this way.

The Dream Team of Mean
Raven

I t's been two weeks in this new world where monsters exist and I'm the monster slayer. My head is spinning. Today we're on our fight schedule and on the way to my Maestro Cali's class that I affectionately call *Intro to Ass-Kicking.*

"Okay, Tyros. Partner up with someone who's not in the same guild." Maestro Cali claps her hands. Everyone quickly buddies up, including me and Dakota.

"Barbie, let's switch it up, since it's odd numbers," Cali yells. "Go join Dakota and Xena: Warrior Princess over there," she says, pointing at me.

"Who?"

"God." She shakes her head and rolls her eyes. "Has it been that long?"

I want to say probably, but I don't want to do laps for my smart mouth. "Is that a superhero or something?"

"Yes. Just one of the greatest shows of all time," she replies in a how-dare-you voice.

She turns to Santa Barbara. "Go join them."

She whistles with her fingers to get everyone's attention. "Spread out, Tyros. We're practicing defense, and today we're tackling barriers."

Dakota groans beside me.

"Is it that hard?" I ask.

"For me, it is." She rolls her eyes. "Who am I talking to…

You'll probably ace this, too."

"C'mon, Dakota." Barbie slaps Dakota on the back. "We'll show Raven the basics."

We walk to the other side of the room. Most students linger in the middle of the dojo near Maestro Cali.

Barbie and Dakota circle each other, and I move near the wall to give them space. Barbie bounces on her feet. Dakota slides back, her hands clenched at her sides.

"Hands up," Barbie commands. "Don't be so stiff."

Dakota bobs her head. "Right, yeah. Got it."

"Okay, I'm going to attack you…for practice." Barbie flicks a look my way, then returns her attention to Dakota. "I need you to pull up that barrier, okay?"

"Yes. Okay. I will."

With impressive speed, Barbie picks up Dakota and body-slams her into the mat. Her back slaps the mat so hard, the sound reverberates in the dojo.

"Ahhh." Dakota rolls like a turtle on her back. "That hurts."

"We've got to work on your barrier. That's the first thing they teach us here." Barbie reaches out her hand to help.

Dakota huffs and pushes herself up. "It's been gone for so long, I've forgotten how to do it. It's like… I can feel something come out of my hand, but I can't see it. How do I know if it's working?"

"You've got to use your heightened senses," Maestro Cali instructs as she walks over to them.

Barbie stops bouncing around like a bunny. Dakota has long abandoned her fighting stance.

"You've got to *feel* it." She walks closer to Dakota. "Close your eyes." She snaps her fingers and points at me. "You too. Come closer."

"Okay." I walk over to the trio, then squeeze my eyes shut, waiting on the Maestro's direction.

"When you think of protection, what do you see?" she asks.

Grandma Lou's smiling face appears in my mind. But that's not the only person. Khamari's face, looking fierce as he fights vampires. And a loving, tender expression. An expression I hadn't really seen before.

Bite your tongue.

"Raven?" the Maestro calls.

"I...don't know."

"Yes, you do."

"I don't." My voice is sharp.

"I could be kicking the sand out of bags right now. Don't waste my time."

"I'll try," Dakota says. "I see...a tall fortress or something. Made of stone. Like a castle."

"Okay, good. Imagine yourself in a room in that castle. You're looking out of a tower. Your enemies surround you from below. What do you do?"

"I shoot fiery arrows. Cannonballs. Oh! And I have a moat, too."

"Someone's into D&D," Barbie whispers.

I laugh, but then I imagine what Dakota and Maestro Cali are talking about.

A warm, invisible energy vibrates around me.

It's working! It feels soft yet solid. Malleable. Like I can make it hard as steel or soft as silk if needed. "A flexible fortress," I mutter to myself.

"Exactly," Maestro Cali answers.

I open my eyes and notice the barrier around Dakota that isn't quite invisible but looks like heat waves on an impossibly hot Texas day.

"You both have got it. Keep it up." She looks at Santa Barbara. "Now Barbie, hit Dakota, then Raven. Raven, you can't hit her back. Defense only."

"What?" Dakota's eyes fly open, and her force field drops.

Barbie cracks her knuckles. "Better protect yourself." She swings her fist back and hits Dakota's shoulders.

Dakota winces. "Ow."

Just before she can lift her leg to kick, I imagine my castle and project my barrier.

"Good job, Raven. Let's go again," Maestro Cali commands.

"Wait!" Dakota raises a hand. Barbie stops her assault on us.

"H-how am I supposed to protect myself? I don't have enough time to imagine all those things."

"You need to get familiar with the feelings and go deep quicker and quicker until it's muscle memory. Now, you've got one more time to put up a barrier. If you don't, then *I'm* going to hit you. And trust me, it's going to hurt a lot worse than Barbie's love taps. Now, Barbie, attack!"

Barbie curls her hand and swings at Dakota, but her fist bounces off the invisible boundary. Barbie's eyes are wide. "You did it!"

"I did, didn't I?" Dakota lowers the shield and gives Barbie a high five. She turns to face me. "Don't leave me hanging."

I don't give her a high five, but I bump her fist. Dakota pumps her fists into the air and does a victory dance. A smile curves across my lips, and I see Barbie laughing at my roomie.

"Very nice, you three," Maestro Cali gives us rare praise.

Barbie shrugs. "That's what we do for each other around here. We're a team." She pats Dakota's shoulder.

"You ladies still have energy?" Maestro Cali asks.

We look at each other and smile. "Yes!"

"Cool. Let's work on how to defend against body slams."

"Oh, God, no." Dakota shakes her head and backs away. Barbie legit giggles at Dakota's antics.

"And you." Maestro Cali points at Barbie. "You broadcast your moves. You need to be quicker, more explosive, efficient."

Barbie stops laughing and nods. "I can work on that."

"And you?" She looks at me.

I rotate my neck and slide into my fighting stance. "I'm game."

Maestro Cali swipes her leg under my feet, and I fall over like a bowling pin.

She doesn't offer me a helping hand, just a smirk. "Let the games begin."

After the barrier practice and spar with Barbie, Dakota, and Maestro Cali, I feel like I can confidently call it *Advance Ass-Kicking*.

Maestro Cali was merciless—kicking, throwing, and punching, she claimed, at 60 percent of her strength. During the fight, when I laid flat on my back, so dizzy I was seeing stars, I wondered if I robbed this lady in a past life. Luckily, I landed a few hits on her and gave her a bloody nose. Before she gave me a swift uppercut, she looked, dare I say, impressed by my moves.

But today's training taught me something—I'm not as strong as I thought I was. I've got a lot to learn if I want to get into the field and earn my code name.

After class, Dakota and I shuffle like battered zombies to the cafeteria.

"You're adjusting really well," Dakota says, unknowingly melting my anxiety with her kind words as she nibbles her veggie sandwich.

I shrug. "I guess I'm doing all right." I've thrown myself into my studies and fighting, hoping like hell the Maestros and Magisters will allow me into the field.

"You're doing more than all right. Let's see, you're acing your classes, all the professors from the Alchemist Order love you—"

"Except Magister Dieter."

"Can't win them all." She swats me with her hand. "Oh yeah, and I still can't believe you beat The Beast on like your first day of class."

I pick at the grilled chicken and asparagus on my plate. "Hm. Not good enough to be on the mission. I know Maestro Cali screwed me out of it."

"Yeah, that sounds like something she would do." Dakota takes another bite of her sandwich and chomps away. "Can I ask you something?"

"Sure."

"Why did you want to win so badly? It was only your first day." Her eyes dart around, looking at the other students. Most of them are sitting by guild, but when I found her, she'd been sitting by herself. "Are you... Are you trying to impress the others?" Her voice is hoarse.

What she really wants to ask is if I want to be popular and leave her behind.

"I'm not here to make friends. And I want to be out there ASAP because, well, you hear my nightmares, right?"

"Your screams."

"Right." I stab my asparagus and avoid eye contact. "I don't want people to end up like me. I don't want people to witness the one they love dying in front of them. And now that I know those monsters are out there, killing innocent people, I can't just sit around on my ass and memorize symbols. I need to fight. I need to...to exorcise this anger inside of me. It's the only time I feel good."

"You like it when you kill?"

"Vampires?" I look at her. "Hell, yes."

"You know all vampires aren't bad, right? In fact, there's a council comprised of vampires, alchemists, and slayers, and they focus on protecting—"

"Vampires have to drink blood to live, yes?"

"Correct. But it doesn't have to be human blood."

I give her a look, and she blushes.

"But, um, I assume they prefer human blood."

I shrug. "It doesn't matter how you dress it up—we'll always be at odds. They want to drink us. It's in their nature. And now... now it's in my nature to kill them. I've got nothing else to lose."

"What about your family?"

I shake my head. I'm not ready to talk about Grandma Lou just yet. In fact, anytime I think of her, I shut that shit down. Khamari is right. It's best that she thinks I'm dead, or better yet, that she has her memories erased. Though, God, she's suffered so much in her life.

I open my mouth to...I don't know, change the subject, but someone's chirpy voice cuts into the tension. "Hey. I don't think we've met just yet. I'm Tallulah."

I look up and find someone from class. I won't even pretend I knew her name before this moment, but I recognize her Kool-Aid-red hair from earlier today. A few Middling students had stopped by to see Maestro Cali wail on us. She's tall with broad shoulders and a wide neck—the perfect physique for killing vamps. Also, she's got a gold-sun-and-silver-moon symbol embroidered on her blazer, which means she's with my guild. There are other patches I don't recognize, but there are so many I'm wondering if she moonlights as a Girl Scout.

"I'm a Middling," she answers my question and points to a patch with a gray *M* in a circle. "I've just returned from a field assignment."

Tallulah smiles wide, and I can tell from the expectant look in her eyes and the fact that she didn't speak for a beat that she expected a congratulation.

"Cool. I'm Raven."

Dakota, seated across from me, fidgets with a ring on her finger, and she's avoiding making eye contact with Tallulah and the crew standing behind her. Which I'm guessing means Ms. T has probably teased her.

"Nice right hook to Maestro Cali. Wish I knocked her out."

"Oh, yeah?" I ask. Don't get me wrong, the Maestro can be a little rude, but I like how she took the time to personally teach us how to erect a barrier and spar.

"She's, like, miserable or something. But anyway, good fight. And I heard you defeated The Beast, too."

Or something. I have a feeling she wasn't here for sweet salutations and cheery congrats. There's this look in Tallulah's eyes—a mixture of nosy and mischief. I'm not sure if it's aimed toward me or Dakota.

Dakota hadn't exaggerated when she said people talked behind her back *and* to her face about her weak fighting skills. And now I'm feeling a little protective of my roommate.

"Thanks." I nod toward Dakota. "But I've gotta give Dakota some props. She told me about the Latin words to propel the invocation."

Two points to me for using the right terms.

"Dakota helped? Really?" The girl snorts and tosses her orange-red hair concoction. She smirks at my roomie. "Good for you."

Dakota's mouth pops open.

"You kinda bombed the last time around, Mouse. But maybe you're, like, learning and growing?" She shrugs. "Anyway, guilds sit together. The Distorters usually sit over there." She points to the other side of the cafeteria.

I already noticed them clustered toward the back of the lunchroom. A few of them are eating. Most of the long, rectangular tables are cluttered with pieces of metals, silver, and old machine parts. Honestly, it looks like a junkyard. I see a small spark, and then a cloud of smoke bursts from an experiment.

"You should join us," Tallulah says.

"I already have a lunch buddy." I wave toward Dakota.

"She'll be fine on her own. Right, Mouse?"

"Okay, bye now, whoever you are." I scoot my chair closer to Dakota, as if I can protect her from across the table.

The girl crosses her arms. "Wow. Rude."

"What? You get to be rude, but I can't? Girl, bye."

Tallulah storms off.

Dakota isn't looking like a poor little duckling anymore. She's laughing. Loudly.

"What? I told you I don't do people."

She stops laughing. "If you want to sit with the Distorters, you can totally do it. I'll be fine."

I peek back at my guild and shiver. "No thanks. I can't eat my food around all that filth." Grandma Lou would have a fit if she witnessed food and scraps of junk on the table.

But the other guilds' tables don't look so bad. The Evokers have greenery and beautiful flowers decorating their tables. I've seen them replant or pot their flowers each day after school. The Internists are the minimalists, and there's nothing on their tables but their food trays and cups. Dakota and I are seated at a round table near the entrance. It's the admin and teachers' section, but Dakota never sits near the students in the cafeteria to eat. Since Dakota works for the school and I'm her roommate, I assume we're allowed to sit here.

"I think I get it now." She nods, staring at me. "You want revenge, and I w-want respect. Everyone around here thinks I'm weak, but I'm not." Her shaky voice firms. "I'll show them."

"Damn right you will. We'll help each other."

"As friends?" She wiggles her eyebrows.

"Still up in the air." I try nibbling on the rest of the grilled chicken, but I end up tossing it back on the tray. "This isn't good."

"Yeah, I don't trust the chicken here." She lifts her sandwich, takes another small bite. A *ping* comes from her phone, and she checks it. "Commander Paris needs me," she says, then wipes her mouth with a napkin. "What are you doing for Open Period?"

"Sleeping for a thousand years."

"Living the dream." She stands. "If you're asleep by the time I'm back from work, I'll see you in class tomorrow."

I don't sleep for a thousand years, but I do sleep through the alarm, and I'm five minutes late for my Alchemy History and Philosophies class. When I enter the auditorium, Magisters Corrine and Dieter are chatting softly at the front of the room and the door bangs behind me.

"Nice of you to join us." Dieter's dry voice grates my skin.

"Sorry. I overslept." The magisters were generally cool, except for Dieter and his wife, Corrine. And right now, I wish I didn't have him for this class and European Alchemy.

"Make sure it doesn't happen again, hm?" Corrine says. "But I imagine one's body would need rest after being brutally defeated by Maestro Cali." She gives me an unkind smile.

The rest of the classroom chuckles around me. In the words of my Grandma Lou, this raggedy heffa.

Magister Corinne says ta-ta (no, literally, she says ta-ta and wiggles her fingers at her husband).

Magister Dieter walks to the board. His arms are lanky as the rest of his body, yet he holds himself up like a T. rex, his wrists bent as he stomps to the whiteboard. He points at a timeline.

"These are the important dates. The Alchemist Order was established in 323 B.C. Tell me, class—what spurred this?"

Someone's arm shoots up.

"Lexington?"

"Alexander the Great conquering Egypt. He wanted the alchemists to find a way for him to become immortal. They were afraid of his growing power and sought to overthrow him. So, they concocted a way to defeat him."

"Exactly. We alchemists are the reason slayers can fight vampires. By utilizing the transmutation circles, our chants and prayers will give you the blueprint to create weapons to defeat evil. Throughout history, famous alchemists have banded together. You have Albertus Magnus, an alchemist and a saint. He is my ancestor," Dieter reminds us again. "Isaac Newton, Francis Bacon, and Jan Baptist Van Helmont. These families still uphold our fathers' legacies. And we...we are the heartbeat of this organization."

I raise my hand.

"What is it, child?" Dieter growls.

"I want to hop back to the Alchemist Order being established. Alexander still ended up being immortal."

"He's dead now."

"Right, but according to your timeline, he didn't die until...1805. I mean, that's over two thousand years."

"I'm delighted you can count. But that won't help you," he answers.

"What I'm asking is, *how* did he become a vampire?"

"An experiment gone wrong. The alchemists of that time transmuted him to death, and he then became death itself."

"Holy crap. So it's your fault? The heartbeats of this organization?" I cackle.

The room goes silent. In fact, it's like my very astute observation has sucked the oxygen out of the air. Dakota, with wild, wide eyes, motions the kill signal with her hand, making a slash motion across her neck.

I mean, did I say something incorrect? I shrug, but then I look around the room and notice every student is avoiding making eye contact with me. One guy has wrapped his head inside of his blazer.

Oh, come on. What's the Magister going to do…chant me into timeout?

"Get out." Dieter points to the door. "This is the last time you interrupt my class. Don't return until you can learn to respect your superiors," he says among a smattering of "Ooooo"s.

Heat slaps my cheeks, but I clear my throat and cloak myself with bravado like it's a winter jacket.

"Sure. I'll just do some light reading." I pick up the brick of a textbook, though I'm sure that little oopsie didn't make it into this tome.

I take back my sentiment — alchemy classes are a joke. They're nothing but a lovefest about the five families that comprise the Alchemist Order.

I whistle when I step outside. I'm looking forward to having the room to myself, since Dakota is in class and then has to work with Paris during open period. When I return, I listen to music and zone out.

I jerk awake, and the sun shines through the window. Dakota is straightening her side of the room, her headphones on as she bobs to her music.

When she notices me awake, she greets me. "Morning." She lifts the headphones from her ears.

"Did I… Was I loud last night?"

"You were screaming, yes. Charlotte came. She tried to wake you, but you wouldn't budge. Sorry I forgot to order the soundproofing stuff on the 'Zon, but I did last night, and it should be here in a few days."

"Shit. I'll pay you back. Sorry."

"No worries."

"Speaking of… How often do we get paid?"

Charlotte, in her campaign to win me over and make me stay, mentioned that students receive a stipend from the government and benevolent benefactors.

"Training and studying to save the world is hard work. You all deserve to be paid."

And, like any other government job, we have different pay grades depending on experience and level of difficulty of the gig. We even get kill bonuses for certain vampires. "Every two weeks," Dakota says. "You can get an advance from the admin office, too, if you make a good case."

A knock on the door interrupts our convo.

Dakota opens the door, revealing Charlotte standing on the other side. Her eyes hit me.

Charlotte looks concerned.

My face is hot because I know why she's here.

"Oh, hey." I wave.

Charlotte doesn't return the gesture. In a formal voice, she says, "The Ankh Elder Council has convened, and they have specifically asked that you partner with their prince to hunt made vampires."

Okay, so maybe I don't know.

"As in *vampire* prince?" I clarify.

Charlotte nods. "Affirmative."

"No, ma'am," I say, shaking my head.

"I don't understand the problem. I thought you wanted to go into the field."

"Yes, but with other *slayers*. Not a freaking vampire."

Charlotte sighs. "This is nonnegotiable, unfortunately, and trust me, I tried. Meet me in the parking garage at seven p.m. Don't be late."

"And if I don't?"

"The Elders and the king will take it as a sign of disrespect. They may...break off diplomatic ties. That means all the peace treaties such as the no-hunt and kill clauses for humans will be null." She clicks her tongue and crosses her arms. "Put on your big-girl panties. You're going."

Charlotte turns to face the door. "Oh." She stops and says over her shoulder, "You need a code name. A city, country, or state."

I hide my squeal with a strangled squeak. Dakota gives me big eyes. The code name—exciting. Working with vampires? Not so much.

Charlotte stares at me from where she's leaning against the doorjamb. "Have you given it any thought? I would avoid small hometowns. Nothing that can easily trace back to your loved ones."

"It's probably taken, but I'd like to be known as Texas."

Charlotte smiles. "Oh! That's available."

"Yeah, the last Texas died last year, right?" Dakota mumbles.

Charlotte shushes her. "That was years ago."

"No. Last year," Dakota reminds her. "And the others said there were two more before him in under ten years."

"Is that name cursed or something?" I cut in.

"It's not cursed," Charlotte says with a wide smile. "Now, it's totally up to you if you want the name."

I look at Dakota, who shakes her head. I ignore her.

"Yeah. I like it." Maybe I'm being a little conceited, but I kinda like the idea of the code name waiting for the right slayer.

"Great." Charlotte gives me a decisive nod. "Be there at seven...Texas."

After she leaves, my mouth falls open. My heart pumps like it's on speed, but *my brain*, hasn't processed the news.

I turn my attention to Dakota, who's giving me big, stretched-out, *Looney Tunes* eyes.

Finally, I figure out my feeling (anger, definitely anger). I kick over a chair. "I cannot believe they're forcing me to work with vampires."

"It feels a bit…extreme. Especially someone at your level." She gives me a painful smile, and there's a hint of jealousy in her voice. For what, I cannot fathom. Did she not hear that I had to work with those bloodsucking scumbags live and in color?

"You know what? I quit. I'm packing my bags and going back home to Texas!"

"Babe." Dakota shakes her head. "You *are* Texas."

They're Taking Over Buckhead
Texas

I drag my ass to the parking lot, stomping in silence as I follow Charlotte to the car.

"Stop pouting. I promise you will be safe."

"Uh-huh."

"Unfortunately, the vampire elders claimed this is the best solution for remuneration."

"Remuneration?"

"Yes. In this instance, we are paying them back for breaking the treaty."

"I know what it means. I'm just…just pissed that y'all are forcing me to do this. The dude killed my friends. Now, I'm being punished because of your stupid little rules?"

"I warned you to not touch him. In fact, I blew him away with the wind."

"And he came back like a boomerang and tried to kill me."

Charlotte stops walking, and her hand fists and hits her hip like she's Supermom. "It's not fair. Not at all, Texas. Trust me, I am deeply aware of how unfair life is. But we must do this because there is a greater impact if we don't."

"Which is?"

"War. And there are no victors in war." Charlotte clicks a key fob, and a Mercedes coupe beeps on the other side of the garage. "Ready to take Sadie out for a spin?"

"Can I drive?"

"Absolutely not." She opens the door and slides in. "But you can have a phone."

She hands me the latest iPhone, fully charged.

Before I can say thanks, she launches into conversation. "Don't add any apps or credit cards, and don't take any pictures outside of what you need for missions. You'll upload it to our secure server and delete daily."

I nod. Everything she said made sense. It wouldn't be good for anyone—vampire or human—to come across a slayer's phone.

Charlotte exhales. "Good. Now, we're meeting the prince at a neutral location. Our allies in Buckhead." She turns up the music that's synced to her phone. The music is good—she's playing everything from The Jackson 5 to Chloe x Halle, my favorite music duo.

While she drives, I play on my phone, figure out my number. Forty-five minutes later, Charlotte swerves us into the cul-de-sac of a fancy-ass mansion.

As she shifts into park, a lanky man with strawberry-blond hair graying at the temples stands near the driver's side. He motions toward the door, and Charlotte nods. Once he opens it, Charlotte immediately goes into PR mode.

"Nathan, sweetie, how are you?"

They prattle on while I unbuckle my seat belt.

"And who is this lovely young lady beside you?"

"Texas, one of our most promising slayers," Charlotte replies.

Oh, shit. I'm promising?

"A pleasure to meet you, Texas." He bows. Meanwhile, I'm still preening over the compliment.

"Likewise."

"You have friends outside of the Society?" I whisper to Charlotte.

"We have allies with every species."

"What other species are there?" I know about vampires and

werewolves. "You mean like aliens?" I look at the sky.

"Texas?" Nathan offers me his other arm.

I place my hand on the bend of his elbow as I look around the neighborhood and whistle. "Fancy."

He guides us inside. The interior of the mansion is as magnificent as the outside. Marble floors and bright, bold floral arrangements decorate the home. Near the entry is a collection of art that looks like framed pictures of colorful circles and squares and rectangles that a toddler could've drawn.

To each their own.

A pleasing smell of lemons and roses perfumes the air.

While we walk deeper into the home, Nathan speaks warmly about the fabulous theater, library, and chef's kitchen. Finally, we enter a room with a cherrywood table that's so large it can easily seat thirty or more guests. The tabletop gleams. A large tangerine-and-indigo-colored bowl sits as the centerpiece, polished to perfection. Inside the bowl is an array of fruit artistically grouped by color: green pears and grapes, yellow lemons and bananas, and red apples and plums.

That's when I notice a vampire staring at me from the doorway.

My eyes narrow as she enters the room.

"Texas." Charlotte grabs my shoulder, dragging me closer to the creature. "I'd like for you to meet a member of the Prussakov family." She nods at the tall redhead with arresting blue eyes. "This is Ludmila, the matriarch."

In no time, the vampire appears in front of me and Charlotte. The wind from her speed swishes Charlotte's locs. Enormous power exudes from the old vampire. It sticks like humidity to my skin. There isn't enough soap in Georgia to wipe this devil off me.

She must be a Royal.

Ludmila offers her hand to me. A pale, cold, murderous hand.

"It's great to meet you, Texas. Please call me Mila. Charlotte has told us all about you."

I stare at Ludmila. She's beautiful. Her eyes and smile are as soft and inviting as a warm mug of cider. I'm sure Hansel and Gretel felt the same way about the witch. Or poor Little Red Riding Hood with the wolf. They lure you in with their innocent act, and then bam! They eat you.

"Aren't you going to shake her hand, Texas?" Charlotte asks in a reproving voice.

I clasp my hands behind my back. "Nah. I'm good."

"I'm sorry you can't meet the rest of the family today," Mila replies with humor lighting her eyes.

I'm not.

Charlotte shakes her head and continues. "She will one day soon. And of course, you've already met Nathaniel, who is also a human relative."

"Jesus," I mutter under my breath.

Mila moves to the head of the conference table. "Let's convene in the formal room, shall we? We'll have more space to accommodate the prince and anyone else who's in attendance."

Stupid vampire prince.

We follow Mila through an open entryway. A gray stone fireplace stands in the middle of the room. Not one of those fake gas ones, but with legit logs. Mila stands by the hearth, one arm resting on the ledge, while she quietly chats with Charlotte. I pace the room.

A light rap on the door catches everyone's attention.

Nathan sticks his head in and focuses his attention on Mila. "So sorry to interrupt, but the Ankh prince has just arrived."

Berries and spices invade my senses.

I reach for my bracelet. Just in case the vampires double-cross us. Despite my dislike for the creatures, I have to admit my interest is piqued. I've never had the displeasure of meeting a vampire prince.

The doors open. The prince's back is to the room as he turns down the glass of scotch Nathan offers.

Nice ass.

And the navy-blue suit he's wearing is clearly custom-made.

Navy-blue suit?

He takes a deep breath and then turns around.

Waves of power waft off him. My heart climbs up my throat.

Pinpoints of awareness hopscotch over my body when I see those familiar whiskey-brown eyes. Unnatural, with a glint that doesn't belong. With a light that shines from his dark soul.

"Pretty Boy," I growl.

"Prince Khamari," he answers.

He prowls into the room like he pays the rent.

I don't like it.

I don't like him.

And what's more, I don't like the way he makes me feel—like my skin's been flipped inside out.

"We should talk," *Prince* Khamari says.

"You should go to hell."

"Texas!" Charlotte strides toward me. "He is an important ally and he—"

"Was there the night of my attack! When I turned into…into a killing machine." I motion toward my body.

Charlotte's attention snaps to him. "You left her at that crappy motel? By herself?"

"I thought I was protecting her. I erased all traces of myself. And I wonder…still wonder how they found you."

I look away. The chain, his chain, burns in my pocket. Yeah, I keep it close, like a talisman or something, ever since seeing him at that club. He's never getting it back now.

I clear my throat. "Then you know damn well what happened that night is not my fault. So whatever punishment you came up with, you can shove it up your ass."

A very fine ass, but still.

"I'm not here to punish you. I'm here to partner with you. With all of you." He settles on the dark-blue couch and folds his leg across his knee.

"We have a great partnership as it stands, Prince Khamari." Charlotte moves to stand in front of me like a mama bear.

"There are some within the council who feel that not all Mades should be killed. We want to see if there's an opportunity for reformation."

"We only hunt the ones the Royals tag," Charlotte argues.

"What about the government? You work with them, too," he points out.

My stomach goes sour—I know how to sniff out a setup, and this is clear. He wants to get closer to the Society. I know it; Charlotte knows it. And I'm sure that redhead vampire standing quietly by the fireplace knows it, too.

"We have intel on a Rogue who claims an anonymous group has asked him to attend a Made party."

"A Made party?"

"A party to create vampires."

"God." My stomach curdles.

"And they're meeting tonight?" Charlotte cocks her head to the side, still in mama-bear mode.

"Tomorrow night and—"

"Texas is a novice. That type of mission is inappropriate, given her experience."

"I'm simply proposing an observation," he says. "We follow the lead, see where it goes. We won't engage. Then, we'll gather evidence, while also reassuring our Elder Council and clans that we are being fair to our vampire brethren."

"I'll have to run this by Paris." Charlotte folds her arms. "And then we'll come up with a short list of Maestros you can work with."

"Oh, I don't need a list." He looks at me. "I want her."

"Like I've already stated…she isn't ready."

"I've seen her fight. She's better than whoever you'll suggest. And if anything goes down, I'll protect her."

"Fine. But we'll do a practice mission round tonight," Charlotte says, shaking her head. "We have intelligence regarding a murdered scientist."

"Scientist?" both Khamari and I ask.

"Dr. Winters. We need you to do surveillance in the neighborhood where she lived."

"Fine. We'll keep an eye out—"

"Hell no, Pretty Boy." I shake my head and storm out of the room, needing to be outside to air out my anger.

"Wait," he yells from behind me.

I only stop when I reach the front door.

"Wait." Khamari's voice is soft this time.

I squeeze the doorknob. "Why didn't you tell me?"

"I was scared."

"Scared?" I turn around and lean against the door.

"You hate vampires," the royal asshole points out.

"Obviously." I snort. "You would too if… Never mind." I forgot who I'm speaking to.

"They attacked me, too, you know." He points to the scar at this neck.

"What happened?"

He jerks his head toward the wide central staircase. "Let's go upstairs. We can talk, and you can ask me anything."

I cross my arms. "I don't think it's wise for me to go somewhere alone with you."

"You went to a vampire club a few weeks ago and *now* you want to play it safe?" He steps back.

"I was tricked."

"I didn't bite you then, and I won't now." He raises his hands in the air as if to make me feel safe. "Mila and Charlotte will hand me my ass if I try something. I just want to talk, and I want a little privacy before I bare my soul."

I chuckle. "Don't be dramatic."

He crosses his arms and laughs. "That's funny," he tells me.

"What?"

"You just…bring back memories."

"Of your ex-girlfriend?" I lift the corner of my mouth and look him boldly in the eyes, daring him to deny it.

"Yeah. Her." He clears his throat. "Where are my wings, Angel?"

"Nope. My name is Texas."

Angels are soft and kind and forgiving. I'm petty.

"Where is it?"

"Somewhere safe." I walk into the empty kitchen, and he follows me. He wants to talk. And we'll talk, but on my terms. Not in a dusty vampire dungeon upstairs.

"So…" I hop onto the barstool near the counter. "You're a vampire?"

He scoots onto one of the stools closest to me. So close our legs touch. I promptly swivel away.

"Yes. But not always," he says. "I was a human once."

"Huh. So that's why you're hot."

"You think I'm hot?"

"Your body."

"Thank you."

"Temperature!" I want to laugh, but then again, he's a vampire. A bloodsucking vampire.

He tilts his head back, a look of catlike satisfaction in his eyes. "I like it when I can do that."

"Do what?"

"Pull a smile out of you." He points at my face. "You don't smile often, but when you do…"

"What?" I whisper.

"It's like a one-two punch. I can't duck it, and I don't want to."

I cover my smile. He lowers my hand.

Bloodsucking vampire, remember? "Do you kill humans?" I blurt out.

He's quiet for a moment, and as he deliberates on whether he'll lie to me, a knot forms like a tight ball in my stomach.

"Not usually, but I have before."

The knot in my gut doubles.

"For a good reason?"

"I couldn't control my thirst when I first turned, but my grandfather taught me. It didn't take me long, and now I'm an ally of the Slayer Society."

"And also a prince."

"Soon to be king. My grandfather appointed me earlier this year."

"Yay, nepotism." I pump my fist. "Rarely works out for us. But wait...your grandfather is a vampire?"

"Don't do that."

"Do what?"

"Tilt up your nose like you smell trash."

I didn't even realize I'd done that. I sigh, lowering my head. "Better?"

"Much. And yes, as was my father. My mother was human. Both died when I was three or four."

Mine too. But instead of sharing our similar past, I say, "That sucks. How'd they die?"

"He and my mother were killed by another clan. My grandfather put me in foster care to save me."

"How noble." I cross my arms. "And now you're the leader of the Ankh clan."

"Yes. It's a powerful clan. And—"

"You screw with people's minds." My tone is severe, and

the lightness of the conversation is gone. But dammit, now I'm remembering how he manipulated that poor motel clerk.

"You…you tried to screw with *my* mind."

"Yes," he admits. "I can do that, telekinesis, and I'm a dreamwalker."

"Is this a dream?"

"No. It's real. I'm real."

"Before you became a prince," I continue, "what did you do for your clan?"

"What do you mean?"

"Don't play dumb. I know everyone has a role. What was yours?"

"I study blood."

I lean away. "You mean you *drink* blood."

"Both. I don't want vampires to depend on *human* blood. Our clan has ties to the blood bank, and we rely on donations. With Made vampires growing exponentially, we need to find another blood source; otherwise, humans will be overrun by vampires. That's why I'm pushing a mandate throughout all clans to put a freeze on Royals creating vampires."

"Yeah…bet you guys don't want to deplete your food source."

"I don't enjoy feeding off humans. And I don't want a repeat of what happened to you and others like you. No one deserves that. That's why I'll dedicate my life to understanding how to synthesize blood."

He sounds genuine, like he honestly wants to save the world.

But he can't. How can a monster save the world?

"I believe that once we crack the code for blood creation, vampires and humans can coexist peacefully. In fact, the Society has agreed to fund my research."

I laugh, and it's all sarcastic and soulless. "Your kind doesn't want peace. You want to rule and kill and destroy. Have you…" I clear my throat. "Have you killed kids?"

"C'mon now." He huffs.

"Yes or no."

"No." He shakes his head. "This was a mistake. You don't want to get to know me. You want to condemn me."

"We're having a conversation, and you said I can ask you anything. Don't get mad if you don't like my questions."

"I admitted to killing. It's not something I enjoy. No one deserves to be murdered. I'm not perfect, not by any means, but I try to do good now." He pauses for a beat. "Does this answer your questions?"

"I've killed a vampire. Plan to kill more."

"I'm aware. Those who died deserved it, I'm sure. Certainly Ethan."

"You're not upset?" I raise my chin in the air.

"I don't think you would care if it upset me."

"Sure don't." My tight frown morphs into a small smile.

He smiles back, and damn, I mean, *damn*, he's fine, and it feels indulgent to look at him.

He lifts his hand out for a shake. "So, will you go out with me?" He smiles. He knows just how he sounds.

"I'll go out on a *stakeout* with you. That other crap you tried to pull in there…" I shake my head. "Probably not."

"You don't trust me yet. I get it." He leans away, lifting his hand to his chin. Then he looks at me and drops his hand.

"You're going to have a hell of a time getting me to trust you." I shrug. "Doesn't matter anyway. After tonight, it's not like we'll see each other again."

I hope.

"Is that what you think?" His lips curve into a smile.

"It's what I know."

His smile grows wider, as if he's silently telling me: Challenge Accepted.

"Why are you smiling?"

"Just happy to see you," he says.

"After sunrise, you won't be seeing me again."

"Oh, I'll be seeing you."

 I roll my eyes. "In your dreams."

"Don't tempt me."

Mystery Man
Texas

'm the world's worst stalker. Not because I'm not sneaky, quiet, or clever, but because I'm too impatient. Amped-up impatient. As impatient as a five-year-old girl on a road trip who'd just slurped down her fifth juice box.

Even in October, the Atlanta weather drags its ass on ditching the heat. Whatever faction of the Society does recon—count me out. Because sitting here on a roof in Midtown while I make like a hot dog and boil isn't my idea of fun.

Khamari looks…preoccupied. Nervous, even. Ever since Charlotte announced our new stakeout plans, he became porcupine prickly. And maybe even a little paranoid, given the way he checked his phone and sent cryptic messages that, at first glance, I can't figure out the meaning of.

And if he's so damn busy, why did he even drag me out here?

Oh, that's not right. The Slayer Society forced him to partner with me on this "test run" for a slayer-and-vampire partnership. Charlotte told me she'd hope she could satisfy the vampire elders' request while simultaneously keeping me out of harm's way.

After an hour of not speaking, *Prince Khamari* crouches low beside me while sneaking in glances. I guess he's stopped pretending I don't exist.

"You like what you see?" I toss back the callous words he said to me a month ago. And of course, a few hours later, he tried to erase my memories and left me at a shitty motel.

"I've got a pretty good memory." He's not sneaking those glances in anymore. He's staring at me with hungry wolf eyes.

He's truly exhibiting f-boy behavior. I roll my eyes, unfolding my middle finger until it stands at attention. "I'm sure you've collected enough of them."

"Lifetimes," he whispers, but he's dropped that flirty tone.

Good.

"I'm sitting down."

"On the roof?"

"Yes, Prince Khamari," I say, mimicking the royal bathers from *Coming to America*.

"Stop it."

"Stop what, my prince?"

I get a big dose of satisfaction when his jaw flexes like he's chewing steel bubblegum.

"I'm not your prince."

My body hardens to stone. He didn't say it unkindly, but I feel embarrassed.

"I know that—"

"But I can be your king." His gaze drifts down to me, lingers, languishes—lights me on fire.

I swallow. The tension in the air, in my body, paralyzes my throat. Still, I squeak, "I... I'm just playing."

His eyes are still on me. His stare is unyielding. "You shouldn't play with a guy like me."

I nod, though I say nothing.

I pop up to my feet and move as far away from him as possible, pacing around the small corner of the roof like a cornered feral cat. We are awkwardly quiet—zipped lips, crossed arms, avoiding eye contact.

We could really use a vampire attack right about now. But as much as I want to slay, the vampire we're tracking is likely a no-show—just as Charlotte suspected. If anything goes down, I'm ready as I can be. Dakota lent me her flash cards, and, on the way over, I ran through cool new weapons to create.

"Stop pacing." His voice cuts through the silence. "Come over here before you're noticed."

I drag my feet and move closer, then slowly kneel beside him.

A curly curtain forms around my shoulders as I let my hair slip past my face. I peek through and look at him.

My body breaks out in tingles. He's scanning the area like he's Jack Reacher or something—ready to take off his shirt and fight anything that jumps in our way.

He looks down at his large watch with a rose-gold face. Yes, he's got money. Lots of it. Meanwhile, I'm repping 100-percent-cotton yoga pants that make me feel 100-percent busted next to his custom-made suit.

"So, you're rich, huh?"

He takes a breath but doesn't move his attention from the street below. "Very." He says it in a matter-of-fact way. "After you live a long time, you know how things work—how the more things change, the more things stay the same."

I chuckle. "That's what my Grandma Lou says."

"Oh, yeah?"

"Yeah." That's right. That's what I'm here for. Understand how to use my power and… I don't know, visit her. Maybe even undo whatever erasing thing the Society has done to her. Which is pretty crappy, if you ask me, even if it is for the best. But that's kinda what Pretty Boy does, too.

That's right…. That *is* his power.

"I've got a question."

"Shoot."

"If you erase someone's memories, do you know how to, I don't know, bring them back?"

"What?" He finally gives me his eyes. And whoa. *Whoa.* His brown eyes are like beautiful nightlights.

My stomach vaults somewhere in deep space.

"Can you…" I lick my lips. "Can you give someone their memories back? You know, even if someone else took them. I'm, um…asking for a friend."

He shakes his head. "I don't know. I don't manipulate memories unless necessary."

"And I was necessary?"

His eyes hit me like bullets. "Very."

"You say it like I'm dangerous."

"You are," he mutters.

"No, the killer we're on the lookout for is dangerous."

Not that the vampire will show up unless they're stupid. I would hope not even vampires are bold enough to circle their prey's home—unless he's looking for something. Charlotte told us the person murdered was a former alchemist. Maybe they're looking for a clue that points back to the Order.

"Does the Society investigate all former alchemists' deaths?" he asks.

"I'm not sure. But this is a special case because one of your homeboys tore her limbs to pieces and she had fang marks on her neck."

"A Rogue, then." Khamari crosses his arms, back to guard-watch mode.

"Nope. They don't think it's random. Remember how Charlotte said that Dr. Winters specialized in epidemiology?" Before we left, she gave us a five-minute summary. Former alchemist, now epidemiologist. Lived in Midtown, worked downtown. Oh, and Dieter's former protégé. No description of the vampire other than that her office smelled like sewage.

His back muscles go tight—so tight I can see his shoulder blades poking through the expensive material. He's unnaturally still. In fact, he's not breathing.

I narrow my eyes on his back. "Did you know her?"

"No." He looks down before he turns to face me. "I just…find her background in studying diseases interesting."

"Right. That's the million-dollar question: what in the hell did a vampire want with Dr. Winters?"

"I'm not sure how we're supposed to find a random vampire. There are lots of us out here."

"I'll just follow my nose."

"Right, because they smell like sewage." He waits a few beats before asking, "Is that how I smell to you?"

Oh right. He is a bloodsucker.

"You smell…" *Amazing.* "Like a regular dude who doesn't know the correct ratio for cologne," I lie through my teeth.

I take another deep breath. But it's not Khamari's signature scent of all-spice and berries. It's sewage, intense — an all-encompassing, stomach-screwing scent.

I rock on my heels and refocus on the target. I don't need a scope from my vantage point — my superhuman vision is that good.

I slap Khamari's chest with the back of my hand and point to the culprit.

The vampire has a Mad Hatter vibe: funky red blazer, navy-blue pants, and a top hat, of all things. The odd bastard walks to a rhythm that is not of this world. He lifts his legs at a ninety-degree angle from the ground with the precision of a drum major. His neck twists at all angles, ears perked like a canine. A girl dressed in an Emory University sweatshirt stands on the same sidewalk. She isn't moving and just stares wide-eyed at the vampire.

My calves clench. I hold my breath, ready to tackle and slay.

The girl doesn't hurry past like a normal person. She bats her glued-on lashes and gives him a pageant smile.

I shake my head. Even before I knew vampires existed, I had decent instincts, and this guy screams dangerous. But what's weird — weirder than Happy Hannah smiling at a predator — is the vampire's reaction. He doesn't stop or sniff or bite.

Instead, he hustles past the human, reaches into his jacket, and pulls out a cell phone. He ticks something on the screen and then stuffs it back into his pocket.

"Shit," Khamari whispers.

"You know him?"

"Rider. I've been looking for him."

"Can I kill him?"

"No."

"Can *you* kill him?"

"No." He growls low. "In fact, my hands are tied."

"Why are they tied, Khamari?" I ask. This shit doesn't make sense. "I thought your precious Elders wanted you to partner with us?"

"Rider will try to kill you."

"That's what y'all do, which is why we are here."

He lets out a low sigh. "Charlotte doesn't want you to fight. I don't want you to fight. I'll go down, follow him. And if I must, I'll take him down."

"But—"

"I know you want some action, but we've got to do this right. Alert the Society that we spotted him. You can…you can tell them he's part of the Ankh clan."

"Fiiineee."

"Be back in a few minutes… maybe an hour."

"What?" I snap.

"I've got a radio, and so do you. If you need me, call me." He motions to the black backpack behind us. "But I'll telepathically communicate with you." He taps his forehead. *"Like this,"* he says, but in my mind.

His voice rings loud and clear as if through speakers in my head. "You're loud." I gasp at the intrusion and grab my forehead. "Really loud." I know communicating this way is necessary, but it felt too…intimate. I still don't know him like that.

"Sorry," he whispers this time. "Alert the Society. After, you follow him up top, and I'll follow down low. I'll call if I need anything."

"Be careful," I whisper-yell to his back.

"You sound like you care."

"I don't."

"Yeah, you do." He runs off the rooftop and jumps. He's so quiet I can't even hear him land.

I send a text to Charlotte.

Vampire is here. Rider…somebody. Don't know the last name. He's an Ankh. Khamari recognizes him. Don't worry, I won't kill a stupid clan member this time.

I grab the backpack and then creep along the rooftop, moving as the vampire moves. Khamari lags, giving the vamp enough space to avoid his attention.

I flex my shoulders and steady my breathing. It's all I can do to stop myself from giving in to my instinct to kill. Stealth eludes me, but I can't afford to mess up this mission. If I do this right, this could lead to more field time, far away, by myself.

But first, I need to get this thing inside of me under control.

Charlotte informed us that ASS has a policy that requires us to wait until no humans are present before we attack. It's 5:30 a.m., so the vampire has less than two hours before sunrise. If the sunlight hits him, it's a wrap.

The vampire clears another block. If Charlotte's hunch is correct, he's headed to the doctor's apartment.

Careful and quiet, I jump, tuck, and roll onto the roof of a fancy hotel.

The large sign affixed in the middle provides adequate coverage, so I don't have to crawl or crouch.

Taking a deep breath, I try to zero in on his scent. Oh. Yep. There it is—*eau de ewww*. I'm running out of roofs to hop. I crouch on the last roof and watch as Khamari closes in on the vamp.

A loud *ding* blares from my phone.

Shit. A text message. Dammit, Charlotte!

The vampire directs his gaze toward me, and as soon as he spots me, he's looking at me like he's a psychotic puppy and I'm the chow.

It Takes Two
Texas

The vampire growls, saliva seeping down the sides of his mouth. But before he can attack, Khamari lets out a dog-like whistle.

The other vampire turns, growls, and hurtles straight toward Khamari. He slams his body but bounces off Khamari, like a fly against a brick wall.

Shit. "Khamari, look out!" I shout, but it's too late.

Someone else runs behind him, in a black hood and mask. They slash him with a knife, and Khamari just barely dodges. With a swipe of his hand, he swats the air, but the hooded figure stands rooted.

A low chuckle fills the air. I sniff, attempting to place the scent, but I don't smell vampire.

I smell nothing. Nothing at all.

The other vampire gets up, and together, the duo fights Khamari. The other vampire clearly isn't a match, but the hooded figure is a wild card. And with that knife, they're getting closer and closer to nailing Khamari's heart.

"Go!" the hooded person yells at the vampire. Their voice is changed with a distorted, robotic quality.

"Damn." I stand, my heart running ragged in my chest. I can't just stay up here.

Pushing off my feet, I sprint to the edge of the building, pumping my arms and legs, then sail off the gable. I land on the sidewalk carefully.

"I've got him!" I yell to Khamari. He doesn't argue—he nods and focuses on his adversary.

"Rider's no match for you. I'll join you soon. Remember... don't kill him."

I nod and run after the vampire.

The chase lasts only a few minutes before Rider slows in front of the entrance to Piedmont Park.

Before I engage him, I summon my power.

Another cool thing Charlotte gifted me is my blood-letter. The ring on my finger looks like ordinary jewelry to the common eye. But with the press of a button on the base of the loop, I release a mini serrated knife, slice my palm, and press my hands together.

Electric silver-and-gold energy courses through my core, zipping up and down my body. The air stirs, and my palms pulse with power.

White light surges from the alchemy symbols etched on my palm, warming my hand. It signifies a communion between a slayer and The Architect.

Seconds later, I jump over the stone wall, landing in the grass on the other side. The park is massive—two hundred acres of green space with walkways bisecting the flat, green lawn. Lush bushes dot the grass like oversize broccoli. Finding a cluster of trees, I dash beneath the gold-green leaves for cover.

The vampire slows his pace, nose in the air, head swiveling side to side like a bloodhound.

I crouch behind a thick tree trunk, fingers embedded in the bark, knees on the slick grass.

"No need to be shy, human." He pivots to the left with flaring nostrils and squinty eyes. "You've come so far. Step out of the shadows." It isn't a command or a request, but his tone is superior and expectant. No more hide-and-seek.

Fine by me—I don't like playing games. I step away from the

tree and march toward the center of the park.

The vampire looks me up and down. "Slayer, I presume?"

I nod.

"It's not nice to block your scent. I do love the smell of slayers."

"Have you been in recent contact with the doctor?" I ignore his taunts and try to adhere to ASS's stupid policy about asking clarifying questions before engaging in a fight.

He tilts his head. "I know a lot of doctors. You'll have to be more specific."

"Dr. Karen Winters."

His eyes narrow.

"Your scent is all over her office," I tell him. "Don't deny it."

"I won't."

"Did you murder her?"

"Did I murder a human?" He shrugs. "There have been so many, I can't recall."

"What was your relationship with the doctor?"

"What do the kids call it these days? Wikileaks? Sneaky freaks?"

Sneaky link. But I'm not answering him. I move on to the next question. "What business did you have with a scientist?"

"They taste better."

And that's enough clarifying questions for me, thanks.

"Two choices. Come with me and stand trial with the Society. Or...resist and die." My lips stretch into a smile. "Feel free to resist."

Technically, I'm not *allowed* to kill him, but maybe Khamari or another slayer can finish him? This vamp doesn't need to know that small detail.

He points to a tattoo on his inner wrist: the shape of a cross but with an oval loop in place of an upper bar, the symbol of the Ankh clan. I stare at the tattoo—iridescent gold, blue, and red markings. "Even with the precious prince, you can't kill me. I'm protected."

Bleh. Now I wish Khamari were here. I already got in trouble for killing a stupid, protected vampire. I can only slay him if I find him attempting to kill a human or if he attempts to kill me. Breaking into a dead-scientist-slash-former-alchemist's apartment isn't good enough, even if he did heavily imply he's the one who ripped her apart. *Stupid treaty.*

"Your name?"

"Rider Edwards, and God, don't you hate politics?" The vampire echoes my very thoughts. "A few centuries ago, we could duke it out. May the best man or woman win."

One thing we can agree on. But rules are rules, and I'm not ready to be on ASS's shit list for killing another precious vampire.

"Fine." I sigh. "But you'll need to come with me."

And when Charlotte and the cavalry arrives, they can take him to a holding cell in Clayton County made special for supernatural creatures.

"Oh, I don't think so, slayer."

I snort. *Just what I want.* "To confirm, you are resisting arrest?"

"Absolutely."

"Great." I kneel and outline alchemy symbols on the grass. The formula, outlined in white, reflects on the ground like a cheat sheet on test day. The symbols are an alchemical formula to create my weapon, including iron and silver for my chain. A luminous gold glow shoots from the ground, forming the outline of a kusarigama—a sickle attached to a long, heavy chain with an iron weight at the end. In seconds, the outline solidifies into the weapon.

Is it over the top? Why yes, it is.

Do I care? Hell no. My four seasons of binge-watching *Castlevania* will not go in vain.

The vamp's fangs sprout, and thick saliva coats his deadly canines. Rider's mouth twitches at the corners, into a smirk. The extremely good-looking vampire has hazel-green eyes, midnight hair, and a catch-me-if-you-dare smile. It's no wonder Dr. Winters fell prey, even with Rider's horrible fashion sense.

But beneath his devastating smile lurks danger. He looks at me like he's on death row and I'm his last meal. And the jerk had the audacity to lick his lips and grab his junk. My stomach burns. Not from fear but from red-hot hatred.

I wrap the chain around my hands, the metal rubbing against my raw palms.

I made some upgrades to the centuries-old weapon. One end of the weapon—the chain with the weight—can lasso a vampire. Barbie's electric lasso during the simulation sparked some ideas. The other end bears the silver-plated sickle. It's also made of tungsten and houses magma that emits a red-orange glow. Anything it slices will burn to a crisp. And to my delight, that includes the diamond-hard skin of a vampire.

"I've been a bad boy." He shrugs. "Perhaps, too bad."

The glare I spear him with is as sharp as my blade. "Last time I ask: why did you kill her?"

Rider's smile widens into what I'm sure he thinks is a sexy smirk, but it just makes me want to stab him in the eye.

"You have spirit, slayer. I'll tell you what… I'll give you a ten-second head start."

A baseball field stands between us, but the distance means nothing, thanks to the skills I've been honing at Tria Prima. In a matter of seconds, he or I can close the divide. His easy and unguarded posture defines arrogance.

He thinks he can take me.

I spin the chain in a large circle over my head. A fiery sphere forms like a cloud in the night sky. With my free hand, I wave him over.

But in my peripheral version, I spot Khamari creeping near the entrance of the park.

The vampire sniffs and smiles. He pivots his attention from

me and speeds toward Khamari. A bloodied, limping Khamari.

"Watch out!" I yell as I sprint in their direction. The vampire, Rider, grabs Khamari by the throat and slings him across the field toward me. I drop my weapon as Khamari's body slams into mine and we both tumble to the ground.

"Khamari!" I smack his cheeks, but he's out cold. He reeks and smells like fire and brimstone. Like sulfur. I know that smell well from my alchemy classes.

Rider stalks toward us.

There's blood at Khamari's temples. I run my fingers through his hair to check for the source of the wound. He's bleeding. I should've stayed behind to help him.

Just like I should've stayed behind with Deidra.

The girl with the squeaky flute, bright eyes, and an undying love for BTS.

It's my fault. My fault…

So what are you gonna do about it?

Darkness slithers over my fingertips and shoots up my arms until it cocoons my body. I can't stay here, and Rider's coming.

He's coming, and I'm going. Back to the dark place. It feels like the darkness is dragging me by the ankles.

No. Stop.

It won't take no for an answer, shoves the memories into my brain, won't let me forget.

Her wide eyes stare at mine. No impish grin, just crinkled grooves around her lips and between her eyes. She wheezes. Blood spurts from her red-stained mouth and clawed-through neck.

With firm hands, I place my palms on either side of her throat. Red rivers gush through my fingers, and it's hard to keep a grip—the blood makes it too slippery.

"It's not bad. It's not bad at all." Salty tears settle on my lips.

Her eyes lock on mine, asking me all sorts of questions I don't know how to answer.

"Hurts." Tears gather in her eyes, slip down her cheeks.

"It's not bad. I'm gonna fix it. I-I promise."

"Friends forever?" she asks, as she's done time and again.

"Forever and ever."

The dark energy bangs against my body. I squeeze my core, trying like hell to root myself here. I can't let it take over. Something tells me that if I ever let it free, it won't be pretty. But it coats my flesh, and now my palms are glowing like there's a lit bulb beneath my skin. My vision is blurry, and it's hard to make out the vampire's face.

Kill the light, something whispers inside of me. And this bastard is bright white. Before the white light can come closer, I grab Khamari and jet to the other side of the field. I lower him to the ground, awake now, and he grabs my wrist, stopping me from returning to the fight.

"What happened to you? Your eyes are...white?"

Can't see. Can't see.

His face blurs. I blink once, twice, until it clears. When I open my eyes, they're blinded by white light.

I jerk my hand back. Not Khamari. A vampire. Kill vampires. Kill the light. I grab the monster and sling him across the field.

I use the small blade on my finger to dig into my skin, bringing myself back from total darkness, and then grab my weapon.

My vision is still dark around the edges, but I'm able to see Rider leaping midair, claws outstretched and ready to maim. I throw the chain, but the vampire pivots before I can wrap it around his body or slice him with the sickle. Rider lands a few hundred feet away. He tests me, tests my weapon.

I whip the chain again and slice his shoulders. When he yells, my vision clears. The darkness inside me seems pleased. Pleased enough to pull back and curl into the pit of my stomach. It's hidden, but I know it amplifies my movements, my focus, my knowledge.

Rider vaults toward me again, this time like a cannonball. I chant a transfer prayer, transmuting the chain from an ordinary metal to graphene, a pliable but thick material. I catapult the new weapon. The vampire somersaults backward, darting from one spot to the next, on the defensive. His silly top hat topples off his head.

He runs at jet speed toward me, pinging and ponging in different directions to distract me.

I jerk the chain, now lighter and faster and stronger, and pivot on my heel. Like a heat-seeking missile, the weapon speeds toward him, zipping behind the vampire as he changes course. I track his movements, anticipate his next move, and finally shackle his legs and tug him from the air. The other side of the weapon, the sickle, is embedded in the ground.

"Gotcha."

When he falls, he craters the baseball diamond. The ground shakes, as if a huge building has dropped from the sky. A dirt cyclone swirls. I spin around, shutting my eyes and clamping my mouth shut to avoid the grit.

My eyes pop open just as he tries to untangle himself from the chain. Using the distraction, I grab the sickle and launch it, aiming for his head, but he breaks free and ducks.

Dammit. I stomp the ground, pissed that I missed the target until I see the burn mark that curves from his cheek to his collarbone.

A guttural growl echoes throughout the park. He rolls to his feet and crouches low. Now, he's only a short distance away. Sharp nails sprout from his fingers. When his claws rake the manicured lawn, ten rows of jagged earth trail his path.

He's frustrated. *Good.*

"How about I give you a ten-second head start," I taunt. "I like a good chase."

"I'll kill you." Shooting up, he feints to my left, slashing the air with his knife-sharp talons. In one smooth arch, I thrust the heel of my palm into his nose.

The crunch of broken bones makes me smile. Blood sprays like a fire hose.

Rider jumps back a few feet. With an air of defiance, he resets his nose. His gaze never leaves mine as he says, "I'm not so easy to kill."

His saccharine smile, rimmed in blood, makes him look even more deranged.

"Don't underestimate me. I've been alive since before your Grandmamma Lou's grandmamma, so I suggest you pay attention, *slayer.*" He spits the word out like it's poison.

In attack mode, I charge him, slicing the air so fast I create a whirlwind. He spins away, but he isn't fast enough. The blade slides across his chest like a hot knife through melted butter. The wound isn't enough to satisfy my bloodlust—I want to rip out his heart.

The vamp jumps back, as if to reset himself, then rushes me again. He grabs my wrist, forcing the weapon from my hand. Slamming my elbow against his forearm, I break free from his grip, jamming my foot into his torso and then twisting his arm out of its socket. I push him to the ground. I learned that little move from Grandma Lou.

Before I can stomp him with my boot heel, he hops and distances himself again, landing on first base while I remain at the edge of the field.

I sprint to retrieve my weapon. After swirling the chain in the air, I hurl the sickle at full strength, only to cut a scrap of his hair.

"You're going to have to do better than that," he smack-talks as the mask of his humanity fades.

The irises of his green eyes transform to blood red while the surrounding whites become obsidian. His jaw opens wide, and the back of his throat is in plain view. Sharp white fangs dripping with drool lengthen in anticipation.

I launch the kusarigama again, this time chopping off his left hand. He looks at me, then down at his severed hand in shock.

Blood drips from the nub at his wrist. He tips his head back and howls. I run to close the distance, grab his shoulders, and knee him in the groin.

He stumbles back. Taking advantage of his imbalance, I slash his eyes. The magma in the sickle burns him into a gory hot mess.

"Bet that hurt," I taunt, hoping he'll lose all composure and just come at me full force. I want to fight. I just want to pound *something*.

The pain must have dulled his good sense, because he flails his arm, giving me the opening I need to arc my blade into his throat. The thick, gaping wound sprays blood on my face and shirt.

A look of surprise overtakes his smirky expression. He grabs his throat and drops to his knees. On his hand, I spot a black outline of an infinity symbol with a sun overlaying the intersecting hoops.

I raise my hand to deal the death blow.

He drops his hand from his throat. Barely choking out the words, he says, "The P-prince. H-he told me to kill them."

Them? Are there others? "Kill who?" I demand.

A low moan from behind me snags my attention.

Khamari.

"You should go check. You probably killed him."

"Me?"

"You slashed his chest and tossed him against that tree."

I shake my head. No, I didn't. I only attacked the light. The monsters, the—

I glance over my shoulder again. Though he's far away, I can see him. His suit is ripped to shreds. His eyes, barely open, look at me with wariness.

"Send my regards to the prince," Rider spits before he makes a break for it and speeds away.

Something topples out of his pocket, but he's long gone.

"Dammit!" After kicking up grass, I stomp over to whatever dropped from his pants. A flash drive.

Really? Are we in a spy thriller? "What are the vampires up to?" I ask aloud, confused, turning the small black device over in my palm.

"World domination," Khamari answers from across the field.

I sprint across the park and stop just in front of him. His eyes rove up and down my body, then land back on my eyes.

"You weren't yourself."

"W-what do you mean?" Adrenaline, fast and furious, floods my veins and jolts my heart. *He knows my secret. He knows I can't stop.*

"The air went stale, as if you sucked up all the energy. Your eyes went white, and for a second, you levitated. And the way you fought… How did you even know how to make those weapons?"

"Alchemy classes."

"You've been here for what? A few weeks?"

"You can learn a lot in a month." No way in hell am I telling anyone that I see the symbols in my mind as if I wrote them in the sky. Cali already clued me in to my weirdness. Until I can figure out just how different I am, I'll keep my mouth shut.

"Listen." I lick my lips. "I don't know what happened. I was just stressed, you know?"

"That's some kind of stress."

"I know and I…I'm sorry." The pity in my voice makes me feel pathetic. I stare down at my boots.

"You're really powerful."

"So I hear."

"You've got to rein it in. If vampires and even the Slayer Society find out…"

I lift my eyes from my shoes. "Don't tell them I'm like this."

He swallows. "Only if you promise to figure it out. If not, you'll hurt others like…"

"Like I hurt you."

He nods only once. "I guess I deserved it."

"No. It's all on me," I tell him. "Next time, it'll be different. I'll…pull back. Won't fight as hard."

"You already pulled yourself back. How?"

"Don't know."

He can tell I'm not telling the whole truth. His eyes hold mine as he says, "You can trust me with this. I won't judge you. It took a lot of practice for me to overcome my bloodlust, to realize I'm no longer human."

I look at his eyes, and I see his pain, his struggle. He isn't lying.

I lick my lips. Deciding to trust him, I finally answer. "I hurt myself. The pain… It anchors me."

"You shouldn't have to…shit." He stands.

I hear a car door closing just beyond the exit.

He points over my shoulder. "Cleanup crew is here."

Charlotte strides toward us. Her mouth drops open when she surveys the mess I made. "Oh my goodness, what have you two done?" Charlotte rushes to Khamari. "Are you okay?"

"Yes. Rider and someone else did a number on me."

"What happened?"

"We ran into one of my clansmen and another person, but I couldn't make them out. A mask obscured their face. Didn't smell like a supe, so I'm thinking maybe a human. If it were a vampire, they would've used their claws and fangs during the fight."

Charlotte nods. "Must have been a powerful one."

"Very. Anyway, I managed to fight them off. Or rather, they ran away. Rider attacked Raven."

She pulls me away from Khamari, at least several hundred feet, before she whispers, "Did you go dark? Like at the motel?" She looks at me. "You're practically radiating with energy."

"I didn't kill a Royal this time. Two points for me, right?"

Charlotte pulls me into a hug, and I don't push away. She feels safe.

And her hug makes me forget, for just a minute, that I'm dangerous.

"I knew this was a bad idea. I want you in my office tomorrow, noon."

I nod.

"And I expect the truth. All of it."

As Charlotte stares at me, the intensity of her gaze suffocates me.

I drag in a breath, nod, lie.

I'm not ready to admit that something is wrong with me.

16

He Did It All for the Nookie
Texas

Before I'm summoned, I make the trek to Charlotte's office. When I arrive, the smell of fall wafts through the doorway. I bang on the door like I'm the police.

"My goodness, come in," I hear Charlotte snap from inside the room.

After I open the door, I place a fist over my heart and bend. I noticed students do that to Charlotte and Paris whenever they enter the room.

Charlotte rolls her eyes. "Somehow you even make a gesture of respect look sarcastic."

"Sorry, my liege." I wave in a flourish, then raise my head. "You told me to come to your office."

"Close the door, sit." She points to the door, and I do as I'm told.

"I read the status report and looked up his name. Rider Edwards. He's a member of the Ankh clan, but just last year, they listed him as a Rogue. No mention of his powers, either."

"Yeah… I kinda figured he wasn't a Tick from the way Khamari talked about him."

"Don't say Tick." She tsks. "Our allies hate that name."

I give her the blandest of looks. By now she should know that I don't give a damn about a vampire's feelings.

"Not all vampires are evil. Some are even pacifists. It's the reason our Rogue Elimination Program is so effective. Who do you think feeds us the intel?"

"You think they're doing this out of goodwill?" I suck my teeth. "C'mon, Charlotte. You know better. They're using us like exterminators to kill their pesky little rodents when they get out of line."

Charlotte twirls her fingers in the air. It's her fancy way of dismissing something unpleasant. "Did you attack the vampire before you verified he belonged to the Ankh clan? Also, did you confirm he killed Dr. Winters?"

"Yep. He admitted to everything. Said his prince told him to kill her. Actually, he said *them*. So I'm thinking he offed multiple people."

"Prince Khamari?" Charlotte scrunches her button nose. "That doesn't sound right, but I will investigate it."

"It doesn't sound right that a vampire prince orders his clansman to hunt humans?" I roll my eyes. "Right."

"I mean, you certainly know him better than I do." She crosses her arms and rocks her neck.

I knew she wouldn't let me knowing Khamari go, but I really don't have the energy to talk about our tragic meeting, or the fact I saw him in that bloodsucking club. "No, I don't."

"Why didn't you tell me you had a boyfriend?"

"Because I don't." I grab a pillow and hug it to my chest. "Pretty sure dating a vampire is against the rules," I mumble into the pillow.

She shrugs. "We don't exactly encourage it. For one, they can't enter headquarters and they sure as heck won't invite you to visit their nests."

I roll over to the side to look at her. "Ugh, nest. Is that seriously what they call it?"

"No. They call it a home. We call it a nest. It's…easier to think that way." She props her elbows against the desk, her doe eyes as big and expressive as a Disney princess.

"What?" I snap. "Out with it."

"You've got a lot going on right now. Maybe you should come to one of our group therapy sessions. Slow down and take it all in."

"I'm fine. Perfectly fine."

"You're already over the fact that the guy you like is a vampire?" She slaps the back of her hand. "The very thing you loathe?"

I shrug in the most casual way possible. "Sometimes life gives you lemons." *Rotten, gnat-infested lemons.* "But you've gotta just add lots of sugar, maybe even a little Kool-Aid packet, and make it tasty."

"Mhmmm." She gives me the side-eye. "He seems nice, progressive, and he'll make a great king and powerful ally. I do hope Rider's allegations are untrue."

So do I.

"Who knows, but I sure as heck don't trust the guy."

"You don't trust him, or you don't like the fact that you're attracted to him?"

I narrow my eyes. We have a stare-off for a full fifteen seconds before I bite out, "Whatever."

"Okay, back to the Royal." Charlotte clasps her hands. "He admitted to killing Dr. Winters. And we've recently discovered there have been a few other doctors that have suffered from huge memory lapses in the metro area. Did he, by chance, mention anyone else?"

"I didn't have time to question him further, seeing as he ran away. But"—I pull out the flash drive—"he dropped this little beauty while he tucked tail and ran."

Charlotte wiggles her fingers. "Give me."

I hand over the drive.

She tucks it into her desk drawer.

"You aren't going to pull up the files?"

"I think that's something I'll do later."

"Spoiler alert: I've already copied the files. So you can show me now, or I can look at them after our meeting."

Charlotte sighs. "You're a mess." But she still pulls it out of the drawer. I smile, pumped by my minor victory.

I nod at the black thumb drive. "It's a good thing vampires don't use the cloud, huh?"

"Hopefully, this isn't a virus or something. We should run it by IT." Charlotte nibbles her lips, her fingers gripping the drive.

I sigh. "Let's live a little."

Charlotte shakes her head, likely convincing herself to break protocol. "I'm sure it's fine. But to be safe, I'll disconnect from our network." She pushes the drive into her laptop. Two files appear on the screen, labeled Personal and Research.

Charlotte looks at me, her eyes bright with the unspoken question.

"Personal," we both agree.

Charlotte clicks on the folder, and inside of it, a movie file pops up on the screen. "Here we go."

A queen-size bed with a black-and-gold comforter appears on the screen. A few minutes later, Dr. Winters and Rider enter the bedroom.

They immediately get down to business. As in ripping off each other's clothes, tongues everywhere. It's not soft—it's hard, panting, ruthless.

And not cute. Not cute at all.

"Oh no." Charlotte blocks the screen with her hands. "Cover your young, sweet eyes!"

I roll said eyes. "This ain't my first rodeo. Just keep it going."

After ten minutes of watching hardcore, XXX content, I ask, "How long is this video?"

Charlotte hovers her mouse over the video. "An hour and a half."

"Jesus."

Charlotte tsks again. "Don't say the Lord's name in vain."

"All I know is that I'm not sitting here for that long. Fast-forward it."

Charlotte skips ahead a few minutes at a time until the fifty-minute mark.

Rider is talking now. Charlotte rewinds it and then presses play when Rider moves his mouth. They're lying in bed in post-banging bliss.

"Did you get it?" He smiles, his voice smooth and seductive.

"Get what?" She bites her lip as she strokes his chest.

He wraps his hands around her throat. She gags, but she doesn't seem taken aback by the violence.

"The scroll."

"H-he…" She taps his hand. He loosens his grip, but his hand remains around her neck.

"He said he couldn't get to it. Too many eyes."

"You told me no one knew about it."

"I… I think he's getting cold feet." She flicks her eyes toward the camera.

Rider follows her direction. "Something I should know?"

She shakes her head. "No, baby. I'm trying my best." She gently pries his fingers from around her throat.

I really wish I'd killed him. Elders and kings be damned.

"Let me help you relax." There's a hint of desperation in her voice.

"I'm relaxed enough. What about the—" He looks toward the camera again, suspicion darkening his green eyes. "The…parcel."

"I set everything in motion," she says. "Should be any day now."

"It better be. Any more delays and it's your sweet ass."

She nods and looks away. He doesn't say another word, just leaves the apartment at vampire speed. Her attention returns to the direction of the camera with a knowing look in her eyes. An acceptance. She knew she was in too deep.

She walks toward the camera, pulls over a chair, and then the screen blinks black.

"Dang." I rub my temples. "You said she's a former alchemist. Do you remember her?"

"Yes. She was nice enough, extremely intelligent. Dieter's protégé." Charlotte clicks open the folder labeled Research. There are dozens of files.

Inside the files are pictures representing the vampire clans. The Saqqara clan with a bird to symbolize teleportation. The Hekau clan with a double infinity sign. Underneath the symbol, a description in italics: *The power lives within us.*

She clicks on another document—yellowed parchment captured by a phone. "It's a scroll."

She zooms in and squints her eyes. "Probably not *the* scroll that they're looking for, but it looks to be a copy of the *Book of the Dead.*"

Book of the Dead? We haven't gotten that far into the curriculum. "Let me guess, it's about how to raise the dead?"

"Not exactly." Charlotte shakes her head, still examining the file. "It's funerary text, more like guidance on how the dead navigate their afterlife. It's on display in the British Museum."

Charlotte pores over the other files. She gasps when she sees more signs, as in our signs from the Slayer Society and Alchemist Order.

"Do you see this?" Anger infuses her tone as she rattles off the notes. "'The Eye of Ra. The Internists are healers and invoke the god within. Distorters' symbol is the sun and the moon. They find true beauty in the secondary forms of materials and objects. Evokers harness the cycle of life by using elements and nature.' I mean… I cannot believe this. She should've had her memories erased."

A chill marches up my spine. "So the Alchemist Order didn't

erase her memories?" I ask.

She shakes her head and mutters, "They were supposed to."

"Who are they?"

"Dieter."

I tap on Charlotte's desk. "Looks like someone needs to speak to Dieter."

"Well, not you. Either I or Paris will speak to him."

"Yeah, of course. Sure thing." I glance at the clock and see that it's a quarter to three. "I missed my class, anyway." I shrug. Though I plan to swing by his office and get the assignment.

"Do not speak to Dieter," Charlotte warns. "He is your superior."

"The only thing he's superior in is being an asshole."

"Texas."

"Fine." I raise my hands. "I won't. But do you think Dieter is the 'he' Dr. Winters referred to? The one who's getting cold feet?"

"We can't make assumptions. I'll bring Paris up to speed."

"About Khamari, too?" I hold my breath, waiting for a response.

"Yes, of course. But I know there is always in-fighting within the clans. His ascension to the throne will probably be bloody."

"Why?" I ask.

Charlotte shrugs. "It always is. Add to the fact he's a half-breed. But we will verify."

"How?"

"We have our ways of pulling out the truth. Don't you worry." She gentles her voice as if I'm a ten-year-old in need of comfort, or apple juice, or whatever a worried ten-year-old needs.

I nod and stand, heading for the door.

"Texas?"

"Yeah?"

"You did an amazing job last night. You battled a Royal vampire and identified Dr. Winters' killer. Paris will want to talk to you."

"Why?" I've seen the older woman in passing, and honestly, she scares the bejeezus out of me. Like she can look into my soul and see the lie.

See the darkness.

"She'll want to thank you directly. Get to know you."

"Great. Looking forward to it."

"I know *she* is." Charlotte smiles and wiggles her fingers. "Be in touch."

Why, oh why, does that sound like a threat?

When I enter the auditorium used for alchemy classes, it's completely empty, save for Magister Dieter, whose back is facing the door as he scribbles on the whiteboard. He turns around when the door bangs behind me.

"Class is over, Texas. You'll get docked for participation, and you can catch up with one of your classmates." Professor Dieter turns around and writes more alchemy symbols and Latin on the board.

"It's not like I skipped it on purpose." I march down the stadium-style steps until I reach his desk. There's an empty chair near it, and I sit.

"No excuses, dear one," he says in a so-not-endearing voice.

"Didn't you hear? I was in the field with the Ankh prince. I nearly killed the vampire who murdered Dr. Karen Winters."

His hand flinches ever so slightly.

Boom. I'm in.

"I heard she was a student of yours."

"She was. Exceptionally talented and respectful...unlike you."

Oh, really? Because this untalented slayer used complex alchemy. *Nope, don't go there.* Cool and collected is the name of the game. I kick up my boots and plop them on Dieter's desk. "So why didn't you erase Karen Winters' memory?"

He turns around. "Excuse me?"

Okay, shoot, so maybe I'm not exactly cool and collected. Sue me.

"Why. Didn't. You. Dose. Dr. Karen Winters? Your protégé? God, don't tell me you were banging it out with her, too."

A strange look crosses his face. "No, I did not diddle her. She was too young—barely twenty." He sighs, and a haze shades his eyes. "God bless her, but I believe she may have had a crush on me."

I lift an eyebrow and scan the ornery alchemist. Ain't nobody peeping for Mr. six-foot-two, one hundred and ten pounds of pale, saggy flesh.

"Sure, she did," I mumble under my breath.

His angular cheekbones are even more pronounced as he hovers over me, and his long, beak-like nose points down at me.

I don't see auras like Charlotte does, but I can practically taste the black cloud of hatred rolling off of him.

Alchemists are our guides, our keepers, and our teachers. Magisters, the highest order of their group, teach slayers and practicing alchemists the science of alchemy and how to maximize our power. But if you ask me, I think Dieter hates his role more than the other alchemists.

"What makes you think I didn't clean her memory?"

I shrug. "Just a hunch."

His face is Lake Placid calm, and his eyes affect a look of pure boredom. His signature style, but I hear the jackhammer rhythm of his pulse. The speed of his heartbeat.

In the words of Grandma Lou's favorite artist, Aretha Franklin, he's a liar and a cheat.

"You know anything about a scroll?" I ask, not answering the question that clearly makes him nervous.

"Which scroll? There are so many, as you know."

"That's your final answer?"

"You are a student. Get out. Now. I'll make sure Charlotte and Paris will hear about this…this disrespect."

"And what exactly will you tell them? That I asked questions about a student? I'm just trying to learn, here."

"You're a little shit, is what you are. There is an order to things—"

"I don't care about order or titles," I snap through gritted teeth. "I do care if we have a snitch in the house."

We stare at each other, our anger tangible. I never knew that silence could be so violent.

Three firm knocks interrupt our stare-down. "Dieter. Open up. I need your help."

Through the clear rectangular window on the door, blue eyes stare at us. It's the Maximus, Rich, who pushes the door open.

"I have company. Unwanted company." Dieter glances at me.

"Rich." I study him a few seconds longer. Maybe I'm being petty, but he looks a little haggard. The low cut has grown out, and his usually clean-shaven face has a five o'clock shadow. Though I don't care for him, his life can't be easy. I don't envy the life of a Maximus—always on the road, killing Rogue and Tick vampires, saving humanity, and bringing in new slayers.

Even so, I thought we slayers don't age and mostly look fresh as a spring rose until the day we age out. And even once we age again, it's supposed to be slow.

Rich flexes his gloved hand. Wincing, he cradles it to his chest like a newborn lamb.

"You okay?" I point to said hand—the one that bears the Philosopher's Stone. I narrow my eyes and lean in to get a closer look. "Is that why you need help?"

He jerks his hand away. "I'm fine," he snaps, his voice sharp and high. "Just had a run-in with a vampire. Just because I'm the strongest of us all doesn't mean I don't get an occasional injury."

"I thought we healed quickly?"

Rich narrows his eyes at me. "What are you doing down here? Extra credit?"

"Just here to learn." I return my attention to Dieter.

"Yeah, I heard about your run-in with the Royal last night." He looks at Dieter. "Apparently she did a complex transmutation chant."

"Is that so?" Dieter looks mildly interested.

"Yeah, watch out for this one. She's cocky and thinks she's hot shit. And maybe you are?" His eyes rove over me, like I'm a new and interesting species. "But you'll never be stronger than me."

"Pluck the stone out of your hand and let's see how strong you are."

His eyes stretch, as if I'd suggested something blasphemous. "Dieter and I have an appointment."

I glance at my watch. Ten minutes until my next class. I swing my feet off the desk and stand. "I'll be seeing you, Dieter."

"It's *Magister* Dieter to you. And I'm looking forward to it," he replies through a steel-clamped jaw.

I would've slammed the door behind me, but the pressurized door makes it hard to use it as intimidation.

All he's gonna do is lie to Charlotte and Paris. But for now, I'll wait him out to see if he rats me out.

17

Walking in the Spiderwebs
Texas

After my run-in with Dieter, I return to my room and lie in bed. Between that conversation and last night's shenanigans, I'm done for the day. Tria Prima can shove their little participation points up their ass for all I care.

I don't rest, though. I can't. I mean, the guy who saved my life is a freaking vampire prince. Why in the heck do they have royalty, anyway?

And don't royals have arranged marriages or something? I pull the angel necklace out of my pocket. Now that I look at it, it's pure silver, which I'm sure vampires are allergic to.

I drag my fingers across the etchings. The wings are heart-shaped with tiny diamonds.

When I rub too hard, the wings break apart. It's not broken but by design. "Huh." I snap the wings back together.

In Alchemy 101, they said every object has a history. That's why we chant—to cleanse the object and purify its energy.

This necklace radiates with energy, with history. And as clear as my own memories, I can imagine Khamari and…her.

Night and constellations.

Fleece blankets and cheap wine.

Kissing under the cold, pale moon.

My heart squeezes, and I close my fist around the charm. The mature thing to do is to explore my feelings.

But I'm not feeling very mature. Nope, today I'll pretend that

Pretty Boy, aka Prince Khamari, isn't a blood-sucking monster.

Okay, now how do I forget?

I could do homework and figure out a way to create some cool new weapons.

No.

My eyes drift to my laptop. I can crack open Dr. Winters' files.

I open my laptop and hop back into bed, propping myself against the headboard.

"All right, Dr. Winters. Talk to me."

I randomly click on a JPEG file and silently pray for G-rated content this time around. The picture file reveals a scroll. On it is an image of a justice scale—a heart on one scale and a feather on the other. There's a man on either side, so to speak. One is wearing the head of a jackal, and the other, a bird. I remember this image from my Egyptian Alchemy class.

Then, I find another picture. This time it's a dog with a crocodile head. Small, black and white, and no bigger than a profile picture for the socials. Fuzzy, too, like someone had pressed paper over an etching and shaded it with a pencil. "Who's that?"

I google "Crocodile head + Dog's body."

Nonsense returns from the search results. Cute pictures of a dog in a croc costume. A news article about a dog eaten by a crocodile after biting him. I wince. "RIP Fluffy."

I change my search and add the word "Egyptian," since that's the start of Alchemy.

A picture of the image I saw earlier appears at the top of the page, but this time it's big and in color. "Much better." I scan an article. "Ammit. Devourer of the dead. Part lion, hippopotamus, and crocodile, and eater of hearts. 'If the man's heart is deemed heavier than the feather'…well, that's not fair."

I toggle back to the picture with the scale. I read on, learning that the god or deity lived near the scales of justice in the Egyptian underworld. "Oh. That's the same as Dr. Winters' picture." I recognize the familiar piece of the scroll. "It's Judgment Day. The underworld."

I type some notes in a document and then open another file.

There's a bunch of text in another language, and embedded is the picture of the ibis-headed man, which is Thoth, the Egyptian god of wisdom and writing.

There are two triangles, one much larger than the other. In the second figure, the two triangles are combined, forming a six-pointed star.

I copy and paste the text, translating the content online.

"As above, so below."

That, I know. It's been drilled into our heads from day one of training. It was an alchemical phrase that means whatever you do to the physical can reflect on the inside, as seen in the Emerald Tablet by Hermes Trismegistus. It explains how the universe works. Everything corresponds to everything. There is a balance—light and dark. Good and evil. When there's an imbalance, it all goes to shit.

Maybe Khamari and I can balance each other? "Ugh. Shut up. We're pretending he doesn't exist, remember?" I admonish myself.

There's more text—notes typed by Dr. Winters, I presume. I read it out loud: "'To revive is to bring imbalance.'" I look up to the ceiling as if I can find the answers. "What in the hell does that mean?" More notes. This file details something about a vampire breeder's project. I scan her notes, and it looks like she's tracking the uptick in vampires breeding with humans and other supernatural creatures.

To be honest, most of the things Dr. Winters wrote are above my comprehension. I need an expert, an Egyptologist outside of the Alchemist Order. One in Atlanta, if that's possible. I plug a search for what I need, and what do you know—there's a research center in Atlanta. I click the events calendar.

HIGH MUSEUM OF ART: A NIGHT UNDER THE EGYPTIAN SKY.

INVITE ONLY. OCTOBER 10TH.

I snort. "I'm sure Charlotte has connections to get me in," I mutter as I text her.

Me: Have you read the stuff from Dr. Winters ? I think the spider web is getting even more tangled…

Charlotte: Yes. I have. So has Paris. Speaking of, she'd like to meet you today.

Me: Fine. When?

Charlotte: Now.

I listen for the buzz from my phone, but someone knocks on the door.

"Who is it?"

"Commander Paris." I hear a voice that is stiff and stern from the hallway.

Well, damn. That's quick. "Ummm…one second."

I run to the door, sliding in my socks, but even when I get it open, I still can't believe what I'm seeing. The commander of the American Slayer Society is standing on the other side.

"Would you like to come in?"

"Yes. Please." She steps into my room, and the energy seems to…I don't know, interact with hers. She turns to face me, and I know she's studying me. I just can't figure out what she thinks. What she sees.

But I'm staring, too.

She's not a baddie when it comes to looks, but she has a face that no one can forget, with a short, glossy white bob, steel-blue eyes that reflect shrewdness, and a wide-set mouth that's quick to smirk but never manages a full smile. From what I can tell, she has the admiration of slayers and even the alchemists.

"Texas."

"Commander." I wave at an open seat. She nods at me and sits in perfect posture. I sit on the chair across the coffee table, a mirror to her posture, with my knees at ninety degrees.

"It's been a month. How are you settling here?" Her alto voice, a blend of European accents I can't place, rings with authority.

Seeing as I have no choice about being here—not if I want to stay alive—I think I'm doing well-ish. I clear my throat and say, "Good enough, I think."

"You like your classes?"

"Sure."

"Professors?" Her eyes spark with something.

"Most of them. Magister Dieter doesn't seem to be a fan of slayers."

"That is true. But he is renowned for his brilliant alchemical inventions. Have you learned from him, despite his prickly bedside manner?"

I like that she's straight up about her feelings, and I try to give her a straight answer.

Though he's dry as the Sahara Desert, I have learned a lot, much to his dismay. I can tell he doesn't like it when I have the answers.

"I'm learning, and I'm not failing class. That's a good thing, right?"

She doesn't answer directly. Instead, she says calmly, "Charlotte believes you're somewhat of a prodigy."

I shrug. "I don't know about that, but I just…see things differently."

"How so?"

"I, um… The formulas come easy to me."

"Ah, you have an excellent memory."

"Something like that," I answer in soprano.

"I know someone who could see the formulas as clear as their own hand."

My stomach clenches. *Someone else can do what I can?* "Oh, really? Who?" I ask in my most nonchalant tone, which wasn't really "chalanting" today.

"Another story for another day," she says. "But I'm glad you have a good recall." She gives me a tight smile. "And your fighting skills are impressive, too. Maestro Cali says you're a dynamo."

"I've got to give my grandmother credit. She taught me everything I know. I just have more oomph to my punch now."

"Your grandmother taught you how to fight." She kinda smiles to herself, and her starch voice loosens. "That's wonderful to hear."

"She's a tough old lady."

"You must miss her."

"Every day." As every day passes, I feel more and more strongly that I *should* get out of here and go find her. If they haven't erased her memories, then I'll figure out a way to let her know I'm okay. I'll just tell her I work for a top-secret sector for the government or something.

"I'd like to have you tested. See if we can skip you up to Middling, maybe even Maestro."

A smile spreads across my face. "Does that mean I can go into the field for good?"

"Yes. It means exactly that. But these tests aren't just about strength—they're about emotional intelligence, control, teamwork. Especially if you are to work with a vampire."

My smile wavers, but I still nod. For one, I hope the tests won't reveal my dark side. Also, there's no way I'm working with Khamari again, but I'll agree for now. Let me get my Maestro rank before I talk shit. "I can do that."

"I'm hosting a meeting today. I'd like for you to attend it."

"What time?"

"Five o'clock. It's in the War Room. Ask Dakota or Charlotte how to get there if you don't know the way."

"I'll be there."

"Wonderful." Paris stands and glides to the door. Without turning around, she says, "I'm looking forward to seeing what you're made of, Texas. I have a good feeling about you."

Stone Love
Texas

The door closes behind me, but firelight from the torches on the wall illuminates a sliver of a path down the curving stairwell. The sound of my boots clomping against the steps is the only noise cutting through the silence, but that doesn't bother me—I need the silence. Need to think through why the commander is calling a meeting and inviting me to the War Room.

My arms prickle from the cool temperature change. I pause at the entrance and inhale the stale, musty air.

The underground chamber looks like something out of the fabled King Arthur stories—a large, square room with carved gray stone walls and floors. An obnoxiously large and round glass table sits in the middle of the floor, and in the center of the table are hand-painted sigils from each guild. About fifty square seats surround it, and a few people are seated at the table.

I frown a bit as I pivot away from the seated people, hands clasped behind my back, and continue exploring.

A calm energy oozes in the room, just like the classrooms upstairs. Our Internist alchemists must have blessed the rooms with some kind of relaxation magic.

The stained glass set into the stone walls is crafted in the colors of the three slayer and alchemist guilds. Although we're hundreds of feet underground, the glass emits light, as if sunshine streams through. The mural reminds me of the windows in my Grandma Lou's old-timey church in West Texas—the church she used to drag me to every Sunday.

But the stained-glass scene isn't a serene picture of Jesus strapped on the cross and dying for our sins. This mural looks like something out of a Brothers Grimm tale. Fanged, demonic-looking creatures with red eyes and sharp talons. Mutilated human bodies. Slayers wielding swords, balls and chains, and curved daggers.

"This is the Blood War," I whisper to myself. The slayers and alchemists versus the vampires during the fourteenth century.

The worldwide battles had nearly outed vampires to humanity, but the Alchemist Order and Slayer Society had altered history and hidden it behind the guise of the Black Death. I get a pretty big kick out of that little-known fact, now that I've mulled it over. I swear people will believe anything printed in a textbook.

I wander back toward the table and find Charlotte chatting with some dude I don't know.

She looks up and waves. "Over here, Texas."

I nab the seat next to her. "I thought this was a...slayer get-together?"

"We've had some recent developments, and we're meeting with Maestro-level slayers and government."

I glance around.

"If you're looking for Cali, she's not here. She's in the field."

"Then why am I here?"

Charlotte shrugs. "Paris asked that you attend, so I'm sure she has a reason. She always does. How are you feeling?"

"Me? I'm walking on sunshine."

"Is that right?" she asks slowly as she scans me from head to toe.

"About Dr. Winters—"

"Not here. Not now." She shakes her head.

"Fine," I sigh. "So what's this meeting all about, anyway?"

"You'll have to wait and see like everyone else."

"Then what's the point of me being friends with the second-in-charge?"

She ignores my comment and does the fake-smile-and-wave thing to someone across the room.

There's already two dozen alchemists and slayers in the room. A group standing together wears slouchy black suits with either long, homely ties or low-heeled pumps. They have to be government agents.

"Can't wait to get the hell out of here," one agent whispers to the others.

"Yeah," a brown-haired man agrees. "This place gives me the creeps."

We can hear you, dumbasses. I shake my head. "And why are they here?"

"Agents typically never attend meetings unless there's a major public crisis."

"So they come here to complain."

"No." Charlotte emphatically shakes her head, but she's smiling as she explains, "We need the government as allies to alter videos, tech, keep us under the radar. And when, say, a human posts a video of a vampire online, they quash it. And then we come along and alter their memories with our serums."

I snort. "Except for Dr. Winters?"

"Well, yes. And I'll get to the bottom of that mystery."

"You know who it is." I roll my eyes. Magister Dieter is the obvious choice, since that's his former protégé.

Before she responds, I spot another familiar face. Seated beside one agent is Rich.

"What's he still doing here? I thought he was back on the road."

I'm sure Rich hears me, because he's frowning and squinting in my direction.

"Shhh." Charlotte drops her smile. "I'm not at liberty to say…" She clears her throat. "Especially with so many ears around here."

She straightens in her chair and taps her fingers against the table as if she's doing Morse code. She has a nervous energy that makes me anxious. I don't know her that well, but I've yet to see her act fidgety. She's sunny skies and rainbows.

What in the hell is going on? Between Charlotte's tense behavior and Bitch Rich's presence, I have a feeling this meeting isn't about third-quarter killings. "What's up? Seriously?"

Charlotte pats my thigh. "It'll be fine," she tells me, but her melodic voice is borderline shaky.

We wait another thirty minutes as more slayers and heads of the alchemist families trickle in.

Paris finally arrives. And though she doesn't have a head spot at the table, she exudes power and leadership, and all eyes gravitate toward her. Everyone stands, placing their left fists over their hearts, and they give her a deep bow. I clumsily mimic their movement.

Paris tilts her snow-colored head. "Please be seated."

The commander takes a chair three spots away from me, next to Rich. Dakota settles to her left, a pen and notepad in hand. Probably since she still works part-time for Paris and Charlotte. She gives me an energetic wave, and I give her a head bob.

"Thank you, everyone, for meeting here at such short notice," she begins, her voice serene. "I know many of you have traveled a great distance. And though not all our key members of the Order and Society are present, we must move quickly. Time is not on our side."

I lean forward in my seat, ready for the hammer to fall.

Paris turns to Rich, who gives her a nearly imperceptible nod. "There's a lot to be discussed, so I'll jump right into it. I ask that everyone holds their questions until I have finished."

There are a few grumblings, but after a regal sweep of her hand and the hard glint in her eyes, the room grows silent.

"Richmond has aged out."

I grab and squeeze Charlotte's hand. "Does that mean what I think it means?"

Charlotte squeezes my hand back. "Yes. He's begun the aging process again."

"Oh, shit," I whisper, releasing her hand and tucking mine deep in my pockets.

"Richmond has bravely borne the stone, ending the existence of countless Rogue vampires and defending humanity for over six centuries." Paris inclines her head toward him. "We appreciate your service, Richmond."

He grunts, then rubs his ever-reddening neck.

Paris' eyes scan the room, and for a second, she stops on me. "But now it's time to select another. With the help of our alchemists, who concocted a potion, The Architect chose Richmond to be our Maximus. It is imperative that we quickly conduct the ceremony to transfer the power."

"Power transfer?" a suit asks.

Paris gives him a glare as snowy as her hair. "Mr. Donovan, as I already stated, we will hold all questions until I've finished. There is much to discuss." She clears her throat. "Since Richmond is aging, his strength wanes, and there is no telling how quickly his aging will pass. As such, we must give the stone to another slayer to be our next Maximus. With the power transfer, they will master all slayer abilities and have immeasurable strength."

I want to ask her to quantify it, but I don't want to be on Paris' shit list right now.

"We will have the ceremony in two days."

Two days? Holy crap. That's too soon. Don't they need to plan for training or…or something?

I knock on Charlotte's foot with my own, trying to get her attention. Her eyes are on Rich, hands clasped like a pretty princess in her lap. I can practically smell her pity for him.

"I'm holding off as long as we can," Paris says, her imperious voice reclaims my attention. "I want all the slayers in the field to have time to return to base. If the Maximus does not reside in the U.S., we will conduct the ceremonies abroad until the stone has found its match." She lifts her pointed chin. "I believe this goes without saying, but no one can know outside this room. No. One. Not even our vampire allies. We will let them know of our newly appointed Maximus once the ceremony has concluded."

Vampire allies. I roll my eyes. All of them are E.V.I.L.

"Questions?" Paris finally invites.

"What about the students?" an alchemist asks.

"The students aren't to know. Telling them would add undue stress and create chaos. If The Architect chooses one of them as Maximus, we will then explain. Does that answer your question?"

The alchemist nods.

"Excellent. As for the transfer, we already have the slayer and alchemist induction ceremony scheduled for next week. We will push up the ceremony and use it as a guise."

I don't bother raising my hand. "How do you know who The Architect chooses to be the next Maximus?"

Rich folds his hands together as he answers, "This is only the second ceremony. As you know, *I* am the first. After the souls of one hundred warriors were added to the stone, the Internist division of the Alchemist Order concocted a potion for all slayers to consume. Once I drank it, I immediately glowed. That was the sign that The Architect had selected me."

A potion and a glow? I'd always imagined he levitated in the air and a mighty voice boomed and said something like, *"Thou art chosen to protect my lambs."*

"That's it?" I figure my tone was a smidge rude, because Paris twists her lips into a scowl.

"Yes, Texas. That's it," Rich drawls, voice dripping with disdain. "During the ceremony, I will remove the stone from my palm. Slayers at every level will drink the potion. Once the potion is consumed, the stone will gravitate toward the new Maximus."

"Commander?" Magister Dieter stands and bows.

"Speak," she says through clenched teeth.

Good to know the commander and I are on the same page.

He clears his throat. "Since it was my ancestor who boosted power into the Philosopher's Stone, I'd like to propose the Magnus family create the potion."

I snort. Didn't take long at all for Dieter to mention Eduard Magnus, the great-great-who-the-hell-ever of Albertus Magnus. Once, in class, I counted how many times he mentioned his great-however-many-times uncle.

Fifty! It was fifty times. And I know Eduard Magnus' story, too.

After sixty percent of Europe had been slaughtered and infected by vampires, Eduard devised a plan to overpower them. The 100 Powers Oath is an agreement for Middling- to Maestro-level slayers to sacrifice their powers to augment the Philosopher's Stone. We also had one vampire ally who sacrificed his power. With their powers combined and full access to their skills and talents, the Maximus, formerly Bitch Rich, became the most powerful being on the planet.

Well, he isn't anymore. I want to snicker, but not when there are so many lives the Maximus saves.

"While I appreciate your eagerness"—Paris inclines her head to Magister Dieter—"the Internists are best suited for this task."

Dieter throws the commander a tight smile and sits down.

"And how do we plan to protect the stone until the transfer happens?" Magister Robert Bacon, another top alchemist, asks. "I know you're a mighty slayer and all, but are you still strong enough to keep it safe, Richmond?"

Ohh, burn. No one, not even an aged-out slayer, wants his strength questioned. All attention swings to Rich, whose cheeks are a lovely shade of red.

"Oh, Robert," he responds. "Still the jealous little boy who so wants to be superhuman but is only…human."

"Please." Magister Robert snorts. "Without us alchemists, you slayers wouldn't know which hole your power comes from. Which is why my question bears repeating. Are you strong enough?"

"Yes, Robert. I am powerful." Rich's voice rumbles as he says, "Why don't you come over here, and I'll prove it."

"Gentlemen," Paris interrupts. "There is no need to engage in fisticuffs. To answer your question, Robert, the Maximus still has adequate powers. We have also incorporated other measures. The Magnus family has added protection over Richmond and the stone."

"The Magnus family? Are you kidding me?" Spittle spews from Magister Bacon's mouth. When it settles on an agent's hand, she dives for something in her pocket—hand sanitizer.

Magister Bacon slams his meaty hand on the table. "Why weren't the Bacons consulted? We have just as impressive a lineage as the Magnus family. Why are we just learning about the stone needing a new host?" the portly alchemist demands.

Dieter gives him a slick smile and a simple shrug. "Because they wanted the best."

"Oh no, he didn't," I whisper to Charlotte.

She shushes me.

I need popcorn and soda. It's like I'm watching *The Real Housewives of the Alchemist Order*. Each of the five major families think themselves more talented than the others. Not to mention their jealousy of the Slayer Society. I caught that just as soon as I took my first class, and Dakota later confirmed our complicated relationship. But long story short, they were the coaches. We were the quarterbacks. Some people like to coach; some people want the glory of playing on the field. The only way alchemists can wield powers is through potions, and those are only temporary—a few hours, maybe.

"Richmond skipped protocol"—Paris' voice shifts from

patient to hard—"and informed the Magnus family when he aged out. Dieter had already added protections prior to my knowledge."

Paris turns to Dakota. "Please make a note to adjust the Society and Order charter to always inform the commander first when one has aged out. The consequence of this insubordination is death."

"Yes, ma'am." Dakota jumps in her seat but then scribbles down the order.

Rich snaps his head back as if he'd been slapped.

Paris ignores his wounded look and continues fielding questions until she raises a closed fist in the air. "This concludes our meeting. Send your questions through Dakota." Paris stands.

We do the antiquated-bow thing.

I grab Charlotte so we can gossip, but she shakes her head and whispers, "I've got a meeting with Paris and Richmond."

I want to process this whole power-shift thing with someone, and I look at Dakota from across the room and wave at her to come over. This news is huge, but I agree with their approach. They need to find the next Maximus ASAP. If the vamps find out, they will try something. My stomach clenches at the thought. If all hell breaks loose, I need to figure out a way to protect Grandma Lou, maybe even bring her back to headquarters.

I snort. I'm sure Paris would just love it if I brought my eighty-something-year-old grandma to our secret location. "Talk later?" I ask Charlotte before she goes, knowing Ms. Goody Two-Shoes will say no.

"You know I can't." Charlotte shakes her head, and the corners of her lips turn down in a regretful frown. "But trust me, it'll be okay." Her voice is steady, but the ghosts in her eyes are all too real. She pulls me into a hug, and I don't push away. We're kinda-sorta friends now, I guess. She'd been more than kind to me since we met at that crappy motel.

"If you say so," I whisper, but she's already on the way out.

My gut spins like a tilt-a-whirl. Between Dr. Winters' death, her research, and Rich aging out, I know the vampires have their filthy claws in this.

After the meeting, Dakota and I return to our room and gab about what just happened—including speculating about why *I* was there, but her best guess is that I was Maestro Cali's replacement to keep up numbers in front of the government people. I wanted to resume my research, but I was dead tired after hearing about the new Maximus transfer and the prince who must not be named. It's only seven p.m.

Sleep isn't an elusive flirt. Tonight, it comes easy. And so do the nightmares…

I stare at the blue charter bus in the ditch. The blinking lights look ominous and—

"Stop."

I see Khamari in my dreams, and he feels all too real.

Light floods the darkness, and I'm no longer on a stranded highway but in my old room back home at Grandma Lou's, standing in the doorway. Posters with my favorite artists cover the walls—John Coltrane's *Giant Steps* album cover. Nina Simone in all black, crouched low with a serious expression. And of course, my fave, Beyoncé's *Formation* poster. On my desk near the window is a picture of me and Deidra striking a diva pose in our frumpy band suits and another old picture of Grandma Lou, my two grandpas who passed away, and my mother, who was a teenager in the picture.

Khamari leans against the headboard, *my headboard*, with his arms crossed behind his head and his mouth-watering abs on display.

His eyes are intense. "No more nightmares," he commands,

as if I have control of them.

"You're in my dreams."

"Yes."

"I told you to stay away."

"You did." He bobs his head. "But I can't."

"Why?"

"You know why." His relaxed position doesn't look so relaxed anymore.

I cross my arms. "Right. You thought you could do a little dream booty call. Well, listen up, partner." I lower myself to sit on the foot of the bed, angling my body toward him. "I'm not into that freaky-deaky stuff."

"What exactly is freaky-deaky?"

"You're not sticking your dream peen inside of me."

"Raven, I—" He cinches his jaw shut and takes a deep breath, then says, "I just want to talk."

"Fine." I cross my legs on the bed. "What do you know about Dr. Winters?"

"I don't want to talk about the human. I want to talk about us."

I shrug. "Then we have nothing to talk about."

"I don't understand you."

"Many don't," I quip.

"Stop it."

Khamari sighs, and I know he's annoyed that I won't entertain his small talk. Still, I feign ignorance. "Stop what?"

"Stop pretending like we don't matter."

The hurt in his voice hooks me and stuffs down the sarcasm that's about to erupt from my mouth.

He lifts my hand, kisses my palm. "No more nightmares—I can leave now. Because now I know you'll have sweet dreams."

Then he disappears. Just. Like. That.

And he's wrong. Oh, so wrong. My dreams aren't sweet. They are very, very bad.

Graduation Day
Texas

Ceremony Day has finally arrived.

I'm standing front and center in the room, with four other slayers and three alchemists who will be inducted into the Society and Order.

One set of double doors to the room swings open.

"Enter," Paris' commanding voice rings. The alchemists and slayers march into the long hall in tandem, grouped by the guilds.

The Distorters have donned wool metallic-gold ceremonial robes. Fifty-eight Distorters stand in line in order of rank on the northeast side of the room.

Like the Distorters, each guild wears their house colors and settles at their designated seats. The tables are round, much like in the War Room, minus the creepy stained-glass murals. The walls are lined with oil paintings of the famous slayers who sacrificed for the stone. After donating their powers to the stone, the slayers aged out and had a human lifespan. All died long ago.

The dim lights, cool temperature, and hushed tones create a somber atmosphere.

Small blue teacups are neatly arranged on the table, one for each seat. A sign with fancy calligraphy in the middle of the table serves as a warning for us not to touch the cups. I don't touch, but I look and notice a thick, goopy liquid inside.

Ahh, the infamous potion. Despite the drink's questionable appearance, it smells of honey, clover, and responsibility.

I want more power, but not like this.

My stomach spasms. The cup represents responsibility, and taking the cup means suffering and sacrifice. Being a regular slayer is bad enough, but a Maximus is a whole other level.

I don't want to drink it, but I will.

At the front of the room sit Paris, Rich, and Charlotte.

Paris stands from her chair, her hands clasped behind her, shoulders stiff and squared. Ruby-red earrings stand out against her all-white ceremonial robe and silver hair. She wears a brooch with all the house colors represented.

"Good afternoon." Her tone is light, yet it sounds like she's speaking directly in my ear.

"For those of you who are new to the Slayer Society and Alchemist Order, I welcome you."

Beads of water drip from my hair and down onto my robe. Earlier, the commander had purified us with blessed-by-the-Architect water and oils. Then, they prepared us for induction by ladling water over our heads and chanting. Though I know what to expect, my body is slick with sweat. Goosebumps spread across my skin like a bad case of chickenpox, and something like a tiny earthquake invades my body.

Paris continues her ceremony speech. "Today we celebrate our new slayers, whose powers have been activated. And we celebrate our novice alchemists, who will devote their lives to help the Society and Order."

Paris nods toward the chalice on the table. "The next part of the ceremony is for our new slayers. Completing the purification is an important step. You will sacrifice yourselves for the good of humanity. No matter the race, sex, age, or affiliation humans have given themselves, if you agree to this life — and you do have a choice — please drink from this cup."

The slayers pass along the cup. I grip the cool chalice and, with shaking hands, I tip it back and gulp. Tart red wine splashes against my tongue. I return the chalice to the table. My hands are steady now.

"Now, look at your palms, and there you will see your guild, your destiny."

Though I already know my guild, I look down at my palm anyway. My hand radiates with even more color now.

"Raise your hand, palm up. Show us your guild," Paris commands.

There are two Internists, an Evoker, and a Distorter (yours truly).

"Guild heads, please greet your new family members."

My guild leaders, Tacoma and Cali, do as they are told and greet me.

Cali gives me a smile and squeezes my shoulder, then guides me to join the other Distorters at the table.

After we sit down, Paris addresses the room. "Today, you shed your ignorance of the world as you knew it. There are no monsters under your bed; rather, they live amongst us." Paris releases her hands, leans over, and pushes her palms on the table as she intones, "Before you start your journey, you must understand the history of our kind and how we came to be."

She clears her throat, though she already has everyone's attention, then settles in her seat.

Everyone remains quiet. A hum of excitement fills the hall.

Paris lifts the chalice to her right and takes a delicate sip. "The year was 322 B.C.," she begins. "A young conqueror and one of the greatest military minds of all time set out to rule the world. Alexander the Great was charismatic and calculating and cruel. With the help of his army, he laid siege to many lands."

Paris smooths a stray hair that dared to touch her forehead. "You see, Alexander made many enemies. He drove his army to exhaustion. He thought it was his birthright to take what he wanted. He thought himself a god, but he was only a mortal man.

"Alexander knew that to achieve world domination, he needed to become immortal. Alchemy held the answer. The true power of alchemy is not in transmuting metal into gold. No..." She lifts a finger. "The true power lies in spiritual transmutation. Elongate life, remain youthful, and end diseases that plague humanity. He rounded up the world's most acclaimed alchemists and threatened to kill them and their families unless they figured out the key to immortality.

"In a terrible turn of events, the alchemists stood their ground to defeat him. The transmutation went wrong, making Alexander an immortal killing machine."

I glance at Dieter, who's seated near the front of the room. He and his wife, Corrine, roll their eyes.

"Alexander built his army, but this time, of immortals. Alexander had always thought himself a god. First as the son of Zeus, but then after conquering Egypt and falling in love with their culture and customs, he wanted to become an Egyptian god. He stole their culture and later created the Ankh, Saqqara, and Hekau clans based on his progeny's abilities."

"A colonizer through and through," I mutter.

Cali snorts at my comment and burps. Seconds later, the smell of alcohol wafts beneath my nose. I stare at my fave Maestro. Her nose and cheeks are flushed. Her eyes, glassy. Sure, I've heard rumors about her drinking excessively—I've seen her drunk more than a few times. Some students cruelly call her The Drunken Master. But it sucks to see her like this, especially when we're selecting the new Maximus.

My mind coasts while Paris does the history song and dance. *Blah, blah, blah, they turned Alexander into a vampire in a transmutation gone wrong. Blah, blah, blah he made a bunch of vampires and killed humans... Blah, blah, blah, The Architect created slayers to defeat them.*

Paris' powerful voice pulls me back in. She points to the

oil paintings behind her on the wall. "One hundred warriors' powers were sealed into the stone. The bearer of the stone—the Philosopher's Stone—has access to their power times ten. In other words, they are the most powerful being on Earth. We managed to push back Alexander's undead army, and we even killed Alexander. We have won many battles since, but our work is never done, make no mistake. And now…it is time to pass the torch." Her attention pivots to Rich.

With his eyes forward and jaw clenched, he nods.

The room buzzes with a nervous energy.

"Today, a new Maximus will be chosen. They will fulfill a higher calling and be the keeper of the Philosopher's Stone," Paris announces as she stretches her hand open. "Richmond. The stone."

Rich presses two fingers into his palm, releasing the garnet-colored stone. The dime-sized gem hovers just above Paris' hand.

It splits in two. In the blink of an eye, one half vanishes.

"My God." Rich's voice is reed thin and panicky.

Cali's face transforms to granite. She stands at attention, no longer wobbling.

Teachers and students shout, gasp, shriek. It's like we're witnessing a slow-moving car crash.

Paris closes her hand and reopens it as if the other half will reappear.

It does not.

"What did you do?" Paris' eyes stare straight into Rich.

"N-nothing."

"There is magic in the air." Paris' voice is all hiss. "You've done something to this stone."

I flick my spiked ring and slap my palms together, ready to brawl.

"Seal the room," Paris barks at no one in particular. But no one makes a move at first.

Then, a few Maestros, including Cali, hurry to the wall behind the table and brace their palms against it. Gold and silver hues, along with blue and green, twine and twirl together. Power *booms* throughout the hall.

In my mind's eye, I can see and detect steel covering the dozen windows and the doors at the front and back of the room.

"The ways are shut," Cali confirms as she returns to the table.

While the others look to protect the room, I focus on the biggest threat: Bitch Rich. He had the stone, and now, it's suddenly gone? That can't be a coincidence—not to mention Magister Dieter already had done something to supposedly protect Rich and the stone. It probably happened that day I went to confront him about Dr. Winters.

I grab the knife I'd stuffed under my robe.

Jolts of untapped energy course through my muscles.

Rich's goldfish-wide eyes seem to take in all the sealed exits and his tan, weathered hands grip the edge of the table. His legs shake like a runner ready for the starter pistol to fire. Where he plans on running to, I don't know, but I won't think too hard about it.

I jump on the table in front of him. Cups clatter and topple from the impact. Rich pushes back from the table, scrambling past chairs to get away.

"Sit. Down." I press the blade into his hair-stubbled neck.

Rich conjures a dagger. I kick it from his hand and push mine deeper into his neck. Beads of blood bubble against his skin. "I. Said. Sit. Down."

Hands up in surrender, he returns to his seat. I can damn near hear his molars grating into a fine powder. "It wasn't me."

I sense his strength—as faint as a Middling. Dang, he's weak without the stone. A few days ago, down in the War Room, he had way more power.

He scowls, but his eyes tell another story. They are wild and wide.

"Texas!" Paris yells my name.

"Yes?" I answer without averting my attention from Rich.

"Keep him restrained."

"With pleasure." I transmute my blade into shackles that shock the wearer like a stun gun if they struggle against them, then slap the bonds around his hands and feet.

Rich does not disappoint when he squirms. His body goes rigor-mortis stiff, and the hairs on his arms stand and sizzle. I'm unpleasantly surprised when he doesn't pass out from the volts that zap him.

"No one move. No one speak," Paris says, her voice dripping with menacing authority. "There is a traitor among us, and we will root out this evil, this poison," she hisses, "and cast it out." Paris scans the room. "Robert, come."

The squat and balding alchemist scurries to Paris' side. Sweat drips from his forehead down to his chest. He knows what the halved Philosopher's Stone means. No one is safe.

"Truth serum," Paris snaps. "Can you make it for me?"

"Y-yes." The arrogant alchemist who'd challenged Rich's strength a few days ago has disappeared. He wipes his palms against his thighs. "Though I don't have all the ingredients to make it here. I'll need to go to my lab."

"Very well." Paris inclines her head. The act is graceful despite the rage that cages her voice. "Charlotte, please escort Magister Bacon to his lab." She steps closer to her second and whispers, "Take the tunnels. Be quick."

Charlotte bows with her left hand over her heart. "Let's go, Robert." She guides him to the wall, and Cali lifts the steel. Once they step out of the room, Cali reseals the door.

"Commander Paris," Dieter Magnus addresses her with a plastic deference in his tone. "While I understand we are in dire straits, I would be happy to concoct a potion. After all, my family are masters at elixirs."

Paris ignores him. She walks to the center of the room. "Everyone, please lift your cups."

Each person, except for me and my prisoner, follows her instructions. "Pour out the elixir. Yes, on the floor." Paris waits while everyone follows her instructions. "Trash the cup. Use your power however you see fit to destroy the serum. If you haven't yet mastered your powers, crush the cup and whatever it contains under your heel." A series of whooshes and splashes and crashes reverberates throughout the room.

While this takes place, Paris sits and calmly conjures ceramic teacups. There must be at least three hundred of us in the room.

"Need help?" I ask. Rich's weak ass isn't going anywhere.

"No." Paris shakes her head. "This is oddly soothing."

"Commander Paris," Magister Dieter interrupts again. This time, his voice is less reverent. "I assure you, I have done nothing to the potion. If you'll allow it, I'll—"

"Do nothing," Paris cuts him off, still conjuring cups. "Everyone is innocent until proven guilty, but make no mistake, *someone* is guilty. And I find it's no coincidence that Richmond went to you to *protect* the stone and now a part of it has disappeared, right in front of my very eyes."

I nod when she says this. I've been thinking the same thing.

"I told you I did nothing, I—" Rich, struggling against the bonds, is shocked to silence.

Dumbass. I shake my head. "Rich, dude, you gotta chill out. You aren't getting out of this."

"I don't want to. I'm innocent."

I cut in before he can say more. From Paris' flat lips, I can tell she's on the edge. "If what you say is true, we will find out soon enough. Until then, shut up."

Rich nods, though his shoulders are near his ears.

"No, I don't need your help, Magister Magnus." Paris' voice is hard and as cold as an iceberg. "Those whom I trust are helping me."

My heart jumps at the rare sentiment. *Paris trusts me?*

Before I can bask in my *I'm awesome* glory, someone knocks on the door.

"It's me," Charlotte says from the other side.

Cali raises her arms in the air, lifting the seal again. Charlotte and Robert step through the door with an enormous cauldron and bag.

After Charlotte leads Robert to the corner of the room, she turns to him and asks, "How long will this take?"

"Fifteen, maybe twenty minutes?"

"Make it ten," Paris demands from the opposite side of the room. "Charlotte, Texas, and Dakota will help pass out the truth serum, since it's only potent for a few minutes. Time is of the essence."

Under scrutiny and curiosity, Robert whips the potion together in a little under fifteen minutes.

Charlotte scoops the liquid. Dakota and I hand out the cups. I watch as the alchemists and slayers swallow, and I check each one to verify it's empty. I pay special attention to Dieter, Corrine, and Rich. When I pass the cup to Andreas at the Evokers' table, his hands shake. He doesn't look at me, just grabs the cup and drinks the concoction. I want to tell him it's going to be okay, but he of all people knows his dad.

Does Andreas know what happened between his dad and Rich? I swallow my unkind question and move on to the next student. After I pass out the cups, I return to the front, settle next to Rich, and drink the serum. The potion oozes down my throat like warm honey, but it tastes of sour blackberries.

Paris closes her eyes as she mutters something, interrupted only when Charlotte gently taps her shoulder. "We're ready, Commander."

Paris stands from her seat. "Thank you," she says, then clears her throat. "We do not have the time for individual interrogations, so I'll ask yes-or-no questions. If it's a yes, stand. If it's a no, remain seated. Understood?"

"Yes, Commander," everyone answers like good little soldiers.

Paris lifts her head. "Question number one. Have you ever betrayed the Alchemist Order or the Slayer Society?"

Rich stands along with one other person: Magister Dieter. Everyone else remains seated.

"Well, well." I look at Rich. "Thought you were innocent?"

"I am." He turns to Paris. "*You* know all my deeds. All the things I've done for the Society." His voice holds an edge of menace.

"Very well," she quickly concedes.

What the hell was that? My eyes seek Charlotte's. She shakes her head, brows wrinkling and lips tight. Whatever those *deeds* are, Charlotte knows nothing about them.

"Question number two," Paris says before settling in her seat. "Did you give away or have you ever worked in conspiracy to steal the Philosopher's Stone?"

Rich drops himself in the chair, a look of triumph on his face.

Magister Dieter remains standing. With an elegant sweep of her hands, Paris lifts her pinky finger, equipped with a sharp file on the end. She swiftly slices open her palm. A blurring of colors shines through. Forming a bloodied fist, she fashions the outline of eight cylindrical bars, then slams the holograph-like confine around the traitor.

Magister Corrine shrieks.

Dieter tries to shake the bars, but whatever makes up the cell burns him. He yelps, shaking his hands. "This is ridiculous. I have nothing to do with the missing stone!"

Paris lifts her arms, raising the prison and its prisoner high into the air so all can see. The floating jail cell blinks between red, blue, and green. "We have our traitor."

Noise bursts through the silence. Weapons are conjured.

"Traitor!"

"Where's the stone?" someone yells from the back.

"Kill him."

The air is thick with frenzy and aggression. Everyone needs to calm down before all hell breaks loose.

Andreas walks to the front of the room. "Tell me it isn't true." His voice quivers. A sheen of tears well in his eyes.

"Son, of course not." Dieter shakes his head, his eyes hard. "This is just a misunderstanding. I would never betray the Order."

"You were always jealous." A rash of red creeps up Andreas' neck.

He didn't know.

"Please," Andreas begs. "Please, don't let this be true."

Paris raises her hand. "Andreas, Corrine, go with Dakota." Paris waves her over. "Grab the Emergency Lockdown handbook. Follow it to a T."

"Yes, Commander." Dakota hurries away.

"No!" Corrine screeches. "I want to be here. My husband is innocent."

"Go." Paris' voice is arctic.

The barriers on the exits are removed, allowing for a screaming Corrine and a silent Andreas to pass.

"Charlotte, Texas, Robert, Richmond—remain here. Everyone else is dismissed, but do not, I repeat, *do not* leave the premises. Guild heads, I will leave it in your capable hands to keep your house in order. If you do not have a room here, one will be made available to you. Dakota will ensure this happens once she wraps up with the Magnus family."

Everyone leaves the room. Paris lowers the prison. Dieter is now at eye-level.

"I'm not in the mood for mess, but I will absolutely get down and dirty if I must. Must I, Dieter?" She arches her brow.

Note to self: I ain't never, ever, ever getting on the commander's bad side.

Nobody Move, Nobody Gets Hurt
Texas

While Paris faces off with Dieter, I unshackle Rich. His eyes drill holes in me. "I told you I didn't do it."

"Then why were you meeting Dieter the other day? You were cradling your hands."

Rich shakes his head. "I would sooner cut off my arm than betray the Society."

"But you did betray us." Paris' voice grabs our attention.

"I didn't—"

"You went behind my back and got protection from Dieter. You know the importance of the stone. The sacrificed powers are in the hands of God-knows-who now." She stares at Dieter. "But we will soon find the answer."

Rich flexes his hands and rubs at the red skin that circles his wrist. "I know what I did was ill-advised, but Dieter's family created the contract. He comes from a powerful lineage, and I knew he'd be ready to—"

Charlotte interrupts him. "I know what you wanted, and I don't need the truth serum to get the answer." Her soft voice hardens as she says, "You wanted him to figure out a loophole to bind the stone to you forever. You weren't ready to let go of that power."

A hitch in Rich's breath gives him away.

Bingo.

Charlotte shakes her head. "How could you? I thought you

were better than that. You were our Maximus. Our hero."

"With my powers gone, I'll grow old. Without you."

Charlotte's chin wobbles. "Then so be it. That is the way of things."

Rich nods slowly, seemingly resigned. "Dieter told me he couldn't figure out a way, but he did a protection spell, or so I thought."

Paris points her finger at the old Maximus. "Your greed, your thirst for power, has compromised the lives of your peers," she tells him. "You know very well the sacrifices that were made to create the contract, the risks…" She cuts herself short. "You may not have given the stone to our enemy, but you might as well have put a target on our backs."

Paris turns, facing the jail, and the floating cell disappears. Dieter crashes to the floor.

Paris conjures a glowing rope and straps Dieter to a chair. She steps back once he's bound. "Where is the missing piece to the stone, Dieter?"

"I don't know," Dieter responds.

"Robert. Give him more of the truth potion," Paris commands.

Robert scurries toward the cauldron. He looks down, then back at us. "Par…" He clears his throat. "Commander Paris. It's empty."

Dieter shakes his head, snorting. "This is ridiculous."

"Then make more," Paris snaps.

"We don't have any more sodium pentothal."

"Doesn't the main alchemist lab have any?" I ask, referencing the workshop on the basement level.

"I did inventory the other day and noticed we ran out. I tried to buy more, but it's on back order. Next shipment is coming in a week."

Charlotte crosses her arms. "But you had some in your personal lab."

"I-I... Sometimes I take more supplies. I'm not stealing or anything," he rushes on. "I just have a secret stash." Robert points his shaking, thick finger at his comrade. "Dieter m-must've stolen the rest and made sure we couldn't order more. He knew we'd use it on him."

"Really?" Paris' voice is serene. She claps and leans closer to Dieter. "We will just have to use other methods to get the truth." As she rubs her hands together, a silver glow forms, outlining five-finger claws around her fingers. The outline solidifies.

I look at Charlotte and tip my head toward Paris and her metal claw. "Looks like that's going to hurt."

Charlotte's arms tighten around her torso, and her lips purse, brows drawn so tight her skin looks stretched across her forehead. "Good."

Damn. Even Charlotte wants his blood.

Paris touches the metal talons—there's one on each of her fingers now—and mutters a prayer for justice. "See the tips of these claws," the commander says to Dieter with the patience of a seasoned teacher addressing a difficult student as she extends her forefinger.

Dieter nods, his eyes blinking rapidly.

"Anything I scratch will decay." Paris scrapes a wooden chair with the weapon. The chair transforms from a tree-bark brown to a frosty-snow white. Within seconds, pieces of the chair fall to the floor, and the legs of the chair collapse and wither to a pile of rotting wood. She whispers, "I'm going for your face next."

Dieter tries to jump.

Dayummmm, girl. I'm so adding that weapon to my arsenal. I have to find out the compound elements. The claw is clearly metal, but how in the hell does she add the decaying component? *Is it acid?*

"Do you know anything now? Is this"—Paris flexes her metal fingers—"jogging your memory?"

"Fine, fine!" Dieter shouts. "But I didn't betray the Order—"

Paris swipes her claws near his face.

"Stop!" He takes deep, steadying breaths, and I hear his heartbeat speed up. "I'm telling the truth. I... I almost did, but I changed my mind."

"You changed your mind?" Paris asks, her voice sharp and mocking. "Then why did you remain standing when I asked about the betrayal?"

"Because I... I suppose in the conversations I had with her, I may have accidentally given her information."

"Dieter, please." I stand over him. "You may be a jerk, but you're a smart one. How and who did you accidentally give information to?"

"Karen."

"Dr. Winters?" I clarify.

"Yes. I... I didn't erase her memories when she left the Order."

I roll my eyes. "Duh."

"Why didn't you follow procedure?" Paris demands.

I snap my fingers. "Y'all were smashing." The comment about her having a crush on him makes sense now.

Dieter inhales and shoots me a look like he wants to reprimand me, but then he must've come to his senses, because he lowers his chin to his chest. "I'll admit I was wrong. I should have discouraged her advances. But she was so bright, so promising. I couldn't let her go."

"She left the Order seven years ago." Charlotte paces the floor. "How often did you meet?"

"Not often. Recently, her visits became more frequent. She seemed frantic. Not at all herself. She was babbling on about research and rebirth. She wanted to know what I knew about the *Book of the Dead*."

Icy fear frog-leaps up my spine. "What did you tell her?"

"I may have mentioned that I had some texts."

Paris extends her claws. "Did you give her Alexander's—"

"No." He shakes his head. "No, I didn't give her our scrolls. I told her I was mistaken. She insisted I was lying and then"—he takes a deep breath—"she said that he would kill her if she didn't get it to him."

"Who threatened to kill her?" Charlotte asks.

Dieter shrugs. "I suppose the vampire who killed her. The one who fought with Texas."

"What did Rider want with the scroll?" I mutter to myself.

"Maybe he wants to bring someone back to life?" His eyes narrow on Commander Paris.

"We do not have time for half-cocked theories," Commander Paris interrupts.

"And what about me?" Rich points to his palm. "How did you get the stone to disappear? How did you get me to age?"

A chill skitters over my skin. I don't like that the alchemists have the power to make us prune.

"I didn't do that." He shifts his attention to the other alchemist, Robert. "Make the serum as soon as you can. I'm telling the truth."

"And where is the other piece of the stone?" the commander asks.

"I don't know. But I suspect it's with the same person who afflicted Richmond."

I look at the floor, tapping my forearm, thinking. "Are you saying we have another mole?"

"I'm not a mole, but yes. And there's something else you should know about the stone. Think of it as an act of good faith to show my loyalty."

"Go on." Charlotte waves her hand.

"When my ancestor powered the stone with the souls of the warriors, it became...unsteady. It's no longer pure. It is considered the Materia Prima, the source of the universe. To add or supplement its power source with other supernatural beings' powers is, well, unnatural."

"I am aware," Paris says through clenched teeth, "that those who gave their powers gave some of their life force."

"Yes." Dieter swallows. "The stone cannot remain halved, and we have little time."

My heart *ka-thumps*. "How long?"

"Since the Philosopher's Stone was taken during the autumnal equinox, after the Harvest Moon, we are bound by time to find the other half of the Philosopher's Stone before the next full moon—otherwise, it will be lost to us forever. The Hunter's Moon is in two weeks' time."

Shit. Shit. Shit.

Robert wipes the sweat off his brow. "We can find it. The good news is that the vampires cannot bear it."

"Yes, it drains their life force." Charlotte nods. "But it's not as if there are stones just lying around." She turns to Richmond and asks, "Are the legends true? Did the stone just appear to Eduard?"

"That's what he said, though…though I suspect there's more to the story." Richmond unclenches his palm. In the center of his hand is a mark shaped like a black ring, and it looks like a mini explosion.

When I noticed his hand in the alchemy auditorium with Magister Dieter the other day, I didn't see the black ring. *But wait a minute! He wore a glove.*

"Your hand." I point to Rich. "Did it look like that while you were aging or just now, after it disappeared?"

Richmond studies his hand. "When I started aging. In fact, it was the first sign that the stone rejected me."

Charlotte snaps her fingers. "Brilliant, Texas."

"I know, right?" I grin. "Vampires can't bear the stone. If they've handled it, they'll have that mark."

"And likely die soon after," Rich agrees.

"So why in the hell would they want it?" I ask. "They're the only ones who have anything to gain from slayers being weak, but stealing half the stone doesn't make sense if it was just about getting rid of the Maximus."

"That's the million-dollar question." Charlotte darts her attention to Paris. The Commander doesn't say anything, just paces the floor, eyes flat, looking straight ahead, like she's plotting something.

"I never gave it much thought," Rich says. "But any time a vampire tried to steal the stone, it burned them. And that's what happened to me, albeit slowly. I'm not a vampire. It should've drained my energy, but not much else."

Dieter clears his throat. "As I said before, I'm innocent. And as soon as I take the serum, you'll know for certain that it's not me. Now, may I please be released? I can be much more helpful if you—"

"The very fact that you draw an arrogant breath and make an arrogant request is a gift." Paris stares at Dieter with the look of disgust one would give a pig rollicking in mud.

"Charlotte, throw him in the cellar. Search his home, his lab. Take Rich and Robert with you. I want to know what he gave Richmond, and I want Robert to verify Dieter's statement."

"Yes, Commander," Charlotte responds, hand over heart.

"And make sure none of the students are milling about." She removes the claws from her hand and then conjures them away. "I must leave," she tells Charlotte. "Uphold the security and work with Dakota to ensure everyone is safe and has a place to rest. I'm depending on you in my absence."

Paris turns to me, waving me into action as she says, "Pack your bags. We've got a stone to find."

Who You Callin' a Hoe?
Texas

We're screwed.

We have a mole in our ranks. Part of the Philosopher's Stone has gone missing, and we have no Maximus to save the day. Not to mention the former Maximus is aging faster than a California raisin.

After I finish packing, I head to the underground garage. A series of black government-issued sedans and SUVs litter the three-level parking deck. Nathan, the vampire butler-slash-cousin, takes the bag I'm more than capable of carrying.

"Hello again, Ms. Texas."

"Just Texas. Drop the 'miss,' mister."

He gives me a bright smile, then turns away as he gently places my bag into the trunk of a limousine, handling it as if it were mint-condition Givenchy luggage instead of a ripped and tattered duffel bag.

When he opens the door, I find Paris perched on the edge of her seat. The commander does not turn to face me when I sit beside her. She doesn't say a word.

The limo pulls off, exiting the garage and entering the twisting country back roads of Georgia that shroud our headquarters.

The partition is raised, and I'm not used to being with the commander all by my lonesome. I want mission details, but Paris is just staring straight ahead—not blinking, barely breathing, deep in thought.

After all, a top-ranking member of her trusted Alchemist Order ignored her command to erase his protégé's memory. The deceit has to burn.

When I maneuver to face her, she turns toward the window again.

"Where are we going?"

"Buckhead," Paris answers, her attention focused on absolutely nothing but dirt and trees and cows.

I roll my eyes toward the roof.

"Who's in Buckhead? The person with the stone?"

"No."

"The stone?"

"No."

"A psychic to find the mole and the stone?"

"No…" She taps her long fingers against her thighs and tilts her head. She seems to think through what to tell me.

"Commander Paris." I lean past the console between our seats, getting all up in her space. "I'd really like to understand what's happening."

"We are meeting with our allies, the Prussakovs. I'll need you to work with them."

"Oh, hell no." I cross my arms. "I'm not working with any more vampires."

"More? You mean Prince Khamari?"

"I haven't worked with him. I was told that I had to, since I killed his stupid clansman—who attacked me *first*, by the way."

"Oh…yes. The blood exchange. Seems so long ago," she says, her voice sounding centuries old. "The Prussakovs have worked with us for many years. I'd like you to work with them. Closely."

"Why can't someone else? I'm new, still getting a hold of my powers. You've got other Maestros—"

"With Rich out of commission, you seem to have the rawest power. Charlotte will be busy aligning with our global counterparts and taking care of our students. And Cali is… She needs to attend to a personal matter. She cannot handle the magnitude of this issue." Paris grips her knees.

I nod, knowing the personal matter is the bottle of gin at the bottom of her desk drawer.

"I chose you for a reason. I hope you won't disappoint the Society."

I scoot closer to the window as uneasiness unfurls in the pit of my stomach. Too much crap is happening at once. The stone, Dr. Winters, the darkness…the vampire prince invading my dreams.

Breaking the uncomfortable silence, the chauffeur lowers the partition. He peers through the rearview mirror.

"I was so pleased to hear about your visit with us, Ms. Paris. Tell me, do you plan to stay with us long?"

"No, Nathan, I'm afraid not. This will be a quick visit for me," Paris answers in a sweet voice.

Nathan pulls into the middle of a curved driveway. I've seen it all before, but I still roll down the window to take in the beige stone mansion with off-white columns bisecting the compound. The avocado-green trees, lit by the glow of the streetlamps, stand like sentries, engulfing the mansion as if to ward off unwelcomed guests.

He turns off the ignition, then walks to Paris' door, opens it, and offers his arm. I slide across the seat and exit from Paris' side. Nathan offers me his other arm, and I grab it. "Takes your breath away, doesn't it? You must walk around the back of the property sometime. There's a beautiful view of the Atlanta skyline. When the sun sets, it will bring tears to your eyes."

His icy blue eyes squint at the sky. In his late fifties, his clean-shaven face proudly displays laugh lines around his small mouth.

A reluctant smile spills across my face. "I imagine it will. I would love to see it."

"Come along. You have plenty of people to meet and a lot to

learn," Paris says as we enter the beautiful estate.

Nathan leads us to the same room as before, the spacious living room with the enormous fireplace.

The familiar smell of lemons and roses perfumes the air. This time it's stronger, much stronger, which means more bloodsuckers are inside.

My eyes narrow as they file into the room.

"Texas." Paris grabs my shoulder, dragging me closer to the creatures. "I'd like for you to meet the Prussakovs." She nods at the tall redhead with arresting blue eyes. "You've already met Ludmila."

"Hello, again, Texas." She smiles. "I wish we were meeting under better circumstances."

"Yeah… I wish a vampire didn't collude to steal the stone so that now I'm forced to work with y'all. But, well, shouldn't be surprised. Vampires are gonna vampire."

Paris chops the back of my neck. "We don't know who has the stone."

"Oww." The old woman has hands of steel.

"Don't be rude," she snaps and then looks at the rest of the vampire gang. "Excuse my slayer. She doesn't socialize much."

"I can tell." A younger, spitting image of Ludmilla sneers.

Paris waves her arm toward them. "The rest of the clan is her family of varying relations. This is Evgeny, Lev, and Ludmila Rose, but we all call her Rose."

Mila moves to stand by the fireplace while her doppelganger, Rose, sits on a U-shaped couch that can fit at least a dozen people. Lev and Evgeny flank the door on either side, as if waiting for an attack.

I stand in the back near the window, pacing like a caged animal. Every so often, I press my finger against the spike ring or rub the spike bracelet around my wrist.

Anything goes down, make an AK-47 with silver nitrate bullets.

The window is thick, so I'll need to blast through it. Only three floors down, by my count.

"Texas." Mila is the first to greet me. "Please take a seat." She motions to a blue suede recliner.

Nathan swan-dives into the room with a tray of goodies. Mini cupcakes and a cup of tea. I thank him and bite into the sweets first.

"Mhm. Key lime. It's my favorite."

"Oh, good. We just want to make sure you feel comfortable and well fed." Nathan winks.

More like feed on me. I keep that to myself, since the back of my neck still throbs from Paris' hands of steel.

I take a huge gulp of tea.

Paris waves toward the Prussakovs. "I've already given the Prussakovs an update about what you found in Dr. Winters' files."

"You gave…" I take in a smiling Mila, a smirking Rose, and stoic Evgeny and Lev. "*Them* information?" That part, I missed.

"Yes, just as we've shared pertinent information, too." Evgeny, or is it Lev's, rough voice breaks the tension.

"Quid pro quo, Texas. You tell us things, we tell you things." I can tell Rose is trying to be funny, but it doesn't land with me.

"Why do you sound like that?"

"Because it's Hannibal Lecter?"

"Who?"

"*The Silence of the Lambs*?" her voice squeaks.

I shrug. "Haven't heard of him."

"Ugh. Youth." She shakes her head like it's a curse.

"Whatever. And what have y'all shared, anyway?"

Rose crosses her arms. "There are rumors about a sale."

"A sale?" I frown. "Who would be dumb enough to sell the stone?"

Mila stands. "They either don't realize its potential and want to make a quick buck…"

"Or?" I prompt.

"Or they want to draw us out…kill us, and take the other half."

"But vampires can't use the stone." That's the only good thing going for us right now.

"Yet," Mila says in a low tone, voicing my fears.

"Is there a way for the stone to work for vampires?" I ask her.

"Not to my knowledge." Mila clasps her elbows. "But from what Paris has told us, Dr. Winters seemed very much into Egyptology and alchemy, the start of us all. Perhaps her research centered on leveraging the stone's powers? Perhaps it's why Rider engaged in a relationship with the doctor."

"Prince Khamari, he…" I swallow before I rush through my theory. "I think he knows something about the doctor. Something he's not sharing with the rest of the class."

Rose gasps. "You think your boo stole the stone?"

I cut my eyes toward the irritating vampire. "Who says he's my boo?"

"Aunt Mila said that sparks were flying between you two."

"Do not tell tales and agitate Texas," Mila admonishes her niece.

"First of all, he's not my boo," I clarify. "Second, I'm not accusing him. I just think there's something there. If he comes clean, we can figure out Dr. Winters' and Rider's relationship."

"No." Mila waves a hand. "I do not think Prince Khamari is tied to the stone. His hands are much too full now, between infighting and…other things."

I very much feel like Alice in Wonderland. "Well. Only way to find out is to get out there to the sale, bust some heads, and stake some hearts." I stand. "Where's the meeting for the vamps?"

"El Diente." Rose's voice is chirpy.

"El…" I sigh. Of course. The club where supes drain humans and each other for funsies.

"Shouldn't that be shut down or something?"

"Technically, it's 'unsanctioned.'" Rose uses air quotes.

"Aren't you all supposed to defend humans?" I point at Rose. "Yet you allow an unsanctioned underground club to stay open."

Rose shrugs. "If we tattle on everything, we lose our cool card. Besides, no humans have died. That we know of for sure."

"Whatever." I shake my head. "Pretty sure I'm blacklisted there. How do we get in?"

Rose stands and walks toward the entry. "C'mon, slayer. I know a guy."

Rose and I are given coordinates and instructed to drive a few miles out to conceal the car in a wooded area. I fume during all ten miles there. Not only do I have to work with another vampire, but she's also quite possibly the most annoying vampire on the planet. And for the past hour I've been plotting different ways to kill her.

She drives a cherry red, two-door, drop-top convertible. She listens to eighties music, dancing and singing at the top of her lungs. This isn't a road trip or a damn rom-com. We're on a mission. A mission that hopefully results in vampire remains on the soles of my shoes and the stone in my possession.

A sensible, dark-blue BMW sits idle on the side of the road at our designated meeting area near West Midtown.

I release the "Oh Shit" handle and flex my fingers, wishing they were wrapped around Rose's neck. A tall, blond male vampire steps out of the vehicle.

"Where are we?" I don't hide the suspicion in my voice. I'm still not convinced this isn't some elaborate setup to attack the Society.

"We're meeting our informant, Gregory. He's already been at the location."

"So have I." I don't tell her about how we stupidly infiltrated the supes club with nothing but scent blocker.

"You trust this vampire?"

She shrugs and puffs. "Eh…he's an unwilling informant."

"Meaning what?"

"He works for another Royal. We have information Gregory wouldn't want to get out to his sire and the rest of the vampire population. Let's just say he's sufficiently motivated."

I shrug. I have no problem with blackmail among bloodsuckers.

Rose opens the car door and steps out of the vehicle. "Gregory," she purrs.

"Beautiful Ludmila Rose." The slick vampire takes her hand, giving it a peck. "It's an honor to work with the Prussakov clan once again."

I stifle a chuckle, knowing both vampires probably hate each other's guts but have no choice in working together.

Like me.

My smile drops.

He straightens, taking in Rose, and then he swings his attention to me. He tsks. "This is a formal event." He waves down at his slim-fit navy-blue suit. "It'll be hard to get you in with you wearing that athletic gear."

Rose puts her hands on her hips. "Since when? El Diente has always been casual."

"I thought it was understood." He shrugs, the lie easily detectable in his voice. "When vampire society, especially Royals, get together, tank tops and sports shoes aren't allowed."

"Fine." Rose gives an airy wave. "I have a few dresses in my trunk."

"Why?" I ask.

"Why what?"

"Why do you have dresses in your trunk?"

"I had a few of my dresses cleaned the other day. I'll let you borrow one." She walks around me. "We're the same height, though I'm a little slimmer than you."

I have about ten pounds more muscle in my body. But that doesn't bother me. It's the fact I have to play dress-up. And where the hell will I put my weapons?

"Is this necessary?" I ask Gregory.

"Yes," Rose answers for him. "Something huge is happening in Vampireland, and the only way to find out is to mingle. Think of this as a covert operation. Like *Mission: Impossible*."

"Fine." I wave. "Just pick out a dress."

Rose taps her lips. "I have an emerald green and dark blue that would look good on you. How do you feel about—?"

"I. Don't. Care. Just choose."

"Oh, shoot. I only have one pair of shoes."

I roll my eyes. "I'll just wear my chucks. The dress will be long enough."

Rose shakes her head as she says, "You can't get in with those shoes."

Gregory sneers right along with her. "She's right."

Bougie-ass vampires. "Fine, then." I press the button at the base of my ring and slice my palm. Even in the depths of the night, I can see Gregory's fangs extend past his lips.

"Try me if you want."

He snaps his mouth shut.

Rose doesn't seem bothered by my blood. Instead, she moves to her trunk, muttering something about dealing with tomboy slayers.

I do a series of symbols in the air. A silver mist creates the outline of a pair of gray heels before the shoes take a solid form in my hands.

Rose returns to the front of the car and hands me a dress wrapped in plastic on a hanger. "Good job, slayer. I didn't think you had it in you."

I pick up the shoes and bang them against my hand. A large blade juts from the sole. I smile. "Weaponized heels."

Between the knife in the front and the sharp heels, I can do a lot of damage.

"I'll get dressed in the woods." The back of her car is too small to put on the dress. While changing my clothes, I create a makeshift strap around my thigh and add a small handgun and a dagger. By the time I'm changed, the cut on my hand has stitched together and is fully healed. When I return, Rose has changed, too, and is talking low to Gregory.

"What's the plan?" I ask.

"We'll take my car," Gregory answers. "Rose is my guest, my lover." He gives her a creepy grin. From her fake smile, I can tell Rose is less than enthused.

"And what about me? I'm obviously not a vampire." I've already rubbed myself down with a serum to camouflage being a slayer, but I can't cloak my humanity.

"You"—he points—"will be our blood whore."

"Say what?" I ask in a voice that carries warning, retribution, and certain death.

Gregory tilts his head like a confused baby seal. "You *do* know what a blood whore is, right?"

Rose waves her hands, giving her informant a bug-eyed look. "Gregory, I don't think that's a good—"

"A blood whore"—his voice rises over her protest—"is a human, a prostitute of sorts that allows us to drink straight from the cow. Excuse me, I mean 'the source,'" he says with air quotes. "Throughout the night, you'll need to allow us to feed from you. We have to make it look real, you see." A smirk curves across his lips. "You know, I haven't had the pleasure of drinking from a slayer before."

"And you won't be drinking from a slayer tonight." I whip up the skirt of my dress and pull out the knife from the strap around my thigh.

In three angry strides, I stand in front of Gregory, grab him by the throat, and lift the vamp from the ground. His pretty-boy loafers scrape the pavement as I press my knife against his neck. "Apparently you've forgotten that slayers are stronger than *Made* vampires, you worthless Tick." I angle both our bodies so my back isn't facing Rose. I don't trust her, either.

"Um…excuse you, slayer, but that is not a fact," Rose cuts in. "Some Made vampires can be just as powerful, depending on their lineage."

"Shut up, Mila Jr." I dig the blade into the vampire's skin. Drops of blood seep from the cut. "The only blood that will be spilled tonight is yours."

"Rose," he sputters. "Tell your guest to remove the knife from my throat."

To my surprise, Rose shrugs as she smooths out nonexistent wrinkles in her green gown. "I don't know why you thought a slayer would be okay with role-playing as your blood donor."

I smile. I like the word *donor* much better than *whore*.

When she looks up from her dress, her eyes settle on me. "Have you got a new plan?"

"Sure do." I look at Gregory. "I'm your human *guest.* Now, they can assume I'm a blood donor. But if you try to drink from me, as you so delicately put it, I will shank you. Understood?"

"U-understood."

"Good." I drop Gregory, letting him flop on the ground. "Thanks for listening to my TED Talk." I step over him and walk toward the car. "Ready, Rose?"

"Sure am." She steps over him, too, and snaps her fingers. "Come, Gregory."

"Just one minute." He rubs his neck. "If I have a bruise, we'll need to wait."

"Oh, stop it." Rose waves a dismissive hand. "You'll be healed by the time we make it there."

I roll my eyes. The Prussakovs need better narcs.

Sucker for Pain
Texas

It's only been a few weeks since I last visited El Diente with its expensive-yet-goth feel, so I'm not entirely convinced that this is the froufrou event Gregory claims it will be.

The guard scans us, but his eyes linger on me. He shoots me a stupid grin with too much gum and too many fangs.

Dammit, no matter what I'd threaten or say to Gregory, everyone will assume I'm a blood hoe.

"Password?" he barks at Gregory.

"Et oriri solem."

Latin for *the sun will rise.* Ironic password, but I keep my face blank.

The punk-rock vampire nods, steps back, and waves us in. The same black infinity symbol I'd seen on Rider stands out on his beefy hand.

A chill creeps up my spine. *Where should I begin?*

"Beats me," Rose replies. But her mouth doesn't move.

My eyes flare. *"Get the hell out of my head!"* I yell. First thing tomorrow, I'm getting a Costco-sized mind block elixir from the alchemy lab.

She smiles, all friendly, all fang. *"Fix your face, Slayer. I'll only communicate telepathically when necessary."*

I focus my mind's eye on giving her the bird. I hear a chuckle from Rose. Good. Message received.

Gregory stands in the middle with Rose on one side and me

on the other.

"Bliss?" a voice offers before we make it past the door. A short vampire moves a tray in their direction and ignores me completely.

What the hell is bliss?

Gregory picks up a glass.

Rose declines the offer. *"It's blood and whiskey,"* she so kindly informs me, again in my head.

Gregory takes a sip and then scans the room. "Let's stick together, yes?"

"Nope." I slide my arm away from the crook of his elbow. "See you around."

Rose guides Gregory to the opposite side of the club. I'm surprised she doesn't push back on my desertion. Then again, she probably has her own agenda.

The inside of the warehouse has an industrial-loft feel, exactly as I remember it. A spiral staircase leads to a spacious area upstairs. I don't know what I'm looking for, but I'm willing to bet nothing will be done out in the open.

I head for the staircase that Khamari and I had taken last time. Just before the stairwell hangs a Pop Art–style portrait of Khamari in red, yellow, and blue colors. A crown is tilted on his head.

Dear Lord, please tell me he has nothing to do with this gaudy-ass club.

"Where are you going?" a painfully thin vampire asks just as I place one foot on the step.

I tap my neck. "My services are requested."

"By whom?"

"Me," someone says with a voice thick as grits from behind me. I know the someone. Which is why I squeeze my eyes shut before I paste a bright smile and turn around.

"Prince." The vampire gives him a deep bow. He brushes his

long bangs away from his forehead. "Your pet got loose."

"*She* may roam as she pleases," he growls.

Damn right I can.

Khamari steps beside me, placing his hand on the small of my back. Despite his cool touch, my skin is on fire.

The vampire takes a deep breath. "If I may say, Prince Khamari, she smells delightful."

I smile and give the vampire a regal nod.

"Will you be sharing tonight?"

Sharing? I swear fo' Jesus, if someone else threatens to drink me again, I will burn this building to the ground.

"No." He looks down at me. At six foot three, he towers over me like a sunflower in a field of daisies. "*Come,*" he says, his voice low and gravelly again.

I swivel my hips, stretch my lips into a passable smile, and keep my eyes low. Not out of deference. I know they'll detect the heat in my eyes, and the vampire at the stairs has drained my patience.

The stairs lead to an open hallway. Like last time, the lights are dimmed upstairs, save for the moonlight streaming through the double glass doors. Khamari grips the knob and shuffles me inside of a room.

In the corner stands an old desk flanked by two metal filing cabinets. A long, horizontal closet stands behind the desk, partially covered by an old patchwork curtain that serves as a divider.

He bites his bottom lip as his eyes track my body. "You look—"

"What are you doing here?" I snap.

"Working." He crosses his arms and gives me a slow smile.

"At a club?"

"It's a social for Ethan," he says. "You know, the vampire you killed?"

"Yes. I know. Can't ever forget ripping out someone's heart."

It was only fair—he'd done that to mine when he killed my best friend.

"Well, we had a service. And now, we young ones drink afterwards."

"No Elders?"

"No. Just me and a few other clansmen."

"Huh." I tilt my head, then ask, "Are you following me or something?"

Khamari lets out an impatient exhale. He stares at me for a moment, his eyes soft with disappointment. "Rose reached out to let me know you both were attending."

"Why?"

"It's my club. Or rather, it's under my jurisdiction."

"Well, your club should be shut down, since you're drinking human blood in public."

"Isn't it better to have vampires working, socializing, having fun *inside* of a club, rather than roaming the streets?"

I lean closer and whisper, "The better option is that you all don't exist."

Khamari lowers his mouth toward my neck, and his warm breath shoots tingles across my sensitive skin.

"Jude was right. You do smell delightful."

I shrug. "Two showers a day keeps the BO away."

"No, it's not that, it's…" He takes a deep breath.

I hold mine.

In seconds, he stands closer to me. He leans in and sniffs.

"Watch it." I slap my palm against his chest. A very hard, muscular chest.

"Brown sugar. Spiced cocoa," he whispers, and by God, I swear his breath caresses my skin.

Danger. Vampire. And one day he'll be the king of them.

I take one small step back for me, and one giant step back for my hormones. "If I see anything sharp coming out of your mouth,

I'm going to push something sharp into your heart." I clear my throat. "Anyway, I need to go exploring, and you're cramping my style."

Khamari leans against the desk. "Are you looking for a certain stone?"

"H-how do you know about that?" My heart swan dives to the floor. It's my first mission, and people already know our secret.

"I'm privy to information as a Royal. No vampires know but a select few...for now."

I rub at my temples. "Fine. So, I don't have a lot of time, which means I need to go." I move to open the door.

"How do you expect to get information from a vampire? You can't kill them. All hell will break loose."

"Easy." I bat my eyes. "Seduction." I trail my fingers over my throat. "I'll pull them outside or into a room." I look around the room we're in. It's spacious. Sound carries, but I can gag the vamp. "This room will do. I'll lead them back here. Let them think they're about to get a little sample, and then I'll—"

"No. Too dangerous. You'll come with me."

I snort. "And be your little pet? Um, no. Not an option."

"I'll ask questions. They'll talk. And if I feel like someone's lying, I'll drink their blood and dreamwalk. It's simple, but it'll work. Besides, we're supposed to be working together—might as well start now."

I groan and stare at the ceiling. I promised Paris that there won't be any casualties. This is not a Rogue recovery or kill mission, and it requires a lighter touch. A touch I don't have. I'll play along with Khamari, but if his plans go tits up, then I'll throw the deuces.

Or I can sneak off and snoop around.

I like that plan better. Play the dumb human pet and pretend I don't know where I'm going.

"Deal." I offer my hand. He jerks me close, turns over my

hand, and kisses it, lingering over a vein.

"One day, you'll let me drink," he whispers over my skin.

"Don't bet your afterlife on it."

"If we exchange our blood, I can dreamwalk more easily in your dreams. You won't be drained, and we can—"

"No." I snatch my hand back. My head is screwed up enough, thank you very much.

"Let's go." I march toward the door, yank it open, and wave him through. "Your Highness."

Khamari offers his arm, and I take it. We return to the glass-walled, soundproof room on the third floor that he took us to the last time I was here. The windows allow us to look down at the dance floor. The formal wear brings about a more subtle atmosphere than before. Still, after scanning below, I find a few vampires feeding from humans discreetly in the corners of the room. The humans will feel it tomorrow, even if they erase their memories.

I shoot Khamari a heated look. "Yeah, I'm not sure if this is much better than what's going on outside. And after this stone thing clears up, I'm going after you."

He doesn't seem bothered by my threat. He just lifts his eyebrow and gives me a slow, heated smile. "I'll always want you to come for me." The red lighting in the room makes him look even more dangerous.

"Be quiet." I squirm in my seat.

A tall, slim, and pale vampire enters the room, along with a few others behind her. I guess it's not Khamari's private space—but his face doesn't change as they enter, so I keep my expression neutral, too.

But the relaxed, unbothered vibe is gone. His shoulders square up, and now his eagle-eye attention shifts from me to the vamp.

She sits beside Khamari, leans over, and squeezes her lace-gloved hand on his inner thigh.

I grit my teeth and look away.

"Prince Khamari, it's been a long time," she purrs. "Too long, it seems."

Khamari grunts. "I've been busy."

"Too busy to call or stop by?"

"That's what busy means, Mercy."

"Well, don't be a stranger anymore. Managing the club takes a lot of time. I don't have time to pop by the mansion."

Where is Khamari's little vampire nest? I return my attention to the vampire. A beautiful monster with large, expressive brown eyes and too-perfect features.

She stares back at me, frowning. "Your pet seems so... energetic. Have you been feeding?"

I look down again to hide my hate.

"Yes," he says. "And she tastes delightful. Before you ask, no, I'm not sharing."

Mercy snorts. "You never share."

So, he just drags random women around and sucks on them all night. Blood bank my ass.

"Regardless, I'm glad to see you, Prince, even under the sad circumstances of the death of your clansman. Ransome says a slayer gutted him."

"Afraid so." Khamari frowns. "The slayers cooperated and sent the blood of the one who killed him. It pains me to say that Ethan resisted protocol. Have you heard anything? Heard any rumors about a missing stone? Maybe his death is linked to this."

A large, stocky vampire enters the private room and jumps right into the conversation with, "Fuck the stone. I say you give us the name and we gut them like they gutted my comrade."

"Ransome." Khamari nods.

The vampire, built like an offensive lineman, stares at Khamari.

Khamari stares back and asks, "How's your sore throat?"

Ransome looks away and massages his neck. I can tell that vampire doesn't want any of Khamari's smoke.

The conversation is stilted for a while. Mostly about imports, gossip about other clans. Not so much gossip that I can use it against them, though. Just as I'm about to pretend to go to the restroom, someone slips into the room with us.

Jude, the asshole from the stairwell. "Mercy, your guest has arrived."

Mercy stands, the red light casting an angry glow on her pale skin. "If you'll excuse me, I'll be just a moment, my prince."

Khamari studies the vampire. "Is everything okay?"

"Yes, my prince." She bows. "Just a guest I must attend to. I'll return as soon as I can." Mercy uses her vampire speed to rush out of the room.

Jude sits beside his prince while Khamari resumes the conversation with Ransome. Though his demeanor seems relaxed, the energy bouncing around him is potent.

"My prince." I bow. "May I use the restroom?"

He nods, though his eyes hold a silent warning: *behave.*

Right.

"You may," he says. "But come back quickly."

"I'd be happy to escort your human," Jude offers.

"No need. I've given her orders, and she knows not to disobey me. But please put the word out that she's not to be touched."

I hurry to the door, determined to follow Mercy's tracks before she goes too far. Thankfully, the smell of her expensive perfume forms a trail that directs me to the balcony. Just below the balcony is a small patchwork of grass, where someone in a red hood speaks to Mercy in hushed tones, though it doesn't make a difference—I can clearly hear the conversation.

"You can't be here," Mercy says. "The prince is just upstairs."

"The prince knows nothing." The woman's voice is dismissive.

"Where is the stone?"

"I don't have it." Mercy waves her hands covered in lace.

The woman in the cloak grabs Mercy's hand and yanks off the lace gloves, revealing a large black circle on her palm.

"Liar."

"I—"

"You're already dead." The woman in the hood drops Mercy's hand.

"But you can fix it with your—"

The cloaked woman draws a sword. In a smooth, swift motion, she slices Mercy in half. Blood splashes on Mercy's killer and streaks the ground. Her halved body crumbles to ashes.

I jump over the ledge and step out of the shadows. "Who are you?"

The cloaked woman reaches inside her darkened hood and twists a dial. A loud screeching noise fills the night sky.

"What are you doing here...Texas?" That same robotic voice— the one who attacked Khamari—greets me.

I Don't Know Her
Texas

The cloaked woman pulls back her hood. Tense silence soaks the night sky. I hold my breath, waiting to figure out who she is and what she wants.

A black mask with two pointy ears, a long, pointy snout, and golden eyes obscures her face. I recognize the mask as Anubis, the god of Egyptian mummification, from class. Beneath the layers of perfume, I can't tell if she's human.

Dammit. I exhale my disappointment. On the bright side, I'll just have to rip that mask off.

"You know me?"

"Does anyone ever really know someone?" she replies.

But I'm pretty sure she's the same person who fought Khamari near Piedmont Park while I was fighting Rider.

"What do you want?" I ask.

"Nothing from you."

I tap my spiked bracelet, but I don't draw blood—it would alert the vampires to my presence. The wound from the blood I'd used earlier had healed in under a minute, so I don't have access to the power now. They say the blood of a slayer is potent, and though I'm stronger than most, I don't want to test my strength by fighting off a horde of vampires.

I run toward her and spin around into a kick, knocking her obscured face to the side.

She counters with a gut-punch. And damn, does it hurt.

I stumble back, then land a combo punch to her jaw and ribs.

She falls to the ground and puts her hand up; with the other, she pulls a knife. "Back away, slayer."

I ignore her warning and grab her cloak. She places the tip of the blade in her hand against my neck. "Touch me, and I draw your human blood," she threatens. "The vampires will be here in seconds."

I release her cloak and step away.

"That's right. Back up." With her free hand, she draws a circle and a series of symbols, then slams her palm against the ground.

One minute, she's solid—the next, she's gone.

"Where did she go?"

"Behind you. Watch out!" Khamari tackles me.

We both roll and *thud* onto the ground. The weight of his body is so jarring, I bite my tongue.

He moans, reaching for his back.

"The dagger." I roll out from under his body and quickly yank the blade out of his back. I scan the area. She disappeared again. "Shit. I... Damn, she got me."

"No..." He wheezes. "She got me." He rolls onto his side.

I slap his shoulder. Vampires heal just as quickly as slayers. "You'll live. It's just a stab wound. Also, Mercy and that woman who stabbed you are linked. She asked Mercy for the stone. Mercy had this..." I stop myself from mentioning the burn mark. If the vampires know, they'll handle it differently.

"Why are you still lying there?" I stand and offer my hand, though I'm not sure why he needs it.

"Silver. Alchemy." His voice slurs.

"What?" I scramble to find the tossed blade. The silver gleams under the moonlight. I pick it up, feeling its weight in my hand, and sniff. "Silver...purified silver. Shit." Transmuted and purified silver is deadly to Ticks and, depending on how deep the wound, deadly to Royals. Like certain venoms, Royals can become immune if they've been stabbed and survived it.

"Is it deadly to you?" My voice is calm, but on the inside, I'm a hot mess.

"First time." His forehead beads with sweat.

Time to see if Rose's invasive mind-talking goes the other way. *"Rose! Rose!"*

"Yeah, slayer?"

"Khamari's hurt. Purified silver."

"Shoot. I'll meet you at the car. Aunt Mila can help work it out of his system. If he's...if he's not terribly allergic."

"Just hurry."

"On my way."

"Let's go." I pull him to his feet. He must be at least two hundred pounds, and thankfully I have superhuman strength on my side.

The masked warrior has to be the mole. *An alchemist.*

"Why did you tackle me, anyway?" I berate him, but mostly, I berate myself. The dagger would've slowed me down, but I could've taken her. Silver is deadly to vampires, not to humans. That fucking mole had to have known he was coming. Maybe she smelled him.

"Can't lose you," Khamari mutters in a fevered whisper.

I pick up the pace. Rose beat us to the car, and once we're in, she speeds down the highway like a bat out of hell.

Khamari's breathing is shallow and quick, filling me with dread.

I squeeze his hand, my throat slowly closing. "Just hang on, okay? We've got shit to discuss, you and I."

He licks his lips. "Unfinished...business." His eyes roll back, his breathing slow and labored.

"Wake up!" I slap his cheek. My heart is pounding so hard it feels like a sonic boom in my chest. "How far are we, Rose?"

"Two minutes."

"He passed out! We don't have two fucking minutes."

"Got it." She punches the gas and jerks us into the speed of light.

I won't complain about her speed now. Not a minute later, we pull into the mansion's circular driveway. Mila and Lev meet us at the door, and Lev carries a now passed-out Khamari to a bathroom.

Lev points to me. "Strip him."

Rose helps me with his shoes, and then I strip him completely at the speed of a TV ER doctor.

Then I place him as gently as I can into the clawfoot tub filled with ice. Mila opens his mouth and pours a brownish oil down his throat.

When Khamari's body slides underwater, I pull him back up.

"It's okay," she says. "He can go under the water."

"What did you give him?"

"Detox cocktail: juniper, lemon chamomile, rosemary, and clary sage. The ice bath will cut his body temperature. After he's cooled, I'll take him out, wrap him up, and let him sweat out the toxins."

"Okay, sounds good," I say through chattering teeth.

"Are you cold?" Mila asks.

I look down at myself, realizing I'm shaking. "I'm fine."

After ten minutes of tense silence, Mila checks her watch. "Let's take him out."

We pull him out of the tub. I rub him down with a terry cloth, removing every droplet of water. I'm not sure if vampires can catch pneumonia, and I don't want to find out.

Mila wraps him burrito-style into a clean white sheet and puts him in bed.

"And now?" I ask.

"Now we wait for however long it takes. I wish I could stay, but…"

"Sun's rising."

"Yes. I'll leave him in your capable hands."

"Yeah, of course… Anything I should do?"

"Talk to him," Mila says. "He's in a bit of a coma now and needs an anchor to hang on to."

"Is he… He's gonna make it, right?"

"He's a half-breed, and he's still here. I think it's a good thing. Have faith."

"Right." A vampire telling me to have faith. If that don't beat all.

She gives me a weak smile and shuts the door.

I pull a chaise longue near the bed. *Talk to him.* What is there to say?

I know a bit about his story, and if the wound on his neck is any sign, I'll wager that he probably sugarcoated his transition from human to vampire.

"Life has kinda sucked, huh?" I look at him. His breathing is still shallow, but he inhales and exhales and hasn't stopped yet.

"Mila said I should talk to you. I think it's stupid and you probably can't hear me, but it doesn't hurt to try. Maybe you'll hear me in your dreams." I mimic him in that deep voice of his.

"You probably guessed it already, but I love music. Just about any kind, even country if the guitar and lyrics are good. I like Beyoncé, H.E.R., and Chloe x Halle. But I like the classics, too. Every Saturday, my grandmother would wake me up to clean up the house. We listened to Aretha Franklin, Marvin Gaye, and Tammi Terrell. And then we'd get down into an argument about who did a better version of 'You're All I Need to Get By.'"

I smile, remembering how furious Grandma Lou would get, telling me I don't know nothing 'bout nothing when it comes to the classics.

"Since I became a slayer, I don't play much music. It just reminds me of the past. Music is…memories. Good memories. And it hurts too much to remember what I lost." I lick my lips, look around the room, before I tell him the biggest confession of all.

"Sometimes when I see you, I hear this melody that I can't place. It's slow and smooth—it feels almost like gospel, but there's this part when the piano transitions to these bright runs, and it feels like…like I'm running toward something great. Anyway, stupid, yeah?"

I shrug. "I wish I could remember the song. The lyrics. So there. You should live because you have a soundtrack that plays whenever I see you."

I continue to talk to him for hours, big things about my life, and stupid, silly things, too, about my favorite books and TV shows. Six hours have passed, and he's still barely breathing and beautiful.

"She was still. She was beautiful." Grandma Lou's voice echoes in my head. When I was six or seven, I'd begged Grandma Lou to read *Sleeping Beauty* to me. I don't know why I liked it so much, but I did.

"All right, sleeping beauty. Wake up."

What if it's like sleeping beauty and he can only wake up from a true love's kiss? I mean, we aren't true loves, but maybe a true *like*.

And yes, I can finally admit that I like him, fangs and all.

I check the room, making sure no one will witness what I'm about to do. I lean over and softly give him a kiss on his cheek, mere millimeters from his lips.

"Wake up," I whisper. "Come back to me." I lean away. No open eyes, no gasp of breath, no nothing.

But thirty minutes later, something changes in the atmosphere. His breathing steadies. His dull skin transforms from ashen to bright. Just as my eyes grow heavy, his slowly open.

The piano from that melody plays again. The strikes of the keys are like fire to my soul. My heart soars, and the barbed wire fence that surrounds me crumbles to dust. His survival is important to me. He's important. I just…just don't know how to voice it in a way that doesn't sound clingy.

"You're here," Khamari whispers in that harsh voice of his.

"Yes." I inhale, allowing the cool of the air to dilute the emotional surge cresting inside of me. "Reading you bedtime stories."

He licks his dry lips. "Did you?"

"No, but I...talked to you. Did you hear me?"

"I felt you, but no. I didn't hear you. I was waiting for you to sleep."

"Oh. I stayed awake."

"Because you were worried about me?"

"You stepped in front of a knife for me." I shrug, but the thickness of my voice reveals the truth. He got stabbed because of me. He's been protecting me since the day we met. "It's the least..." I take another calming breath. "L-least I could do."

He glances down at his bare wrist.

"We took off your watch," I say, then check my phone. "It's a quarter till ten."

"In the morning?"

I point at the window—the window with the sun streaming in. "Looks like it."

"I've got to get going." He pushes himself up and rotates his shoulders.

"What? You just woke up."

"Yes, but I've been gone all night and my...the clan will be worried."

The clan. Right.

"You said my... My who?"

"My what?"

"You said 'my,' and then you paused. Do you have a girlfriend, wife, or special someone?"

A weird look crosses his face. "No. As I said, my *clan.* Besides that, I've got responsibilities to attend to." He jumps, yes, actually *jumps* out of bed, searches the room, and throws on his clothes.

"But your clan is sleeping," I say, following him as he stalks through the room finding articles of clothes and accessories. "It's daylight. No one will worry." My eyes narrow. "I swear to God, if you've been trying to get with me—"

"I haven't asked you out formally."

"Stop. You implied it and you know it."

He stops moving and cups my chin. "There isn't anyone else."

"Your special somebody could've been talking to you all night. Checking your temperature and playing doctor and—"

He kisses me. He kisses me *well*. Like, the dude is a pro. Deep, worshipful, his tongue caresses my lips. He pushes us both against the door. Then he grabs my legs and wraps them around his waist, all the time never breaking the kiss. I can't move, can only breathe him in and take what he gives me. And he's giving me everything.

Everything.

He pulls back.

I push on his chest. "What the hell was that?"

"You kissed me. Now I'm kissing you."

"I… You… You said you couldn't hear me."

"I didn't hear you, but I could feel you. Smell you. I knew you were near. Your kiss yanked me out of my dream state."

I push away and step back from him. "It means nothing."

Okay, yes, the kiss means something, but I can't tell him that. I can't be with a vampire—the very creature that tore my life apart and killed my friends. I won't disrespect their memories.

His eyes flare. "It means something."

I hug myself and take more steps away from him—away from my feelings. I shove them down as deep as I can, down beside missing my grandma and my grief for Deidra, and I say, "No maybes. Just plain ol' no. There is no us. You don't know me, and I don't know you."

He's important, yes, but that doesn't mean we can be together.

Besides that, there's something about him I don't quite trust. He's too smooth, too slick. And the biggest red flag: he's a vampire.

"Then let's get to know each other," he says.

"Ugh. Really?"

"Really what?"

"That's what all guys say," I tell him. "'Let's have a conversation,' but they really just want in your pants."

"I won't deny that I want you. But you say you don't trust me. So take the time to get to know me."

"I don't have time for this while I'm chasing the mole and the stone."

"We'll find a way," he whispers, caressing my cheek.

I'd be lying if I said it didn't feel nice, but I still turn away. "How?"

"We find the stone together. And sometime in between, when we're sleeping, you get to know me, and I get to know you."

"You won't like me." I try to hide the insecurity in my voice, but it still pushes through.

"You're beautiful, sarcastic, and can tear through a vampire's heart. What's not to love?"

He opens the door.

Like I said—too smooth. Too slick. "We aren't getting together!" I tell him again firmly.

He shrugs. "You've got questions, right?"

Sure do. Namely, is he involved in Dr. Winters' death, and what's the location of his clan? That way, if any of those fuckers get out of line, I have direct access.

I cross my arms. "We'll see."

He leans against the open door. "I knew you'd come around to my thinking." He shuts the door behind him and whistles as he walks away.

"Freakin' vampires."

Don't Dream It's Over
Khamari

After I return home, I rush to find Khaven. Last night, Dr. Persing texted me that Khaven had fallen ill. A simple cold, but nothing's "simple" with Khaven's immune system.

My insides tangle in coils as I round the corner to his room. I gently nudge Khaven's door, though I want to bust it open. When I open the door, I find him in bed with just a thin sheet wrapped around his legs. The thick goose-down comforter is on the floor.

I lean over his bed, checking his breathing, like I've been doing for the past few months. Doesn't matter that he's older than me by three years—I'll always check on him. The monitor softly beeping near his bed shows that his oxygen levels and blood pressure are steady.

Khaven cracks his eyes open. "Hey…where were you?"

I sit on his bed. "Got tied up."

"Tied up literally? With a woman?"

I wish Raven would tie me up.

Khaven laughs—it's thin, and it rattles his chest.

"Oh. You hesitated!"

"It's not what you're thinking." I cross my arms and look away.

"Whatever. Tell that to the cheesy grin you're trying to hide."

"Khaven, I—"

"Happy for you, little bro."

"Happy?"

"You're focused, driven, approachable, but not happy," he says.

"I know you left your girl behind, and that sucks. But now you deserve…someone great."

"I've been with other women. I'm no saint," I remind him.

And after I returned to my old stomping grounds and saw my ex-girlfriend had moved on to someone else—I kinda lost it. And yeah, I had a few months of running through women. But I discovered I wasn't a fan of one-night stands, so I stopped dicking around and focused on my clan.

"You had one or two hookups, but not something meaningful. You know, a relationship."

I laugh, shaking my head. "Kinda hard being in a relationship when you're about to be king."

"Then find a queen."

Something knocks at my chest. Maybe in another life, in an alternate universe, she could be my queen.

But she hates my kind. She hates me.

The monitor near the bed beeps again. *That's your answer. Don't focus on her. Focus on your brother.* "Dr. Persing and the others will be here tonight," I say, changing the subject.

"Mari—"

"Don't want to hear it, man. You better get your ass to the lab and let them do what they need to do."

I realize how parental I sound, and I wince. "Sorry, I know I sound like Julius, but I'm just… You can't leave me to handle all this bullshit by myself. We're a team, remember?"

Khaven shakes his head. "It's not right, what you're doing. You shouldn't screw with their minds. Look what happened to Dr. Winters."

"What happened to Dr. Winters is unfortunate. But she played with fire, fucked around with Rider—"

"Rider?"

"Yeah. Don't know all the details, but I'll find out."

"Damn."

"Yeah. But we'll have Hilda doing the mind bending. She's not as good as Rider, but she's loyal. At any rate, we've got to push forward. We're so close—"

"We've been *so close* forever," Khaven snaps. "Yet, nothing has changed."

"Ass downstairs. See you at seven p.m. sharp."

"Fine." He crosses his arms and even pokes out his lips like a little kid. "Will you be there?"

"Of course, I… Shit. I can stay for a little while, but I have an event later."

Khaven waves a dismissive hand at me. "The least you can do is watch me get prodded and poked."

"It's not a fun event. We're trying to get a handle on the stone situation."

"Wish I could be there to help you out," he says.

"Keep your eyes and ears open," I tell him. "I'm sure Rider didn't work alone."

"Gotcha. A damn shame we can't just make the stones ourselves…or use them."

Now that's interesting. He was the one who pushed me to form a true alliance with the slayers. "Why? We've got no issues with the slayers."

Khaven rolls his eyes. "The stone has the power to create, heal, everything. If whoever has it can figure out a way to crack the code so that vampires aren't overpowered, the opportunities are limitless."

"Huh. I knew vampires wanted it to shift the balance, but…"

Heal? My mind whirs as possibilities fly past. The main, hulking one is saving Khaven. *If I find the stone first, I can save him, then return it.*

"Yeah, dummy," he teases. "Read a book sometime."

"I'll have to try that." I smack my thigh and push off the bed. "Okay, I've got shit to do."

"Cool. See you later."

"Yeah, but remember, you've got an appointment at seven."

"I guess."

"Need you healthy. Who else is gonna watch my back?"

"Your queen." Khaven wiggles his eyebrows and rolls to his side.

I chuckle on my way out. Raven is definitely able, but she isn't willing. And she'll never trust me if she ever realizes my growing plan to find the stone and use its powers. But I've always been one to believe in asking for forgiveness rather than permission.

I set up the dreamscape for Raven. Since she knows I can walk through dreams, I create a dreamscape, in my bedroom. Tonight, I'll seduce her mind. In order to do that, I need her to relax.

Raven rolls off the couch and hits her knee on the table. "What in the…?" She looks around, and her eyes narrow when they land on me.

"Are you hijacking my sleep?"

"Maybe."

Gunfire blasts from the television.

She groans. "I really need a nap."

"Friendly fire. My bad, dude," I shout into my headset.

"For fuck's sake, K-star. You're such a noob," a voice that sounds like a preteen yells through the speaker. The dreamscape I created happened a few months ago. I like blowing off steam by playing online first-person shooters. If those foul-mouthed kids knew I could ruin their dreams or kill them in an instant, they'd go crying to their mamas.

"Come sit down." I pat the open cushion on my love seat.

"What are you up to, *K-star*?" She crosses her arms and stands in front of me. A large *boom* blares from the television. Raven snaps her head toward the sound, reaching for a weapon she doesn't have.

"What's this?" She points to the screen. Players in blue and red suits lob flash bombs at one another. "Is this some sort of space game?"

I chuckle. Khaven would lose his mind at the description, but she isn't wrong. "Kinda." I wave toward the snacks on the side table. "Cool Ranch Doritos? Blue Gatorade?"

"Ummm...those are my favorites. How did you know?"

I tap my temples. "The subconscious."

"I subconsciously think about Doritos?"

"It's buried in there."

"What else did you find without my permission?" she asks suspiciously.

"Nothing else. I just wanted to know what you like."

"Then ask," she snaps. She sits down on a loud sigh. Still, she reaches for the bag of chips and tears it open. "Still don't trust you."

You will.

She munches on the chips. "For instance, Cool Ranch isn't my favorite anymore. I'm a Spicy Sweet Chili girl." She takes another bite.

"Wish I could root around your brain and figure you out."

I pause the game. Well, I put the controller down, anyway. You can't pause, since it's live. You can just sit there and wait for someone to kill you. "Ask me anything."

"Who does the necklace belong to?"

"That again?"

"Yes. That again."

"Fine. My old girlfriend."

"You mean ex?"

"Yes." Though it stings to think of her that way. But it's my fault—or, rather, it's my genes that screwed me over.

"Is she alive?"

"Last I checked."

"And does she know about your"—she waves at me—"situation?"

"There was an accident when I was turned. My grandfather hired folks to find me. Soon, word got around to the other clans of my existence. They wanted to kill me off because they knew I could be next in line to ascend the throne."

"Who is they?"

"Another clan. We haven't figured out which one yet. They sent Made vampires to kill me off."

"Smart," she says in a dry tone. "That way if you survived, which you did, you couldn't tell which clan was behind it."

"Exactly. I survived, barely." I point to my neck.

"What happened that night?"

"The Made vampire stood in the middle of the road. My girl and I were on the way back from our date. I was driving, and when I noticed him, I swerved. My girlfriend hit her head on the dashboard so hard she went unconscious. A vampire attacked me and tore at my neck, then tried to get to my girl, too. I killed him."

I take a deep breath, trying to rein in my emotions. "Before that happened, I was on the fence. I considered suppressing my vampire half and just...moving on. But I realized there is no moving on. No going back. What solidified it was that my grandfather found out about the attack and came for me. I went by my girl's room and took the necklace I gave her. I know it's selfish as hell, but—"

"You needed something from your old life. You need her."

"I don't want to talk about her anymore. She's moved on."

"That's fine, but what I want to know is why didn't your grandfather come to you before the attack?" she asks with a weird edge to her voice.

"I'm a half-breed whose vampire side didn't manifest. So, after my parents died, he…sent me away." I rub my face. The old man left the government to take care of me. Though I understood his logic—the vampire world was too rough for a human boy—it still burned that he not only sent me away, but he separated me from a brother I never knew I had.

Raven looks away, but not before I see a flash of pain in her eyes. "That sucks. And now you rule a bunch of stone-cold killers."

"We're not so bad."

"Uh, huh."

I push down the wave of annoyance. *Patience.* "Vampire society is different now. I'm sure when Alexander ruled, it was more barbaric. These days it's all about growing the business. During the day, I manage our investments. Right now, there are a lot of promising technology and pharmaceutical startups. I get to invest in the future. A future I'll likely be a part of. And at night, when my clan members are awake, I'm problem solving and managing my clan's affairs."

Raven tugs her bottom lip between her teeth. "Sounds like it's a job."

"I'm no different from a CEO. And besides that, vampires don't go skulking in the night anymore. We contribute to society. Add value. Hell, we even pay taxes."

"What about Ticks?"

"I'm working on a campaign to encourage Royals to welcome Rogues and Mades back into the fold. If they have structure, they'll likely not get into trouble. Idle hands—"

"Are the devil's playground," she finishes.

"Enough about me. I want to learn about you, Raven."

"For one, my name's not Raven."

"That is your name."

"Not anymore." Her voice hardens. She rubs her forearms. "Raven is dead, and I'm not that girl anymore. If you *really* want to get to know me, that's the first thing you should accept."

"Okay." I nod. "Tell me more. What happened after…." I lower my voice.

"After you left me in a shitty motel? I got drafted into The Architect's army." The anger in her voice grows stronger.

This wasn't the conversation I'd planned for tonight, but she needs to vent and I need her to be okay. "As I understand it, slayers don't have much of a choice."

"No choice at all." She tucks a foot under her other thigh. "And that's an ugly pill to swallow. Sure, they say you can leave, and the Alchemist Order can erase your memory. But hell, after realizing there really are monsters and you have the strength to fight them, well…just like you, there's no going back. I struggle…" She clamps her mouth shut while she stares at the now blank TV screen. "I struggle a lot. It's hard to connect to people. I've lost so much—my friends back in school, my grandmother, my parents. I just don't know how to be normal, even before all of this. And besides that, I'm so strong, and I can tell they're trying to figure me out."

"You've got to be pretty strong to take down a Royal," I say, referring to Ethan.

She nods down at her lap. "They want to test me, but Paris thinks I'm at Maestro level in terms of strength. Takes most slayers about fifty years to get to that level."

"How many Maestros are there?" Knowing their numbers will help me plan for contingencies, in case the stone retrieval flops.

"Not too many. Not too few." She finally looks my way, baring her white, even teeth.

I raise my hands in the air. "Just trying to get to know you."

"That question is about the Society, not me."

"Fair enough. Favorite shows?"

"*All American*, *Riverdale*, and ummm…" She clears her throat, and I detect blood rushing to her cheeks.

"Out with it."

"Okay. My roommate got me into *Buffy the Vampire Slayer*."

A little on the nose, but who am I to judge?

"Do you like to read?" I ask, leaning back on the love seat.

A weird look crosses her face. "Who doesn't?"

Khaven would love that answer.

"What do you like to read, then?"

"Everything."

"Including romance?"

"I used to, but now I can't read it anymore. It's hard reading about others getting a happily ever after when I can't."

"Maybe…" I stop myself before I can finish. "You have a lot of years ahead. You never know."

She rolls her eyes. "Yeah, we'll see. Slayers typically don't live long, seeing as we're always fighting your kind."

"You'll live a long time."

"Sure, I will."

"I'll watch your back," I tell her. It's a promise I plan to keep.

"I don't need you to watch my back."

I laugh, shaking my head. "Yeah, you are something else. Something special."

"Oh, I know." She says it with confidence, but it looks like she's fighting a smile.

"I think you can achieve anything you direct your energy toward. And that includes staying alive and maybe finding someone later. Someone worthy of you."

She snorts. "Right. And when I show up to date night bloodied and bruised, I'll just tell my human boo, 'Sorry I'm late. Got caught up killing monsters.'"

"Don't date a weak-ass human. Date someone who knows about this life. Someone who can roll with the punches. Someone you have a connection with, dare I say—"

"I get it." She laughs, but for real this time around. "Maybe you should drink some of that Gatorade," she said, her voice shaking with laughter.

"Why?" I laugh, though I don't know what's so funny.

"It'll help quench your thirst." She laughs with her body, head back, shoulders shaking. Her eyes are warm, soft, unguarded.

"My thirst?" I rub my jaw. "I don't get hungry or thirsty in dreamwalking and— Ohhhh." Her joke finally lands. "I didn't say me. I said *someone.*"

Ego be damned, I'm thirsty *and* hungry for this girl. And seeing her laugh, something she hasn't really done around me, feels good.

"Yeah, just someone like you."

Raven stands and scurries to the other side of the room. "This is nice and all, but I should probably get back. I'm pretty exhausted."

"Yeah. I enjoyed our date."

"It's not a real date. If you want to date me, you should probably stay out of my head. It's only gonna piss me off."

"You're right. Let's call it a conversation. And we should have another one tomorrow night…in person."

"I'm busy."

"How about—"

"Finding the stone is my number one priority," she says.

Mine too. I keep my motivation to myself while Raven continues to push me away.

"I don't have time for in-person hookups."

"Fine. It's settled. We'll continue our conversations in our dreams."

"Khamari—"

"I don't have much time, either. But we have the common goal of finding the stone. Face it—we need to work together."

"And how is asking a bunch of personal questions in my dreams defined as working together?" she challenges.

"I don't have a lot of good in my life. Real or not, being with you is the only thing…" I stop myself from revealing too much. I can't tell her about the things that keep me up at night. Like my sick brother, or how I'm one misstep away from a revolt among my clansmen. "I want to know you. And I want you to know me at my core. I'm not the monster you think I am. I need time to do that."

"It's too complicated. I'm a slayer, and you're a vampire. I mean, it was a cute TV show concept, but real life?" She shakes her head. "I don't do tragic. I avoid that shit at all costs."

I move closer to her and grab her hands. She doesn't pull away. "We don't have to be tragic. We can control our own lives, write our own destinies."

"Since when? Life has never given me what I wanted." Her eyes are liquid. "Life just seems to take and take, and then take some more."

"Then it's time we take back what's ours. Stop asking. Start grabbing. Piece by piece."

"Just like that?" she scoffs.

"I'm not asking for a relationship. I just want you to carve out some time. Can you do that for me…for yourself? In person is fine."

She pulls her hands back and paces the floor. Her mouth moves, but nothing comes out.

Then she stops. I hold my breath.

"Okay," she says. "But I have rules."

"Deal." The muscle that clenches my jaw relaxes. I don't care about her rules. I just want her time.

She arches a brow. "Don't you want to know the rules?"

"Go ahead."

She lifts a finger and points it at me. "No funny business."

"I don't know what that means."

She looks around as if others might be listening. She leans in, then whispers, "It means I'm not giving you my blood."

"I can't agree with that, beautiful."

"Oh, what a surprise. A vampire won't agree to not drinking my—"

"When you wake up after this, your energy will be drained. You'll get it back throughout the day, but that's the drawback when I walk in someone's dreams. But if I have your blood, it's a smoother transition."

She crosses her arms and stares down at her feet. "I need my strength."

"I need your blood. You've got to trust me."

"Sure, I will. Tell me what you know about Dr. Winters."

The clench in my jaw returns. "I already said I know about as much as you do."

"Rule number two. Be honest."

"As honest as I can be," I tell her honestly.

"Do you really want this to work?" She narrows her eyes.

"Yes. And I'm following your rules to a T. I don't want to lie to you."

"Next rule. No more dream crap unless necessary. We'll meet in person, so I don't have to worry about giving you my blood." She offers her hand, and I smile. Honestly, it's more than what I expected.

I take her hand and pull her close. Her pulse jumps, and her breath warms my skin. I kiss her forehead—I'd prefer to kiss her lips in person. "You've got a deal."

25

Hold On
Texas

I stand beside a tall crystal vase at the High Museum. Charlotte was right on the money when she forced me to wear a dress. I pitched Charlotte the idea of attending this event to see if I can connect the dots to figure out Dr. Winters' and Rider's fascination with Egyptology, and she was all for it.

White flowers decorate long rectangular tables. The decorations are sprayed with some manufactured vanilla scent. Patrons mill about the space. From their expensive jewelry and designer tuxes and gowns, I'm guessing they're filthy rich.

"Well, hello. Haven't seen you around here."

Lightly gripping the stem of the champagne flute, I turn around to greet the male voice. A tall man eyes me. His skin is as bronze as the painted pharaohs on the sarcophagi.

Showtime.

"I'm Dr. Trevor Bozeman." He offers his hand, though I can clearly see his name on the *Hi! My name is* tag. The academics—who aren't as expensively dressed—wear the nametags.

"Rachel." The lie slips out easily. "And no, this isn't my usual hangout spot. I'm more of a bar and lounge type of gal."

Dr. Bozeman appraises me like one of the mummies in the thick, tempered glass across the room.

I grin and take another sip while he eyes me again from head to toe. I'm not in my usual getup. Today, I wear a black bodycon dress, strappy heels, and a spiked gold bracelet.

He strokes his salt-and-pepper beard and licks his chapped lips. "Are you a lover of Egyptian culture?"

"Totally." I nod. "I was flipping through the History Channel and saw the great mysteries of Egypt. My friend had an extra ticket and gave it to me."

"Did she?" He wags his finger. "Your friend is naughty."

Gross. "Why is she naughty?"

"This event is for" — he looks around and leans close to my ear — "donors with *deep* pockets," he whispers.

I smooth my hands over my dress. "I don't have any pockets." I smile at him, hoping the smile incites lust. Smiling is not my strong suit.

His pupils dilate.

Yep. Not too bad.

He answers my smile with a grin. A grin that probably would've done something for me if he were thirty years younger… and used lip balm. There's something about a man with well-moisturized lips. I slide my arm, hook his elbow, *hook* him. "What are you raising money for anyway, Dr. Bozeman?"

We stride toward the enclosed exhibit across the room. "Call me Dr. Trevor Bozeman."

I roll my eyes. He can't see me, anyway.

"We're raising funds for an excavation to uncover one of the three great Egyptian secrets."

"Secrets?" I sip my champagne while still clutching his arm.

"Yes." He stops us in front of a clear case displaying a beautiful broad collar with rows of aquamarine beads and gold plates.

"The secrets are the tombs of Nefertiti, Cleopatra, and the biggest fish, Alexander the Great. We're focused on Alexander's."

Champagne spews from my lips and then onto the good doctor's sweater and chinos. Dr. Trevor Bozeman jumps back and dives for the nearest cocktail napkin.

"Oh, shoot. I'm so sorry. It's just… I didn't know Alexander the Great was Egyptian. That's fascinating." I add a little breathlessness to my lie.

He dabs at his wool sweater. "This is merino." He drops the seductive tone and switches to professor mode. "Alexander was not Egyptian. He was Greek. But he conquered many lands, Egypt included. And so, he took on their customs, becoming pharaoh and claiming his birthright as the son of Zeus-Ammon and so on. Anyway, I must get going, I—"

I grab another napkin and dab near his crotch. "Again, I'm so sorry. I'm such a klutz."

He takes a few steps back. "No, I'm fine."

Perhaps my wipes were too vigorous? "Oh, well, I'll just see you around."

"I'm sure you will." He rushes past me to the bathroom. Far away from me.

Okay, so my flirting is a wee bit rusty. No worries. With a few more glasses of wine in him, I can get him talking about Alexander again.

The lights dim as the DJ plays slow jams, taking over for the string quartet that had been playing earlier. Couples, old, young, and in-between, stick together like Velcro on the dance floor.

A forty-something couple dances a few feet away. The woman tucks her chin on her partner's shoulder and wraps her hands around his back. Two silver bands sparkle on her ring finger. Her eyes are closed, her lips parted. The picture of pure bliss.

That'll never be me.

I turn away and shut out the thought as I rub at the phantom wound over my heart. If I leave my feelings unguarded, the wound on my chest will stretch, tugging at the threads I'd carefully stitched together over the past month. In my heart, I know the pain of losing my old life will never fully heal. It'll never scar because I'll never let go of the hate.

I need hate to energize me. Because if I don't have that, I'll have no purpose.

Alabama Shakes' "You Ain't Alone" blares through the speakers. I love the song but hate hearing it tonight.

"Can I have this dance?"

I spin around, knowing who I'll find. "What are you doing here, Khamari?"

His eyes, expectant and expressive, entrap me. A few weeks ago, I would've dug my heels and stood my ground. But now it seems like he's got a lasso around my body and he's tugging me close. Too close. And dammit, I'm tired of trying to fight it.

"Dance with me." In his tone, I can hear what he doesn't say. *Let's be normal. Let's pretend.*

I nod, then rest my head on his shoulder. I close my eyes, pressing my heart—my wound—against him. The sharp pain disappears, and I imagine things that can never be—hot summer nights, backs on the grass and eyes to the sky. Lazy Sundays with just ten square feet to dance.

Bliss. I sigh, and for the first time tonight, my smile is real.

He sighs, too. His rough palms slide across my back. Though the material isn't thin, I feel the tremor in his hand.

"I wish—" He cuts himself off.

"I know," I whisper, brushing my nose against his chest.

He feels cool, smells clean and somehow…deep. Like I could get lost in exploring his depth.

A part of me wants to try.

My heart slams against my chest as the drummer thwacks the snares with building intensity. The lead singer demands for us to *hold on*.

I grip the lapels of his jacket like a lifeline.

Khamari stops moving. I tip my head back, stare at him.

In his eyes, a thousand emotions swirl like a Texas twister.

Agony, tenderness, torture—these feelings are my own. The agony of lives ripped at the seams. The tender moments thinking about what could be. The torture in knowing that we'll never fit together. How can we? Neither of us is whole.

Khamari shakes his head, as if he's dismissing my silent death blow to...whatever we are. "Just dance with me," he whispers.

I lower my chin, dancing, pretending. The artist sings and shouts, demanding that I, that *we*, hold on again.

Khamari's finger lifts my chin. His eyes are glinting with specks of amber. Predatory and beautiful and dangerous.

She "ooohs" with so much pain and longing and angst that if this person doesn't hold on—cry, scream, shout, and fight for them—then all is lost.

I want to hold on, too.

A band loosens around my throat, the freedom of truth swooshing through my veins like a drug.

I'm free and high, and I want more.

I *need* more.

My hands on his chest, I stretch to my toes and kiss him.

Because if I don't, it feels like my world will end.

He tilts my head back and devours. His lips are warm, and his tongue plunders with smooth execution. The control to my frenzy. But his heart gives him away, crashing and raging against my palm.

I break away from his kiss, staring at him as our breathing syncs.

His eyes, yellow now, cast a nocturnal glow.

"Your eyes."

"Blood...lust."

"Geez, Khamari..." I push at his chest. This is why we don't fit. He wants to *eat me*. And not the good kind of eating.

"No, not like you think. Your blood...it sings to me. It's like I'm surfing this gigantic wave, and if I don't steady myself just so, keep my feet exactly right, I'll crash and drown."

"Sounds like you think I'm dangerous."

He chuckles, but neither his eyes nor his chuckle hold humor.

"More than you know."

My skin feels tight and itchy, like a rash overtaking my body. *He*'s the dangerous monster. Not me.

But I'm the monster hunter.

I storm off the dance floor, and he follows. "Why are you stalking me, anyway?" I snap at him as I snatch a champagne flute from a table and chug.

"I'm not stalking you. Charlotte invited me to join you. How did you find out about it?"

"Googled 'Egyptologist' and found this event. Charlotte got me on the list and...here I am."

"I saw you messing with that old guy. I figured you were up to something."

"Sugar Daddy had loose lips, and he spilled all the tea." *He would've said more if I hadn't spilled all my champagne.*

"And you had to dress all seductive and rub his crotch to get information?"

I close my eyes, inhaling for strength and exhaling my irritation. "First of all, I did my research. The man likes pretty girls, and he's arrogant. I safely extracted intel."

His thumb slides down the base of my neck, leaving a cool trail. Despite the cool touch, a jolt of electricity zips down my spine, and I shudder.

"Cold?" His voice is warm and on the edge of laughter.

"I'm fine."

He twines a lock of my hair around his finger. "And what did the good doctor share?"

"It's about this fundraiser. Get this—he's raising money to find Alexander's tomb."

"What? When you say Alexander, you mean—"

"As in your fang daddy." I point to him. "We're working with a missing piece of the stone, plus the dead scientist and ex-lover of your clan. And now, someone's been commissioned to find

Alexander's tomb. I bet it's all linked."

"Do you think… Do you think they're trying to resurrect him somehow?"

It's something I've wondered, too, but I shake my head. "I don't even know if it's possible, but the Philosopher's Stone is capable of unimaginable things."

"We've got to find that stone."

"Yeah. And the first place to start is your clan."

To my surprise, he doesn't argue. "Rider's gone to ground, but I bet he's still in touch with a few other disgruntled clansmen. They want to go back to the old days."

"Really? I thought vampires were so evolved. 'We pay taxes; we don't go bump in the night.'" I mimic his deep voice.

"We have good and bad ones. Just like humans. Just like the mole in your organization."

"Touché." As soon as I figure out who the little rat is, I'll wring their neck.

"I'll search around my clan," he says, "figure out what's what."

"I need to bring Paris and Charlotte up to speed. We've gotta turn up the heat to find our mole." I swallow and look up at Khamari, thinking about my history lesson, the slayer versions that told the true story about Alexander. Pretty much every plague, every war, was started by Alexander and his minions. "Alexander…" I sigh. "He can't come back."

"We won't let him."

The song ends. Someone clears their throat, amplified by the microphone. "Good evening, esteemed guests, patrons, and academics. We have very exciting news."

My attention diverts to the short woman on stage.

"We've just received a large donation and have exceeded our fundraising goals. We thank all of you for the generous donations. But we'd like to give a special thanks to the St. John family. Please, eat, drink." She points to the DJ. "And let's dance."

Khamari and I look at each other.

St. John.

A flash of the name on paper pops in my mind.

Khamari St. John.

I slam down my glass and point at him. "You!"

The crowd turns their attention on us as Khamari grabs my arm and hustles us toward the back of the room.

"No. Not me," Khamari denies. His face turns to stone. "Maybe someone in my family. Or someone else. St. John is a common—"

"It's not that common." I yank my arm away from his grasp. "Are you trying to play me?"

"No. Of course not. I'll handle it."

"You need to talk to your grandfather. ASAP."

I storm away from Khamari. I bet Charlotte didn't know what his little family and clan were up to, funding the discovery and excavation of Alexander's tomb. Hell, maybe Khamari wasn't just guessing about the dig's goal—maybe he knows firsthand that they're trying to bring Alexander back from the dead.

There's no way we can partner with them. Vampires can't be trusted.

That's Just My Baby's Daddy
Texas

I turn the corner and enter Paris' office suite. The receptionist's desk is stationed outside the commander's door. Dakota sits in the front, a pocketknife to her palm, and I watch as she slices it open and emits a flickering blue glow.

"Welcome back, Ms. Texas," Dakota teases.

"What are you doing?" I wave toward her bloody hand.

"Practicing." She presses a cloth against her palm.

"And how's that going?"

"Things are going well," she says, tucking a curly brown strand of hair behind her oversize glasses. "I… I'm nowhere near your skills, but I've been here for three years. Hearing about your missions made me realize I need to be more proactive. I need to train and get ready."

Heat hits the back of my neck. I try to rub it away. Skilled? I can barely control myself. I nearly got Khamari killed the other day, not that I would say that out loud.

Instead of admitting my shortcomings, I say, "You are amazingly talented with alchemy. You're leaps and bounds ahead of the pack."

"Yes, well, I still need to work on my skills, so that's what I'll do. And now we have a new Maestro to help us Internists."

"A Maestro? Who?" Must be from another slayer cell.

"Anton," she answers. "Do you know him? Where he's from or whatever?" A blush spreads across her cheeks.

"Anton? That's not the name of a city. And no, I haven't heard of him. You know more about the Society and Order than I do."

"Once you become a Maestro—"

"Not officially a Maestro yet."

Dakota shrugs. "Do you think he'll teach me some things?"

I chuckle. "What kinds of *things*, Dakota?"

"Not like that, like…Internist stuff. Not the fighting stuff that you're teaching me." She rubs her face.

"I'm just messing with you."

She searches for something on her desk, finds a pen, and throws it.

"Ow!"

"You're so mean."

"He must be cute."

"He's, um, easy on the eyes."

"I'm sure he is. But anyway, is Commander Paris here? I need to see the big boss."

She glances down at the clock on her desk. "I just got back from lunch, but Ms. Paris messaged me and said she's busy for the next hour." Dakota motions to the brown couch. "She usually meditates around this time."

I roll my eyes. "Meditates?"

She offers a notepad. "You can leave a message."

I grab the pad. Streaks of light-brown makeup dirty the paper.

Ol' dude must really be cute for her to bust out the makeup.

I glance at her and shake my head. "On second thought, I'll wait."

Dakota nods. "She has an opening in the next hour. You can come back or take a seat."

The vampires are literally staging a coup, a piece of the stone is missing, and we have a mole, and she wants to be left alone to meditate? We don't have time for chants and crystals and essential oils.

"Sorry, Dakota." I rush past her desk, straight toward Commander Paris' office.

The door bangs against the wall after I push it open. I find her looking like a regal monarch behind her glass-and-chrome desk. Sitting in front of her are Charlotte and some old dude.

Their conversation halts as three heads turn toward me. Charlotte lets out a deep sigh. Paris leans back in her seat and clasps her hands. The old guy swings his cataract-covered eyes toward me and shoots me a get-off-my-lawn look.

"Paris, Charlotte. Sir." I nod at the trio. "Sorry to interrupt, but I need to speak to both of you. Immediately."

"Why am I not surprised?" The old geezer, who must be at least one hundred and eight years old, shakes his head. "I don't know why you put so much trust in her, Paris."

I cock my head, my hands now on my hips. "Look, old dude—"

"It's Richmond, Texas," Charlotte interrupts. She bites her lips, and her eyes are large with alarm.

I raise my fist over my mouth and take a good, long look at Richmond, at the liver spots on his dull and bald head. The deep wrinkles that rival weeks-old laundry that'd been stuffed at the bottom of a drawer.

And my God, his old-man hands are curved around a walking cane. He looks like Brad Pitt. Not regular Brad Pitt, but the Brad Pitt in that movie where he's born old. Grandma Lou loves that movie.

"Oh, shit. It's *The Curious Case of Benjamin Button*." I thought I said it internally, but I quickly realize I said it out loud. I mean, this is the literal case of soul rot—when you stink so much on the inside, it seeps to the outside.

Richmond utters another shaky old-guy sigh. It sounds like someone opened a can of flat soda.

"My bad," I say, and I mean it. I'm not about to kick Richmond while he's down, and homeboy is deep-blue-sea low. Besides that, it's frightening that an alchemist has the power to control our aging.

"The meeting is concluding anyway," Paris replies. "Richmond, have Dakota call someone to help you."

Richmond nods and struggles to get up. Charlotte stands and grabs his elbow. *Saint Charlotte*. She has so many reasons to hate him and yet she helps him.

I sit in his now open seat. "Goodbye, Richmond."

There's a distinct possibility he'll die in his sleep.

I turn my attention back to Paris. I don't have the energy to worry about Richmond. Other lives are at stake.

"Go on," Commander Paris invites. "Charlotte may be a while with Richmond."

"I went to the High Museum's Egyptian fundraising gala last night and met a Dr. Trevor Bozeman, and get this—they're raising funds to find and excavate Alexander's tomb. And one of the major donors is the Ankh king."

The commander's mouth drops open. "He attended the fundraiser?"

"Well, no," I reply, shaking my head. "But the donation is from the St. John family. That's their last name."

Paris drags her eyes away from me and focuses on something over my shoulder. "I was afraid of this."

"Afraid of what?" I ask.

"The vampire guilds want to use the stone to resurrect him."

"But how can they, if—"

"The stone will be the conduit. It requires a powerful host to channel their life force."

"So…the host will sacrifice their life for Alexander's?"

"Yes," Paris replies simply. "Everything requires a cost. The cost of a life is steep."

"Not if Alexander doesn't care about cost," I say. "I mean, who in their right mind would volunteer for something like that?"

"This is true. And as I said, the host must be powerful. The slayers cannot be used—our humanity protects us. They must be supernatural."

"Who knows this is even possible?" I ask her. "Surely they're the ones we need to look at first."

She shakes her head. "I have no idea. For all I know, every vampire clan in the world could know about it by now."

Well, shit.

"If he's brought back to life, will Alexander be immortal? Worst case, if he's back, can we kill him?" I ask her.

"That, I do not know." Her tone is sour, and I can tell she hates to admit her ignorance. "I'd say it's best that he doesn't come back."

An army of goosebumps sprouts and spreads over my body. He's a conqueror; he can kill at will. Run through families, innocents, students…

Blood covers the floor and ceiling on the bus. My lungs burn, my throat raw from the scream I'd swallowed. My boots squish something beneath my feet. I hold my breath, look down. The scream escapes.

Paris taps her manicured fingers against the desk, dragging me back from my nightmares. "What I know is that Alexander wants to use the stone to become the perfect specimen," she continues. "No weaknesses; the ability to walk in the sun. The Order and Society can no longer contain him. He could snap his fingers and be anywhere. He could do anything."

"How can they resurrect him? Does he even have a body now? Or will he just poof from thin air?"

"The Royals will need to secure his remains."

"And his remains are where? In the tomb they're trying to find?"

"His tomb is in a safe location."

"But—"

"I know what you're thinking, but I cannot disclose the location," she says, shaking her head. "It's not just my secret—it's one that must be approved to share by all commanders worldwide. I will, however, ask that I can make you all aware."

"Appreciated." I relax in my seat. "If we can figure out who they're planning to use as Alexander's host, that will give us a leg up." I wonder out loud: "Maybe it's a werewolf or another vampire?"

"No. Not just any supernatural. A powerful being both supernatural and human."

I snap my fingers. "It all makes sense now. Dr. Winters was tracking the uptick in half-breeds."

"Yes," Paris responds in a measured voice. "I suspect that is the reason why. A powerful half-breed can likely resurrect Alexander."

"Like Khamari," I whisper.

"Yes. Though he has already created the perfect specimen."

Vampires have a piece of the stone *and* a host? "Who?" I lean forward. "Is it Prince Khamari?"

"No. Not him. Someone from Alexander's loins."

"Oh. Well, not to be heartless, but shouldn't we just *kill* his li'l evil seed?"

Paris' eyes ice over. "Killing him is not an option."

"Why?" I meet her stare. I have no doubt that she's killed some vamps in her day.

"Because…" A deep voice breaks the stare-off between me and Paris.

I hadn't scented anyone else in the office. I hop from my seat, turning to face the stranger. How the hell is that possible?

A man with odd eyes studies me from the corner. His legs are crossed, a cup of tea in hand. "I'm Paris' son," he tells me calmly. "And Alexander is my father."

Sleeping with the Enemy
Texas

"I… You…" I plop down in the seat in front of Paris' desk.

I slap my forehead as if I can smack the shocking knowledge out of my head. "You and Alexander…did the nasty?" I poke a finger in and out of my closed fist.

Paris' face, her mouth, her expression, are as closed as my fist.

Jesus H. Christ on a buttermilk biscuit. She slept with the enemy. All joking aside, I'm seriously considering if I can take on the commander and her seed. I mean, dayum. No one can be trusted.

I lean over to whisper to Paris. "My offer still stands to…get rid of him."

A wave of power boomerangs throughout the office. My hands freeze. I try to turn my head to face the source, Paris' spawn, but the energy he emits makes it hard to move. It's so binding. My skin stretches over my bones. I slip my hand inside my blazer, a few inches away from my knife. The tips of my fingernails scrape the handle. I try to overcome the power, but it's like I'm moving through a vat of Vaseline.

"Stop it, Anton," Paris says in a seasoned voice.

I bet she never disciplined him as a child. Teeth chattering, I bite my lip until it bleeds, hoping this will suffice as a blood offering to gain my powers. Warmth and light spread through my body. The sacrifice is accepted. Apparently, The Architect doesn't appreciate the spawn's show of whose junk is bigger.

My muscles relax. Taking advantage of the reprieve, I grab my knife and throw it.

He dodges the weapon—fast and graceful and totally unbothered. It takes me a few seconds to realize the knife grazed his cheek. A thin red line beads against his pearlescent skin.

Paris' hands flex around the edge of her desk. Her eyes are ice chips. "If you're both done, I'd like to continue the conversation. Now, Texas, to answer your question, Alexander and I did not—"

"Your seed"—I point to what's-his-name in the back—"would disagree."

Paris rubs her wrist, her eyes clouding over like the onset of a storm. "It's not something I usually discuss, but for the sake of transparency, I'll share this. I met a soldier named John during the American Revolutionary War. We fell in love, married, and he later died. Alexander caught me at a vulnerable time. He swooped into town, pretending to just be a man looking for an honest living. Nine months later, my son was born."

"Okay." I lick my lips, nodding. "You didn't realize he was evil incarnate. Got it."

That sucks. That really, really sucks.

The office door opens. Charlotte strides in and settles in the seat beside me.

I wave. "Hey."

Despite the world being flat and upside down and spinning off its axis, Charlotte looks like a supermodel, with an off-the-shoulder blue blouse and skinny jeans, perfectly slashed.

"You've met Anton," Charlotte whispers as if none of us has perfect hearing.

I turn my head, staring at him with no regard for niceties. "He tried to power-strangle me, and I threw a knife at him. So yeah, we're acquainted."

Charlotte twists her neck to look at Anton. "I don't know what your mama has told you, but we do *not* attack each other.

I don't care who you are and what you know, understand?"
Charlotte has the are-you-out-of-your-mind mama tone down
pat. Paris should take notes.

Anton stands. He isn't as tall as Khamari, but he clears six
feet. Longish, dark brown hair falls just below his strong, angular
jaw. Probably hard to punch it without breaking a few fingers or
a hand. Something tells me I'll try to break that iron jaw sooner
rather than later.

The spawn of Satan tilts his head, a bored look in his eyes,
which I notice are striking: one eye blue as his mama's, the other
a hazel green.

He looks down his perfectly symmetrical nose at me and then
at Paris. "She's the warrior with potential?"

I cross my arms. "*She* has a name."

"Very well." He bows to me, as if to introduce himself. "Anton
Orléans."

"Orléans, huh?" I swing my attention back to Paris. "I finally
know your last name."

She clears her throat. "That's not my name."

Anton clears his throat, too.

Must be genetic.

His weird eyes zero on mine. "Perhaps we can make each
other's acquaintances?"

I raise a halting hand. "Maybe later. Right now, I need
answers, and your mama has them."

"Actually, Texas," Paris' smooth voice cuts in. "Anton can
provide answers to your questions. He's an expert in Egyptology
and has taken a particular interest in studying his father." She
sounds like a beleaguered baby mama. "Besides that, Charlotte
and I have a few things to wrap up."

I turn to face the *GQ* half-breed. "Then lead the way, Prodigal
Son."

. . .

We walk down below to the War Room. It's safe and soundproof, making it the perfect location to dish the dirt. Like last time, the temperature is alarmingly cold down below—and with no one here but us, the echo of our footsteps booms and clacks against the stone floor.

We settle in seats across from each other with the glass round table between us. Anton folds his ivory hands into a steeple under his chin. His stance relaxes, but his body exudes power. More power than Paris—hell, more than Old Man Richmond in his heyday.

More power than me.

I want to test the extent of his strength. In the Slayer Society, we have ranks, and we don't have to guess. "How long have you known?" I ask.

He tilts his head and raises an eyebrow. "Known…what?" he asks in a European accent—British, I think. It's smooth, deep, and slightly arrogant. The arrogance isn't a European thing, it's an asshole thing, and he wears it like a too-old-for-the-club guy who drowned himself in cologne.

"How long have you known that Alexander was your father? You seem pretty calm, given your father is evil incarnate."

"I've always known I'm unique. As a child, I discovered I could do…things." He flicks open his hands, exposing a ball of white light.

I twirl a finger in the air. I've seen better. "Neat trick." I open my palm, clap my hands, and release a flat disc made of light and the size of a card deck. "But I'd expect more from the son of the first vampire and a Maestro slayer."

He looks at me and raises his golden brow again. Clearly, he's not impressed with my display of power. I smother a snort and move my hands apart, forming a large round ball of light, slightly bigger than his. I lower my hand and point my finger, as if I'm cocking a gun. I aim straight at his chest. The current briefly disappears, then pulses forward in a bright flash. I hit the mark. He flies from his seat to the other side of the room.

"That's for trying me back in Paris' office."

Anton stands, patting his chest as smoke rises from his singed shirt. He looks up, a smirk on his face. I didn't take him for a smirker.

He points up above my head. Before I can tilt my head upward, a bright light expands, jarring my vision. My eyes water from the sensation, like they've done many times from the football stadium lights during my marching band performances. The brightness explodes into a sphere of white-hot energy, launching me backward.

What just happened?

Did he somehow place that ball of light above me before I hit him? Is that why that asshole was smirking?

Remembering Cali's training, I imagine a fortress and form an invisible barrier—not that it's doing much good. I can still feel the heat. The rays are hot and hard, the force so strong it pushes back my shield. I struggle to keep my feet planted.

He doesn't let up. Shards of glass explode around us as the heat splinters the table in half.

Shit. I'm not paying for that. Or cleaning it up.

Don't clean it—use it. I see, or rather, *know* the symbols for the formula. In a single, swift motion, I lift my leg and then stomp the ground with as much force as I can manage. The glass shards launch into the air as I clap my hands together. Silver-gold energy darts around the room as I reconstruct the glass in front of me into a makeshift shield. It helps with the light, but the heat is still unbearable.

"Good response. I give it a B-minus," Anton calmly replies

as I widen the shield's radius. "As you probably guessed, this allows me to project light—very hot light, if your sweat stains are anything to go by. The glow burns any vampire in sight. Extended exposure will kill them."

Kill vampires? Hell, this light could kill anything. Including me.

How can I fight it? Buckets of sweat drench my body, gluing my shirt and pants to my skin. Shoulders tight and stomach tense, I dig deep, determined to hold him off. But damn, he's relentless. He wants to teach me a lesson. He chuckles like I'm here for his entertainment.

I've heard that heartless and cruel laughter before—the same laugh as Ethan, the vampire who attacked me and my friends.

His face misshapen by rows of teeth too large to fit his mouth.

Another flashback. Stop, dammit! Don't go back.

My skin prickles and turns to ice. The darkness comes—edges my vision, pushing through my skin and oozing through my pores. The dark shape that now surrounds me becomes solid, enveloping the entire room.

"Kill," I command. The army of darkness shoots toward Anton, cutting through his light.

The white brilliance surrounding Anton vanishes, replaced by darkness.

But I can see him—his confusion, his anger, his *fear.* The darkness likes his fear.

"What the—" He extends his fangs until he pricks his bottom lip and releases a drop of blood. Placing his hands together in prayer position, he blasts light in all directions—except for a sliver that outlines my body. It feels like the heat of a million suns.

Energy zaps my body, jolting me back to the present. Something foreign skitters across my skin. A warning that sends a shudder down to my bones.

"How did you do that?" Anton demands with a scowl I suspect

is his resting bastard face.

"D-do what?"

"Swallow my light? Rob me of my senses?" He looks at me strangely. "This can't be happening again," he mutters, more to himself than to me.

Again? Even *I* don't understand what this is. But nothing good comes from letting the darkness in me loose. "I transmuted the dark energy and absorbed the light. And...you said not again? Have you seen this before?"

"You didn't transmute energy. You *became* the energy source. An unstable one at that." His curious eyes drill a hole into mine. "And yes, I've seen this before. Not to the level you've exuded." Anton looks troubled, like he doesn't know how to process the information. Like he's gonna snitch or tell the Society to terminate me.

"You've seen what, exactly?" I clarify.

"When one becomes the energy source by manifesting dark emotions. I've seen it twice. Both cases happened eons ago."

"What happened? Are the slayers still alive?"

"One died fairly young."

I flinch, then immediately cover up my reaction with a shrug, pretending to not be bothered by the prognosis. "One could say death is freedom."

"She died because I killed her. Because she was unable to control herself. She became a danger to herself and to others."

Heat rays zigzag across my body. "I'm in control."

"Hmm. The other slayer still lives. She's an old lady."

"Good." The stiffness in my neck relaxes. But still, he can't be trusted. "You aren't going to demand my head or try to burn me on a cross, are you?"

"It can be used to your advantage, once controlled." He stares at me, and suddenly his eyes clear. He smooths the errant curl that dared to touch his aristocratic nose and straightens his half-burned tie. "Shall we continue?" He waves toward the broken table.

A bead of sweat rolls down my nose. I wipe it off with the back of my hand and with the other, pull out a chair. "Certainly." My tone matches his formality.

He waits for me to sit before he continues. "When Mother discovered my powers, she realized the drifter was a vampire. For quite some time, we never knew my true origins. But…" He leans back, palms now on the table. "I've always known the vampires were up to something. I followed the trails, found other half-breeds—most are weak; a few, powerful. None, however, who were more powerful than me. I could narrow my lineage down to that of a Royal. I've studied all around the world under various cells for the Order, the Society—"

"How?"

He raises an eyebrow. "I've not revealed my lineage until now. I'm a half-slayer, too. My mother and I thought it would be best that we not…advertise our relationship. There would be too many questions and therefore too many lies. But now it's time for the truth to come to light."

Okay, I can get down with them keeping it on the low, but he could've still fought with us without revealing his background. "You and Paris didn't have to reveal your relationship for you to help the Society. You could've—"

"There is no right or wrong. Black or white. I've met evil humans and vampires and other supernatural creatures. And I've met what you deem to be *good* humans and vampires and creatures."

I shake my head. "There is a wrong side, and it's pretty clear. Vampires violated your mother."

"The Alchemist Order betrayed the Society. Your number one slayer put his desire to keep the Philosopher's Stone over his duty to protect humanity."

"Vampires slaughter innocent families and children and—"

"As do humans."

I cross my arms. "You're just sitting here, a lump on the sidelines, while vampires try to destroy us."

"I seek the truth. I yearn for peace." His tone is even, his eyes the picture of serenity.

"We don't need scholars—we need warriors."

"We need both. Alexander was both." He sighs. "And apparently I am my father's son."

"The vampires are coming for the stone, if they don't already have it. Coming for Alexander, *wherever* his remains are." I massage my temples. "I still don't understand how this all works. If he's dead, how can they bring him back?"

"I can answer that."

"Please do."

"Very well." He nods. "After his turning, Alexander renounced his belief in the Greek gods for Egyptian gods. And for that reason, we could bind his spirit."

"How?"

"In Ancient Egyptian culture, if one desires to ensure a spirit is lost, you can achieve this by several means. You scratch out the cartouche—that's his name inscribed in temples and tombs and the sarcophagus. You do this because if his name is erased, his spirit cannot find his body. Inside the sarcophagus, or what you know as a casket, is the resurrection door, where his spirit can enter."

"There's a door on a casket? Like a door on a door?"

"More like a spiritual door on a physical door."

"All right, that kind of makes sense. So Alexander can't find his door, I'm guessing."

"Precisely. The alchemists destroyed the resurrection door. They sent him to the plane of the afterlife. And now he is set to complete the Hall of Truth, where he must go through several trials to prove himself worthy of having a good afterlife. If we're lucky, he failed and his spirit is already destroyed."

"That's when they weigh his heart, right? Light as a feather is good. Heavy is bad."

He lifts his eyebrows, his eyes brighten a fraction, and his lips sort of curve up into what some would call a smile. "Right. Looks like you know a little about this."

"I've done some research, but I'm still confused. I mean, does the underworld really exist?"

"It does. Where exactly he is within the underworld remains unknown. I believe Alexander will find a way out. And when he does, we must be ready."

"Stay ready so you don't have to get ready." I nod. "So, what's the next move?"

"Mother tells me there's this Prince Khamari who will be in touch with you soon? You two are to work together."

"Yes, uh, he'll be in touch." I try not to blush.

"Until then, we protect our half of the stone. And also, I'd like to train you."

"Train me?" I snort. "Pass."

"I can help you control it."

"Yeah. Like ol' girl you killed? No, thanks."

"Does Mother know about your predicament?"

"Yes." *No.*

"Fine. I'll talk to her about what happened to Ji and why I had to kill her. I'm sure she'll understand she has another unstable slayer among everything else that's going on."

"You're a jerk, you know that?" There's heat in my words, but I'm too drained to do much of anything.

He flicks his wrist. "I've been called much worse."

I don't have it in me to spar with him. He gave me a decent solution, and as much as I know I need help, I still don't trust him. "And you think Mommy will let you play with me?"

"Yes."

I stand and move toward the stairwell. "We have other things to do. Moles to find. Vampire cells to destroy."

"Which is part of the reason I'm here. Everyone and everything leaves behind a signature. I can track the traitor and the Philosopher's Stone by tracking its energy. Mother told me the stone leaves a black mark?"

"Yes. On the vampire's hand and on Rich's. I'm not sure how it'll show on a human's hand."

He nods thoughtfully, rubbing his bottom lip, but doesn't say anymore. He stays silent all through our walk back to Paris' office. The commander left, but Dakota is there and hands us a sealed note.

"Ms. Paris asked that I give this to you." The white envelope has beige fingerprints on it.

I glance at Dakota and her now heavily made-up face. Black kohl sloppily lines her eyes. She smeared green eyeshadow on her eyelids. "S-sorry," she stutters, tossing a side glance to Anton.

I look at her and sigh. Does she even know he's an evil seed? I rip open the envelope and read the message. *Call Prince Khamari.*

Right. Khamari doesn't know about Paris' baby's daddy. God, this is getting messy.

"Gotta go, love child." I wave off Anton and rush back to my room. I don't actually have Khamari's number. I scroll through my dismal list of contacts to text Charlotte, but before I get to the letter C, I see a contact name that stops my scrolling: *Boyfriend.*

"Boyfriend?" I screech.

My thumb hovers over the call button. "No…" I shake my head and instead click the text icon.

Me: Who is this?

Seconds later, my "boyfriend" responds.

Boyfriend: Oh. You finally saw it. I'm your man.

Me: Who? I don't have a man.

Boyfriend: Your first and only love.

Me: Deon Smith? Long time no hear! Are you still fine as hell?

I laugh when the phone rings.

"Who the hell is Deon?" Khamari demands.

"My first love. Broke my heart when he moved to Denver with his parents at the end of freshman year."

"Bet he had a big head."

"Not as big as yours." I laugh at him.

"You know how to kill my ego."

"Whatever. You know you're good-looking. Big head and all. But anyway, I'm not here to stroke your ego. We've got some new developments."

"More? You spoke to Paris about the museum?"

"Oh yeah. That's where the new developments came from."

"All right. Let's meet up," he says.

"I can just tell you over the phone."

"Too many ears. Too many enemies. We need to meet somewhere else. Somewhere discreet and in daylight. Are you available in the next hour or so?"

I glance at my phone. "It's three p.m. Yeah. I know of a good place that's low-key. Not too crowded this time of day. I'll send you the coordinates. Meet you at four thirty."

"It's a date."

"No, it's not."

"Sure, it is. And since it's our first date, let's go somewhere nice. Discreet but romantic."

"It's not our first date. Because we aren't technically together," I say a little too forcefully.

"True…" He sighs into the phone. "Just trying to keep it light. We can at least be friends, right?"

"Friends trust each other. I don't trust you."

"What do I have to do to convince you to trust me?"

"Tell me the truth. Why'd you rush off the next morning after you were stabbed with silver? Or, I don't know, how are you connected to Dr. Winters?"

Another ragged breath rattles the receiver.

"Right. See you soon." I hang up before he can argue. "Secretive bastard." I stomp to my drawers and select my usual attire for fall in the South: a fitted black tank top, black yoga pants, and a light pullover jacket. Black, of course.

"How does he expect us to be…" I struggle for the right word. "Boyfriend" sounds too juvenile for who we are. For how I feel. "*Anything* if he can't be honest?"

I yank the tank top over my head. The only thing I know is that he's the leader of a murderous clan. A few, if not all of them, are plotting humanity's demise.

"Bet I could get them to talk," I mutter aloud as I pull on my yoga pants. "If only I knew where he lived."

A brilliant thought pops into my head, and I can't keep from grinning. "I'm gonna track his ass."

I have the perfect way to commemorate our "first date."

28

The Whole Truth and Nothing but the Truth
Texas

Right on time, I pull my car into the parking lot of our meeting spot.

Khamari stands outside, decked out in his signature navy-blue three-piece suit and white shirt, but instead of a navy-blue tie, it's pink this time.

"A little overdressed, huh?"

"If you had told me we were meeting at the Waffle House" — he waves his hand toward the gold sign — "I would've dressed appropriately."

I tug his tie and pull him toward the restaurant. "C'mon, Mr. Fancy Pants."

He pushes the door open for us. As I suspect, there aren't many people here. A beefy guy in a trucker hat, a guy our age, two servers, and a cook.

"Let's sit in the back."

"Near the bathroom?" His tone is scandalized.

"Afraid of a few germs, Pretty Boy? I'm sure you get your fair share when you plug your fangs into randoms." I take off my jacket and then slide into the booth seat facing the door.

Khamari slides in beside me, and his hip bumps against mine.

"What are you doing? Go over there." I point to the empty seat across from us.

"I never sit with my back facing the door."

"Neither do I."

"Then sitting beside you is the perfect solution."

A server with a visor and collared shirt places a menu on the table. "Hey, babies. Let me know when you're ready to order."

"Sure will." I smile, and the server walks off.

Khamari sighs. "What's good here?" he asks me.

"Everything. Can't go wrong unless you're craving something with a little more hemoglobin in it."

"I can eat table food."

"Table food?" I cackle.

"You know what I mean. Help me."

"Well...the waffles are bomb."

"What else?" He leans closer. His stubble scrapes my bare shoulder.

"Hmm...hash browns are g-good. You can add just about any topping. And my favorite is the Texas cheesesteak."

He pulls my tendril. I slap his hand away, but with little effort. "I think I'll go with the waffle," he says. "And I've got a taste for Texas."

"Cheesesteak," I finish for him.

"That's what I said."

I clear my throat. "Excellent choice."

The server returns and takes our orders. Khamari somehow scoots even closer in the tight booth before she delivers a cup of coffee and tea.

He leans closer and whispers, "Pass me the sugar, will you?"

"Scoot over." I plop a few packets in front of him and then nudge him with my shoulder.

He lifts the steamy mug to his mouth. "At least you didn't punch me."

This game of physical chicken isn't working for me. "I need to get up."

Khamari stands, and I slide out of the booth, settling in front of him on the opposite side. If anyone tries to assassinate me, I'll have to depend on Khamari to warn me.

My pulse rages like a wild river. I take a deep breath to calm the swooshing sound rushing through my ears.

Khamari gives me a cat-that-ate-the-canary smile—total satisfaction from the rise he's getting out of me. No, sitting across from him is just making things worse. Now I can see pure hunger in his predatory gaze.

What happened to just getting to know each other?

I massage my neck and focus on the jukebox. "Once she returns with our food, we'll talk. I don't want any interruptions."

"I've thought about what you said. About building trust. I agree with you."

My eyes snap back to meet his. "You do?"

He nods only once. "I have an idea for a game."

"This isn't a game. I'm a…" I lean forward, lowering my voice. "A slayer. You're prince of the underworld."

He simply leans back, looking unconvinced and unmoved by my declaration.

"Being together or friends or…whatever would be unnatural."

"Unusual, yes. But for you and me, there is nothing unnatural." His voice is low and intense.

We stare at each other. He's got that special glow in his eyes, and I can tell he wants this—he wants us. And to be honest with myself, so do I.

"Play the game with me, Queen."

"Queen? Is that a pet name?"

"Just your name."

"Oh, right because you'll be king."

"Something like that."

When our food arrives, I dig in, not saying a word. Occasionally, I glance up to find Khamari's eyes on me. His mouth is a work of art as he devours the sandwich. The look in his eyes broadcasts a clear message: *this could be you.*

"What's the name of the game?" I hear myself whisper.

"Two truths and a lie. You tell me two things that are facts. You tell me one thing that's a lie. But let's make it interesting. The other person gets to choose the subject. But you can't ask which is true or false. No follow-up questions. Deal?"

I nod. I like the idea of the game. I can ask Khamari my burning questions, and baked somewhere in his answers will be the truth. Even better, I'm an ace at lying. Something that used to piss Grandma Lou off to no end.

"We'll play after you give me the update."

And so I do—about Anton, Alexander, and how our theory about his resurrection is likely true.

He slouches back in his seat, a stunned look on his face. "When it rains, it pours."

"How bad is it at casa de Ankh? I mean…how many of your clansmen hate you?"

"Not hate—they just don't trust my vision. The younger ones get it. The Elders don't, but they'll still support me. It's the ones in the middle, not too young and not too old, that I'm not so sure of."

"How old are we talking, the ones in the middle?"

"Between mid-two to three hundred."

"As in years old?"

"Yep."

"So, Alexander turned them, but they had little time with him before he was killed?"

He shakes his head. "Right. Some are Made."

"I think it's the old heads you have to worry about. The ones who have more history with Alexander."

His face blanks. "No. Impossible. Like I said, the Elders support me."

"Is your grandfather an Elder? Did you figure out if he cut that fundraising check?"

"Yes, he's an Elder. He knows about my plans to be less reliant on blood and build our portfolio so we can maintain our lifestyle. He agrees with me and wants me to be his successor. He'd never betray me." His eyes go all dark.

Oh. So the subject of his grandfather strikes a nerve. "Know what else is fishy? Your grandfather just decided to help after your attack, huh? And then suddenly, you go from human to half-breed. You know there's some shady shit going on with half—"

"If you have any more questions, we can play our game." His voice is cool.

"Fine." I squint my eyes. "Tell me three things you've done after you were turned that you aren't proud of."

"*That's* what you want to know about me?"

"Yes."

"So, you want more ammo? Another excuse to hate me and my kind?"

"No. I want to know you. All of you."

"One: I became a henchman for my clan. I killed enemies seen and unseen. Mostly vampires. A few humans." His cold eyes freeze me in place.

He resents me for asking, but I need to know who I'm working with.

"Two. I targeted criminals in major cities to control the crime in the area, killed them, and drank their blood because I didn't know how to control my bloodlust."

"And three. I told my ex-girlfriend that I'm a vampire, and she rejected me."

What?

"You told her?"

"Two truths and a lie. Think about all three statements. Which one is likely false?"

He was a henchman, a Rogue who killed humans, or he told his little girlfriend that he sucks blood. A triple whammy, and I don't like any of the options.

The girlfriend rejecting him—I betcha he wants me to feel sorry for him. Still, I don't like that he chose that as his lie.

He wants to get a rise out of me.

"Your turn." I wave at him to get on with it.

"What are some unhealthy ways you've coped with being a slayer?"

Easy. "One: I've dedicated every waking hour to honing my skills so I can kill vampires, because I hate them. It gives me great pleasure to dole out justice."

He smiles at me. "Truth."

I continue. "I have nightmares about what happened."

"I know that already."

"You should've been clearer on the instructions." I shrug. "Three. A few times…when I've gone out to kill, this darkness takes over me and I lose control."

"Lie. You never lose control."

I clear my throat. *Sure, I don't.*

"Your turn. Tell me how you're connected to Dr. Karen Winters."

He adjusts in his seat. His eyes aren't hard this time—he had to know I would ask. "One. She dated Rider. Likely, she used him for intel. He caught wind of it and killed her." His voice is smooth, with no uptick in his tone. His eyes are steady and calm.

Liar.

"Next one. Should be the truth this time." I smirk.

"Two. I leveraged Dr. Winters' expertise to synthesize blood."

"But how did she—?"

"No follow-up questions," he cuts me off. "Number three: I have a sick clansman who is dying of a rare disease. I needed her help to find a cure."

I nod. The last two sounded feasible, since she studied epidemiology.

"Last set of questions," Khamari announces. "Do you have

any suspects for the mole in your organization?"

I scrunch my nose, a little disappointed by his impersonal question.

"Could be anyone." I prop my chin against my fist. "I honestly don't know."

"You're smart. I know you have suspects and your theories."

"Fine…" I blow out a breath and look at the ceiling. "Bitch Rich, our Maximus. Maybe he got tired of hunting vampires down. Maybe he did something to permanently screw up the balance."

"Hmmm…maybe. I've met the guy a few times. Arrogant, but I don't get 'evil mastermind' from him." Khamari drinks from his coffee mug and eyes me over the rim.

"Yeah. True. Like I said, no idea who it is. Ready for my next guess?"

He waves a hand for me to continue.

"Paris."

He chokes on the coffee. "What?"

"She had sexy times with Alexander. Gave birth to his spawn. Maybe she fell in love and figured out the stone is the only way to resurrect him." I cut into my waffle and watch the syrup ooze to the side of the plate. "Stranger things have happened."

"Like Spike and Buffy."

"You've been watching *Buffy*?"

He looks away, sipping more coffee. "A few episodes. You said you liked it, so…" He returns his gaze to mine. His eyes are a little darker now. "Last guess?"

"Dieter is my number one guess. He's a Magister in the Alchemist Order. I don't think he directly stole the stone, but he had something to do with it."

"He's the guy that was Dr. Winters' former mentor, right?"

I level a stare at him. "How do you know?"

"Rose."

"Then why are you asking me when you know the answer?"

"I trust your gut. You've got good instincts."

His expression is serious. I look back down to my waffle. "You don't know me well enough to say that."

"Maybe," he admits. "Bonus round?"

"I'm out of questions, but go ahead," I invite.

"How do you feel about me?"

Goddammit. I hate this game.

I grab my tea and swallow. The liquid scalds my throat. Serves me right for getting sucked into this game. "One: I have…strong feelings toward you. Sometimes you intrigue me. Sometimes I wish I could have feelings for a regular dude."

He clenches his jaw. He doesn't like my answer. Well, too damn bad, because it's the truth.

"Two. You're on my mind. A lot. Sometimes good and sometimes bad things."

He looks away. "You already said that. Next." He sounds defeated.

I grip the mug in my hand and lick my lips, debating if I should share another truth. "Three: Sometimes…" I look down at the table. "The good stuff is that I think about how you feel. I want to kiss you again. And sometimes I pretend that we're normal people who met in school. The guy who plays football, the girl who plays in the band."

He sucks in a breath, and his eyes…his eyes are so intense, so emotional, I know he can imagine a reality where I'm just a girl and he's just a boy next door.

My eyes rake over him. Never mind. Nothing about him screams "boy next door."

I clear my throat. "Which one is the lie?" I arch my eyebrow. None were lies. Everything I said, I meant. I'm terrible at this game.

He leans over, his hand cupping my face. "Fuck fate." His lips own mine in an impossibly passionate kiss. I return his kiss, no longer holding back. Besides, holding back my feelings is like holding back a tidal wave with a picket fence.

Someone clears their throat. We break apart, just inches from each other.

"Check." The server slides the bill between us with a sly smile. "You can pay up front."

He grips my neck. "Come with me. Be with me."

Be with me? What does that even mean?

"Just one night," he murmurs. "I know we can't... I know there's much more important shit going down right now. But if we can just get each other out of our systems, maybe we can focus."

I lower my head and stare at the off-white table. No feelings, just fun. I'd done that before with Cam, and it hadn't ended well. Because eventually, someone wants more.

I lift my head, stare at him. Last time, it was Cam who wanted more, but from the way my pulse throbs, my heart 808 booming in my chest, I know I may be the one left with hurt feelings.

He bites his lip. I can tell he's holding his breath, waiting for my answer, and wanting it to be yes.

I want the yes, too. I want many more nights, but the one will have to do...for now.

I nod. "There's a Hilton Garden Inn right off the highway. Follow me."

He grabs my hand, tosses three twenties on the table, and yells at someone to keep the change.

When we step outside, I reach for my car door handle. He pulls me away before I can open the door, kissing me senseless.

"Just up the road?" he growls.

I lick my lips, nodding.

"Hurry," he commands.

I hurry.

Pinkie Promises
Texas

We drive just two exits south like we're in a high-speed car chase. We swerve into the hotel's garage, near the valet stand. Khamari is next in line for the valet. Instead of waiting, he parks, hops out of his car, and tosses the keys to the harried valet. Before I can pull into a space, he opens my door and shifts my car into park. He unbuckles my seat belt and tosses my keys to the scared guy behind him.

"Khamari. Calm down."

He growls. Since it seems like his animal side is taking over, I give the front desk the alias the Society provided me, Rachel, handing over my fake driver's license.

"Hi, Janice." I glance at the agent's name tag. "Do you have a room available?"

"Hm." Janice types on the keyboard "We've got a double queen."

"One bed," Khamari snaps.

"Oh, um…yes, sir." Janice clicks and clacks on the keyboard.

I'm not prone to embarrassment, but my cheeks are blazing. I squeeze his hand—a hand I just now realize I'm holding. He squeezes back. Not hard but firm.

"Looks like we have a cancelation. Here are your keys, room 235." She hands me a card. "Check out is at eleven a.m. and—"

We don't hear the rest of poor Janice's speech. We jog to the elevator. Khamari pulls open a closing door, startling another guest and her yappy dog. In ten seconds flat, we arrive on the second floor.

My fingers are shaking. Khamari's hand covers mine, and this time, his hands are warm. Together, we tap the card on the key fob. For a second, we just stand in front of the door. Taking in the room, the forbidden moment.

Khamari growls, tugs my hand, and we fumble inside. He pushes me against the wall.

But then he goes still, his eyes transfixed on my body. Though the lights are off, I see the determined glimmer in his eyes.

"Ready?" I ask.

He nods, but he doesn't move an inch. I quickly take off my clothes.

"You're still dressed?"

He nods once. Otherwise, he's still as a statue. I slide his pants down, then his boxer briefs, from his waist down to his feet.

His chest heaves, his stormy eyes glued on me. I reach out and touch him. From his low groan, I know he loves it.

"Raven." My name seems to be ripped from his lips, from the depths of his soul. I'm dizzy, tipsy with the power I wield over this royal vampire. My fingers trace his lips, and I'm pricked by his sharp, lengthening teeth. A small pearl of red bubbles on my finger.

I hiss, but not from the pain—from the heat of it all. "Khamari, you better not…"

His blazing golden-brown eyes are focused on my face, not on my blood, not even on my chest. I swallow hard like I'm choking down cinnamon.

"My Raven," he whispers with reverence. Then, at hurricane speed, he steps back, scoops me up from my knees, and swiftly enters me. My back slams against the wall, scraping against the textured wallpaper. His nails dig into my waist, the pain adding to my pleasure.

He pulls back and rocks into me again. A framed picture drops to the floor, the sound swallowed by the plush carpet.

He stands there, his cheek against mine. His warm breath tickles my neck. An electric current binds us together. Not fluid, but a link. Flexible, yet fragile.

"You feel it, don't you?" he whispers against my ear.

My throat closes. I don't know what the *it* is—destiny or trouble.

Probably trouble. The frenzied energy clears, and he walks us to the bed, pulls back the covers, and hovers over me.

We stare at each other. My heart leapfrogs into my throat. His fangs slowly descend. "Khamari, n-no."

"I'll make you ache," he says, kissing my neck. "But I won't hurt you. I'll *never* hurt you. Understand?"

I nod, my eyes squeezed shut as a tidal wave hits.

"You feel it?" he asks again, this time with more urgency.

"Yesssss."

He slides inside of me again. My eyes fly open, back bowing up from the bed. I want to touch him, to grip him, to go toe-to-toe, but I am helpless. Bound. Trapped.

A large tsunami builds inside of me. Everything feels so big— this moment, my emotions. Everything about him feels secure and amazing and absolutely right.

How could that be? How could I feel good being with a monster? But staring into his eyes, I know he isn't some mindless, uncaring villain. He strokes my cheek, whispering words that I'm too far gone to decipher. But what I notice is the way he looks at me—like I'm apple pie *and* the à la mode and he wants to devour me.

I wrap my legs around him tighter. I don't care how, but I want to meld myself to him. "Mari. I feel like I'm falling," I breathe.

"I'm Mari now?" he asks roughly, though from his eyes, he's pleased.

I don't answer him. I can't. I'm still melding, still in need of him.

He jerks down his chin, veins bulging from his neck. "We don't fall. We fly."

He shows me just how. Picking up the pace, we soar to the finish. Our desire catapults us warm and wild, cresting and crashing over me.

He pulls me close. Our skin, once heated, is now cool from our sweat.

"Stay with me." His demands are less urgent, now, but still earnest.

We don't fall asleep; instead, we talk all night. We don't hide behind two truths and a lie when we share our pain this time.

"Can I ask you something?" Khamari whispers beside me.

"Shoot."

"Why do you fight?"

I exhale in the darkness. "I don't know if you've noticed, but we're not given much of a choice."

"If you packed your bags and left the Society, would they stop you?"

"No. Probably monitor me for the rest of my life and blank my memory, but they'd let me go, I guess."

"Then why do you stay?"

"I genuinely want to kill vampires."

"Raven." He sighs. "It's just me and you. Your secrets are safe with me."

"Vault?" I ask him.

He smiles. "You don't even have to ask."

"That night..." I squeeze my eyes shut to brace myself. "I have nightmares, but sometimes I have dreams. Good ones, where Deidra and I get to grow up and complain about our bad-ass kids. I dream about becoming a composer and band teacher." Tears fill my eyes and force them open.

"Queen, I'm—"

"It's fine. I'm fine." I cut him off and rush on. "Anyway, all of that is to say, I don't want anyone to feel what I feel. I don't want the world to know what goes bump in the night. I want people like Grandma Lou to think the worst things out there are human criminals. I want people to live their lives in ignorant bliss. As much as people think I'm cynical, I don't want others to share in my misery."

"You think ignorance is bliss?"

"In this case, hell yes." I narrow my eyes. "Why are you helping the Society?"

He's quiet for a long time. So long, I check to make sure he's still awake. "Tell me."

"Maybe I'm trying to buy my way out of hell."

"What do you mean?"

"Sometimes I worry that whenever I die—and as much as vampires think we're immortal, one day we'll all die—Heaven's gates will close in my face. And you'll be on the other side."

I snort. "I'll probably be on the same side as you."

Khamari tosses the blanket off and sits on the edge of the bed.

"You don't think that... God, you can't be serious? You think you're going to Hell?"

"I am a monster."

Even I haven't thought much of my destination. Yes, I know God exists, and I'm all too aware that Hell is real. I figured all the lives I'll save would be my ticket in. But will that be enough?

And here sits Khamari, his chin on his fist, looking as if the weight of the world sits on his shoulders.

I thought all vampires are mindless killers, but this guy in front of me cares. "Not that my opinion means much, but I'd say you have a good shot."

"You think so?"

"I do." I wrap the blanket around us, hugging him from behind. "Tell you what. If I happen to be on the other side of the gate, I'll sneak you in." I put up my pinkie finger and lift it in front of his face.

"You…" He laughs a bit. "You still pinkie swear?"

"Not in a long time." I wiggle my pinkie. "Now take it."

He hooks his finger around mine.

"It's a promise. I'm sure God or The Architect honors pinkie swears." He'd better. He owes me.

Sometime around dawn, we fall asleep, warm in each other's arms. Sunlight streams from the window. I wake up to a piece of paper wedged underneath my nose.

Morning Queen,

You were snoring so loudly, I ~~was afraid~~ didn't want to wake you. Duty calls, and I have business to handle. You've got my number. Squeeze me in. If not, I'll be in your dreams.

Always,

Your Mari

P.S. Dreamwalking would be much easier if you gave me a little blood. I promise it won't hurt.

I roll my eyes. "Still not happening." Last night, he'd tried to convince me to give him blood after I told him how tired and woozy I'd been after he'd walked my dreams the other night. After five minutes of hearing his pleas, I snapped and told him I wasn't the American Red Cross.

I return my attention to the letter.

P.P.S. I wasn't snooping or anything, but I found the box on the floor and found the cufflinks with my initials. Pretty nice for a first date. I'll bring you a gift next time.

The cufflinks have a tracking device inside of them. I'd planned on gifting them to him before…before everything.

Unease pools in my stomach. Am I being dishonest? Sneaky? I know I'd be pissed if he put a tracking device on me.

"I won't use it unless I have to," I vow out loud. Only if he or his cronies cross the line.

I shower for a long time, taking care of the deep aches that even my accelerated healing hasn't fixed yet. Hard to do when we were at it all night.

I smile as I soap my body. I want him again and for more than a night. And heck, both of us are kind of immortal. We might never have normal lives, a normal love, but we might as well take advantage of living forever once we find the stone and restore order.

They Smile in Your Face
Khamari

"Khamari." Something pokes my face. "Wake up, dude."
I smash whatever smacks my face as my eyes fly open.

"See, that's why I didn't touch you." Khaven pulls back his dented EZ Reach stick. "You just got home. How are you sleeping so hard?"

Flashes of warm, silky skin flood my memory. We talked; we made love. There was no time and no desire for sleep. But after I returned to the compound, I found my eyes drooping, and instead of getting ahead in my research, I crashed.

Khaven scoots closer to my bed, keeping his voice low. "Remember when you asked me to keep my eyes and ears open?"

"You don't have to be quiet, Khaven. It's daytime."

He shakes his head and pulls out a gadget from what I call his spy bag.

It looks like one of those old GPS devices, but instead of easy-to-read directions, there are blue and green lines on the monitor.

He depresses a button. I don't hear anything at first. Then, after a few seconds, I hear static, like a white noise.

Khaven takes a deep breath. "Inaudible white noise—well, inaudible to humans. But it's jamming any microphones or spyware in your room."

I sit up straight, heat melting my insides. "Someone's spying on me?"

"Yep." Khaven places the jammer by my bedside. "You haven't

had any sensitive conversations here, have you?"

"No, I... Shit. Maybe. Just once." If anyone listened to the conversation I had with Raven yesterday, it probably sounded like flirting.

I reach for my phone on the nightstand. "Can you scan my phone?"

"I've already been doing that, which is what led me to check your room. For the past few days, someone's been trying to hack your phone. I've been pushing them off...but you need new tech. I'm cooking up something for you."

"Fuck. Shit's getting weirder and weirder."

"What do you mean?"

"It's nothing—"

"Little bro," he interrupts, "I think we both know I can handle it. Don't let this chair fool you." He waves a hand over his wheelchair. "I'm stronger than you think."

"I know that."

"Then lay it on me."

"Okay, but just the pertinent information." I toss him the phone I found in Rider's room. And then I give him the highlights of the museum theory around resurrecting Alexander and the potential link to our family.

"You think Julius has something to do with this?" I whisper, despite the security from the white noise.

Khaven nods. "Why do you think I modified his watch? I've been on to that old bastard since I..." He snaps his mouth shut.

"What is it?"

My brother shakes his head. "Nothing proven. Just a conspiracy theory. I haven't found anything concrete yet, because he keeps anything important in his room, but if you're asking if the Ankh king is looking for a way to bring back Alexander by any means necessary? Hell yeah. And it's something tied to the *Book of the Dead*—I'm telling you."

"Yeah, well." I slide to the edge of the bed. "Time for me to recon and figure out who's spying on me."

I'd been so busy trying to get with Raven, my priorities weren't top of mind, and time was not of the essence. *Never is.* "You cover the skies, and I'll do the groundwork."

Khaven pumps his fist. "Hell yes, Robin."

"Robin?"

"Batman's sidekick."

"Nah, man. I'm Batman. You're more like Alfred."

"A frail old guy who serves tea?" Khaven looks at me like I'm gum on his shoes.

"You know what I mean. You're smart. Hold down the fort and keep my sanity."

"Hope you're smoother at complimenting your girlfriend."

Heat creeps up my neck… I cut my thoughts short. Nothing worse than getting a hard-on in front of your brother. I place a pillow on my lap. "I don't have a girlfriend. I told you—I'm too busy right now."

"Yeah, yeah, yeah." He hits reverse on the controller to his scooter. "While you're looking around, I've got a few things you can plant in the offices." Khaven stares at me a bit, as if waiting for me to catch on.

"Sounds good." Only the Elders have offices, but if this person has resources to spy, it's coming from someone with deep pockets. The clansmen with the most money are me and the Elders. "We can't leave a stone unturned."

I follow Khaven to his room. He supplies me with pens and little bugs that'll fit nicely under a desk.

"No pens." I shake my head. "They'll notice something new."

"You're right." He takes all but one back. "Maybe put the pen on your desk? That way, if someone comes into your office, you'll know."

I stuff the pen in my pocket and stash the tech in a bag. "No more talking out loud. I know you have a jammer, but you can never be too careful. If we have new info, I'll use telepathy. And I'll only do that if it's mission critical. I know how it drains you."

"Agreed."

I step out of his room. There are four offices to hit today, and I start with Aldercy, Garin, and Maab. After a few hours, I only find loose papers, old vampire fables, and financial earnings—nothing out of place. The ominous, opaque cloud that hangs over my head lightens. The only space that remains will be the easiest to scratch off my list—my grandfather's room. I'd already searched his office, but as Khaven pointed out earlier, all his important documents are in his room.

Raven suspects him, but she's wrong, and I look forward to proving it. One day, I'll convince her that not all of us are evil.

In a few hours, darkness will descend. For now, the clansmen, along with my royal grandfather, are dead to the world.

As the leader of our clan, I'll have to adopt the nocturnal ways of our vampire culture, but for now, I'll remain awake and alert as I please.

Today, it pleases me. I open Grandfather's door and shut it behind me.

He's sleeping in bed. An old book sits on the edge of the nightstand, next to an empty tumbler that smells of his favorite scotch.

I scan the room. Although it's spacious with a hotel-suite feel, there aren't many places to stuff things. I try the small desk by the blackout curtained window. Opening the drawer, I find nothing but paper clips and a few old pens.

I check the nightstand drawer. Nothing. Completely empty. "Where else?" I ask, thinking through other places. *Suitcase?*

I open the closet and pause at the door. There's a risk that the old man will smell me in his room when he awakens. And if I rifle through his personal things, my scent will linger. I step back, shutting the door.

What am I doing? This is Grandfather—Julius, to his friends, and he has many. He wouldn't betray me. He's patient, understanding. Khaven said as a kid, he played hide-and-seek with us. When it was Grandfather's turn to hide, he always hid under the bed, where we could find him.

Under the bed. My muscles bunch.

As I walk closer to the bed, I double-check to make sure my grandfather is sleeping.

Then, I crouch low and lift the covers.

A long metal box is just out of reach. I lower myself to the floor, crawl under the bed, and pull out the lockbox. A few dust bunnies float in the air. The box has a combination lock, and I roll through the numbers, inputting a date important to both of us—Khaven's birthday.

The lock clicks, and the lid pops open. Inside the box are dozens of papers. I flip through them, stopping on one that has red marks and yellow highlights.

Name: Anton Macedon

Species: Half-Breed

Power: Unknown

Breeder: Slayer

DOB: 9-21-1782

Potential Candidate: Yes

Son of Alexander. Candidate seems to obscure his identity; however, sightings have occurred. Father can sense his presence when he's near but has not been able to reach him. Once contact is established, we may be able to amplify communication.

"What the hell is this?" I whisper to myself, wanting to stop reading but needing to know more. Anton... This is the guy Raven mentioned. She called him Paris' spawn. I put the page aside and flip through more, hoping like hell there aren't other bastard children of Alexander. My heart stops when I see a name. *My* name.

Name: Khamari St. John

Species: Half-Breed

Power: Dreamwalker, Telekinesis, Telepathy (May be able to bend reality like mother)

Breeder: Witch

DOB: 1-23-2003

Potential Candidate: Yes

Candidate displayed no power as a child. Vampire genes activated. Work with Marcy to get blood and DNA samples.

Marcy? Dr. Persing. *My* Marcy? The human I recruited on my own—or so I thought. She's been working with me closely for over a year. I shake my head. He's been playing me since day one. I thought he supported my vision of creating synthetic blood.

Pawns. All of us are pawns. The proud smiles, the pats on the back—he knows my weakness. As much as I show the world my hard edges, all I've ever wanted is family.

He's using me. But for what? A *potential* candidate for some secret project because my mother is a witch, my father a Royal. All this time, I thought my mother was a regular human.

Does Khaven know?

Something big is happening. Something that I know bone-deep I don't want to be a part of. *I need answers.* And I won't wait another minute to get them. I sit in the chair beside Julius' bed, relaxing my muscles, and slip into meditation. I close my eyes and enter a dream state. Pinpricks of energy shoot from my feet to my head, and that energy manifests into light. Power flows through my body. Tiny translucent balls tightly woven together hover in front of me, and then they blast into a brilliant light in an explosion that represents reality breaking apart.

The solid foundation beneath my feet transforms into water. I enter the dream realm. A place where I can create a "new reality." And I, the dreamwalker, will put the pieces back together as I see fit.

I center my breathing and create the setting. I opt for Julius' study and recreate everything from my eidetic memory. The dome ceiling with gold, green, and peach accents. The horrible salmon-and-green-patterned carpet Julius refuses to replace. The white marble fireplace. Above it, an oil painting of Julius and my grandmother, who died well before I was born. Two gold couches flank the fireplace. An extensive library on built-in shelves lines the wall near the door. I add finishing touches and hang a few more pictures on the green wall.

Now I just need Julius. I connect to my grandfather easily. It's just a virtual tap on his brain, but a vampire of his power must allow me in.

"Khamari." Julius looks around the room. "Why are you in my head?"

"I have some private things to discuss. I don't want the others to hear."

"Okay." He waves a hand. "Wish my power was this strong…so much detail." Julius smooths a hand over his slacks. "Telekinesis and telepathy have their uses, but you have those powers *and* you're a dreamwalker. You are so much more," he says with pride. "Everything from taste, sound, and touch feels real."

He looks to his left and notices his favorites—a glass of cognac and his poetry collection by Langston Hughes.

"Drink?" He points to the decanter of scotch on the serving cart.

"Yeah." I grab the empty rocks glass and pour the drink, then take a deep gulp. The brown liquid burns a fiery path down my throat until it numbs.

Bottle still in hand, I refill the glass. "I need to ask you something." I slam down the scotch. The glass clacks against the mirrored surface on the serving cart.

"You don't need liquid courage with me, son." He points toward the armchair opposite him. "What's on your mind?"

"I don't know how to say this, so I'll just shoot it straight. Did you have anything to do with my turning into a vampire?"

The fingertips of his index fingers rest on his mouth. It's a familiar move—one he uses when evaluating a threat.

"That's a bold accusation." He drops the warmth from his voice.

I meet his stare and hold it. "An accusation you haven't answered."

"I've never lied to you, boy—"

"Boy? I haven't been a *boy* in a long time." I lean forward. "Not since my guardian burned cigarette butts on my chest. Not since I was a starving runaway, digging through the trash for scraps. And not since I was caught stealing food and beaten within an inch of my life." I try to wrangle my rage. It's sharp, tearing a bloody path down my throat. I gulp it whole.

The pupils of his brown eyes enlarge to the size of pebbles. "Yes," he hisses. "I did it. I had you turned."

I squeeze my eyes shut. He couldn't have known his words were like a punch to my chest. He couldn't have known his confession left a gaping hole in my heart.

"Why did you do it?" I ask, opening my eyes to…everything. "Why did you allow your grandson, your blood, to grow up that way?"

"Son… I… I knew your childhood was bad. When I received word that you were a street urchin, I arranged for you to be in a home. And yes, I eventually found out about your foster parents'… proclivities. I wanted to kill them and everyone else who hurt you, but I knew what you went through would only strengthen you."

He sighs, lowering his head. "Our world isn't a place for children. It's not a place for half-breeds. Hell, you see how they treat Khaven, and I'm the king. Most of your kind never survive the transition. I had to protect you."

"From whom?"

"From us!" He jumps from his seat. "You know how it is—

politics and power, always a struggle, everyone always grasping for the throne. And your father" — he jabs his finger toward me — "he got us into this mess. He should've done what he was told, but instead he chose to die for that woman. She didn't want you and Khaven with us! She... She seduced him into leaving his family."

"My mother is a witch?"

"A priestess, a mare — nothing more than someone to breed the next generation." He waves as if swatting a gnat.

"And my mother was a candidate for this breeder shit."

Julius narrows his eyes. "I had to get our clan out of that mess your parents caused." He smoothly skips my accusation. "Your father turned his back on us."

I unlock my clenched jaw. "Sounds like he grew a conscience. He saw more to life than power and killing."

"He died a traitor."

"Tell me what really happened to them," I demand.

He looks away but returns to his seat.

"Tell. Me."

He lifts his head to meet my gaze straight on. "When the priestess, your mother, wanted to hide your vampire heritage and have you live as a human, I issued a death warrant for her." He looks away.

A coldness sweeps through my body. I'm not angry. I'm...in pain. A wound leaking and never healing. A bold strike of evil dealt by the hands of my flesh and blood.

Fate or life or God or *something* had done it to me before I even realized — robbed me of the people I love.

"Your father found out and fought against us. Since his betrayal, I've had to shuck and jive to pull together the tatters of our reputation. I've recruited the strong and pruned the weak. Our clan is the strongest in numbers and abilities. As the new king, you're inheriting everything I've built. The keys to the kingdom."

Recruited the strong? He forced me into this life. His words unstick me from the paralyzing shock.

"You dragged me back into a life my parents died for me to escape. And what did you do? Kill your own damn son." My voice garbles as the monster inside me claws to the surface.

"He killed himself!" Spittle dangles from his lips. His fangs jut from his gums, sinking into his bottom lip. "He was the one who decided to change the plans. To run away with a witch. When he made that decision, he was as good as dead."

"You should've protected him." I thump my chest. "Protected Khaven and me."

"And then what? Die along with him?"

Those are the thoughts not of a father but of a selfish man. For the first time, I see him as a monster.

"Don't look at me like that, Khamari."

"Like what? Like I've lost respect? Or is it the look of a man betrayed? Which one do you see?"

"I know it was selfish, but I wanted you to know me. To be a part of our family and to pass on this legacy."

His tone rings just below insincere. "Why all the other half-breeds? Why all the documenting? The secrecy?"

"We need the half-breeds for the Philosopher's Stone."

My stomach drops to the floor at his casual confession. The Philosopher's Stone. The very thing Raven and the others have been chasing. It's been here, with him, all along.

"*You* stole it?"

"Rider brought it to my attention a few months ago. He found a link, which is why we moved to Atlanta. I thought it was a long shot but worth a try. But then...then we discovered something more heinous."

I thought I made the decision to move to Atlanta to save Khaven. How much control have I really had over anything? And what could be more heinous than what my grandfather has done to us?

"What?"

"The slayers lied to us. They never killed Alexander. They never can, and they never will. He's hidden in this very city. We will find him, and we will crush all who lied to us about our father."

"No." I jab my finger at him. "Don't go off half-cocked. I'll schedule a time to meet with Paris and—"

"The time for peace and politics with the humans and their protectors is over. It will happen. Tonight."

The fuck it will. I'll end this dream. Warn Raven. The vampires can't move during daylight. I have time.

"As your future king, I command you to cease this mission. We will not kill or attack based on hearsay. We will follow procedure and—"

"It's too late," he says. "They know."

"They, who?"

"The Elders. The Saqqara and Hekau clans, too. They are on the way to our headquarters, tonight."

"The fuck? How dare you—"

"I dare because I know what you've been doing. Screwing that slayer." Julius' eyes narrow to slits.

"You're the one who's been spying on me?"

"She must go, Khamari. She has her hooks in you, like that priestess did with your father. Did you think I wouldn't put it together? I've watched you for years. You were ready to give up everything you worked to achieve for that girl."

Raven. Cold creeps up my skin.

"Yes. I know you erased her and your friends' memories back when you were in high school. And I know she's back, though I'm guessing she doesn't realize who you are to her. And I wonder what'll happen if she finds out the truth. That you crept into her room—"

"Shut up."

The corner of his mouth tips up to the right like the Joker.

Julius knows he's hit the target, the heart of me—the very thing he'd tried to crush.

"Kissed her goodbye and told her to forget about you."

The room spins around me, getting smaller and darker.

Dark like the night I left my Raven with a bandage wrapped around her forehead. The Percocet on her nightstand hadn't been opened yet—my girl didn't want to dull her senses. She knew something weird had happened the night of our car crash. And every waking moment she asked, "Did you see him? That monster? He's after us."

"I had to leave her. Had to erase her memories. She wasn't safe," I say, trying to convince myself.

"Heh. And now I know she's a slayer. Should've killed her when I had the chance."

He knows my secret, and now Raven's identity is compromised.

"Oh, yes, fate is a bitch sometimes, but I refuse to allow you to make the same mistakes as your father." He keeps talking while I seethe. "And lately, you're always gone, risking everything we've worked for over the same girl. A *slayer* of all things."

"You screwed me over." I slam my fist against the cart, then get a tight grip on my rage before I continue: "I was doing just fine. I was going to play football, marry her one day—"

"And be a sheep. I gave you power."

"You stole my life, but now I'm taking it back. I'm warning the Society. They'll be ready, and our clan's blood will be on your hands."

"Do what you must, but it's already done. My blood is surging. I'm awakening."

He's been keeping me here, stalling me with irrelevant stories. The sun will set soon—I can feel it now. "Fuck you, old man."

"Watch your tongue. You're important to me, so let me give you a fair warning. Whatever happens, do not implicate yourself. As long as you abide by the rules, I will keep quiet about your dalliance."

My body rocks as I open my eyes to end the dream. I look out his window. He's right. The sun dips just below the horizon. I have an hour to warn the Society to get somewhere safe. I open my phone and rush to my room, dialing Raven.

After several rings, the phone goes to a robotic voicemail.

"Call me. Now."

I throw my phone on the bed. She should be at headquarters by now.

"Damn!"

I snatch my phone back up and message Rose Prussakov. Email Charlotte, since I don't have her number.

"Maybe she's sleeping." I rush to my door, lock it, and relax into the dream state.

When I discovered I could dreamwalk, I hated it. It's intrusive, entering someone's private domain. There's so much information to be found. People are softer, more amiable, and open to suggestion when they're sleeping. It's an invasion of privacy, and I feel like a peeping tom. But today, I'm grateful for the power.

I close my eyes, relax my muscles, and steady my breathing, listening for the calm hum that cocoons my body.

"Raven," I whisper as I envision her and slip into her dream.

She lies on a bed. Her arms cover her eyes, as if to ward off the world.

"Raven, it's me."

She blinks and rubs her eyes. "Oh. Hey. Here for another round." She gives me a sleepy smile.

I sit beside her, resting a hand on her thigh, the other on her cheek. "I'm so sorry. We've run out of time."

"Have we?" She looks confused. "The dream just started and—"

"Raven. I'm sorry, Queen, but I've got some things to tell you."

I grab her hand. It's callused and warm—I hope, after tonight,

I can touch her again. "There'll be an attack at the Slayer Society tonight. As soon as the sun sets."

Her eyes shift from soft kitty to killer feline. "Who's coming?"

"I don't know. I…I just found out an Elder betrayed me."

"Saqqara," she whispers. "They can teleport like that." She snaps her fingers. "Get in and out quickly."

"Sounds likely."

"I'll warn the others. Protect the stone."

"It's not just the other half of the stone they want. They think Alexander's remains or body is there."

"That's not possible. He's dead. He's… Oh shit. Right." Her eyes widen. "Tell me more about the attack. How many vamps?"

"I don't know, but prepare for Royals. Either way, you need to evacuate."

"Make no mistake, we'll get the Tyros out of here. But the rest of us will fight." She twists her lips, then says, "Khamari?"

"Yes?"

"You better not be there."

"I don't have the strength. I've dreamwalked twice tonight. Be careful, Queen."

Her eyes turn to slits. "I'm not a queen. I'm a slayer."

Nowhere to Run
Texas

My heartbeat thumps like a bass drum. Blood rushes through my pulse—fast and relentless, overtaking my senses, rattling my bones, rippling my skin.

Am I dying? No, but others will if I don't move it.

My eyes fly open. *Alexander. Attack.*

Memories tumble in my head as I scramble out of bed. My feet tangle in the sheets, and I plank face-first on the floor, which doesn't help the wicked headache that holds my body hostage.

"Dakota!"

No one answers. Palms against the floor, I struggle to push up. Down is up, and up is down. My gut spasms as I'm overwhelmed by nausea. I bear-crawl to the trash can and heave. Nothing comes up but dry coughs.

After wasting precious seconds, I grab the bedframe and pull myself up.

My eyes dart toward the clock on the wall. 6:00. *Morning or night?* There aren't any windows to confirm.

If it's p.m., I have no time to waste. I search the room for my phone. It's charging on the dresser, just ten feet away. Sweat plasters my T-shirt against my torso. I grab the dresser and shuffle to the phone as steel needles prick my legs.

What did Khamari do to me?

I grip the phone. My fingers slip on the screen as I dial Paris' private line. When the phone screen lights, I notice the time.

6:00 p.m. "God dammit!"

The phone rings only once. "Yes."

"Paris, it's me. I spoke to Khamari…" I exhale, trying to gather my breath and wits. "In a dream. Vampires are coming to attack headquarters. They want Alexander. D-do we have him?"

Please, God, let him be in Europe or Hell or something.

She sighs and asks, "When?"

"Tonight, when the sun sets in forty-five minutes. I didn't… Couldn't get up in time, I…" Fear and hysteria squeeze my throat. Feels like I strapped one-hundred-pound weights to my arms. *There isn't enough time. We aren't ready.*

"Effects of Khamari's dreamwalking," Paris cuts in, her voice a soothing, beachy breeze. "If he doesn't have enough blood from you, it's tough on the body. Where are you?"

"I'm not the American Red Cross." I wince, remembering my reaction. He'd warned me, but I was too proud.

"Texas!" Paris' sharp voice interrupts my misery. "Where are you?"

"My room." My knees buckle, and my butt hits the floor.

"Can you make it to the War Room?"

"I can't…" I clench my fist and bang it against my thigh. "I. Can't. Move." My voice shakes. What good was it to get a warning if I can't get up in time?

"It'll wear off in a few minutes, but since time is of the essence, I'll send someone to you. We meet in the War Room ASAP."

Five minutes later, I still can't move. Two knocks on the door jolt my nerves.

"Just a second."

As I try to get myself up to answer, the knob twists and jiggles. The door pops open. Anton stands at the doorway, staring down at me as I lie soaked in sweat and shame.

"I can't—"

"I know," he answers swiftly. "Mother told me." He

immediately opens drawers and pulls out a clean shirt.

"Hey."

"You'll be like this for another five minutes or more. Minutes we don't have. May I remove your shirt?"

"Yes." I hiss as he works the wet shirt off me to replace it with a clean one. Cool air hits my skin, but I don't have time to be a prude. Thankfully, I have on a sports bra, so we don't have to struggle with undies.

He tugs my shirt down, staring into my eyes. His blue and hazel eyes dilate. "Let's go." He scoops me up, but it hurts—I yip, bucking like a newborn foal.

"Don't fuss." Anton's voice is just as cool as his mom's. "We're going to be late." He speeds down the back hallways into the underground chamber, holding me like I weigh nothing. The wind from his speed whips his hair into my eyes. Once we enter the War Room, he settles me in a seat and sits beside me.

Charlotte, Cali, and Paris are deep in conversation at the table.

"Hey! You're back from the field," I greet Maestro Cali. Honestly, I'm relieved to see her. It feels like it's been ages since we were training in the dojo or practicing in The Beast.

"Happened to be in the neighborhood." She gives me a quick salute.

"Anyone else coming?"

"The Prussakovs are already on the way," Anton answers. "Prince Khamari got in touch."

"How? The sun is still up."

"The how is a secret of their own, but they have a blacked-out vehicle," Paris confirms. "Texas, please tell us what the prince relayed to you."

"The Elders are sending goons to get Alexander and the other half of the stone. They'll be here tonight. Not sure if it's right at sunset, but we don't have time to waste."

"Alexander?" Charlotte shifts her attention from me to the

commander. "He's dead, right?"

Paris rubs her right temple. "No. Not exactly."

"How?" Charlotte yells. "I've read the archives. He—"

"We don't have much time to explain, but in short, Alexander has an enduring spirit," Paris interrupts. "We starved him of blood and completely dehydrated his body. With the help of the Alchemist Order and a few slayers from the Internist guild, we forced him into a trance. After that, we mummified his body."

"I wasn't your second, then," Charlotte mutters under her breath. "If I were, you wouldn't have lied about something so important."

"Hey." I clap my hands. "Back to the issue. Where is Alexander right now?"

Paris frowns. "We placed him in a life-sized statue to shut out his senses. He hasn't been active since, but he is technically alive. Just trapped in another plane."

"Wait." I raise a hand. "Alexander's mummified body is in the statue in the lobby? In plain sight?"

"Correct," Paris confirms.

Charlotte's eyes dart from Paris to me. "Do we know how many vampires they're sending?"

I shake my head. "Khamari doesn't know. I'd guess the Saqqara Royals. They can teleport in and out easily."

"I'll check registration numbers, but to my knowledge there are only thirty registered Royals in that clan."

"Only?" Cali snorts. "Charlotte, darlin', I know it's been a while since you've been in the field, but thirty Royals might as well be three hundred well-trained Mades."

Charlotte shoots Cali a hard look. "We'll handle it. We have to."

"Sure, okay." Cali turns her attention to me. "How do they know about our location?"

"Likely the mole."

"No matter," Paris answers. "We have to prepare for the attack and protect the stone at all costs."

The numbness in my legs lessens. I wiggle my toes and sigh, relieved that I won't have to kill vampires while strapped to a chair. Still, I'm not at 100 percent.

"Where is the stone?" I ask my commander.

"It's safe," she replies, her voice curt.

I don't press for an exact answer—not until we figure out the identity of the mole.

Paris continues. "Dakota's gathering the students in the hall. The doors there will lead them into underground tunnels to our secondary location, which is about ten miles away. Dakota and Tacoma will lead them."

It'll take them at least an hour to cover ten miles. "How many Middlings and Maestros do we have at headquarters?"

"Ten Maestros and sixty-eight Middlings," Charlotte rattles off.

I tilt my head back, thinking through a strategy for our numbers. "I thought we had more Middlings."

"We have one-hundred and five, to be exact." Charlotte purses her lips. "The rest returned to field training after the botched ceremony."

Right. The advanced Middlings returned to their internships, where they partner with different slayer cells throughout the world. The ones that could use more in-house training had to stay back.

If I had woken up sooner, we could've avoided this. I glance at my phone. "Thirty minutes until sunset. We've gotta get the Tyros on the move and then gear up."

"Right." Paris clasps her hands together, her eyes on me. "You and Anton will defend the statue."

I look at Anton. His eyes are bright, his mouth tight.

I put my hand out for a fist bump.

"I don't know what that means," he says primly as he covers

my fist with his hand.

"It means there's no time for peace. We've got to defend the homestead."

"I know."

"Good. Let's kick their—"

Ka-boom!

The War Room shakes as wisps of dust spin up like cyclones. The ground shudders, shifting the heavy round table and toppling the chairs.

"It's coming from below us," Anton announces.

"The tunnels." I study the floor. "They're trapping us. That fucking mole told them how to trap us!"

"Upstairs, now," Paris commands as she runs toward the stairs. We follow behind. The closer we get, the louder the screams.

They're here.

By using the tunnels, they didn't need to wait until sunset. Those fuckers crawled right into the main hall and had access to shoot us like sitting ducks.

The door swooshes open. Full-out battle wages in our hall.

Tyros and Middlings, Maestros and vampires brawl with weapons, fangs, and claws.

Andreas has a vampire in a bear hold while Lexington slices off its head. An explosive light burst from a Middling's hand, forming a golden spear that strikes a vampire mid-flight. Even Magisters from the Alchemist Order are in the mix and form a barrier around some of the newer Tyros. Within the protective bubble, the Magisters bark out formulas to the Tyros, creating light bombs to lob at the flying vamps.

"There's too many. Close to one hundred of them." Cali shakes her head and then yells at me: "Duck!" She spins away from a vampire's attack and then plows her blade into the beast's heart.

I borrow the blade from the vampire's disintegrating chest and fling it into a vamp that flies in our direction. My hands shake from the power surging inside of me. I stumble back, ready to reel myself in, when Charlotte bumps into me.

"Don't be afraid to let loose." She unhooks a flask from her waistband.

Charlotte flings the water in the air, with her palms stretched, freezes it, and then rams a vampire with an icicle to the heart. The vampire claws at the ice in the middle of his chest. But it doesn't move, and soon, neither does he.

She slaps my shoulder. "We need your power," Charlotte tells me, looking straight in my eyes before she runs into the fray, going into attack mode. In mere seconds, she plows through three vampires.

I nod at her words. Her acceptance of my imperfect power lessens the weight on my shoulders.

"I'm coming."

32

The Night the Lights Went Out in Georgia
Texas

I t's chaos. Pure chaos. No one will notice if I go dark.

Instructors, slayers, alchemists, and a select group of vampires cloister together, fighting against legions of teeth and claws and power. Barbie and Dakota are fighting back-to-back on the other side of the room. Another student lops off a vampire's head with a scythe.

Something claws at my shoulder. I pivot away too late. My movements are still sluggish, like I'm underwater.

A vampire snarls and swipes its claws at me again. Springing into action, I jump on his shoulders and wrap my thighs around his neck. With my momentum, I swing us to the ground. The floor cracks and splinters like river deltas, making the ground uneven. My hip hits a sharp piece of rubble, and pain rings throughout my body like a church bell. I ignore the ache and tighten my legs around his throat as the vampire claws at my legs.

"Just die." My thigh muscles squeeze. My movements aren't as fast and smooth as usual, but the Tick is no match for me. I snap its neck and roll away.

At some point, Rose joins the fight. Using dual curved daggers, she slashes away at vampire throats and hacks at limbs. Her lips snarl, her fangs bared, but her eyes are lit like a child's on Christmas morning. "About time you showed up!" I yell as I throat-punch a Tick.

"Don't worry." She knifes a vampire in the center of its chest.

"I'll catch up."

"Plenty of them to kill." I give her a chin dip and return to the fight. I flick my ring and drip blood as a sacrifice. I tear out throats, lop off heads, and stab hearts, but it seems to do nothing. Sweat drenches my face. There are just too many of them.

Collectively, their power surpasses our own. Although some are Ticks, a good number are Royals. Us students are out of our depth, and the licensed slayers are tiring out.

I hop on a table, scanning the crowd.

On the other side of the hall, Andreas and Lex continue to work together to take out a trio of vampires. Blood splatters in all directions.

Barbie fights a few hundred feet away. She has a lasso in the air and a pile of vampires at her feet.

The girl is kicking ass. No hesitation.

"Barrier!"

Dakota rushes to her side, forming a defensive wall around them.

A Royal vampire follows my attention. He looks at me and winks. "Friends of yours?" The Royal leaps over the fray, heading toward Dakota and Barbie.

"Oh no, you freaking don't."

I run, hopping on shoulders, nearly getting pulled down into the brawl of claws and fangs. I donkey-kick a handsy Tick that won't get out of the way.

My heartbeat triples. *They'll be fine. They'll be fine.*

I finally make it to them, but the Royal beats me. His claws curl around Barbie's throat. Dakota chucks a piece of rubble at the vampire's back.

"Stupid human." The Royal tosses Barbie like a doll to the ground and stalks toward Dakota. She forms another protection barrier, but he rams into it like a bucking bronco.

Hand spread, I touch the debris beneath my feet. "Malleus."

The rocks transform into a hammer. I pick up the mallet and chuck it at the vampire's back.

As it lands, I jump between him and Dakota. "Go away." I give the bastard an uppercut to the chin. He sails across the room, crashing into a painting on the wall. I'm right behind him, and before he can slip to the ground, I grab his neck and body-slam him. The vampire grabs my shoulders, lifting us both into the air.

The Saqqara are slippery bastards. I tighten my grip around his throat, but the air shimmers. He's gone. He teleported away.

I fall to the ground, slamming into another student. I scramble to my feet and help him up.

"You okay?" I steady the wobbling Middling.

"Y-yeah." He shakes his head, his eyes clearing. "Yes."

Barbie stands and yells, "Watch out!"

I turn to face the Royal bearing down on me, mere feet away. Barbie lassoes the vampire's wrist before he can swing his claws into me.

It would've been a death blow.

The vampire vanishes again and reappears in front of Barbie. Dakota claps her hands. A barrier sonic booms in front of Barbie before the Royal can thrust his claws into her torso.

He doesn't hit Barbie, yet blood oozes from his claws. I look at him, at Barbie.

Then Dakota.

A buzz careens in my ear, as if a bomb explodes.

Dakota sways on her feet. Barbie yells something. She catches Dakota before she hits the ground.

My mind struggles to process the scene in front of me. Dakota had thrown her body in front of Barbie. The barrier temporarily stunned the Royal, but he pushed through the defense. Dakota hadn't solidified the barrier completely.

She's still learning. Still growing.

Now dying.

Blood gurgles out of Dakota's mouth and trickles down her chin as a red stain blooms at her center.

"No!" I roar. Taking a cue from Barbie, I slap my hands together and form a lasso.

I know his tell. He shimmers again, but before he can melt away, I wrap the rope around his neck. "Chalybe," I hiss, my voice gravelly as I utter the transmutation. Rope transforms to steel, and with a smooth snick of the blade, the vampire's head topples to the ground.

I hurry to Dakota's side, gently lifting her hand from the fist-size hole in her stomach. Her fingers emit a dim blue light. She's trying to heal herself, but her power isn't strong enough.

"Somebody help me!" I yell, though it's impossible to hear me above the clash.

I gather Dakota close in my lap. She doesn't deserve to die, especially not scared and alone. Her brown eyes are surprisingly dry. In their depths is a quiet, heartbreaking acceptance. She knows the price of this life. Cali drilled it into us, making sure we understood death always lurked around the corner.

Barbie forms a blockade in front of us. "I've got you, Tex."

"I'm so sorry," I whisper to Dakota. "I'm so sorry."

"Not your fault. You t-told me that I needed to practice the barrier. I should've—"

"You did nothing wrong. You saved us."

"That's what friends do," she says, coughing up blood.

Dakota's face fuses into Deidra's. I blink twice, taking a deep breath. Black dots rush my vision. *Stay here. Don't drift.*

"Yeah—friends." I smooth her matted brown hair away from her forehead. The darkness edges away.

Her eyes close.

"No! Stay here. Please."

"I'm sorry I have to leave you." Dakota's breathing is ragged, and her eyes are still shut. "Like your friend Deidra. You call for her at night. That's why you didn't want to…to be my friend."

Tears and guilt burn my throat. All this time, I've tried my best to not form attachments, but it's all a waste. Because it hurts like hell.

Despite my intentions, tears drip onto her face.

"Don't be sad." She opens her eyes, but she's not looking at me; she's focused on the ceiling. "Be happy for me. My work here is done." She takes a long breath and releases it. She doesn't take another. Her hands go lax. Her eyes close for the last time.

Just. Like. Deidra.

The lights in the hall blink. I rock back on my heels. *Everyone dies.*

Don't let them in. People make memories. Bad memories.

Don't let them in. A low keening fills my ears. I slap my hands over them.

Block it out. Block it out.

"Texas?" Barbie whispers, her voice delicate like fine china.

Ripped.

Torn.

Shredded.

"It hurts." Tears gather in her eyes, slip down her cheeks.

"It's not bad. I'm gonna fix it. I-I promise."

"Friends forever?"

"Forever and ever."

People die. Always in my arms. I'm too late. Always, too late.

Ice skin.

Ice heart.

No light, only darkness, only death.

White light surrounds me.

Follow the light. Extinguish the light.

The darkness is insidious; it locks my soul and seeps out of my pores, slithers around my body. Rising like a mist, it twists itself around limbs and necks. It squeezes like a python. Power surges through my body. The white dots squirm and struggle against my shadowy traps.

"Die," I command with a snap of my fingers.

The shadows surrounding the white dots absorb them. Eat their bodies, devour their souls. The white light disappears. The darkness inside of me is satisfied.

My body slumps to the floor. My vision clears, and I awaken to find Dakota's lifeless eyes staring back at me.

Steps thunder across the floor. Cheers erupt throughout the room.

"Texas." Someone slaps my cheek. "Texas!"

The darkness isn't done just yet. It swallows me whole.

Pop. Pop. Pop.

Someone snaps their fingers by my ear. I keep my eyes closed, aware of the fleece blanket swaddling my body.

"That was insane, amirite?"

Ugh. Rose. I do not want to deal with your mile-a-minute mouth.

"It was certainly unexpected," a cultured voice responds. *Anton.* "I didn't see her when it happened, though I saw a flicker of her talent the other day when we were…showcasing our skills to each other."

Rose snorts. "That sounds hot. Anyway," she continues in a whisper. "She was floating in the air, hair blowing in the wind like a Beyoncé video, and her eyes were all white. Then she just went berserker. Tore through those vamps like she had a homing beacon on all the bad guys."

"Yes. I would agree. It was very…frenzied. Destructive. I've seen this level of power before."

I clench my jaw. Anton claimed he would keep my dark secret

SIGN OF THE SLAYER

between us. Well, to be fair, that was before I tossed the feral cat out of the bag.

"Reminds me of Dark Phoenix," Rose says.

"Who?"

"Dark Phoenix? You know, from *X-Men*."

"I do not know of such an organization. Are they a sect of the Alchemist Order?"

"Dude, it's one of the best comics of all time," Rose says in a who-are-you voice. She snaps her fingers by my ear again. "Hey. You. Wake up, chick," Rose whisper-yells in my ear. "Looks like she's still out."

No shit. Go away.

"It seems that way." From the way Anton emphasized *seems*, I'm starting to think he isn't convinced by my Sleeping Beauty impression.

"Maybe we should slap her?"

Maybe I should stab you.

"*I heard that, slayer,*" Rose responds to my thought.

Shit, how does this mind thing work?

"*Don't worry,*" Rose whispers, but again, in my head. "*Mum's the word. I know snitches get stitches.*"

"*What's the situation out there?*"

"*I don't know if we should talk about it right now.*"

"*I need to know. Just tell me.*"

"*Fine. I'm sorry to tell you, but they've taken Alexander. We still have our piece of the stone, but at a significant cost... A third of the students died.*"

A violent eruption jolts the speed of my heartbeat. I bet Anton and Rose can hear me.

"*Santa Barbara, though. She's a tough cookie. She stood over you and refused to leave your side. Charlotte had to coax her away.*"

Santa Barbara, huh. I don't know anyone by that name.

"*Big blue eyes. Blond hair. Stocky. Cute as a bunny but*

tough as nails."

Must be Barbie.

"She said they took Dakota."

"Dakota is dead."

"Dying, not dead. Charlotte suspects they know she's Paris' secretary. Though she may as well be dead now."

"I'm going to kill those fangy bastards." I don't know how this berserker thing works, but this thing inside of me seems to be linked to emotions. Easy. I have big fucking feelings right now.

"Three Maestros," Rose continues, as if she hadn't said one of my classmates is in the grimy hands of vampires, likely getting tortured for information.

"Charlotte?"

"She's alive. Paris, too."

"Cali?" I ask, taking in a deep breath, waiting for the crash.

"Yeah. She didn't make it."

My nose burns.

"Whatever the hell you did, it changed the tide. Not one of them survived. It was like you manifested some weird dark matter and you kind of just steam-rolled them. Nothing's left except carnage."

Shit. Not again.

"This happened before?"

"No. What do you mean by carnage?"

"Heads rolling, blood on the ceiling. We definitely sucker punched them."

"Them, huh?

"Yes, them, slayer. I am not one of those monsters. Otherwise, you would've killed me, right?" Rose's voice is sharp.

I didn't mean to call her a monster. But damn, she's the one in *my* freaking head.

Rose gives a deep sigh, out loud for Anton to hear. "Looks like she's still recuperating. Let's give her time. She deserves it."

"I suppose my questions can wait."

I hear shuffling feet and a door closing.

A few minutes later, I release a deep breath. I can't sleep the day away. We need a plan. There must have been at least one hundred vamps, mostly Ticks, but twenty or so were Royals, so losing them had to hurt their numbers. Royals are a lot smaller in numbers than slayers.

We need to find that mole. Gotta talk to Khamari. Figure out if the mole has outed themselves, but there's no way I can reach out to him—his powers aren't a two-way street. And someone probably now monitors his calls.

No. There is a way.

I know where they live.

Save Dakota. Kill them all.

Alone.

There were already too many lives lost. Knowing Charlotte and Paris, they'll want to recuperate and plan the next steps. But our enemies are growing stronger, and God knows what else they have up their sleeves.

Time to get up.

No way in hell I'll allow Alexander to come back to life.

Sometimes They Come Back
Khamari

"Khamari." Someone shakes my body. "Wake up, son."

I open my eyes and focus on my grandfather's face. No, he's Julius to me now.

His lips relax into a serene smile. His eyes are bright and eerie. "It's done. The father has returned."

Is she alive?

I glance at my phone on the nightstand.

"And the stone?" My muscles tense, tight like a rubber band, ready to pop.

"No such luck."

Before I can relax, his eyes glint. "But we've got a workaround. The informant led us to someone who knows how to resurrect him with just half the stone."

"Willing or unwilling?"

"Does it matter?" He steps away from my bed. "Most of the clan leaders are here or on the way. Your presence is required."

I can't move. I drained my energy dreamwalking. There's only one thing that can charge me up enough for tonight's meeting, but my stomach twists at the thought.

"Before this…this girl, I've never had to question you, Khamari. I came in earlier and you were dead asleep. You warned them." He pounds a fist against the wall and caves a hole. "Twenty-five Royals died. If anyone else finds out about this, you're dead."

"Then tell them. I'll leave, step down."

"This isn't the Mickey Mouse Club. You leave in death only."

"I'll kill—"

"You'll kill yourself, your brother, and me. All the leaders are here, and they sorely outnumber you. There's no turning back, *King* Khamari."

"I'm not the king."

"You will be tonight."

I feel like I've been tossed into the bottom of a pit and my adversaries are piling dirt on me, burying me alive. Enemies surround me, and if I show my hand, we're dead. I don't care about my life, and my hate for Julius is growing with every passing minute. But Khaven doesn't deserve this. *There's gotta be a way out of this.*

"Son." He reaches for my shoulder, but I knock away his hand. He takes a step back, takes a deep sigh, and stares at the ceiling. "Whatever you think about me—a monster, a killer—you are right. I am all these things. But nothing has changed. I still want what's best for my grandsons. We can still save Khaven. This stone presents opportunities beyond your imagination, and those doctors haven't gotten anywhere."

"Because you sabotaged me. You sabotaged Khaven."

"I would never hurt Khaven. There is no cure for what he has. Nothing *medically*."

I turn my head to face the window, staring into the thicket of woods that surround our compound.

Julius dials something on his phone. "Bring him in."

"Bring who?" I ask after he hangs up.

"You're too weak. We can't have that. It'll make me and the entire clan look bad. So, I took the liberty to help you."

Etienne, a member of the Ankh clan, enters my room. In his grip is a young man struggling against the vampire's chest. "Get off me!"

"You may leave, Etienne." Julius waves the other vampire

away. Etienne shoves the human into my room and slams the door.

The human pounds on the door and yells.

"No. I'll just…hit the blood bank," I shout over the yells.

The young man pulls a knife out of his jacket. "I don't know what kind of kinky shit y'all got going over here, but I'll gut you like a pig if you touch me."

The human stands as tall as a center on a basketball team. Dirt-brown hair, dirt-brown eyes, with a long scar that bisects his cheek.

Julius lifts his eyebrow and turns his back on the human. "You need to feed."

"I—"

"Don't worry." Julius rolls over my protest. "He's just your type. Felon. He's killed men, women, children, and baby kittens. Soul as dark as night."

The human spits on the carpet. "And you two will be next."

He turns to face the human and wags his finger. "Tut. Tut. Didn't your mother teach you any manners?"

"Not soon enough. I killed the bitch."

My stomach twists again, this time from hunger. Claws sprout and incisors break through my gums. My eyes lock onto the human, on the sweet song of his heartbeat and the exciting rush of his blood. No one has tempted me like this in a while. I avoid humans, especially the bad ones. "Just this once," I whisper to myself, already tasting the nectar that will soon gush from his neck.

I push myself out of the bed, slit his throat open, and feed until I drain him dry. To confirm his death and make sure my blood did not mix with his, I check his pulse. I don't want this bottom-feeder in our clan.

The felon's blood gives me the energy I need to deal with the den of devils. After I've fed and showered, I meet the rest of the clans in the basement.

Everyone is on high alert and hungry for revenge. Brothers and sisters, thousands of years old, have met their last death.

Julius, ever the politician and peacemaker, works the room, offering a firm handshake, shoulder clap, and somber eyes. I hear a few repeated phrases. "He was a strong vampire...the best of our lot."

And the funniest of them all is: "Gone too soon." As if living for centuries isn't long enough.

Vampires are arrogant. It isn't the loss of Royals' lives that upsets us—most vampires don't have friends outside of their clans.

No, they're pissed the slayers got the upper hand. Vampires, the ultimate predators, lost to humans. And from the rumors swirling around, one slayer had killed most.

Who killed them? The slayer must be mighty powerful. Maybe the Maximus has enough power to defeat them?

"Let us begin." Julius beckons everyone to gather forward.

He's selected the Throne Room as the setting for our meeting in the basement. It's not the official name of the room, but it's a place befitting a king. A gold throne with a plush cushion sits on a raised platform at the front of the room. The obnoxious symbol of power is nestled beneath an archway with a stone wall as the backdrop, and there are at least one hundred feet between the throne and the tables and chairs. The plastic and dust from renovations are clear; however, a few poles are stacked neatly in the corner.

Someone has arranged four rectangular tables in a U-shape for the Ankh, Saqqara, and Hekau clans, with my clan at the center. Our name plates have numbers beside them—a ranking system for the Royals. Though we all know them by heart, we never display them like this.

My rank has changed to three. For the past year, I've been number two, just below Julius, and soon my power will exceed his.

But we have a new number one now.

Alexander.

From the stares that burn a hole in my chest, the other clans don't like the ranking spectacle. They especially don't like that I'm not even a century old, yet I hold more power. Julius did this on purpose.

I don't care. I never wanted this power. And I sure as hell don't want to be their king.

They don't want a leader or progress. They want to descend into mindless killing.

There's a small pressure at my temple. *Julius.* The criminal's blood isn't enough to bring me to full strength, so Julius can easily access my thoughts and emotions.

"Do not show your anger. We must be united."

I push my chair back a few feet from the table and cross my legs. My hands clasp into a steeple, a look Julius had perfected.

A strain compresses my heart, as if someone has reached into my chest and squeezed. My hands and my body shake from the strain. I want to reach out and clutch my chest, but I can't show weakness. Sweat beads and bubbles along my hairline like hot grease on a skillet. My attention sweeps around the table to find a vampire who dares to harm me by pitting his strength against mine. At a clan meeting, a show of power can elevate his rank. Asen, a two-hundred-year-old vampire, shoots me a fanged smile. The dumb fuck doesn't even know how to conceal his hatred. Nah. He just doesn't care.

I concentrate on the pain and, as Julius taught me, imagine that it's a small ball. I press and smash until it becomes dust and disappears.

Blood spurts from Asen's nose.

Taking a deep breath, I swipe two fingers in the air. Asen's lean body lifts from the seat and crashes against the stone wall. I adjust my black silk tie, looking straight ahead. He doesn't deserve my full attention.

"Release me." Asen squirms like an earthworm hit by the sun. I'll allow him to do that much—to struggle. Outside of the Ankh, I've never displayed my power of telekinesis.

"Oh, ho. That's what you get for messing with the future king, boyo." David, fourth in the Hekau clan, laughs.

"Idiot," Baris, one of his kin, mumbles under his breath.

"Number twenty-one." I refuse to acknowledge him by name. By the end of the night, he won't rank high enough to be in this room.

With my other hand, I raise a steel pole, striking him in the chest, just missing his heart. Blood blooms beneath his pale shirt. A hoarse cough rattles his chest as fat blood drips from his fangs and dribbles down his chin.

Asen's hands wrap around the pole. He grunts and yells something in his native language—Bulgarian, I believe—while he attempts to pull out the pole.

Julius nods, a smile on his chiseled face.

I lean back in my chair, my attention now on Asen. I tilt my head, furrowing my brow as if interested by his predicament. "You reach into my chest again, and I'll do the same. And I'll leave with a parting gift—your heart." My voice is subzero, but I'm not cold. I'm hot.

Anger coats my skin like a rash. Rage stands on the brink, ready to crash and crush everyone around me. I'm tempted.

But emotions siphon power, make you a target, and cloud the mind.

A blast of cold spreads across the room, startling and smacking us like an icy whip to the face.

"Royals." Julius stands and moves to the center of the room. There's no outward sign he's the source of the cold, but there doesn't need to be; everyone knows that strength came from him. "We have an alchemist who has given us the keys to true immortality. Bring forth the human," he yells to Etienne.

He drags in a pale, skinny human by his collar. His hands are bound and covered—likely because he's an alchemist. Blood drips from his nose, and from the snarls and hungry, low growls in the room, they want his blood.

"Hold your fangs," Julius commands. "This alchemist has much to share with us."

Alchemist? Is it the one Raven mentioned?

Julius cuffs the back of his neck, as if he's pulling up a dog by the scruff. "Tell them what you told me."

"Why should I?" He shoots Julius a bold look. "You're just going to kill me."

"Eventually, yes. But if you prove useful, we'll keep you around. If you last long enough, *maybe* you can figure out a way to escape." Julius' lips twist into a Grinch-like smile. He enjoys cat-and-mouse games. "But if you don't tell us everything, everyone will feast on your entrails." Julius waves about the room.

The Alchemist's heart thumps like a jackrabbit running from a pack of wolves.

"What will it be?"

"Fine." He nods, looking down at his feet. "I'll do it."

Julius lets go of his neck. "Speak."

"O-over two hundred y-years ago, there was another war spinning up. Alexander had a personal vendetta against the commander, and for good reason."

"We know the reason." Julius takes on a bored tone. "He wanted his son."

"Yes, but do you understand why?" He straightens his posture. The tremors are fading.

"Tell us," Julius growls.

The alchemist continues. "He knew half-breeds—*powerful* half-breeds—are needed to bear the stone and its power. It's always been the factor vampires could never get around. But...

but if the half-breeds are recognized as more human by the stone, Alexander hypothesized he could use it. Use them."

Julius shakes his head. "Alexander would never share power."

"No. He didn't plan to. As you well know, he'd been creating half-breeds over the centuries, but there's more. He wanted to transmute his soul into their bodies, then use the Philosopher's Stone to cheat death, to make his body perfect."

"He wants another body," Julius mutters under his breath. He snaps his fingers. One of our clansmen appears in front of him with a yellowed scroll. The scroll isn't paper—it's thinner but somehow woven together. Papyrus, I think.

"This will tell us how to bring him back."

Everything inside of me freezes.

The alchemist tries to reach out but realizes his hands are bound. "You stole this from me!"

Julius shrugs. "Rider did, yes. Through your old protégé."

"You killed Karen."

"You humans and your silly, messy emotions." Julius chuckles.

"But how did you—"

"Never mind how we got this," he cuts off the human. "We are asking the questions. Explain."

The man's eyes, hazy with emotion, refocus on Julius. "Alexander deemed himself a pharaoh, and this is a funerary text. This"—he swallows—"this is his addition to the *Book of the Dead*."

Aa, one of the Elders from the Saqqara, stands and zooms toward the human. "May I?"

Julius nods as he gently passes the papyrus into Aa's hands.

"You can read hieroglyphics, correct?" Julius asks.

"Yes…" Aa's hands shake. "This isn't the proper way to handle something so ancient."

"What does it say?" Impatience creeps into Julius' tone.

"This is no ordinary passage. These are resurrections. You see the picture of his mouth, the fangs?" He points to the paper. Julius nods. "This was written after he transformed into a vampire."

"You're right," the human agrees. "While the other pharaohs focus on the trials for the underworld, this one tells a different story. He doesn't use spells to praise the gods—he views himself as one."

"They…" Aa's voice shakes, not with anger but with wonder. "The alchemists must have deconstructed the spells to bind him. Tell us how." He takes two menacing steps toward the human.

"No. I've done enough damage." The alchemist shakes his head. "Kill me if you must."

"I wanted the others to hear you. But it looks like I'll have to do this myself," Julius says, then turns to face the room. "Brothers, sisters, do you trust me to translate the truth?"

"Yes." There's a mixture of shouts and mutters. I don't say anything. I can't. Khaven's life hangs by a thread.

"Very well." Julius grabs the human and lifts him from the ground. He closes his eyes, sucks in a breath, and I know he's listening to the alchemist's knowledge.

Julius tosses the human to the floor. "We must use the spell from the *Book of the Dead*. The spell of the gods. Then we must use a human, a powerful being, to wield a stone. We will then use the stone to reverse the damage to Alexander's resurrection door. To remove the stain on his name."

Aa tilts his head, staring at the human. "The human is too weak to use."

Julius nods. "We cannot use an ordinary human. This person must have access to extraordinary power. Otherwise, they'll die. And die before anything can happen. We need Alexander's son. He has the power of the father and the humanity of his mother. But we could not retrieve him. He is too strong." He looks up at the ceiling and sighs. "There's no choice," he seems to whisper to himself. "We'll just have to go with the second best." Julius turns to face me. "Khamari."

All eyes snap to me.

"What?" I shake my head. "No."

"You are powerful. The son of a priestess and Royal."

"My mother wasn't a human. So I can't be your guy," I bluff.

"A human witch. An immensely powerful human witch. It is your destiny, son, to resurrect our father."

An Elder comes forth with a bright red shard. Half of the Philosopher's Stone. My heart beats fast, furious, like a high-speed car chase down I-75.

I can't do this.

Julius walks to me.

"There is no choice," his voice whispers in my head. *"If you deny us, you will die."*

"I'm already dead if I do this."

"You won't die. You are too powerful. Don't you feel it? Royal and priestess blood. You are the most powerful of us all."

"A powerful tool."

"Not a tool—the key. Alexander will reward your sacrifice and bravery. He'll help Khaven."

"What I did to Asen is child's play. Take one step toward me, and I'll kill you," I warn the den of angry vampires.

An Elder from the Hekau clan enters the room, but he's not alone. Khaven struggles against him.

"What is this?" Julius turns to face the Elder. "Why do you have my grandson?"

"The prince is hesitant. We must shore up his heart."

Everyone else in the room nods and grunts. They seem to agree with the traitor.

"Mari." Khaven shakes his head. "Don't do this."

Whatever it takes. I can fix this. Alexander will be weak, and with the stone, I'll be more powerful. I'll kill him and then return the stone to the Society, and I'll save my brother in the process.

Risky, too risky, but I have no choice.

I turn to face the Elder, his arm wrapped around my brother's chest. "We need to be logical. This alchemist is intent on killing all of us, and we are playing into his hands. But, if the Elder Council believes this will resurrect our father, then I will accept this challenge to prove my loyalty. Even if I must die." The lie rolls smoothly from my tongue.

"Bring forth the statue and the sarcophagus," Aa commands.

"Khamari, no!" Khaven's voice shakes as much as his body.

"Let go of my brother now, or this is over."

The Elder releases him, sending Khaven toppling to the ground.

Khaven pushes himself upright, lifting his upper body. "It can end with us. You don't have to do this."

"*Yes, you do.*" Julius' harsh voice grates against my gray matter.

"Listen to me, Khamari. I'm not afraid to die," my brother pleads.

"*But you're afraid, Khamari. You can save him, son.*"

"*Get out of my head, old man. I know when to fold.*"

Someone rolls the limestone statue into the room. Though any vampire has the strength to carry it, they handle Alexander with care.

I walk the green mile to face the father.

The life-size statue has gold-plated armor around his chest. A maroon fleece blanket is draped around his waist. His glassy brown and blue eyes stare at me—like he's accessing my worthiness. It seems to me his soul is trapped in those ivory eyes.

"Place the stone in the middle of your palm." Julius, now equipped with the alchemist's knowledge, begins the ceremony. He picks up the stone with a pair of tweezers and drops it into my hand. It immediately sizzles like a hot poker to my skin.

I grunt, swallowing my urge to yell. A cyclone seems to tear a path through my stomach and chest. I'm burning alive.

"Did you hear me, Khamari?" A hand shakes my shoulders.

"Khamari? Shit, is he dying?" Khaven's voice is panicked. "Khamari!"

"Repeat the incantation quickly before it drains you." Julius' sharp voice is the anchor I need to rise above the pain.

In my mind, Julius says: *"Hail to you, my ka, my spirit. I have risen as the sun. I am immortal. I stand on the shoulders Amun-Ra. I do not need purification, for I am perfect. Open the gates, and ba will soar. Open the gates, and ba will soar. Open the gates, and ba will soar."*

I repeat it. The statue shakes and topples over with a loud smack against the tile floors. Despite the crash, the statue remains intact.

Something scorches my hand. A black mark that looks like a tire tread appears on my palm. My limbs are heavy, and the burning sensation hasn't stopped. My knees buckle, and I drop to the floor so I'm eye to eye with the statue. My mind and my body are too tired to react when I see the eyes glow.

A whirlwind blows through the room, revealing the ancient vampire now sitting on the throne.

A hushed silence fills the room. It's the infamous father: Alexander.

He's hard to look at, but I stare on. Death is ugly, but he is more. If a strong wind blew, pieces of his skin, decaying and dark as soot, would flap from the pressure. His eyes are iridescent— blue and brown and brutal. Limp, reddish-brown hair plasters across his forehead and hangs just below his ears. And the smell, my God, the smell is everything rotten you could think of— sewage and landfills and death.

A black beetle with spindles on its legs crawls across his chest. Alexander doesn't kill the bug. He just sits there, regal, as if his skin isn't crawling with bacteria and insects. It saps all my energy just to look at him, to be in his presence.

This vampire, barely alive, exudes strength beyond imagining. A hole forms in my stomach. With each passing second in the presence of pure evil, the hole expands until everything inside — food and fear — gushes out.

"Behold the father, the Vampire King, Alexander." Julius places an arm across his waist and bows.

Murmurs rise in the room. The older vampires stand and bow. The younger ones mimic, including me.

"Royals. My kinsmen. My children. Warriors. Greetings." Although his body is decomposing, his voice rings clear and strong. "Julius, an update if you would, please."

Julius nods and squeezes his eyes shut. They are communicating telepathically. Julius grabs the tweezers, plucks the stone from my hand, and then passes them to Alexander.

"Very good. We have much work to do. We have yielded a glorious victory in obtaining *part* of the Philosopher's Stone." He lifts the tweezers with the stone in the air. "This powerful gem has allowed my body to regenerate. But..." Alexander's piercing eyes scan the room. "This is only half the stone. I'll need the other."

An alarm blares. Security. Someone tripped our system.

I sniff the air.

Human.

Slayer.

Raven.

I bury my smile.

"Secure Alexander!" Julius yells. "We're under attack!"

Kickin' Ass and Takin' Names
Texas

I trigger the alarm—on purpose. They're probably trying to resurrect Alexander, and they have all night to do it. Before sneaking out of headquarters, I brought a few things with me.

One of them should work in 3… 2… 1…

A loud *boom*, and the ground shakes. Vampire minions rush to the courtyard.

"Hope they have homeowners' insurance." Rose crouches beside me on the roof. We scaled the ivy walls of the mansion, all six floors.

Light work for me and Rose.

She's the other thing I brought with me from headquarters. The irritating vampire caught me sneaking out and wouldn't shut up until I shared my plan.

Instead of snitching, she told me she was "coming with," unless I wanted to be ratted out to Paris and Charlotte.

"Stick to the plan. Find Dakota and stop Alexander's resurrection," I remind her.

"Right. Hopefully, *you* remember the plan, Dark Phoenix."

"Don't kill Khama…the prince. He's important to our mission."

Rose snorts. "More like important to your lady parts."

"Shut up."

Rose chuckles. "Don't worry." She bumps my shoulder with her own. "He's a friend. I know he's a good guy."

I sigh. Whatever happens, I don't want him to die. Not until we figure things out.

"And if I fall behind, get captured—"

"You're too mean to get captured and stay down. I have no doubt we'll be walking out of here."

I grab my blade and slide it across my palm. "You pick 'em off. I'll get up close and personal." I jump from our vantage point into the middle of the vampire herd.

We planted little bombs throughout the nest. With Khamari's intel, we know there are vampires from different clans. Rose brought some goodies from her little blackout van, which we used to get here, and we laid them precisely but quickly before triggering the alarm. The placement of the traps is cemented in my mind as I perform a deadly dance with vampires. A sword in one hand, a gun in the other, I fire off rounds into one vampire's chest and slice the other one in half. I transmute my sword and bullets to silver nitrate, an insta-death for the Ticks and probable death for the Royals.

"Nine o'clock," Rose warns.

Twisting to my left, I squeeze the trigger—a shot to the head of another vampire. The vampire's head explodes. Blood and chunks of skin gush onto the dusky brick floor, and I spin away before his ashen remains pepper the ground.

"Saqqara coming overhead."

"I thought I killed them all." I run toward a tree, jump, and launch myself into the air, swinging my sword in an arc, a clean swipe to the vamp's throat.

Up above, Rose is making herself useful by sniping the vampires with some sort of specialized rifle.

The horde thins out to just under a dozen vamps—not all of them Royals, based on the zombie-like grunting and weak power they emit.

"I've got eyes on me. I don't think we have any Saqqara outside, but I'm leaving while the getting is good. R&R for Dakota now."

"Good. And…thank you."

"Was that gratitude to me, a lowly vampire?"

"Find Dakota and try not to die," I reply, shooting through a few more vamps that attempt to surround me.

I finally clear out the courtyard. Spinning my sword, I sling the blood from the blade and march toward the entryway. There could be more vampires waiting for me beyond the entrance, but Rose went in a few minutes earlier, so the coast should be clear.

I enter the mansion. Dangerously dark and quiet, I push my back against the wall, tiptoeing through the house. I settle my breath and listen. A low hum fills the silence, and after a few quiet seconds, I hear the scuttle of feet just below the living room. *A basement?*

If vampires have any sense at all, the doors to the basement won't be apparent. A floorboard creaks. The hum grows louder. Gripping the hilt, I ready my sword. A quick slash to the head won't alert the others. *Unless I don't catch the head.*

A boy who looks my age wheels in front of me. "Are you the slayer?" he whispers. He moves into a sliver of moonlight from the window. Though he looks to be around my age, he sounds like a man. I sniff. Not a full vampire, but I can see that from the wheelchair.

Unless he's trying to get close and kill you. I point my gun at his temple. "What do you want?"

"The rest of them are down below, in the basement."

"No shit."

"Follow me. You're looking for your friend, right?"

Dakota. My heart speeds. If I can find her, get her the hell out of the way with Rose, I can handle the rest of the clans. Or die trying.

"If this is a trap, I'll kill you."

He snorts. "Don't worry. I'm already dying."

Despite my brain demanding that I drop him, I follow him.

There's something familiar about him.

Overturned lamps, sofas ripped to shreds, and dead bodies litter our pathway. The dude swipes his hand in the air and seems to move the objects with his mind. After levitating the obstacles, he tosses them across the room and away from our path.

With the power of telekinesis, he must be a part of the Ankh clan. He belongs to Khamari.

"Where is your prince?"

"He…" He takes a deep breath and stops wheeling. "Why do you want to know? You can't kill him. He's not like the others."

"I know. He's a, um, friend."

"Is he?" He searches my face. His eyes spark with hope, but then it dulls. He's guarded. I know all about that.

"Yes, he is. Now take me down below."

"Okay." He opens the door leading to a stairwell and, right beside it, a ramp. I opt to walk behind him in case of an ambush. We descend into the basement.

The smell of thousand-year-old garbage invades my nose. "What in the hell?" The smell even attacks my taste buds.

"Alexander," the guy answers.

I'm too late. "I'll get him."

"He's gone. They took him away."

Shit. Shit. Shit.

"That's why it's so quiet."

Khamari is lying still on the floor. Beads of blood dot his forehead.

Fear stabs me over and over, like a shank to my heart.

I'm too late. Too late again.

I rush to his side. "Khamari," I call through the pain that sutures my throat shut.

His dark eyes rove me. "Alive."

"Hey, little brother. Glad you're okay." The boy wheels to his side.

"Brother?" I choke.

"Your friend…" Khamari's brother, I suppose, points to a body in the corner.

He completely averts my attention with the statement. I rush to the body and turn it over. "No, that's not Dakota. It's Dieter." I sigh. He isn't my favorite, but I can't help but feel something when I notice they ripped his throat open.

I return to Khamari. "They used him to resurrect Alexander?"

He avoids my gaze, but he nods and swallows.

"Where did they take Dakota? Did they kill her?" My voice is curt and snaps like a whip.

"Who's Dakota?" Khamari's voice croaks.

I ignore Khamari and focus on his brother. The brother he never mentioned. "You didn't see her? Average height. Curly brown hair and kind brown eyes."

"No. I…I thought he was the friend?" The brother jerks his head toward the dead body.

"No. Just a liability." My eyes shift back to Khamari. "You've got a brother?"

Khamari's eyes drift to his brother. "Can you give us a minute?"

"She's the one," his brother whispers.

"It's not like that. It's…" Khamari's eyes dart to me.

"Complicated," I say while I stare back at Khamari.

"I'll just be upstairs."

"No, that's too far. Across the room is fine."

We wait for his brother to cross the room. I hear my pulse—I hear his brother whispering, *"She's the one."*

"His hearing isn't as good as ours," Khamari says softly as his brother moves away. "So now you know."

"That game, two truths and a lie. I guess he's the reason you stuck with your clan."

"Right. He's very ill—a rare blood disease. It's like his human and vampire sides are colliding, and I need to find a cure, which I've been doing with the help of the Slayer Society. They're giving me the means to research and keep my brother alive. I want us to be more than that one night, but Queen, my hands are tied. One misstep, and Khaven's life is in jeopardy."

That's why he keeps running off.

Khamari continues talking, but the words whizz past. "That's the link between me and Dr. Winters. I... I targeted her and other doctors who could do further research. Rider manipulated their minds to help me."

"You brainwashed a bunch of doctors?"

His jaw is granite. "I'll do whatever it takes to save Khaven. I'm his brother. And among my clan—even my grandfather—I'm all he has, and we're a family."

"I get it." I raise my hand. "Enough about family." Because family makes my mind drift back to homemade pies, Saturday mornings, cleaning up the house, and listening to music. And going to church from sunup to sundown.

"Texas." Rose jogs down the stairs. "No sign of Dakota, but I smell her."

"Dieter's dead, and they've resurrected Alexander. We've got to warn the others," I tell her.

"I know. I already sent a message to Aunt Mila. She deserves to know after everything he put her through." Her eyes train on Khamari. "Oh good! You're alive. Texas was worried." Rose holds her hand up to give him a high five.

He frowns and then slaps his palm against hers.

His blackened palm. A palm that must've handled the Philosopher's Stone. A palm that resurrected Alexander.

My heart stops beating. But I'm still moving. Still shaking.

Khamari betrayed me. Of course, a *vampire* betrayed me.

Maybe he didn't really do it. My attention drifts to the black scar on his hand.

He did it.

How else could the vampires handle it? Dieter wasn't powerful enough. I look across the room, my attention darting between Khamari and Khaven.

He did it for his brother. I'm so cold, so damn cold that my body shakes and my teeth chatter. I can't clench the feelings away.

I shake my head, willing my body, my mind, to still, but it feels like I'm holding myself together with floss. He's endangering the world because of Khaven. He lied to me, to the Society, because of Khaven.

"Your brother—" I cut myself off. Khamari could be useful. But we are no longer friends, and no more screwing around. We can never, ever go back.

But the enemy of my enemy is my friend.

"Don't contact me unless you have intel on Dakota or Alexander."

I stomp up the stairs.

"Bye, Texas." Khaven waves with a sad look on his face.

He's kinda cute and nice, but still, my blood burns.

When we return to headquarters, Charlotte runs out to meet us. In her hand is a crumpled piece of paper.

"She's gone," she says, and my heart lurches.

"Who?"

"Paris."

History Lessons
Texas

The musty smell from the underground quarters gives me an odd sense of comfort. Everything else is spinning out of control.

Rose sits beside me, sharpening a blade. Charlotte has her lips poked out like someone stole her puppy. Anton, looking thoughtful, has his fist under his chin.

I lean back in my chair and stare at the tapestries, trying to figure out what the commander was thinking by leaving us eight days before the Hunter's Moon. Dieter had warned us that the other half of the Philosopher's Stone had to be found before the next full moon or it couldn't be made whole again. It's kinda ironic that the Hunter's Moon is also called the Blood Moon. Hopefully, we'll be the hunters and not the hunted.

I can't believe she left us a note, like a twelve-year-old runaway.

I must protect the stone. It's not safe here.

"Let's think about this. Does anyone know where she would've run off to?" Mila asks, her voice calm amid the storm.

"I don't know." I drop my chin to my hands and face the rest of the table. "Do you know where Mommy is?" I ask Anton.

"No. We are not close. Because the act of my conception was less than ideal, I don't think she enjoys being around me," he says in a matter-of-fact voice, as if we're talking about the weather.

Still, it doesn't excuse her for dipping out. "Your mom is so triflin'."

"Oh, I think being the Commander of The Slayer Society would make her very much important."

"Not trifil*ing*. Trifl*in'*. A liar, a wuss, a hot mess."

"It's a cultural reference," Rose whispers to Anton. She winks at me.

Anton rolls his eyes. "I haven't heard of such a word, but yes, on that we can agree." He grinds his teeth.

"Let's focus, please." Mila taps on the marble-and-wood table. "We do not fully understand why she left. We mustn't assassinate her character just yet."

"That's just the problem—we don't know her character." Rose clangs her dagger on the table. "Her own son doesn't even know her."

He doesn't, but we know someone who knows Paris. Someone who'll take her secrets to the grave. "Charlotte." I point to her dramatically. "Where's your homegirl?"

"I honestly don't know." She shakes her head, her eyes dazed. We lost a lot of good people today, and she was deeply embedded in their lives. I can't help but empathize, but I need her with us on this.

"Charlotte." I soften my voice. "There has to be something. You've been her second for, like, five hundred years."

"Two hundred and twenty-three years. Yes." She shrugs as if to say, *so what?*

"After centuries together, you've probably learned something." Charlotte has a way of making you comfortable telling her about your business. No way Paris kept it all inside around her.

"I know she's from France, but other than that…" Charlotte shrugs. "She's a closed book, Texas. No one knows her origins, but…" Her eyes widen. "I have an idea. Richmond would know. I overheard them talking. He was there when her powers were activated."

"He's still alive?" The last time I ran into him, he looked like the crypt keeper.

Charlotte nods. "Barely."

"Well, send the old gentleman down." I wave at no one in particular.

"We'll need to go to him," Charlotte says. "He's too fragile, and it's too cold in here for his old bones."

"It's decided." Mila stands. "Let us make way to Richmond's quarters. I'll ask the questions, if you don't mind."

"Very well," Anton agrees.

"Fine by me," I mutter. Mila's approach probably doesn't include a fist down his throat.

"All right." Charlotte pushes up from her seat, seemingly reenergized. "Let's take a field trip upstairs."

After a five-minute trek to Rich's room, Charlotte gives a light and respectful tap on the door.

"Richmond," she calls out and waits a few beats. No answer. "Richmond." Her voice is stronger now.

"Probably dead," I whisper.

"Let's hope not," Rose responds. "Then we'll be back at square one."

"Richmond." Charlotte taps the door again.

"Girl, move." I push through everyone and twist the doorknob. "It's locked."

"Stand back," Charlotte says, then effortlessly kicks the door open.

I raise my eyebrows. "What happened to Ms. Goody Two-Shoes?"

"We need answers. People are dying."

When we open the door, we find the old asshole in bed, reading a book, his glasses propped on his nose.

"Richmond." Charlotte walks into the room. "Did you not hear me knocking?"

"I did. But I can't get up. My voice is weak, and I don't want to be bothered."

He's definitely embracing his inner grumpy old man.

His rheumy gaze studies us. "Why are you all here? You're crowding the room."

"We have a few questions for you," Mila answers from the doorway.

Except for Anton, we all step into the suite. It's far nicer than what he deserves. Plush maroon carpet. A king-size four-poster bed. On either side, there are retractable blackout curtains. Fortunately for the vamps, the blinds are completely closed, since it's an hour before sunrise.

A bright lamp sits on the nightstand. Richmond tosses a book near a pillow and waves his liver-spotted hand. "Ask your question. I hope it's only one."

"We're in a bit of a bind." Mila moves to the side of his bed and settles on a chair. She smooths her dark slacks, then continues: "You see, Paris is gone. She left a note, stating that she must protect the stone. She said it isn't safe here."

Richmond sighs. "I don't hear the question." His tone is nasty and spiteful.

I slap my hands together. "The question, you old geezer, is do you know where she went? Charlotte said you know where Paris was born. She may have gone somewhere that's a secret yet familiar place."

"Yes. I know many things about Paris. Many things, I dare say, would help you find her and the stone." He chuckles to himself. "But I won't help you."

Everyone is quiet, likely shocked that he plans to take secrets to the grave.

We could torture him for answers, but he's knocking on death's door. Guess we'll have to ask nicely. Maybe beg.

Gag. I laugh at the irony. We shouldn't be surprised by Rich's last act of defiance. From day one, I noticed he always looks out for himself. He's the reason half the stone is missing.

I move closer to his bed. "Let's be real. You're aging faster than a banana, and you don't have much time. Do the right thing, don't be a dick, and tell us what we need to know."

"Excuse me. I misspoke. I'm willing to help you, but I'm not sufficiently motivated to do so."

"What do you want?" Anton calls from the door. He doesn't seem perplexed by our situation. He just leans against the doorjamb with a bored look on his face.

"Well." Bitch Rich folds his wrinkly-ass hands across his lap. "As Texas so eloquently puts it, I'm dying. Every breath I take is pure luck. I want my youth back."

"We can't help you there, Rich." I toss my hands in the air. "We don't know who put this curse—or whatever it is—on you. Maybe if you ask The Architect, he'll help."

I give him my most evil smile.

"I've asked. We aren't on speaking terms."

I snap my fingers and point at him. "Did you say pretty please?"

"The longer you provoke me, the shorter the time you have to find a solution."

Charlotte holds a fist over her mouth. "One of the alchemists could help. Maybe Robert?"

I shake my head. "Are we sure we want to do this? Rich could play us."

"You have my word," he says, and his voice shakes.

"Your word means nothing to me." I get in his face. "Before we get you this potion, you need to give us something. Think of it as a down payment."

"Fine." He sighs. "Come close, Anton."

"No," Anton declines from the doorway. "I can hear you just fine from here."

"Very well. Anton, what is your last name? Your *given* last name."

"D'arc."

"And there you go."

"There you go?" I cross my arms. "Are you kidding me? We don't have time to go on Ancestry.com, Rich."

"It's a good clue."

"I will pull up a chair and sit by your bedside until you die, you living prune. Tell us something else."

"You're all so dense." He sighs. "Fine. She is the Maid of Orléans. Born of Domrémy."

"Whoa." Rose gasps. She points at Anton, who looks dry-eraser-board white. "Holy cramoly. Your mom is…is Joan of Arc."

Rich nods. "If she's gone anywhere, it's home, where she first received her powers."

Charlotte crosses her arms. "We will ask Robert to assist you."

"D-does, that mean…" Rich asks in a tragically tired yet hopeful voice.

"You've got yourself a deal," Charlotte finishes for him.

I look at the rest of the group. "I guess we're going to France."

A Father's Wish
Khamari

The clans move to Jeanne-Pierre's mansion. He doesn't live with the Ankh after asking for special permission, which Julius granted him nearly a decade ago.

Once I clear out our home and ensure all bugs and traps are gone, I meet the remaining clansmen at Jeanne-Pierre's home in Alpharetta, Georgia. As soon as the sun sets, we convene in his living room.

"Son." Julius reaches for my shoulder, but I jerk back, away from his touch. He lets out a nervous laugh and looks about the room, checking to see if anyone noticed. I don't give a damn.

He killed my mother, my father. He tried to kill my ex-girlfriend. Me.

I can feel the lava building, ready to erupt. An energy, none that I'd ever felt before, flows through my body.

"Khamari, I—"

"Step away, old man."

Something presses against my temple. He wants to get in. Envisioning a fly, I swat him away.

Julius' neck snaps back. Blood trickles down his nose.

"Hey!" He covers it with his hand.

I grab his arm and move us clear across the mansion, away from eyes and ears and ancient monsters.

He grabs a towel from a closet and applies pressure to the bleeding.

"I can't hear you. I can't get in." When he lowers the towel, his eyes are wide. "Was it the stone? Has it made you more powerful?"

"Don't know." I step back, pacing the floor.

"It's a good thing. If I can't get in, no one else can. Except maybe…"

"Yeah. *Him.*"

Julius jerks his head up like a basset hound scenting his prey. "He's returned."

"From where?"

"Hunting. We've got to go back."

We return to the living room, walking in on a tense conversation among the Mades and Royals.

"We need to double back. Kill that slayer bitch and the rest of them," one Tick yells.

You won't lay a hand on her. I clench my fists, wishing I could wrap my claws around the Tick's throat. He's not strong enough to kill Raven. Most of the Royals can't take her one-on-one.

Alexander sits in a silk chair embroidered with floral patterns edged in gold. There's a naked man in his lap, pale, panting, and minutes away from death.

In a matter of twenty-four hours, Alexander's skin had shed the decay, and he looks almost human. *Almost.* The way his eyes dart around the room and he tilts his head as if he's listening to something hundreds of miles away reveals the true story. When the human's eyes glaze over as he draws his last breath, Alexander pushes him from his lap.

"You." He points to the Made vampire who threatened Raven's life. "Dispose of the human."

The vampire leaps to obey.

"Julius." Alexander turns his head toward him. "I am ready."

"Please be seated," Julius directs everyone. We are in a scaled-down version of the Throne Room. There aren't any tables or rankings or designation of clans, though we all sit with our kin. Instead of tables, there are overstuffed sofas. Seats have been moved from Jeanne-Pierre's dining room to the living room.

"Thank you all for the sacrifice that was made for me. Though I am grateful, it does not go unnoticed that many of you have lost men and women dear to you."

Alexander's words are perfect, but he looks unbothered—like death and time mean nothing to him.

"Some of you," Alexander says, somehow in my head, "think that I am unfeeling. But I assure you, that is not so. Your hurt…I feel it." He taps his heart. "I am your father."

He stands, no longer emaciated but solid and stocky. He clasps his hands behind his back. "As a human, I lost many brothers. Lost them as the unrelenting sun beat down our backs and our blood spilled on foreign soil. Horse to horse, steel clashing with steel, mere inches apart from our enemy, the hot breath of death scorching our necks."

He cracks his neck as he turns about the room. "As a vampire, I've lost sons and daughters. In the lifestyles I've lived, in all the wars I've waged, both known and unknown to you, none of their lives were lost in vain. I assure you, this still holds true.

"Tell me, Jeanne-Pierre"—he waves toward the blond vampire—"do you know why we fight?"

Jeanne-Pierre clears his throat. "For our way of life?"

"That is not an answer, Jean-Pierre," Alexander lightly scolds him. "There is no confidence in your voice. There is no surety in how you sit, in who you are." Alexander moves toward him. "I do not say these things to embarrass you. This is correction. As a father would correct his son and teach him how to be a man, so shall I do to all of you. Someone else, tell me, what is the purpose of the death of our kin? What are we fighting for?"

No one answers.

"There is no penalty," Alexander assures us, his voice as

soothing as a mother to a child. "No silly ranking systems in place. We are a band of brothers."

Alexander switches directions in a smooth about-face. "You there. Khamari. The dreamwalker and telepath. The one who can use telekinesis. Future leader of the fearless Ankh clan. Tell me why we fight."

This is a test. Of loyalty, of intelligence? I'm not sure. But from the way he sizes me up—chin high and face tight—he either wants me to succeed or to expose me.

Can he read me?

Think. *Think.*

I researched him all morning. Some historians hypothesized he wanted to unite the world. He is a romantic, a musician, a philosopher. But no one drives an army to the brink of death so many times for cultural unity. No, he's *the* OG colonizer.

Immortality? Glory? He has that. Even with humanity assuming he'd died, a brilliant leader wasn't enough. Notoriety, maybe. He's tired of living in the shadows. He's a leader, a predator, not the prey.

"Khamari." Alexander's voice, still patient, cuts into my theories. "Your answer, if you please. What are we fighting for?"

"We are conquerors, yet we hide in the shadows. We should be at the top of the food chain. We should influence the economy and culture. We are immortal, yet we do not live."

Alexander's chin rests on his chest, his eyes closed. "Yet we do not live, indeed. Bravo, Khamari. You have told me exactly what you *think* I want to hear." His eyes spear me. I can feel an invisible force pressing against my temple, digging and drilling into my brain. I fight it. Blood pumps and pounds through my skull, rushing through my prefrontal cortex, fighting off the foreign entity that lays siege to my psyche.

"Drop your magical wards, young one. I will not harm you. I only wish to understand."

"Magical wards?" I shake my head. "I have no use for magic, sir."

"Do you lie to me, young one?" His voice is guttural.

Julius raises his hand. "He does not lie, Father. He uses no magic; however, it flows through his veins. And it has been magnified after your resurrection."

Alexander stares at Julius. There seems to be some sort of exchange.

"Very well." He looks at Julius and then finally back at me. "I cannot read your mind. No, I cannot see your memories, but I see your soul. One foot is in the human world, and the other in the vampire."

I don't refute it.

"My associates tell me you seek to find sustenance elsewhere. Do you believe we should coexist with humans? Treat them as equals?"

I lean back, stretching my legs under my seat. Julius' jaw is stone.

He shouldn't be surprised. And though my synthesizing blood is no secret, someone like Alexander—a warrior who takes pleasure in slaughtering and conquering—will view it as a weakness. But I won't fall into the Elders' trap.

I nod. "I believe it's wise to exercise our options."

Alexander dips his head, signaling me to continue, so I do.

"There are seven billion humans. Vampires aren't even half a percent of the world's population. If we out ourselves, we must think of the Alchemist Order, the Slayer Society, and humans banding together. Though Royals are powerful, most of our vampire brethren can be killed by simple means—fire, silver, pierced through the heart, and beheading. If there is a strategic military effort from these parties, we'll be wiped out."

Like we almost were during the American Revolutionary War. I keep that thought to myself, and luckily, he can't hear me.

"True." Alexander clasps his hands behind his back. "That doesn't tell me why you want to coexist peacefully—why you want us to drink fabricated blood."

"If we mindlessly slaughter humans or try to enslave them, we run the risk of killing them from mass consumption. They cannot be continually bled, even if we're careful. And if we farm human blood, it'll require billions of dollars in proper facilities, storage, and resources. Not to mention we run the risk of contaminating them with the vampire virus. Simply put, we may eventually run out of resources."

"Yes, but that would take hundreds, maybe thousands of years," another leader from the Saqqara clan replies.

"Are we not immortal?" I ask no one, though I direct my attention to our so-called father. No one answers. They don't need to. "Then we should consider the long game."

"You answer well, young one. Your logic is sound, yet still I wonder... Do you mean what you say?"

"I've done the research and—"

"You had a human life before this one. Did you love them?"

"Love who?"

"Humans. Your mother, perhaps? Or a lover? What is your *true* intention? Why do you want to save them?"

"I have no ties to humanity. Everyone that I may have...had an affection for"—I power through my lie—"has died."

He stares at me for a moment, and our gazes clash, but I don't look away. For some reason, I can't move.

"Very well." Alexander turns his attention back to the group. "We have gotten off track, though I appreciate getting to know our promising new generation. Elders, you have chosen well."

Alexander seems to float back to his chair. "Khamari is correct. We must rely on blood for sustenance. We cannot walk in the light—well, most of us." He inclines his head toward me. "It is my intention to remove our weaknesses. To live as freely as humanity has done. We did not choose these bodies, but we will achieve perfection. And anyone, or anything, that tries to stop us from achieving our goal will die."

His nostrils flare as he makes eye contact with everyone in the room individually. "No one, not even God himself, can stop us. Because what good is a god whose followers are dead?" His eyes glow like a predator's at dusk. "We will have our time with Him, but until then. We. Do. Not. Cower." His voice roars. "My sons, my daughters, are you with me?"

"Yes!" vampires shout throughout the room. Some raise their fists in the air.

Once everyone quiets down, he continues. "Finding the other half of the stone is of the utmost importance. If they find another Maximus, they have the potential to overpower us."

His eyes narrow into darkened slits. "This must not happen. We will make every effort to recover the stone. The mole had to leave the slayer headquarters, but they've bugged the offices within the Society. They've told me that Paris, the commander, has taken off to parts unknown. There is a team that will search for her whereabouts. I want eyes on the headquarters. What can we do for technology?"

Mary Catherine, a high-ranking Hekau clan member, raises her hand. "We have facial recognition technology. Our government contacts can help us."

"Very good. Mary Catherine, you will head this, and I expect regular reports."

"What of the slayer? The one who killed our Royals?" Julius asks. "We have identified her as Texas. I'd like eyes on her as well."

Dread swirls like a maelstrom in my stomach. Who is this source? It has to be someone close, someone maybe even in a position of power.

Julius puts a hand on my shoulder. "I don't mean to boast, Father, but my Khamari is a skilled tracker. If he can get a way to ingest her blood, he can enter her dreams and maybe influence her more easily. Our insider can help us."

A smile curves on Julius' face. *He thinks he's setting me up to be Alexander's confidant.*

Alexander nods. "Very well. Watch the slayer. Dreamwalk or not, at the first opportunity, kill her."

"Of course." I take a deep breath, relaxing my muscles.

Alexander's eyes drill into mine. "We have one week until the Hunter's Moon to rejoin the broken pieces of the Philosopher's Stone. Otherwise, the powers of the stone will dilute and eventually vanish. This cannot happen. Does everyone understand?"

"Yes."

"Yes?" He laughs. "Whom are you addressing?"

"Yes, Father," we all answer.

"Very good. That is who I am. I am your Father. I am your God. Succeed, and I will reward you. Failure, my children, is not an option."

He slumps back into his seat, saying, "I am famished. I need something more substantial." He snaps his fingers. "I'll be needing to drink from a vampire. Find me a volunteer," he commands no one in particular. Yet the vampire leaders scramble out of the room. Each leader returns with a low-ranking member of their clan. Torrin, the Hekau, is the only one with a Tick.

The Tick, a middle-aged man, trembles in Alexander's presence. Unlike most Mades, this vampire has his sensibilities. Julius told me once that for some reasons unknown to him, Torrin had taken a liking to the Tick and dedicated much of his time and resources to bring the man back from the brink of losing his humanity.

Alexander closes his eyes. "Torrin. Come forth," he commands the ranking member from the Hekau clan.

"Yes, Father." He kneels before him, trembling just like his Made vampire.

"Since you have disrespected me with the offer of your prized pig, *you* will be the one who feeds me."

"B-but—"

"This is your punishment. Your neck, if you please."

Torrin's hair falls over his eyes. He places his hands on Alexander's knees. "I-I'm sorry."

"Of course you are." His voice is soothing. "But you must learn." He scans the room, his eyes settling on me. "All of you must learn."

Quick as lightning, he sinks his teeth into Torrin's neck, like a starved man eating his first bite of steak. He sucks and grunts and moans, his eyes darting their attention among the witnesses in the room. Torrin tenses, but he doesn't yell or struggle.

I steal a glance at Julius. Even he looks disturbed. Long ago, Julius decreed that no vampire should take the blood of another. Mostly it was out of self-preservation because our blood made each other ill.

But not Alexander. Before my very eyes, his skin blushes red with vitality and youth. His hair glows, the tips curling into loose tendrils.

A minute ago, Torrin's heartbeat thundered like a roaring bull. Now, it's slow and faint. Seconds skip by between his heartbeats. Just before his heart stops, Alexander jerks away from his neck, taking a plug of flesh nestled between his razor-edged teeth.

Torrin pushes himself up, teetering side to side as if there's a string tugging at his limbs.

Alexander grabs him by the neck. His eyes are pitch-black. "Have you learned your lesson?"

Torrin doesn't speak. I don't think he can, with the amount of blood gushing from his neck.

"Did you learn your lesson?" Alexander roars, his voice thick with rage. "Never bring your Father a subprime vampire."

Torrin opens his mouth. His eyes close. He utters something unintelligible.

"I guess you haven't learned." Alexander swings his nails across Torrin's neck, slashing at his throat. Blood splatters across Alexander's face, and Julius hurries to offer him a handkerchief. Alexander takes the cloth and licks his lips and the blood dripping from his talons.

Now it's my heartbeat that's out of control. But I'm not the only one with a racing pulse—the rest of the vampires are just as alarmed. One even stares at Julius with a what-have-you-done look on his face.

After licking his fingers clean, he dabs at the blood on his cheeks. "I hope you learned a lesson from our Torrin. May my son rest in peace." His tone is no longer angry, but calm. Too calm. So calm it makes the hairs on my nape stiffen.

He waves his bloodied handkerchief at us. "Now, go. You all have work to do."

After our "Father" dismisses us, I hurry out of the room, unsure of where I'm going. Jeanne-Pierre's house is unfamiliar to me, but it's big enough to house our slimmed-down troops.

Rose and Raven killed twenty-plus Ticks and ten more Royals at the Ankh clan headquarters.

She could be an asset. Your queen.

Enemies surround me, and she's eliminated most of them. It's too damn bad Alexander's been resurrected. He was a wild card, the way he killed Torrin just because he felt disrespected. From the look on Alexander's face—the satisfaction he found in our shock, the terror that reeked in the room—he wanted us to fear him, to reestablish his Alpha status.

After I return to the guest room Jeanne-Pierre prepared for me, I pull out the papers from Julius' lockbox, spreading them across the bed. I'm still pissed that Julius used me as an experiment, but Khaven warned me to watch my front, my back, and my sides when it comes to vampires.

Julius has what he wants—his beloved father—but he lost his sons.

"Fuck you, old man," I mutter.

"You've found out about your turning," I hear from the doorway. Alexander steps in and then sits on the love seat near the door like he owns the place.

Guess he does, in a way.

"I didn't hear you."

"Of course not. I come and go as I please. I felt something was wrong, and here I am to help." Alexander lifts an eyebrow. "All of this must seem very confusing to you."

"You wanted to find a half-breed to handle the stone. And you found your chump—me. That straightforward enough?"

Alexander's eyes darken. "Tone, Khamari." He speaks to me like a disobedient child. I nod and check myself. Just minutes ago, he killed a Royal for giving him what equivocated to chuck eye steak.

"You and I, Khamari, we want the same thing."

"I don't think so." I shake my head.

"You want us to be free of drinking human blood; so do I. Your brother is dying, and like any sibling, you want him to not only live but thrive. That is what I desire. Therefore, we, Khamari, are cut from the same cloth."

I want to save lives. Alexander only wants to destroy.

"No, we are not the same," I reply. "I don't stalk people and change them into monsters against their will. I don't kill in the name of science, no matter how much progress it can bring."

"What happened to you was unfortunate. Yes, your grandfather activated your vampirism, but he had no intention of harming your friend." He waits for a few beats. His odd eyes dilate as he studies me. "You lost someone dear to you."

Julius. Did he tell the "Father" about my ex-girlfriend being the enemy of our kind?

"Yes," I simply answer. I have to trust Julius to keep his mouth shut. For now.

"I'm sorry about your girlfriend. What was her name?"

"Olivia." I say it so smoothly even I believe it.

Pressure fills my head, as if something's squeezing my temple. There's a tap, soft at first, and then growing in intensity. Focusing my energy, I push the foreign interloper away.

I toss Alexander a bored look. He's trying to get inside, and he nearly succeeds.

"How is Khaven feeling today?" Alexander asks casually.

"He'll be fine."

"Very well," Alexander agrees. He inclines his head. "As much as you think I do not understand, I do."

Oh, here comes the *I'm just like you* speech. But why the hell is he bothering me with this? I'm powerful, yes, but not nearly as powerful as he is…or will be.

"Being a vampire can be a very lonely existence," he continues.

I sit, giving him the attention I know he desires.

"Humans are fragile, and I found it…difficult to maintain connections. But after I found out that I could create others like me, in my image, I grew my family. Others tried to form clans based on their inherited powers. They tried to reproduce but found they rarely could do so with other vampires. As I'm sure you know, the females, it seems, cannot carry the baby to term."

I nod. It's one of the first things I researched. Most times, their bodies can't provide sustenance to both the baby and themselves. And so, many vampires breed with child-bearing humans.

"Ordinary human females, we found, could not transfer our power to the child. So, then we tested breeding with *others*. Not completely human or vampire. Witches are quite capable. The magic in their blood allows a fetus born of both worlds to thrive.

It delighted us to see some half-breeds are daywalkers. But I had another theory. Slayers—well, former slayers—would be the perfect breeders. I tested my hypothesis, and I sought a slayer. I bred with her. She became pregnant and had a boy. She hid my son away, though. And now she's hidden the stone."

Paris.

Alexander sucks in a deep breath, as if he's trying to fill his lungs with enough oxygen to last a lifetime.

"I'll admit that I did not react well. I waged a bloody, open war on the slayers. When they captured my essence and transferred it to a different source, they won the battle. Tell me, dreamwalker— how would you address the Slayer Society, our supposed allies?"

He doesn't want my advice. He wants to understand my approach.

"I'll answer your question if you answer mine first," I say.

"Go on."

"What do you plan to do with your son?"

"Anton is mine. Once I've transferred my soul into his body, I'll wield the stone to help my vampire brethren. That includes your brother, too."

"Using the stone is that easy? You make a wish and like that"—I snap my fingers—"it comes true?"

"For someone who studied the Philosopher's Stone well before Christ walked the earth…yes, these are the steps one must take."

"And you will keep your word?"

"As long as you are loyal to me, then yes, your brother will be restored to his former powers and abilities." Alexander taps the tips of his fingers together. "Now that you are sufficiently motivated, what would you do about the stone, dreamwalker?

"The problem of your son or the stone?"

"Both."

"Your son will eventually come to you. He needs answers.

He'll want to understand his true nature."

"What of his mother? She'll have some level of influence."

"Your son is older, and he'll understand complexities. He'll ask questions when he is ready to understand your motivations. To see if you and he are alike."

"Perhaps you are right, young one. And the stone? Where would you look for this...the slayer, Paris"—he spits it out as if he were cursing—"who has taken away everything?"

"When I dreamwalk, or rather, when I construct the dream world, it's important for me to understand the subject. If I don't know them, I scan their memories. Usually, I go to the beginning. Right before a catalyst—in her case, before Paris became a slayer."

Something sour hits my stomach. It doesn't feel right, telling him this. But I need to gain Alexander's trust. Not too much—just the potential for loyalty and brotherhood. Khaven's life depends on my acting. Once we possess the stone, I can give it back to the Society.

"Hmmm." His eyes brighten. "You are right, Khamari." He smiles, but this time it seems genuine. And in his eerie eyes lies a glimmer of respect. "I will take this advice."

"What do you want with all this power?"

"You want to know my motivation?" He gives me a look one would give a bumbling lamb. "I'm not all good, and I'm not all bad. I'm ambitious. I've found a way to make things better."

"And how's that?"

"Once trust is established, I'll reveal all. But until then, I'll leave you with this: every decision a human makes is out of fear. Do good for a small blip in time or punishment for eternity. Tell me, Khamari, is this the infamous free will that the gods throughout the ages deliver as propaganda? If one could live forever, without fear of the afterlife and a scale to weigh the heart of a man, how would one act? If one could not be judged based on one lifetime, one could be themselves, their uninhibited self."

"And you'll allow us to have free will?"

"No." He laughs, looking away from me. "History has proven that man is incapable of making sound decisions. But unlike the gods, unlike this Architect who is determined to destroy our kind"—he points to the sky—"I won't *pretend* it's free will. There are rules, simple rules; follow them, and live forever. If you don't, you will die. Whatever god they serve can take over the rest. Is that answer good enough for you? No." He waves a hand. "I see it in your eyes. It's not enough to motivate you, but your brother is. Help me. Join us. Let's find the stone and in doing so save your brother and others like him."

"And humans?"

"If we cure ourselves of bloodlust, we won't need them." He shrugs. "We can coexist. Though I imagine that because we are superior beings, we will naturally rise above them." He stands and walks toward me. A pale hand juts in my direction, but I don't shake it. A deal with the devil is no simple deal.

Alexander drops his hand. "Think on it, Khamari. You have until tomorrow. I will not ask again."

He won't have to. I have no choice. And we both know this.

All the Stars are Closer
Texas

After our negotiations with Rich, who has graduated from regular asshole to supreme asshole, we quickly fly to France. Nathan, apparently a pilot, navigates us to Paris. After we land, Nathan arranges it so that we have a mid-size SUV driven from Paris to a small French commune in the tiny town of Domrémy-la-Pucelle.

"Shotgun!" Rose shouts and settles in the front seat. The *Yay!* Team, as Rose calls us, includes me, Anton, Rose, and Charlotte. Mila opts to stay behind to protect the students, along with a few other slayers and alchemists.

Nathan slams the trunk and then hustles to open the back door of the car for me. Charlotte has already let herself in on the opposite side. The stuffy butler pops his head inside of the car and wags his finger at Charlotte. "Next time, please allow me to open your door, Ms. Charlotte."

I jerk my head toward the car. "Anton, you go first."

Anton chuckles, though it's a high-brow, my-shit-don't-stank chuckle.

"Don't be ridiculous. I'm several inches taller than you. I'll not be sitting in the middle."

"Nope." I cross my arms. "I'm not sitting in the middle. The middle sucks."

He looks down at me with a frown on his face. "I don't even know what that means."

"The dreaded middle seat," I reply with an English accent, "is for one who is short or is considered a less superior being."

Anton observes me like a scientist who discovered a new species—slightly confused yet fascinated. "You certainly aren't less of a human being if you sit in the middle."

"I'm not sitting—"

"Here. I'll show you." He grabs me by the hips and lifts me in the air. My chest bumps against his. When I gasp, I take in a big whiff of his scent: lemons, cool water, and a hint of salt.

He freezes for a sec and then lowers me into the car—right smack dab in the middle. "We need to buckle up." He reaches for the lap belt, stretches it across my waist, and clicks it in place. "See there," he whispers in my ear.

I lick my lips, my heart clanging like cowbells. "W-what?"

"You're still you."

I clear my throat before I say, "Don't pick me up again." I can hear my breathlessness. "I mean it."

"Duly noted." He slides in beside me and straps the belt over his chest.

Charlotte nudges my rib and mouths, "Hot."

I roll my eyes.

She smiles back.

I'm not trying to get boo'd up…again. The only guy in my life who has my undivided attention is Alexander.

"So…what's the plan to find our missing saint?" I say aloud to no one in particular. "What does Paris like to do for fun, outside of praying ceaselessly and receiving heavenly visions?"

"Who knows if that's even true?" Charlotte pouts. "Everything we've been told is a lie."

All right, now.

Just as I'm about to applaud Charlotte for her rare show of pessimism, she sighs. "Sorry. I'm in a foul mood." She clenches her fist. "I just…" She shakes her head. "I just thought I knew her better."

"Girl, it's understandable." I bump her shoulder with mine. "You've worked with her for what? A million years. You have a right to be pissed. She owes you an explanation."

Anton chuckles. This one is a tsk, tsk, you-are-so-very-wrong chuckle. "She doesn't owe anyone an explanation. Including me."

Charlotte slowly bops her head from side to side. "I guess."

"The hell if she doesn't owe Charlotte an explanation." I try twisting my body to face him. I turn only my head instead. "Paris knows everything about Charlotte."

"And Charlotte?" Anton inclines his head toward her. "Did you volunteer the information?"

"Yes. Yes, I did."

"Then, no offense, but that was your choice. My mother is… complicated. She kept the past to herself, but I now see the wisdom in her decision. She knew Alexander set out to use me, so she kept my whereabouts and parentage a secret…even from me, until they mummified him." He whispers the last part.

I also hear what he's trying to hide: the confused little boy who doesn't understand why his mother shipped him off to the other side of the world.

Charlotte shifts in her seat. "What's on the agenda? It's not like she's going to be in her childhood home from centuries ago."

"We're on the right path," Anton says with confidence. "I can feel her."

"How?" I ask.

"We're connected somehow. When I'm within a certain radius of her, my body temperature rises. It's like a game of hot and cold. I can detect her. That's how I knew she was here the moment we landed."

"All righty, then." I slap my thigh. "Scooby-Doo here will hunt down his mom. Sounds easy enough."

"Does it go both ways?" Rose looks at us through the mirror

in the sun visor. "Can Paris feel you? Can...can Alexander feel you?"

"For my mother, yes. I am not sure about my father."

We sure as heck don't need an Anton detector.

"Yet another complicated layer," Charlotte says. "How far away can you feel her?"

"Not extremely far. Around two hundred miles is my limit, I believe. I haven't had many opportunities to test this out." Anton sighs like the fate of the world is on his shoulders.

It's kinda true. At this very moment, Anton's freakish internal radar could sound off and give away our location. Maybe Paris was right about running away from headquarters.

Did we make the wrong decision? Are we leading Alexander right to the stone?

"One thing at a time." Nathan's words break the silent tension in the car. "First, we find Ms. Paris. We secure the other half of the stone, and then we hold the ceremony for the Maximus immediately after. If we can get the Philosopher's Stone to its rightful owner, we can at least have someone of equal power to slow down Alexander."

"Thanks, Nathan." Charlotte smiles directly into the rearview mirror. "We have to stay focused. Paris first, then the stone, then the power exchange. We've got this."

I'd forgotten about the ceremony. So many slayers have died—what if one of them should have been the Maximus?

My heartbeat thunders like a thousand wild horses. I turn to Charlotte, who nibbles her bottom lip. My money is on her. She's friendly and fierce and has a good head on her shoulders. After this whole thing is done, I plan to sit down with her and grow my powers.

"We've got a few hours before we arrive. I'm driving you all to a house about fifteen minutes away from Domrémy," Nathan informs us. "We should rest until Anton finds Ms. Paris."

The rest of the bumpy ride is silent. I close my eyes and rest. It's just after midnight; we have plenty of time before sunrise.

I wake up when the car slows. Charlotte snores beside me, but Anton's eyes are open.

The car seems to amble down the narrow roads, giving us just enough time to take in the duplex-style homes, a mixture of muted pastels and earth-brown houses. In the front yards are tall bushes and boxed flowerbeds. There aren't other cars around—in this small town, I'm sure our SUV sticks out far too much, given the mission.

There are a few medieval-looking buildings intermingled within the town. But just outside of town are wide-open pastures with trees standing tall and flowers dusting the green grass. Focusing on the village gives me peace. The knots coiled tightly in my stomach loosen.

We finally stop in front of a beige house on top of a hill surrounded by meadows and forest.

Nathan waves us away as he unloads the car. Anton stays behind to help, which surprises me because I pegged him for a ring-a-bell-for-service type of guy.

When Nathan gives me the evil eye as I attempt to grab luggage, I hustle inside.

Rose immediately scouts for the best room. "Thank God," she yells from upstairs. "All the windows have blackout curtains."

"Special order," Nathan yells out. "You're welcome."

I poke my head into the quaint kitchen equipped with a small four-seater table and an ancient-looking stove and fridge. Around the corner, a set of stairs leads to the second floor. The steps dip and groan under the weight of my heavy boots.

I stop at the first door and take a quick peek. "This one's mine," I yell to no one in particular. The room is as small as my old room back home, with simple furnishings, including a bed, a chair, and a pullout desk. But the best part is that it has a veranda.

After I open the long wooden panels on either side of the window, I step outside and breathe in the fresh country air. The wooden railing is just two steps away. Gripping the rail, I lean back and tilt my head toward the sky.

The world fades away. Just me, blessed silence, and the starlight so bright, it gives my heart a big dose of hope.

Hope. Such a soft word. It has no place in war, but it seems to always float in the hearts of warriors. On this night, after hours of travel and grieving and anger and guilt and fearing the unknown, fearing myself, for the first time in months, I let hope take root. The moon kisses my face, and the stars fill my eyes as thoughts of Khamari fill my head. I think he would love a night like this. And with my newfound hope, and against all common sense, I wish upon a star that he'll come to me in my dreams.

When my bare legs rub against a soft suede couch, I know I'm not in France anymore. I'm in Khamari's dream world.

The modern setup—green and brown pillows, a beige fleece blanket, and a woven table—is in deep contrast to the quaint countryside house in Domrémy.

"Did you find Dakota?" I ask without preamble.

He shakes his head. "No. I haven't heard anything about her."

"Then why am I here?"

The sofa cushion depresses. Khamari runs a hand across his face. "My grandfather... He set me up." Khamari goes into an explanation about half-breeds used to eventually handle the Philosopher's Stone.

"So...Alexander plans to use Anton's body?"

"Yes."

My stomach tumbles. I can't imagine moody Anton turning into the father of vampires.

"They made me… They used Khaven as leverage to make me resurrect Alexander. I'm sorry. I'm sure you hate me and my kind even more now."

His confession dilutes my anger. "No," I whisper, prying his fingers from his face. "No." I focus on his guilt-ridden eyes. "I saw your hand. I already figured out what happened, but I didn't know why. I'm glad you told me. I…" My words trail off. I don't know what to say or how to comfort him.

"I…I thought about you," I say eventually. "I was outside, staring at the stars. It's so peaceful. You can see Andromeda." I trace an upside-down *V* with my finger.

"You know about Andromeda?"

I laugh. "Learned it in…" I frown, trying to remember. "School, I guess."

"It's hard to see Andromeda near the full moon. You must be in a darker sky area."

"Hmm," I reply noncommittally. He truly has no business knowing where I am, but I can tell he's just geeking out over the conversation. The weight in the air lifts. He smiles—a wobbly smile, but it still counts.

He leans back, smile still intact, and says, "In Greek mythology, Andromeda's mother, Queen Cassiopeia, bragged she was prettier than the sea nymphs."

I feign a gasp. "How dare she?"

Khamari chuckles. "The nymphs didn't take too kindly to the insult. They complained to Poseidon, and in his godly wisdom, he demanded that the queen sacrifice her daughter, Andromeda. If she didn't, Poseidon would destroy the country."

"Nope, nope, and nope again." I shook my head. "I couldn't do it."

"Do what?"

"Sacrifice someone I love. I would've told Poseidon to go eff himself."

He looks like someone knocked the air out of his lungs. "Really?"

"Yeah, really. I would help the country, of course. Figure out a way to evacuate them. But my loved ones are off limits. Well... if I had someone to protect. That's a moot point now."

He stares at me, his eyes filled with tenderness. "You understand why I have to stay."

"Yes, for your brother." I understand, but it stings. "Tell me about him?"

Khamari smiles like a proud father. "He's...smart, like genius level. Loves to read and loves technology. He's brave—hell, he's saved my ass a few times."

"Not into studying blood like his brother?"

"No." He shakes his head, a ghost of a smile on his face. "I don't blame him. As many times as I drag him to my lab, take his blood samples, and hook him up to monitors, I think it's safe to say he hates anything about medicine. But he's a great brother. He welcomed me with open arms when I first arrived. Taught me about who to trust, who to look out for."

I sniff away the tingle that attacks my nose. "Finish the story about Poseidon and the Andromeda chick."

He strokes my cheek. "The queen doesn't tell Poseidon to go screw himself, but it still ends well, so to speak. That's why the *V* is upside down—it's Andromeda's head. Right before the monster attacked her, Perseus, a demigod and son of Zeus, saved her."

"Those Greek gods were a hot mess."

"What's wrong with the Greeks? I like them."

I'm sure Alexander will appreciate that sentiment. I snort at the irony. "They just seem to dip in and out of human affairs, playing with them like toys."

Like this Architect.

It's like he reads my mind as he asks, "Is that how you feel? Like a puppet?"

I cross my arms. "I've gained my powers from some dude who used to be an alchemist and now he's a god or whatever. Haven't met the guy a day in my life, yet he's forced this shit on me and now he's redesigning my life. So yeah, I'm feeling a little like a Muppet right now."

"Yeah?" He looks amused.

"Let's just hope he has a plan for that asshole Alexander."

"Yeah. Alexander's a tricky one."

"What's he like?"

Khamari rubs his palm on his jogging pants. "He's approachable, unpredictable, but very dangerous."

The "dangerous" part doesn't surprise me, but "approachable" does.

"Approachable." I snort.

"I think that's his gig." He stands and walks to the other side of the room. His hands ball into fists. "He—" Khamari clears his throat. "He figures out what motivates you. Dangles the carrot low enough for you to go for it. But I think there's something else there. Like when the alchemists sent him to the underworld, something happened to him. I think he's scared of death."

"He should be. We have no intentions of letting him live."

"Agreed, but I've got to play this carefully. Better believe if I don't fall in line like a good soldier, I'm as good as dead."

"You're already dead, Pretty Boy."

Khamari's deep laughter makes me warm. But when he looks at me, his laughter dies.

Crossing the room, he tips my chin up and kisses me. Hard and deep and fully. I want to stay here forever, to say to hell with the world. But his brother needs him. And the world needs us slayers.

But his kiss feels so warm and lonely and sad and familiar.

Finally, I realize why he came to my dreams—it's not about Alexander or his grandfather. This is goodbye. We stare at each other.

Don't let me go.

And that sad tune, Khamari's soundtrack, the one I can never place, blares in my head.

A tear rolls down my cheek. Before it can fall onto my shirt, he catches it with his lips.

"I love you, Raven. I love you so much that I'll protect you from myself."

"Y-you don't. You can't. You don't even know me."

"Yes, I do. And I know how I feel." He kisses my cheek, my neck; his warm breath caresses my skin.

It's not fair.

"Baby, I—"

I cover his mouth with my finger to silence him. "One last time."

Even if it's not real.

"One last time," he repeats before he attacks my mouth.

After he assaults my mouth in the best, most wonderful way possible, he lifts me from the couch and tosses me onto his bed. I reach out to him, but he moves my hands away.

He props me up against his broad chest. His strong, muscled arms clasp around me like steel bands. I can't break his hold even if I want to—and I *so* don't want to.

His warm eyes, brimming with love, pin me in place.

"I know you think what you're feeling is imaginary, but I want you to know, for me, this means everything."

"Me too," I say, shyly smiling up at him.

My confession must have loosened something within him. He kisses me again, pulls me close, and makes love to me.

I gasp in shock at the power that flows from him. Heat radiates from his body, drawing me deeper and deeper, drowning and overwhelming me until the only task I can conceive is to meld together until we could never, ever part. How could his imagination conjure this moment?

He lays me down. The cool air that hits me does nothing to cool my skin.

I roll away, but he pulls me close. My eyes are heavy. I fight against it, knowing that if I fall into a deep sleep, he'll release me. My back is now against his heaving chest.

Then he sings softly, his baritone voice in my ear. It takes a moment to recognize "Seems I'm Never Tired Lovin' You"—as he ends quietly, "all in all" seems to echo in my soul.

I rub at the pain in the center of my chest. The lyrics, so achingly beautiful and familiar, bring tears to my eyes.

I'm a Sinner, I'm a Saint
Texas

When I come downstairs, Nathan's butt is swaying to the music blaring from Rose's phone. She alternates between sucking blood from a bag with a straw and belting out some song called "I'm a Bitch." Meanwhile, Charlotte bobs her head and hums along with the music, completing the musically challenged trio.

Blood dribbles down Rose's chin.

"Can you stop?" I roll my eyes and pull out a chair.

"Stop what?" she asks with bloodstained teeth.

"Drinking blood and singing. It's gross. And besides that, why are you drinking blood with a damn straw?"

"Do you think it's gross that your *boyfriend* drinks blood?"

I cross my arms. "Khamari and I aren't together."

"Why not?" she asks after she finishes ruining the chorus.

"Because…stopping Alexander is our focus."

Charlotte, who's seated at the head of the table, claps her hands. "I agree with Texas. We've got to stay focused right now. Love can wait."

"Really?" I'm surprised by Charlotte's reaction. She gives me the impression that love conquers all.

"Yes, really." Charlotte nods. "Once this is all over, I'll be the first person to buy you matching sweaters."

I try swatting at Charlotte's head, but she ducks.

I look around the room. "Where is Anton? Are we going to

get started on the search for his mother?"

"He's in meditation." Rose clasps her hands in prayer while bowing her head. "Anton's trying to triangulate her location. I can't wait to see her." She grins with a dreamy look in her eyes. "I have so many questions to ask her. And I have this new weapon I want her to check out." She rubs her hands together.

"Why?" I shrug. "Mila or your uncle-cousin-or-whatever-the-hell can help."

"She's freaking Joan of Arc. Led an army at eighteen."

But before we can dig into that, Anton bursts into the kitchen, sweating, eyes wide.

I jump from my seat. "What is it? Who's here?"

His gaze drifts to the kitchen door an instant before the knob twists.

Paris strolls in.

I clutch my chest and lower the knife I don't remember pulling from my sheath. My breathing returns to normal. "I almost stabbed you."

Paris isn't in her usual attire. She's wearing multiple necklaces and a long gray shirt dress that hangs from her body like a burlap sack. Her eyes are bright, otherworldly. "I knew the moment you arrived," she whispers. "Richmond revealed my secret, I presume."

"Yes," Charlotte answers from where she now stands at the head of the table, her voice soft and wounded. "We would not have known otherwise. We need to return home."

"Our home has been compromised."

"We're scouting locations," Charlotte counters. "We've got the alchemists strengthening our protection in the meantime, and Maestros from Europe, Asia, and Africa are coming to assist. Just come back, please."

"I can't." Paris shakes her head. "Not yet."

Charlotte guides Paris to a seat and sits beside her. "What's going on? Are you okay?"

Anton takes the vacant chair that was once mine. Nathan stops buzzing about the kitchen and leans against the stove.

"I hear them again," Paris said.

I lean on the table. "Hear what?"

"The voices. The Architect. I couldn't hear them for a while. They were upset with me." She turns toward Anton and grabs his hand.

He doesn't jerk away, but his eyes are blank.

"They stopped talking when I sent you away when you were a child. I'm sorry. I told myself I was helping, but I hurt you with my selfish actions."

He clears his throat. "It's fine. Now that we're all together, let's figure out a way to protect the stone and retrieve the other half."

"We are here, and here we shall remain." She pats his hand. "So please, let me explain. We have time and perhaps…perhaps my explanation can give you clarity. Give you peace."

"Go on," he encourages her.

"Should we leave?" Charlotte has the good manners to ask.

Paris looks at Anton. He nods his head by just a fraction, like he's unsure of his answer.

"Very well. I met a man. To put it simply, I fell in love. He was a soldier in the American Revolutionary War, and as you know, when there's blood and death, vampires will run amok. When the English went to war with the Colonies, I felt obligated to help. After all, I still had a bone to pick with the English for their attempts to burn me at the stake."

"Did you actually burn?" I wince, thinking of the unimaginable pain.

"In a sense. My faith was tested by fire. Richmond—rather, The Architect—transmuted the fire and gifted me the powers of a slayer."

"Was it painful?"

"Yes. Very. It's not something I like to think on often—the horrors of humanity. But I bore the brunt of their paranoia. I became anew."

I shiver, imagining them burning a young girl alive. "So when you got your powers, how come you didn't get your revenge? I would've burned that village to the—"

Charlotte kicks my feet. "Finish your story, Paris."

The commander nods and says, "John was hands down one of the most handsome men I'd ever met. He had dark hair, penetrating, dark-brown eyes, and a mouth like an angel." Her eyes sparkle.

Surprised by her quick candidness, everyone laughs—even me.

"I wanted to fight and monitor vampires, so I pretended to be a man yet again. We became best friends, to my displeasure. Every battle we fought and all the free time I spent with him was pure torture. I was absolutely in love with him, and he was in love with a busty blonde who followed our camp."

She sounds very much like a young slayer girl, even though it happened hundreds of years ago.

"After the war ended and America gained its independence, I felt I could safely be myself. I'd already grown my hair back. I scrubbed the dirt from my face, marched right up to him, and smooched him square on the lips. I said loudly, 'I'm not Jacques, I'm Joan, and I'm in love with you.'"

"What did he say?" Rose asks in an excited whisper.

"I imagine he felt many emotions. Confusion, anger, betrayal. You see, he'd told me many things about himself that weren't appropriate for a young woman's delicate ears. That's what he told me, anyhow." She smiles in a Mona Lisa way, a satisfied grin with a secret lurking behind her eyes.

"I told him all about my past—my true identity and occupation when I wasn't a soldier. He didn't believe me until he saw me fight a vampire. I held back a little as a soldier, but he knew there was something extraordinary about me. He wanted to be my partner and help."

She rocks back in her chair with a casualness that I'm not used to seeing from her.

"Although he didn't have slayer powers, he was still strong and fought by my side—even saved my life a few times. We got married after the war. We were happy. *Truly* happy. We knew we had a small window, as I couldn't age, nor could I have children. But he always thought I was worth the sacrifice. We settled down in a small town where he became sheriff. I was so proud."

She wrinkles her brow as if she's remembering something unpleasant. "But I felt so guilty that I couldn't give him the normal life he deserved. Countless times, I prayed to The Architect. I wanted him to have one normal thing from me—a child.

"One day, he was called to investigate a murder scene. Sometimes I would go on assignment with him, but I couldn't this time because I'd received a lead on Alexander. The trail took me all the way to England. I fell ill during the mission, which is quite infrequent for a slayer. Nothing debilitating, just inconvenient stomach cramps. I later discovered that my menstrual cycle started. It had been centuries, so I honestly did not know."

She looks over to me, imprisoning me with her arctic blue eyes. "I was overcome with joy. I could finally be free, be a mother and normal wife to John. I rushed home. When I returned, I found out that he'd been missing for the two weeks that I'd been gone. Two precious weeks I'd wasted hunting down Alexander. They suspected John was dead." A lone tear escapes, but she breathes deep and continues in a shaky voice. "I was devastated and inconsolable. I waited around for almost a year. I didn't kill or hunt vampires."

She swipes at her tears. "And then, one rainy night, after all my searching, a man knocked on my door. He needed shelter from the storm. He looked just like my John. Tall, dark, handsome. The prettiest eyes I'd ever seen. He looked a bit worn for wear, but I didn't care. I cleaned him up, tried to feed him, but he wasn't hungry." She taps a weird rhythm on the tabletop. "The voices, The Architect, they told me to turn him away. That he was not what he seemed. The voices whispered *vampire*. But the voices didn't help me save my John, so what did I care? I'd given up being a slayer, and this was no longer my war. I wanted to feel. And so…I ignored them." She lowers her head.

"The stranger left the next day. Nine months later, I gave birth to a little boy. *You.*" She squeezes Anton's hand. This time, he gives her a little squeeze back. "The day you were born, the stranger returned."

"Alexander!" Rose yells.

"He told me he had killed my husband and that he had planned to pretend he was John. But he'd been studying me. As a sign of respect, he did not resort to deception. He said…" She shakes her head. "He said that he knew what it was like to pine for someone who would never return. Instead, he came as himself, with the intent of seducing me. He wanted to take you." She stares at Anton. "My son. He wanted to create a new race of vampires, and our son was the key."

"He told you all this?" I interrupt. "He showed his hand. Why?"

"He thought I would give up. He thought he was too powerful and I was too broken. Alexander possesses the power to manipulate the mind, and he attempted to erase Anton from my memory. But a mother's love is too strong. We fought, destroying a good chunk of the town in our struggle. I gravely wounded him, but he escaped."

"He seems to be good at that," I mumble under my breath.

"I asked The Architect for forgiveness and strength. That day, my full powers were restored, but I still aged. I was told to lead the Slayer Society in America." She sighs, looking a bit lost.

"And now, I'm sure all of you are putting the pieces together. Alexander used me, because somehow, he's figured out how to use the stone to become impervious to vampires' weaknesses."

I rub my forehead. "Khamari studies blood. He'll want Khamari to figure out an angle scientifically."

"We've got to go back"—Charlotte leans back in her chair—"and complete the power transfer."

"The voices—"

"What about them?" Charlotte cuts in over Paris. "How am I—are we—supposed to trust you and these voices when we've never heard of them?"

Paris swallows and gives Charlotte a pitiful look. "You don't believe me, either?"

Does Paris realize how she's fractured Charlotte's trust? Running away without telling us didn't give us trust in her or her little voices.

"Give us the stone," Charlotte gently demands. "If we give it to the rightful owner, the person will be strong enough to defeat Alexander."

"You've got to have faith." Paris leans closer to her second. "Faith in the unseen. Faith in the One who gave us the power to defeat evil. I'm sorry for leaving you behind, but the voices told me to leave."

Paris shifts her attention to her son. "I'm sorry," she repeats. "But I will not disobey the voices again. We will wait. We will let this unfold as The Architect would have us—until their plan is revealed."

Somebody That I Used to Know
Khamari

I stare into the bathroom mirror, brushing my teeth. Back and forth. Up and down. The low buzz from the electric toothbrush soothes me. A simple human ritual.

When I was human, I was good, and I cared about people. Growing up with a bunch of adults who don't care about you usually has two outcomes: you stay in the system, or you break the chains.

I smashed them.

Now, I am not a good guy. But one trait that remains from my human side is focus. I will lie, cheat, steal, and kill to make sure Alexander does not achieve his goal.

Alexander will never be okay with simply coexisting with humans. He encourages wars and chaos. He wants us to call him Father, but in his eyes, I see the truth. We are his subjects, not his children.

History will not repeat itself. And there are ties I'll have to cut. Send my brother away. Let Raven go. Not even twenty-four hours, and I'm already breaking my promise to her.

No. I'm not a good guy, but I can sacrifice — I've done it before.

"Son. What are you doing? You've been staring at the mirror since I've been here." Julius' voice interrupts my trance.

He's sitting with his legs crossed in the recliner next to my bed. I can see him behind me, in the mirror. He's a living sculpture. Mouth set in a frown, body still and erect, his heartbeat low and slow.

Before I shut down my thoughts of Raven, I try to send her

a message, though telepathy isn't my strong suit. *Be safe, Queen. Wherever you are.*

Likely somewhere in the Northern Hemisphere. Since it's nighttime, she's likely somewhere in Europe—not in a major city with light pollution, but a small town with darker skies, since she can see Andromeda.

I turn around, enter my bedroom, and then lean against the wall. Julius and I stare at each other for long seconds. I tuck away the last of my memories and focus on the cold bastard in front of me.

"I'm a bastard now?" His raspy voice dips low. It would make vampires step outside during daylight.

"Get out of my head." I stay put, eyes to the ceiling, hands cradling my head. Memories of Raven left me soft and open enough for Julius to slip past my barriers. "What do you want?"

"Are you for us or against us?" his voice whispers in my head.

The steel fortress shutters my defenses. I straighten, eyes and energy focused on him.

Julius slaps his hands against his temples and lets out a howl. Blood seeps from his ears and nose. The vessels in his eyes pop. The power that surges is so much stronger than it was a few days ago. It's thick, pulsing, potent. It wraps around me like a slithering snake, but it doesn't squeeze, doesn't take away from me. It becomes me.

I'm leaping.

Every few years, a vampire's power and abilities increase, usually triggered by fighting.

"Stay out of my head. You want an answer? Ask out loud, and I'll give it *if* I want to. Understood?"

"Khamari." His voice shakes, weary, worn, and for once, he sounds his age.

I release my hold over him.

"I just want what's best for you and our clan."

"I will fall in line with whatever Alexander wants."

"That's great—"

"Only because his goals align with my own. I'll need to hire new staff to oversee Khaven's care."

Julius wipes the smear of blood from his nose with his embroidered handkerchief.

"I'll have Jeanne-Pierre find some candidates right away."

"No." I shake my head. "I'll vet my people. I'm fully aware that between you and Alexander there'll be spies. Nevertheless, I want to choose the one who will have a hand in evolving our species. Understood?"

He nods. "As you wish."

"My second requirement: I will not hunt or kill that slayer, and you will not encourage her demise. She lives, or I go."

Julius doesn't respond immediately. He nods again, but after a few beats, he lifts a finger. "I know how you feel about her. But she's a liability."

"Does Alexander know about our history?"

"No. Not yet." His threat is obvious.

"Not only will I walk away. You will die."

"You would kill me over a piece of ass?"

"Yes, I will. I do not make idle threats—you know that well."

"Very well. I will not go looking to kill her. But if she's at the wrong place at the wrong time, it's out of my hands." He pauses for a beat. "You'll need to be ready to move in the next few days."

"Why? Where?"

"Not sure. Just received some…intel, and I need to follow up."

"*Where?*"

"I'll need to vet it first. I'll be in touch with Alexander's directive." Julius stands, his hard eyes on me. "Word of advice."

"I don't want it."

"Too damn bad. I'm giving it to you." He crosses his arms. "There'll come a time when you'll have to make a tough decision. Not about me or your clan. But between that human and your brother. They are the two who are going to end up hurt."

I already made the choice. I said my goodbyes.

"You can go now," I tell him, pointing to the door.

Julius leaves, but his warning lingers.

Another knock sounds on my door.

"What now, old man?" I growl.

The door opens, but instead of Julius, Khaven enters.

"It's me."

"Sorry. I thought you were—"

"Julius." He stares down at his feet. "Seems to me that things would be easier if I were gone."

"I've got a plan. Don't worry about it."

Khaven smiles a little. "Figured. Anyway, I come bearing gifts." He reaches under his blanket and pulls out Rider's burner phone.

"I got it to power up. Haven't been able to do much else without the others getting suspicious."

"Where is Rider, anyway?"

Khaven shrugs and admits, "That's been bothering me. You would think he'd return when Alexander arrived. Maybe he's doing something else. Something we don't know about."

I walk over to grab it. "Did you read anything on it?"

"No. Not with Alexander having the ability to read our thoughts. I figured it would be best if I don't know anything."

"Good. Smart." I nod. "As of right now, we are suspending the hacking. Alexander's back now. Nothing we can do about that."

"It's never too late. Don't give up."

"I'm not," I say as I read through Rider's text messages. "As you can see, I'm… Shit." My eyes widen when I discover who he'd been working with. It wasn't an alchemist like Raven thought.

"What is it?"

I shake my head. "No. You don't need to know this."

I can't afford to dreamwalk Raven to warn her. I need all my strength to block out Alexander.

Besides. I have a slayer to hunt.

Fear of the Black Planet
Texas

There's been a whole lotta nothing happening in the days since we got to good ol' Domrémy. Charlotte and I explore forts, churches, and other places that exalt our fearless leader. When we aren't out and about, Anton forces me to meditate. The days are lazy, and it *seems* like we're on vacation. But each night, the moon grows brighter and rounder and more beautiful. Each moon rising feels like the Grim Reaper breathing down our necks. The Hunter's Moon will rise tomorrow night.

If Paris has a plan, she's keeping it to herself. Like if she says something out loud, the plan will be foiled.

Paris alternates between quiet meditative moments or being hopped up with energy. The voices are talking to her again, and they seem to have a good effect. She looks ten years younger. The shadows under her eyes have disappeared, and her hair and skin are glowing.

Every day, I ask Paris what the voices are saying, but she only replies in parables. I consider myself smart enough, but without truly having context, her li'l stories are confusing the hell out of me.

The sun sinks past the horizon, and minutes later, the moon rises. Paris and I sit on the balcony. Nathan had gone to the market yesterday and returned with the most delicious apples I'd ever tasted.

"When can we leave?" I bite into the juicy fruit.

Paris pauses mid-bite and closes her eyes. "This vision is for a future time. It describes the end, and it will be fulfilled. If it seems slow in coming, wait patiently, for it will surely take place. It will not be delayed."

"Great...another Bible verse from 'the voices.'" I take another bite. Juice splatters my chin.

She opens her eyes. "Aren't they delightful?"

"They're something."

"You don't have to do that, you know."

"Do what?"

"Push people away. I know what's inside of you, because at one time, it was inside of me, too."

I snort. "What is it?" I ask, knowing that she does not know. Neither do I.

"Rage."

I stop chewing, the apple turning into dry chalk in my mouth. I swallow before I ask, "Rage?"

She nods. "For me, it was like a venomous viper living in the pit of my stomach. For some time, I tried to control it. I suppressed, suppressed, suppressed, until I snapped. Then everyone within striking distance, friend or foe, tasted my poison."

She lowers her eyes and clasps her hands. "It took me a while to realize that I had to let the viper simply be. Let it slither around my skin, let out the poison so that it doesn't kill me."

"What do you mean, let out the poison?"

"Fight. Exercise and funnel that rage. When I let it roam free is when I'm my best self."

"Are you saying your...your snake makes you balanced?"

"That, yes. Also, powerful, invincible."

It makes me feel like a hot mess.

"But what if I... What if I hurt people?" I ask. "I've done it before."

"With whom?"

"Henry," I whisper. "A boy from middle school."

"Why did you do it? Was it unprovoked?"

I shake my head. "Henry, ummm… He and his friend teased me about Grandma Lou. They called her a witch and accused her of murdering my grandpa and mom. They followed me home. Things escalated, and they started throwing rocks. By the time I got home, I was over the teasing. I was ready to fight. My grandma rushed outside when she heard the commotion. She tried to grab me and bring me inside, but I wouldn't budge. Anyway, they hit her right in the head with a rock."

My hands curl into fists. I see them tossing rocks. Hear them saying cruel things.

"I snapped. I was…mostly mad at myself because I know Grandma Lou could've dodged the rock easily if she wasn't struggling with me to get inside."

"It's not your fault. It was an accident."

I shake my head. "Yes, but then I made it worse. I finally broke free of Grandma Lou's arms, and I just blacked out and whaled on Henry. I busted his lips, blacked his eye, punched him so hard he lost a tooth. His parents were upset."

"Naturally, they didn't fault him for following you home and resorting to violent acts."

"Of course not. Henry's dad worked for the mayor's office. Two weeks later, I was sent to juvie, since his parents filed assault charges."

I only stayed for a few days. Somehow Grandma Lou got me out of there before the six-week sentence ended, though I'd been expelled for the rest of the school year. But it taught me a lesson. Never lose control. Never let people know how they affect you.

When Commander Paris turns to face me, her dark blue eyes are so intense they feel like lasers. "You are no longer a child. You must trust yourself to know that you can pull yourself back. But first, you must let loose. Then, you must learn your limits and push past them," she says, pushing her palms through the air.

"You did that?"

"Yes. I learned to trust myself, and then, eventually, those around me. And that, my dear, is what you must learn in order to step into your power."

Trust? Yeah…not so good at that one.

Before I can respond, Rose stomps outside, sighing and pouting. "I'm bored." She yawns and bends her back into a deep stretch. "Let's go fight, slayer."

We've been training together, and I have to admit the girl can fight. She doesn't just focus on brute force alone, unlike most vampires. She's studied fighting styles and, in her spare time, creates badass weapons that I'm determined to recreate with my alchemy.

I scramble up from my seat, ready for any excuse to leave. "Meet you downstairs."

I walk to the door.

"Texas?" the commander calls to me before I can leave.

"Yes?"

"Remember what I said. Don't be afraid of who you are. Trust the voice inside of you."

"O…kay."

When she nods, I race down the stairs. Rose skips out of the house and winks as she passes me.

"Do you…" I start to ask when I catch up, following her across the front lawn, but the words catch in my throat.

"Do I what?"

"Do you think I push people away?"

"Yes," she answers so quickly, I wonder if she really heard my question.

"I'm being serious."

"So am I, slayer."

I roll my eyes. "Whatever."

"No, you asked, and I'm giving you my opinion. You don't like help, even when you know you need it."

"Like when?"

"Like when you didn't want me to follow you to the Ankh clan headquarters to find Dakota. I was useful, right?" She holds the front gate open for me, gesturing with a flourish for me to pass. Her eyes glint playfully in the moonlight as we head away from Domrémy.

"Right," I reply. I won't pretend. She's good at vampiring.

"I've lived several human lifetimes. And one thing I can say for sure—when it comes to saving lives or making change, you can't do it alone. Not even the Maximus. That's why we have the Alchemist Order and Slayer Society and other key alliances."

I nod.

"I've made enemies into friends. We need humans to camouflage our existence. And sometimes, we've got to work with bad guys to catch the badder ones."

"I know, but…" I lick my lips. "How do you… How do you trust people?"

"It takes time—fighting back-to-back, digging each other out of the trenches."

I don't say anything. What is there to say, other than I suck at peopling.

We amble down the hill, over a patchwork of brown and green grass, mixed with petite purple flowers and gray gravel. A mile ahead at our destination are thousands of tiny brown bricks that look like an incomplete Tetris puzzle.

I'm not into old, musty churches, but nature I can do. It's nice, and for once, Rose is silent.

The nocturnal sounds of nature fill the air. An army of chirping crickets pulses through the night. Rodents scuffle as they dash among the jagged rocks and soft pastures. About two miles south, swooshing water rushes downstream. It's the only thing hurried in this peaceful town.

"It's like you humans learning to ride a bike for the first time, yes? You fall down, but you get back up."

"No. It's not like riding a bike. I can't kill someone by mistake with a tricycle."

Rose slows the pace of our walk. "The point is, you've got to keep trying. Go back to the academy, train, learn. I'll help you get a hold of things. Deal?"

I bob my head, a little smile forming. Look at me, making a fangy friend. "Yeah, deal—" I lift my hand, halting the conversation. The air feels heavy. Something's not right.

Rose lifts her head and points her nose straight into the air. A pebble tumbles slowly downhill.

Crickets cease their mating call. The critters stop moving.

Many times, animals run away when Rose or even Anton stroll the rolling hills. They instinctually recognize a predator. But it's never *this* quiet.

Rose lowers her head, her attention on me. *"Vampires,"* she says in my mind. *"Three miles south."*

Dammit. That only gives us minutes, and less than that if they have teleporters, though we eliminated a good chunk of those at headquarters. We're less than a mile away from the house. We can warn the others, but we won't have much time to prepare.

"I'm sending a message to Charlotte. Run, as softly as you can," she warns.

I give her the okay signal. A split second later, we run up the hill, traversing the rocks, taking maximum effort to minimize sound. I relax my bunched shoulders, unclench the cramps in my core, and count my breaths like Anton taught me. It's not working, and my lungs are burning.

Growls and snarls and shrieks sound behind us. If they're making noises, they know we've discovered them. But the smell alone gives them away. The smell would've made a normal human grab their stomach and retch. The vamps are using it as an intimidation tactic.

But we aren't regular humans.

Ticks and Royals are coming. A lot of them.

This is it—our standoff between Alexander and his merry band of Royals.

The cottage comes into view. My pulse skips, skitters, sprints.

Anton stands at the door, his brown and blue eyes pooled with intensity. He waves at us to hurry. We make it to the house and leap inside.

The smell of honey and clover cuts into the odor of decomposing flesh.

Paris stands by the stove, stirring up something. *The Maximus potion.*

I shiver, my temperature below freezing. The vampires are coming, and we need to prepare to fight.

"We're losing the deposit on this house." I cut my palm and let the blood drip to the floor. I can't afford the energy it'll take to create a barrier, but we need the time for Paris to finish.

As a Distorter, breaking stuff apart and creating weapons is easy. Doing it in my mind's eye, without being able to see the results of my effort, is something I haven't mastered. But I'll try.

Mind clear, I focus on the metals in the house. I slap my palms together and jerk them apart. Like an architect, I draw the blueprints of a door in the air. With both hands, I push, and a small gust of wind makes the curtains dance and topples the lamps. One by one, I block off doors and windows.

The blockades are up, but they won't last long against the army outside.

Charlotte must've thought the same thing, because a blue ball of light forms in her hand. She swirls the ball, massaging it as if it were dough, making it bigger. She lifts the blue light, now shaped like a perfect sphere, into the air, then tilts her head back and blows a long stream of breath into it.

Goosebumps race up my spine. I'd never seen the technique, but I've heard of it. She's putting her life force on the line.

"Charlotte, no."

The loud crack at the door and the sonic boom from her barrier drowns my protests.

Howls and hisses at our doorway shoot shivers of panic through my body. The air wavers around us as they test the barrier.

Charlotte scrunches her brow as beads of sweat roll from nose to chin. Her hands, dripping with blood, shake from exertion. "Too strong." She pants. "He's here. He's…in…my…mind." Her voice is shrill and thin and terrifying.

"Mental block, Charlotte," I urge, but my voice cracks.

She shakes her head. "Not. Working."

Someone grabs my shoulders. Paris puts a ladle to my mouth. "Drink."

I freeze. She grabs my jaw, forcing it open. Heat sears my tongue and throat as the potion sloshes in the pit of my stomach.

Paris moves on while I grab my neck and suck in air. Outside of the fire in my throat, I don't feel different. More or less the same. Bitch Rich mentioned there would be some sort of feeling, right?

It's not me.

My shoulders sag at the small bit of good news, though we could use the powers of the Maximus right about now.

Paris offers the elixir to Anton. She steps next to Charlotte. "Drink."

Charlotte remains still, both hands in the air, legs spread, and feet planted on the floor. "C-can't."

"Open." Paris forces the liquid down her throat. Charlotte chokes and sputters. Nothing went down.

Paris lowers the spoon. "We fight this night. Blood will spill." She makes eye contact with everyone in the room. Charlotte and

Rose, Anton, and then me. "Destinies are written. We must stay the course." Her blue eyes are glowing.

I break our gaze, looking at everyone else but Paris. "Where's Nathan?"

"Market."

Rose sharpens two blades together. "I sent him a message telepathically. Told him to stay put."

"Good." I nod.

Paris scoops from the small pot, then offers the potion to Charlotte again. "Drink, then release the barrier."

"No!" Charlotte's voice doesn't sound like her own. Her eyes glaze over as her hand shoots out and wraps around Paris' throat.

Before I can jump Charlotte, Anton whacks her on the back. Charlotte releases Paris, who slumps to the ground.

I rush to Paris' side while Anton faces off with Charlotte or whoever the heck it is.

"Get out of her head, Alexander." Anton throws her across the room. She lands on the couch near the window.

"Be careful! She's still in there, somewhere," I yell at Anton.

Paris coughs and massages her throat, grabbing my attention. "I'm okay." She waves me off before I can help. "Suit up."

Blood sacrifice complete, I close my eyes and let the power of the slayer course through me. "Curvam pugione." Anton and I have practiced this a dozen times over the past few days.

Silver-and-gold mist swirls around my arms. A series of curved blades form along my forearms.

Charlotte must be back to herself, because when Paris offers her the ladle once more, she takes the potion with little protest.

The barrier is breached. The windows shatter from the impact. Vampires fly through the windows and sprint through the doors. Sweet and sour smells—honey and cinnamon mixed with decades-old decay—overtake the house.

"God," I gasp. The urge to gag squeezes the muscles in my

throat, but the power inside me sings with energy. I crack my neck, bend my knees, swing, and hit the vampire that rushes me. His head cracks against the wall.

Rose runs and then leaps through the frame where the front window used to be.

"Lots of Made vampires but a good number of Royals," Rose informs us. She's already engaged in battle, taking on two vampires.

A vampire tries a sneak attack. I swing my forearm to his neck, activating my retractable blade, and cut clean through. His head topples to the floor as I step through a cloud of ashes.

Another Tick yanks my shoulder, jerking my body toward him. Swinging my arm around, I elbow him in the chest and with my other arm stab straight through his heart.

Blood oozes from both blades. I flip over the couch and jump through the broken window.

I need more space. And another weapon.

Paris is already outside, surrounded by nearly a dozen Royals in a tight circle. Two vamps rush her. One lifts a boulder into the air and lobs it toward our commander, but Paris rolls away just in time. The vampires' circle breaks but doesn't scatter.

Hold on. I'm coming.

As I run toward the commander, firebolts scatter and light the night sky. In seconds, bolts of electricity smash together, forming a ball. The Hekau clan are masters at manipulating all forms of energy, like electrokinesis, and from the power swirling over our heads, this Royal is strong.

The energy ball plunges downward, sailing straight toward Paris. She can't avoid the hit. The power ball strikes Paris in the chest so hard, it knocks the commander clean off her feet.

"No!" I rush toward her, throwing knives at the vampires that charge at me from both sides. I leap into the air, push off the shoulders of a vamp, and dive into the circle where Paris was fighting.

Smoke rises from her charred blouse.

One knee on the ground, she grabs the other leg, panting. "I'm fine."

An idea forms in my head. "Stay close and get them closer," I direct Paris. "Harenae." I speak the command in Latin.

Paris smirks and gives me a little salute. She knows what to do.

"Very good. I'll hold them off," Paris says. Her skin is a dusty gray, but she gets up and slaps her hands together. A swirl of green and blue and gold and silver surrounds her. A lance with spears at both ends appears. Spinning the weapon, she impales a vampire through the heart and then slings him off the weapon. Crouching low, she throws her lance like a javelin at the vampire coming toward her. Paris yanks two knives from her utility vest.

She pushes to her feet, sails into the air, and slams into the vampire. They scuffle midair until Paris body-slams him to the ground.

"Closer," I remind her.

While she kicks ass and guards me, I clap my hands together and kneel to the ground. "Ferrum." A long, sharp blade forms.

"Now, Paris."

"Harenae." She utters the oath, changing the solid ground to sand. The earth trembles around the small radius where the vampires are standing. They sink into the hilly mounds, which are no longer solid earth but quicksand. Clawing and scratching on rock bits and dirt clumps, the monsters' shrill screams rattle my teeth and bones. In seconds, quicksand swallows the howls.

Some of the stronger and smarter ones grab hold of tree roots, their heads just above the ground like daisies.

"Nolite Obdurare," Paris yells, pounding her fist into the ground and hardening the earth.

With my blade, I lop off their heads.

"Good work, Texas."

I scan the field. "Where's Alexander?"

"He's around, but he hasn't shown himself yet. He's waiting for this…" She yanks a necklace from around her neck and crushes the blue stone in her fist. Within the blue stone is a small red one: *the* Philosopher's Stone.

She's chanting something that I can't quite make out, but I know it's Latin.

"What are you doing?"

She doesn't answer. Her pale hand reaches for mine. While she chants, the stone levitates and whirls in a circle.

Vampires surround us. "Get the stone," a monster with dark, familiar eyes and a salt-and-pepper goatee commands the others. Paris doesn't pause her chant—the stone is whirling faster and faster now.

Someone in a hooded robe and Anubis mask steps from behind him.

The alchemist from El Diente.

The mystery person juts their small, pale hands in the air. The person chants, and their voice is strong and sure.

Still in the air, the stone stops moving as if it's…deciding.

The electrified air prickles the hairs on my arm. A small cyclone forms in the air, then speeds toward the clearing, whipping my hair in my face as I struggle to remain standing. The windstorm ceases, revealing a man.

Shirtless, with tattoos of ancient symbols on his chest and along his muscled torso, he has a ghost of a beard. His eyes, one brown and the other blue, glitter with rage.

Oh no.

"It's him. Alexander," Paris announces.

Eye of the Storm
Texas

Alexander is here.

Seeing the ancient warrior feels surreal, feels…dangerous. The stiff hairs on my neck warn me to move. My legs are shaking and God, I want to run. Run far away from the evil energy that is warning every living thing in its path that fighting is futile.

But I can't run. I have to stay and try to fight. Experiencing his aura and feeling the waves of power flowing through him, I know I'm not enough. We need a Maximus to defeat this beast. The cloaked person who I believe is a woman walks to his side, still chanting in a language I don't recognize.

"She's a witch," Paris whispers.

Rose, Charlotte, and Anton rush up beside us.

"We've got to stop him," Anton says to Paris.

She lifts a halting hand. "Wait."

Alexander thrusts out his arms, his palms open. The Philosopher's Stone is now floating toward the ancient vampire, but it doesn't go to him. It dances beyond his reach, as if teasing him.

"Tell it to come, witch," Alexander's gruff voice commands. He stretches out another hand and diverts his attention toward Anton. "My son," he whispers.

"Alexander," Anton acknowledges with no warmth in his voice. He sinks his long incisors into his palm, biting hard enough to bleed. Then, he presses his hands together. An impossibly tall sword forms from a swirling blue mist. Instead of a solid steel blade, the sword is made of solid white light.

But he's an Internist, right?

Anton rises into the air, levitating. "Rose, house," he snaps, and she nods and runs inside.

"Protect the house with the orb!" she yells inside my head.

"What?"

"Embrace the darkness. Anton said you'd know what he means."

"Darkness?" I can't control that. I shake my head, though no one else knows the conflict inside my mind and heart.

"Hurry," Rose hisses. *"Otherwise, I'll burn."*

Paris stalks toward the witch, but the Anubis-masked figure lifts her hands and blows the commander away with a gust of wind.

I start toward Paris, but she waves me away. "I've got it. Go help the others."

I close my eyes, focusing on the darkness.

I can't do it. I can feel the darkness recoil in the pit of my stomach, curl up into a ball like a little child.

I reopen my eyes, turning around to watch Anton swing his light blade. Alexander meets him blow for blow, levitating and teleporting at different angles. Alexander doesn't use a weapon, just his claws and fangs.

They're doing a dance, and Alexander is leading. He hops on his feet, spins and slashes and swerves away. Anton isn't a noob, though. The wind and heat from his blade boomerang in the sky. He's even killed a few vampires that have gotten in its path, their flesh burning from the heat. Alexander seems impervious, but then again, Anton hasn't sliced him yet.

"Texas. Do it," Anton yells, his breathing labored.

I close my eyes again.

Get mad, get angry. I think about Deidra and Grandma Lou, but adrenaline overpowers my anger.

The smell of berries and spice startles me. *Khamari.* My eyes pop open.

My smile falters when I see the look in his eyes. Dark, blank.

"Khamari?" I whisper, taking a step back.

He shakes his head and stumps toward me. With his claws, he slashes and hits my arm.

I grab my shoulder, grunting from the pain. *Quit playing, Khamari!* I know he needs to make it seem like he's team vampire, but his claws hurt.

"You." The vampire with the salt-and-pepper goatee points at me. "You will die tonight."

I grip my blade in my hand and move into attack mode. "Nope. I've got plans this weekend."

"Stop. I've got this, Julius," Khamari says through clenched teeth.

Julius? His grandfather?

"He gave you up, you know." Julius nods his head toward Khamari. He's speaking in my mind, like Rose.

I shake my head. "Fuck you. He did not," I say out loud. I look at Khamari, begging him with my eyes to dispute the claim.

"How do you think we found you, silly girl?"

I never told him. I never... *Andromeda.* Ice skitters up my spine. He figured out my location from our conversation about the stars.

If looks could kill, Khamari would be dead ten times over. "Asshole."

"That he is." The other vampire laughs. "And he's done much more." The vampire speeds beside me and grabs my forehead. I don't know what the hell is happening, but between one breath and the next, I'm no longer in Domrémy. I'm in Alpine, Texas.

Pinpoints of awareness hopscotch over my body when I see those familiar whiskey-brown eyes. But these eyes are different. They aren't unnatural, with a glint that doesn't belong and a light that shines from his dark soul.

This pair of eyes is warm. And this guy's hand is holding mine. We're driving on the way to Norma's Diner. Khamari is talking about the football season.

Night and constellations.

Fleece blankets and strawberry wine.

Kissing under the cold, pale moon.

And then…the car swerves, skids, slams into a tree.

Screams. God, the screams.

Fire and fangs.

Pain and death.

And death.

And death.

And death.

And death.

His death.

Not the death of a man—death of a life.

Death of a dream.

A thousand tiny needles prick at my feet and my hands. My bones turn to sponge, and my knees can't hold me. I slump to the ground.

A shock of pain rolls over me. I clutch my chest—it feels like something has cracked it open. Someone or something put a pestle to my heart and ground it to dust.

A high-pitched keening like a boiling teapot rings in my ears.

The screaming. *It's me.*

I stop because I must—air isn't coming in or going out.

I can't breathe.

This is how I'll die. From shock. From God kicking me straight in the ovaries. From life's cruel irony.

Sharp nails claw at my throat.

"Make him stop," someone yells.

"Texas! Snap out of it." I think Rose is speaking to me.

Something releases my throat, and I suck in air.

What's happening to me? Everything.

Weary, whiskey-brown eyes bear into mine.

Hot tears slip down my cheeks. I can't stop.

Khamari. I knew him as a human, loved him as a human. And he erased my fucking memories.

The deep scar on his neck—he got that from the attack.

This is an illusion. I scramble from the ground, away from Khamari, and roll onto the balls of my feet.

"Texas," Khamari whispers. He sounds different now. The old Khamari's voice was deep, but this version of Khamari is different—his voice is deeper, gravelly. Like his vocal cords were mangled in a blender.

"No!" I scream, tripping over my feet. "This isn't real." I shake my head, attention darting from the imposter Khamari to his smirking grandfather.

I'll kill him.

What should I summon: A gun? A stake? Thor's mighty hammer? Maybe a light like Anton. I look at him while he continues to battle his father.

I clap my hands together. I don't feel the warmth or the light to alchemize my weapon. Something is going on with my power, like...like I've lost my connection. I slap my hands together again. "C'mon." I clap over and over, my hands slipping and shaking. "Please. Don't."

"Oh, this is much more fun than I thought it would be," Julius purrs in my head. *"By the way, I ordered the hit on your marching band. Khamari is much too attached to you...his first love."*

Anger boils my bones. Khamari's grandfather is the one responsible for my friends' deaths, too. The vampire who destroyed my life.

Destroyed the man I loved, because this person in front of me is no longer mine.

What happened in the past few days? Is he being manipulated, or had he been playing with me the entire time?

Heaviness crushes my chest. My hands itch to push it away, but I know it's in my head. The weight becomes larger and unbearable and plunges to the bottom of my stomach. It takes every square inch of space, rolling over my organs and destroying something else, something intangible.

Hope.

Screw hope.

A strange rhythm hits my heart. It's no longer steady—it slows down. My heartbeat slows like the scene in front of me.

Darkness surrounds me, covering everything in sight, narrowing until there's only a keyhole left—a keyhole that outlines Khamari's body.

He's reaching for me, a wide-eyed look of fear in his eyes. Energy explodes from my hand, hurtling straight at Khamari. I blast him. He sails into the air and then flattens to the ground.

I hurt him. Hurt him bad.

I'm too far gone to care.

Do You Hear What I Hear?
Texas

Heat blasts from somewhere outside of the orb. The stomach-screwing smell of charred flesh wafts inside.

Julius stands inside the dark orb with me, protected from the blast outside of us. I can feel him flailing about. No, he won't die by the heat of a thousand suns. That'll be too easy, too merciful. He's killed my friends, my bandmates, my Deidra.

I release the orb. Darkness bumps against my skin like a cat seeking attention. Tingles prickle my scalp as wisps of my hair duel with the wind.

The darkness doesn't want to leave.

I don't want it to leave.

I look around at the ashes, the only thing left from the vampires. The heat from my orb—my rage, my darkness—incinerates them all. A tree traps Khamari to the ground.

Alexander is still alive. Barely, but he stands, his chest heaving. The witch stands beside Alexander. She emits a force that I can't see but can feel.

Undeterred, I grab Julius' throat and squeeze.

"Oh, Texas," the witch taunts. I glance away from my prey.

She removes the jackal mask. An odd smile appears as she reveals her identity.

"D-dakota?"

Julius takes advantage of my surprise and scrambles away.

"Surprise!" she says, looking all confident, cocky, cruel.

Khamari carved a hole in my heart as wide and as deep as the Grand Canyon. But seeing Dakota with a smirk on her face fills the hole with acid—with hate—and it spreads like wildfire, burning me from the inside out.

I grieved for Dakota. Risked my life to save her. And now she's standing there with the enemy, looking as pleased as punch, as Grandma Lou used to say.

"All this time, you thought I didn't want to fight, but I do. Just not for the Slayer Society."

I don't know her motivation, and I never will. *Because she won't make it through the night.*

Charlotte and Paris arrive on either side of me. Charlotte forms a barrier around us.

"Maximus!" Paris yells.

The Philosopher's Stone stops its spinning in the sky and barely dodges Alexander's open palm. Another stone, a jagged piece, emerges from the ancient vampire's grip. He growls low and deep with unmistakable fury.

The two halves click together. A red light forms a circle around the stone, growing bigger and brighter and bolder. Now in one piece, the stone zips high into the sky, gleaming with a perfect red light.

Time's up.

Alexander gives a bloodcurdling roar as the stone flies into the stratosphere, so far up I've lost sight of it.

"Venerunt ad Alexander," Dakota yells to the sky.

Julius steps into our circle and yanks Paris away. His gnarled claw rips through her chest and tears out her beating heart. Thick, red blood coats his hand. His fangs drip with saliva as he tips back his head and howls at his prize.

"No!" My hands reach for Paris, but my legs won't budge.

No thrashing, no fear. Paris' eyes are serene. The corners of her bloodied lips tip up in pure satisfaction. She's the peaceful eye in a violent storm.

Charlotte pulls Julius off of our commander and throws him nearly a hundred feet away.

Anton is still fighting Alexander, but his moves tire. He stumbles when he notices his mother's lifeless body.

I run to Paris' side, sliding to my knees, slipping on her blood. Paris tumbles to the ground, bloody, bruised, a blissful smile still on her face. Why wouldn't she be smiling? She's ascending to Heaven while we battle in Hell.

"Paris."

"Don't look down. Look up," I hear her whisper.

But she can't be speaking. She's dead.

"Embrace the power. Embrace the stone."

"The…what? The stone?" War drums bang my chest.

I shake her body while shaking my head. My darkness can't handle the power of the stone. "I can't… I won't do it!"

Julius steps our way. I lift my hand, releasing a barrier. Before I can complete the task, the stone pierces my hand. Heat blasts into my palm and spreads like a forest fire.

"No!" Darkness surrounds me again. "Get it out!"

Energy explodes inside of me. My muscles contract, my blood soaring as the power of the Maximus melds into my body.

But there's something else already inhabiting me. Something dark, raw, unstable. The energies feud inside my body, fighting over me.

Fighting for my soul.

Ripping me to shreds.

I yank at my hair. Then someone or *something* roars.

My attention is drawn to the sky—on the pale, pregnant moon. I can hear voices rising in crescendo, men and women, baritone, alto, and soprano. I'm no longer in the heat of battle but transported elsewhere.

Piles of lifeless bodies, my bandmates, my *friends* are stacked on top of one another near a fiery pit. Visions of vampires feasting on their bodies and gorging on their blood. This isn't what happened the night of the attack. This nightmare is much worse.

Kill them. Kill them all.

Darkness shrouds my vision.

Listen, listen, listen.

Texas, Texas, Texas.

Listen, listen, listen.

My blood runs hot, blistering my skin as if I'd jumped into a boiling lake.

"Texas!" someone shouts, but it's muted, like someone's speaking inside of a tin can.

"It's too much for her."

I strip off my shirt, down to my tank. I tilt my head back, eyes on the sky. I can see again. Clouds rush to cover the moon—only a crescent remains.

I look down at the horror in front of me. Two vampires feast on Deidra. One tears through her neck as the other bites her leg. Her lifeless body is held between them, parallel to the ground. Deidra's closed eyes open. Her bright irises twinkle in the moonlight.

I freeze. Just as I did the night of the massacre.

"I'm so s-s-cared, Raven. I c-can't move my feet. Kill them, Raven. Kill them for me." Her sweet melodic voice is raspy, fierce. Her eyes are now dark as the night.

Khamari sits near the pile of bodies, ass on the ground, his face in his hands. He rocks back and forth, sobbing. His body shakes from his despair. I float toward him, past the bloodthirsty vampires and burning bodies. I reach out to touch him. His shoulders stop heaving. All goes still, quiet.

"I'll save you," I declare.

"No," he says, his voice thick with misery. "I'm a monster."

"You're not like them. I love you."

Khamari turns around, his mouth dripping rivers of red blood. His claws have bits of flesh on them, and his white T-shirt looks stained like a butcher's apron.

"Do you still love me?" he asks around his rows of shark-sharp fangs. His mouth is so wide it distorts his beautiful face, forming a maniacal grin.

"Kill him. Kill him. Kill them all," Deidra chants. The bodies, the band members, join the chant.

Listen, listen, listen.

Texas, Texas, Texas.

Listen, listen, listen.

A low hum fills my ears.

"No!" Deidra shrieks. The hum cranks in intensity to a high screech like train brakes against a railroad. "Kill them. Avenge us. Avenge *me*."

I grab my ears, rocking myself back and forth. "Yes," I whisper, or maybe I yell.

My answer echoes as if I'm in an open field, but the voice isn't my own.

Not me.

Not just me.

A legion, an army. Powerful. Mine.

Ours.

I can use this power. My power. Their power. The one hundred souls in the stone.

Kill Alexander. Kill Khamari.

The screeching reaches a fever pitch. Wind smacks my face as it lifts me into the air.

Blobs of light litter the ground. Little white lights.

Not light—people.

A white light disappears and then reappears before me.

Kill.

I grab someone by the throat. *Enemy. Kill.* The white light morphs into a body. My vision returns. Julius. I wring his neck tighter.

Pain shoots through my head, like someone is drilling a dull screwdriver into my temple. Julius smiles. The pain increases as memories flow like an oil spill.

The memories are of Khamari, always Khamari.

"I will draw him out like a poison," Julius threatens.

"I'm going for the draft next year, Queen." Khamari scoops me into his arms. "Will you move with me when I get drafted?"

Another whack against my skull. My head rings like a bass drum thwacked by a mallet. The dark void disappears, replaced by more sweet, tortuous memories.

"Little spoon," I demand. I wrap his arm around my waist.

Khamari scoots behind me, his warm body better than Grandma Lou's world-famous quilts.

"How many kids do you want?" he asks out of the blue.

"Meh. Too soon to be talking about kids, don't you think?"

"I know what I want."

"And what's that?"

"You."

"And your kids." I roll my eyes, thinking about all the stinking diapers and snot in my future.

"Kids are optional. You are not."

I'm yanked from another memory.

The pain returns. Julius' fingers dig into my temples, even as mine dig into his throat.

"Hurts, doesn't it?" He smiles. "Even with the stone, you're pathetic. But don't worry. I'll free you. I'll *heal* you from the painful memories…by ripping them from your head."

Heal me?

I'll heal him. I pry his sharp fingers from my temples and punch him in the face.

Julius stumbles to the ground and wipes his bloodied nose

with the back of his hand.

His eyes morph from irritation to fear. "What is that...that thing on you?" He points to my head.

There's something weird and warm orbiting my hair. I can't see it, but I can *feel* it. I lift my hand to touch it. The energy is warm, comforting, but then something sharp pierces my finger.

I wince and stare down at my finger, welting with ruby-red blood.

Julius points as he stumbles away from me. "It's a...a crown with a cross," he whispers and looks like he wants to cross himself. I don't care about crowns and weird shit on my head. I just want him dead. The one who destroyed my life.

The one who destroyed Khamari.

He's gotta die. *Painfully.* Vampires are leeches, and vampirism is a disease. *I'll cure him to death.*

"Heal," I command.

At the sound of my words, blood ejects from Julius' mouth. He coughs, attempting to speak, but spews more blood. Twin feelings twine up my spine—a tingle of glee and a tinge of guilt.

"He belongs to our family. A vampire. You can't change his nature." Julius' words liberate me from guilt. I rip tree roots from the earth and wrap them around his body.

"Your body is healing itself at an accelerated rate," I tell him. "You see, I'm curing you. It's what Khamari wants."

His cheeks and chest cave in, and his skin shrink-wraps around his bones. The whites in his eyes are bloodshot. His eyes bulge, rolling in his eye sockets like a Halloween skeleton.

"Julius!" Khamari rushes to his grandfather.

He's alive.

Lifting my hand, I swat Khamari away like the Tick he is. Khamari falls hard to the ground. He doesn't get up.

Julius' emaciated body slips from the root prison and rolls on the ground. I walk toward him and stomp my combat boots against his chest, grinding my foot to his sternum. "Any last words?"

"Khamari doesn't belong to you."

"I know that." I lift my boot and crush him like a cockroach. I don't want to hear his grandson's name.

"Julius!" Khamari grabs his shoulder to reset it and crawls to his crushed relative.

"You want to kill me?" I taunt. "Avenge your precious grandfather?"

He shakes his head as he stands. *"You don't understand. He was in my head. I didn't realize until it was too late that he'd read my mind."*

"Liar." I spin around and kick his face.

Khamari staggers back. A red glob of spit hits the ground. He wipes the remaining blood and smears his sleeve.

"Shut your mouth. I don't want to hear it."

"I—"

"Or I will cut out your lying tongue."

"Listen to me!" he roars out loud.

"Am I a joke to you?"

"No." His voice is hushed. He glances at the son and father titans fighting hundreds of yards away, at the field of blood and carnage. "You're everything."

I shake my head, shake away his lies. "You used me, erased my memories, just…just pulling me along and dangling my heartstrings." I suck in a ragged breath. "You like dangling people along like little puppets, huh?"

I snap my fingers, like I've seen Rich do in fights, and summon strings as thin as dental floss but hard as diamonds. I stretch the strings as I stare at Khamari.

I hate him.

Hate the way he makes me feel.

Hate how he used me.

After I wind the thread around my hands, it bites into my skin, sinking deeper into my flesh as my anger mounts. The scars on my hands will heal. So will my heart...eventually.

Khamari raises both his palms. "Listen, I—"

I fly in his direction, landing on his shoulders. I wrap the strings around his throat. He grasps at the strings, bloodying his hands in the process.

I jump from his shoulders, landing in front of him.

I want my face to be the last thing he sees. My anger. My pain. My vengeance. He grapples for the filament again, but I'm stronger.

He falls to his knees. His eyes water from the lack of oxygen.

He stops struggling and stares at me. I'm not sure why, because I can feel his strength humming beneath his skin. He can break away if he tries.

I shake my head. *Doesn't matter.*

Someone pulls at my shoulder. Charlotte.

"Let him go," she says.

I shrug away from her hand. "He's the enemy."

"We have the stone. Focus on Alexander, not revenge."

I pull tighter.

"Focus, Texas, or Alexander will get away. Anton is tiring."

Hearing Alexander's name is like pouring gasoline onto the fire. "Where is he? Where's Dakota?"

I loosen my grip and then press two fingers against Khamari's pulse, letting the flow of my power lull the vampire to sleep.

With the strings still wrapped around his throat, he slips to the ground. This is my last gift to Khamari. If he stands in my way again, one of us will die.

"Dakota escaped." Charlotte returns to Paris and lays her palm against our commander's chest. She recites a prayer. I don't have it in me to pray.

Alexander. I turn my attention toward the ancient vampire.

He and Anton are blurs. The fighting styles change in an instant—from martial arts to all-out brawling. Grunts and groans and roars ring throughout the open field. Sometimes they stop for a second or two, circle each other, Alexander with his chest singed by Anton's light sword, Anton's face covered in blood and sweat and in various stages of healing and bruising.

Anton whips his sword in the air, causing a whirlwind. Gaining momentum, he slashes at Alexander's body, carving him like a roast. But the old vampire heals too quickly. I study Alexander's movements. He dodges, feints, rolls away, slicing at Anton with his claws, but defensively. Seems like he doesn't want to hurt him.

Because he wants Anton's body.

"I'll get him."

"No. Stay back," Anton orders as he continues his fight. "I've got him."

But he doesn't. Alexander heals too quickly, regenerating in seconds. Even Anton's excellent sword skills aren't enough. I need to figure out a weapon to weaken him.

A bomb? No one would survive. But if I move Anton out of the way…

I look for an opening.

I turn around. Rose and Charlotte are still lingering near Paris' body, since the rest of the vamps are dead. "Rose, Charlotte. Run."

"What are you thinking, slayer?" Rose asks. "Don't do anything rash."

"Go. I'll give you a head start." I flex my fingers.

Charlotte stares at me, her mouth wide open, as if she can guess my thoughts. "No. You aren't ready for the Maximus powers yet. You can barely control yourself."

I don't look or listen to Charlotte or Rose as they plead with me. I wrap the same roots I used on Julius around Charlotte, Rose, and even Khamari, then slingshot them across the field. They're fast healers. They'll be okay.

Magnesium, sodium, zinc... My mind whirls as I make a powerful bomb. *Burn him from the inside out.*

Bomb configured and now in my palm, I wait for an opening. Father and son break apart and do the circling thing. Taking the cue, I zoom toward Alexander, shoving the bomb into his chest. I try. He grabs my hand, twisting my wrist until the bomb drops to the ground. Alexander teleports from the explosive.

"Texas!" Anton yells, rushing toward me, scooping me in his arms. The fiery explosion blasts us up into the sky. The heat singes my legs, feet, and arms. We finally drop and roll onto the ground, and agony shoots through my skull as it makes contact with a sharp rock. Anton's pale, worried face fades until there's nothing.

Rolling in the Deep
Texas

The smell of the sea wakes me.

The sea? I scramble to my feet, my heart clanging like an old church bell against my chest. The sun glares from above me, toasting my skin.

"Where am I?"

Listen, listen, listen.

Texas, Texas, Texas.

Listen, listen, listen.

Texas, Texas, Texas.

Listen, listen, listen.

"Listen, Texas," Paris' imperious voice shouts from behind me, slamming into me like a wrecking ball.

My fists clench. I turn slowly, afraid of what I'll see. Afraid to witness her wrecked body.

"That's it. Listen to me." Paris stands behind me in a white robe, surrounded by an ethereal white light. She stands at the shoreline, a mixture of blues and greens.

Birds chirp, and a breeze blows, soothing my nerves. "No." I shake my head. "You're gone." Tears slip down my cheeks. Salt lingers on my lips. I lick them away. "You're dead."

I unclench my hands. My nails had dug so deep, indents remain in my palm.

"Silly girl, did you ever pay attention to the Internist classes?"

I snap my head up.

"Those classes…" I search my memories. I blanked out those classes. I never really paid attention to the self-reflection, spirit-is-everywhere classes that our Internist members taught us.

"Death, child, is only the beginning. My soul continues and is eternal. I live on."

"Oh, well, okay then. Can I go down the hall to your office and speak to you? Can I touch you? Can I talk to my mother, to Deidra?"

"It's too soon. But one day you'll understand." She shakes her head as if convincing herself.

Everyone dies. Friends, family, classmates, bandmates.

Paris.

"You're not real," I say to my fallen commander.

The gentle wave from the sea laps the shore. I move closer until the cool waters kiss my toes.

"Where are we?" I whisper, not wanting to break away from this place.

"Your charging station. Your version of paradise. You'll need this place when you overdo it. And knowing you, you'll max yourself out often."

"What was that thing on my head?" I ask her. "Julius says it's a crown or something?"

"A manifestation of your nature. The rays of light surround your head. You are light shining through the darkness. You are hope for future generations, yet should anyone cross you, they will find despair. The cross is sharp steel—a warning to all that you are deadly. As you gain control over your powers, your crown will transform."

"No pressure." I let out a humorless laugh. "No pressure at all."

The sun sinks into the horizon. I tilt my head back and let its light warm my skin. I need silence, the serenity, the light. I wait for the familiar feeling of anger to fuel me—for the balloon in my chest to pop.

But I'm tired of being angry. I want peace—not just snatches of illusions from my dead commander or altered dreams from my ex-boyfriend.

I walk farther into the ocean, my jean-clad legs now wet to my knees. *Keep going. Don't turn back.*

Can I just walk away and let the current take me?

"Stop!" Paris' voice snatches my attention. I turn to face her, where she still stands on the shore.

"Stop what?" I keep my voice light. She doesn't know what I'm thinking. Dead people can't read minds.

"Don't stand there wishing for another life. You've got the one you were given. Like it or not, you are the Maximus."

"More like I was the only slayer around. I mean, between Anton, Charlotte, and me, the odds were favorable."

"You were always the one destined for Maximus. Things have been set in motion, even before you were born."

"Maybe. Just wish someone would've relayed my destiny and all." I roll my eyes.

"Be that as it may, Alexander suffered a blow today. But he will retreat and grow stronger. He knows you are the Maximus. He'll study you and engineer ways to observe you again. You mustn't fall for his traps. Trust in The Architect."

"Why should I?" I snap. And there it is. The old, familiar anger deep in my psyche. I kick the water, causing violent ripples. "What has he ever done for me other than rip away my dreams and force me into this life? Huh? Tell me, *please.*"

"You may not like The Architect—you may not understand. But they... I... I have given you this power."

"You...you aren't Paris?"

"Yes and no. She is a part of me now, as are most fallen slayers."

"Most?"

"There are a few souls that still need to come home. That, my dear, will come later."

"I'm still…" I grapple for the right words to address The Architect. "Why did you choose me? There are so many other people who could do this better."

"Your powers were activated much earlier than they should have been."

"When I was twelve?" I whisper to myself. "With Henry?"

"Before him. When your mother and grandfather were killed by vampires."

My gut twists. The warmth of the sun no longer reaches me. "V-vampires?"

"You had the gene, forced to awaken before its time. That was not a part of the plan, though you bloomed beautifully. You've had the control and care to nurture your power until the right moment. Now is the time. No more holding back. No more hiding from the dark. Fear is the enemy, not the dark. Embrace it."

"I'm not afraid."

She stands next to me now. Her hand rests on my shoulder. "But aren't you? You're considering walking away. You view attachments as weaknesses. But you cannot cut off people, *beings*. Their life cords endure, and no one and nothing can sever those ties. People you have loved, even at a distance, have still died. And it still hurts. That is the human experience."

Tingles spread across my chest. For better or worse, I'm Maximus. But the thought of being someone's hero terrifies me.

"I don't want this."

"I know you don't. But I know you'll do it and do it well."

I shake my head. Tears break free and fall down my face. "I… I can't do this on my own."

"You're never alone. I'm with you."

"I still don't know you. I don't trust you."

But I do trust others. Like Charlotte and Rose. That's a start.

"Doesn't matter. I'm listening. I still care."

"I need someone *here* who I can see, touch, feel."

The Architect shakes their head, sighs, and looks to the heavens. Maybe Paris really is in there. "Charlotte is the commander, now. She will lead our slayers and allies. You will be our protector."

"I'm just the muscle, huh?"

"You are so much more," The Architect whispers, their eyes bright with emotion. "You are limitless. One day you'll believe me, and best of all, you'll know it. Now…" They step back. "You need rest. Remember, the stone keeps us with you. It's a bond. The power of slayers and the vampires who dedicated themselves are with you. You only have to listen." The Alchemist taps their heart.

Paris turns around, and ripples in the sea follow as they walk out of the water. "Charlotte should already know this, but the commander's manifesto is in the cellar. Merlot, 2012."

"Are you really leaving?" I yell to their back as I follow them to shore.

"Yes. And tell Louisiana I said hello," they say without looking back.

"Louisiana? Never heard of them."

The Architect doesn't answer. Just disappears through the forest that banks the beach.

I slide to the ground. Birds chirp again. The sun still holds its position, warming my skin. The cool ocean breeze strokes my cheek. I hear it—the song. *His* song.

I take in my charging station, unhurried, until my eyes close, letting the peace flow over me.

Because when I wake up, nothing will ever be the same.

As You Like It
Khamari

The whiskey burns a path down my throat. I slam the glass on the large oak desk and pour myself another round.

Julius' desk is old-world and old-school, like the man, made of dark wood with a glass top. The only thing modern is the laptop I'd forced on him.

Poetry, art, and classics are scattered, along with uprooted plants and my footprints through the dirt on the carpeted floor.

He liked things neat, but I tore through his office with a rage so heavy all I could do was destroy. I even slammed the framed picture of myself, Khaven, and Julius against the wall.

He was proud of his family. I never doubted that. He just didn't know how to love. He squeezed too tight, wanted too much control, just like he did with my father. A generation later, the story remains unchanged.

It's been a week since the old man's memorial, and after that, the Ankh clan members returned to our mostly restored home, though we'll have to move soon, since our location has been compromised.

If he were alive, I'd tell him he was a damned fool. I'd also tell him I loved him.

My attention focuses on the family portrait hanging above the fireplace. Julius, my father, and my grandmother, who died shortly after my father.

I look just like my father, Odell, who looked just like Julius.

Same hazel eyes, cleft chin. Dad had dimples in his cheeks, like his mother, but I do not.

Another shared trait: the St. John men can't keep a woman. My grandmother was Julius' third wife. The other two died, and I'm not sure how.

My mother died at the hands of my clan.

And Raven, no, *Texas*—I have to think of her as Texas now. She's alive. But I'm dead to her. In her eyes, devastation—a look that'll haunt me to my grave.

I raise my glass and silently toast to my shitty luck.

A soft knock sounds on the door, but I know who the visitor is before she enters.

"Dr. Persing. Come in."

"Yes, King Khamari."

Am I the king? Titles don't seem to matter anymore. "Take a seat."

"I'm so sorry about your grandfather. I know you loved him very much." She adjusts her glasses as she settles in the chair in front of the desk. She glances around the office, then at me. She has the good sense not to comment on the disarray.

I open Julius' laptop. Khaven cracked his password for me earlier today. I turn on the jammer and white noise to block our conversation, like Khaven taught me. The sun will be setting in just two hours. Alexander sleeps with the others, but I know now to never underestimate my enemy.

"I found some interesting results from Khaven's bloodwork," I tell her. "Some interesting notes, too, that you sent to Julius."

Her eyes flare with fear. "Let me explain."

"Let you explain what? That you worked behind my back? Impeded my brother's progress?"

"I am sorry." Her eyes mist behind her oversize glasses. "Your grandfather recruited me, a-and he wanted to k-know things before I told you. I sat on this for a while, thought long and hard about things, but I knew if I didn't tell your grandfather, he'd hurt me. Not to mention that he could read my mind. I had to come clean."

"And what did you tell Julius? What did you find?"

"Julius wanted to understand more about Khaven's unique blood type."

"The golden blood?"

"Y-yes. He hypothesized that Khaven's blood holds the key to daywalking."

My nails grow, curving into talons. I claw the desk to stem my anger. "And he just happened to come up with that theory, huh?"

"I…" She licks her lips. "I thought of it first. You see, vampires always receive nourishment from humans. Rarely from each other. But what if Khaven's blood could provide the cure needed to correct the buildup in the red blood cells? We can figure out how to produce enough enzymes so vampires can convert protoporphyrin into heme and…and—"

"I didn't pay you to figure out how vampires can walk in the sun. I paid you to find a cure for Khaven."

"I know, but don't you want to cure vampirism? It's a secondary goal, yes, but Khaven could be the key."

"He isn't. Who else knows?"

"No one. I… Julius wanted to test it out before he announced it. He preferred that we talk to you first. Make sure you were on board."

I shake my head. "Bull. He knew that shit wouldn't fly with me."

"He suspected, yes." She looks away from my hard gaze. "But he said he had a plan to turn you around."

I hope you're burning in Hell, old man.

"If you ever repeat what you told me to anyone else, I will destroy you."

Her eyes snap to meet mine. "I…I would never. I respect

you too much."

Anger boils my blood. I feel my eyes turning, my fangs descending. "Run, Dr. Persing. Run and don't look back. Never return."

"B-but we're at the edge of something miraculous!" Dr. Persing's eyes are bright. "And now that Julius is gone, I can help! I can—"

"I can't trust you. If it's not Julius, it'll be Alexander to use you, and he doesn't suffer fools or loose ends. He'll get what he needs, and then you'll be ten pints lighter and six feet under. Pack a bag and go far away."

She nods so hard, I hear her teeth rattle.

"Even though I'm letting you go today, I can't promise how I'll feel tomorrow. But I promise you this: if my brother doesn't survive, I will find you."

"I'm so sorry." She takes my advice. She runs.

I count to one hundred, making sure I don't give in to my instinct to hunt her down and drain her dry.

A few hours later, after I calm down and delete her files, I go outside to the gardens—my energy won't allow me to sit idly. The rain trickles from storm clouds. They're soft and misting now, but the smell of a storm charges the air.

Hurting Texas is like sticking a sharp, hot blade to my heart. But I can't twist out the knife—it's jammed in too deep.

The choices I made for me, for my brother, endangered the world and put me on a dark, shrouded path ten million miles away from righteousness.

I can't see the light. But you don't need light when you've made a deal with the devil.

One of my foster parents—the only good one—used to say that the rain is just as good as a baptism.

"Surrender to the rain, open your heart, and call on the Lord. He'll answer. He'll wipe your slate clean."

I tip my head back and pretend the cool drops baptize me, washing away the blood on my hands, the sin that blackens my soul.

I'm not good. I'm not clean. But I don't want to do this anymore. The storm rolls in. Sparks of light shoot through the clouds, followed by angry cracks of rolling thunder.

The rain pounds my skin, punishing me.

Someone, maybe The Architect, answers. It's just not the answer I want to hear.

The sin can't wash away; it's glued to my soul. The blood on my hands is too sticky, too thick. Rain can't wash away the sins I've made against humanity.

Against my heart.

I stumble back against the raging storm, fall to my knees, yell at the sky. The hard water drowns my eyes and fills my mouth. I slam my forehead to the ground, coughs and shivers racking my body.

"It's not my fault. I was born this way," I growl.

Lightning crashes into the pavilion. Orange and black shadows blur before me. The scent of smoke mixes with the storm, and the malodorous cloud hovers above me, stinging my nose.

"Our Father is ready for you."

I lift my head, blinking. Julius' former secretary, a Made vampire, calls to me from the back door.

I stand and then turn around. An inscrutable look crosses her face.

My throat is raw, so I nod to let her know I received her message.

"Alexander is in the throne room." She steps back with the door still open.

The sky lights and swirls in a majesty of purple and royal blue. "Do you see this?" I ask her, my voice filled with wonder.

The sky blinks purple and blue, like it's relaying a message.

"King Khamari? He's waiting for you."

The sky blinks faster: blue and purple, purple and blue. It's an anomaly, a miracle. *Is The Architect trying to tell me something?*

But the burning smell still coats the air. The smoke rises, and with it, my faith vanishes.

"Yes...I'll be there."

The sky stops blinking and blanks to black, as if an electric plug has been yanked.

I return to the house and navigate through the halls to the Throne Room.

As I enter the room, a woman with wire-rimmed glasses and wild, dark curls steps out of Alexander's office. This must be Dakota, another person who betrayed Texas.

She smiles. "My King."

I scowl.

She frowns. "I'll be seeing you. Seeing *her*, too."

I lock my jaw, biting back my threat to stay away from...Texas. I can no longer protect her, not openly. What's done is done. I knock on the door.

"Hello, Kha-mar-i." Alexander sits on the throne. The room is different now. The U-shaped tables were moved around to form long rows. A screen and projector hang just beyond Alexander's seat.

The throne hasn't been moved. It's still front and center, but the platform is raised. It's high enough that you have to jump to get on the stage.

My old English teacher, who loved quoting Shakespeare, comes to mind. *All the world's a stage, and all the men and women merely players.*

"Alexander." I bow.

Alexander peers down at me. "How are you feeling?"

"100 percent better." I know what he wants. Gratitude. So, I give it to him. "I must thank you. You saved my life."

"That, I did. But I want to know how you feel. About Julius? About your girlfriend."

He knows. I bite back my grimace. I don't speak for a long while and let the silence hang between us. Finally, I rally myself to respond. "Alexander, I—"

"One foot in the human world, and the other with vampires." He clasps his hands. "Just as I suspected. You are young and foolish. I have been all those things in my youth. But I must know this now... Are you with us? And not just because your little Maximus plaything hates you."

"Yes."

"Will you kill her, if given the chance?"

"If we meet again, she'll kill me. And if she kills me, then I can't save Khaven. So, yes, if I must. But it won't be my first choice. I loved her, yet I betrayed her."

"Loved? Past tense?"

"We aren't the same people, and we'll never have a chance to fall in love with our new selves. So, no, I don't think it would be fair to the old me or the old Texas to say I love her. I've shown her repeatedly that I don't. I always make the wrong choice."

Alexander folds his hands across his lap. "I think this is the first time you've been completely honest with me. You don't have my trust, but you will have the chance to prove yourself."

"Thank you, Father."

"One chance, Khamari. I cannot read you, and for that alone, I am tempted to kill you."

"Understood."

"I'm not your little bird, Raven," he continues.

I wince when he reveals his knowledge of her identity. That alone could compromise her grandmother. I'll have to figure out a way to protect Grandma Lou, to keep her out of Alexander's path.

"I won't give you chance after chance. One more strike, and you're dead, and your brother essentially is dead, too. Do we have an understanding?"

I nod. My throat is too tight with emotion to speak.

"Good. Now, the Maximus tired herself out. We must strike before she gains full control over the stone."

I clear my throat to loosen my muscles. "Now that she possesses the Philosopher's Stone—"

"She can keep the stone. For now."

He twists his neck from side to side, a crack sounding with each oddly angled twist.

"Do you remember what I told you when we first met? About us being the same."

"Yes."

"Our common goal is to perfect vampirism. To remove its weaknesses. Though we have suffered a defeat, we will win the war. Once we create another stone, we can do so."

"We can create another stone?"

"Yes. The slayer-witch confirmed a theory to create another through the Emerald Tablet. It contains the secret of the Prima Materia and transmutations. We can create any reality we want, like, say…saving your brother."

My breath quickens. "When do we leave?" I ask.

"You will leave in two weeks' time. The Elders and I will need to focus on rebuilding our ranks, training our Royals, and creating new ones. Since my time away, the clans have gotten weak and unfocused."

"More vampires?"

"Royals first. They'll be intelligent, influential, and skilled in combat. Then the Royals can make thoughtful selections for the Mades. We need our spear-wielding foot soldiers, so to speak."

"You intend on announcing our existence?"

He nods slowly. "We'll focus on establishing influential Royals around the world, maybe even world leaders toward the end. We'll need to set up a new council, including humans.

The world needs to know there's a new world order and I am its leader."

I rub a hand over my face. "There's a lot at stake. Humans won't take the existence of monsters well. This could very well result in a world war."

Alexander's eyes harden like diamonds. When he flexes his fist, a ripple of muscle shoots up his forearm.

I spread my feet apart, bracing myself for the earthquake.

"Then I will scorch the earth, burn down their beloved cities, and erase their existence. I've done it before, though I do not prefer such extreme methods."

"But—"

"I've considered all possibilities," he tells me. "I am not some mindless conqueror. I have plans for vampires, humanity, the world. Do you trust me to do it, and can you help me?"

I reach for a kernel of truth and hold it. "Khaven needs a cure. If this tablet can save him, you have my loyalty."

"Good. There is no turning back. Your feet are solidly on the side of progress, the future, me." His eyes return from the dark abyss. "Do not fail me again."

Louisiana, the Baddest Chick Alive
Texas

"So...bored. How long is Dark Phoenix gonna be out for, anyway?"

Dammit. Why is Rose's voice always the first one I hear? And why am I always fainting?

"She exuded a lot of energy. None I've ever felt before." Anton's steady voice pours over me.

"Yeah," Rose whispers. "Charlotte said she had more power than even Richmond."

"She's had it rough, my Texas. She needs her rest." I hear the most delightful voice—one that reminds me of sweet tea, front porches, and rocking chairs.

My eyes fly open. *Please, God, don't let this be a dream.*

"Grandma Lou?" I try getting up, but it feels like a one-ton weight sits on my chest.

"Hey, baby girl." She rushes to my side. Still fit, still spry. Her lean muscles are apparent under her short-sleeved shirt. She doesn't look a day over sixty.

Then she smiles. God, her smile makes me smile. It's infectious and warm and kind. It's apple butter and biscuits—warm and flaky and just right.

Goodness personified.

"Well, look at you, gal. You gone an' got yourself all mixed up with Alexander."

"What are you doing here? H-how do you know about...me?"

My voice sounds rusty, and it croaks like a frog. I look around and finally realize we're back at headquarters.

"I made Paris promise me she would call if something serious happened to you. Charlotte, by proxy, called me. She told me about the stone, gal." Her lips turn down, and her brown eyes fill with tears. "It's my fault, what happened to you. It's my fault about you and your sweet mama. But I know...I know The Architect don't make mistakes."

The Architect? She usually says the good Lord. Maybe she's been meaning The Architect all along.

"What do you mean? What are you talking about?"

"Honey, I was a slayer, too. We'll talk about me later. I'm here to help you control those new powers of yours."

I hear Paris' voice echo: *"And tell Louisiana I said hello."*

My grandmother, Granny Lou, is a slayer? I shake my head as if the action can shake the world into making sense. The woman knits booties. She's the mother of the church, which means she sleeps with the Bible clutched to her chest. And she wears those giant hats on Sundays that block the view of the congregation, but she doesn't give one damn because it's her right. She got mad when people—mainly me—cursed or raised their voice. She didn't allow television or video games when I was younger because of the violence, even though she kicked my ass in trainings.

Ha.

"And what year were you a slayer?" I've seen her birth certificate, and I know she was born in 1939.

"It isn't nice to ask a lady's age."

"I think you can make an exception."

She shakes her head. "I'll tell you my story one day. Right now, we need to focus on Alexander."

"I have the stone." I shrug. "We've got some time."

"Girl, this ain't no holiday. I'm givin' you one day to get yourself outta this here bed."

"But I'm sick." I cough a few times like I used to do when I wanted to skip school or church.

"And the Academy Award goes to…" Rose wiggles her jazz hands toward me.

"He's after the tablet. 'Cording to my sources—"

"You have sources?" The woman has a landline that sometimes doesn't work when the weather is bad.

"Yes. Got this here satellite phone. All retired slayers have 'em to use in case of emergency."

"Why didn't you call me?"

"You know the rules, gal. You can't keep in contact with surviving family. 'Sides that, we didn't want them vampires to figure out there's a possibility of second-generation slayers. You're the first one of our kind, and—"

"Lucky me." I roll my eyes.

"Gal, if you cut me off again, we're going to have words, and strong ones at that."

"Yes, ma'am."

"So that's where she gets her sassiness from," Rose observes to Anton, pointing to Grandma Lou.

"Remove the word 'sassy' from your vocabulary, Rose," I snap. I don't have time to save the world *and* school Rose.

I refocus my attention on my grandmother. "Grandma Lou, back to you being a slayer. Why didn't you tell me?"

"The same reasons you didn't tell me, I suppose," she responds in—I admit—a sassy tone. "But I've been around for a century… or two."

"Dang, Granny! Just how old are you?"

"Old enough to teach you a thing or two—and Anton, for that matter. Now, rest up. We've gotta get movin'. The war has yet to come."

Everyone files out, Grandma Lou last. My eyes are heavy. Exhausted, I pull the blanket over my shoulders. It feels like something is tugging at me to go to sleep. Right as I close my eyes, Grandma Lou covers my hands.

"I'm gonna help you, gal. Help get that thing inside of you under control."

"I need to figure out my limits. I'll train. Maybe even ask Richmond for advice."

"No, baby. The other thing. The darkness," she says in a hushed tone.

"Y-you…you know?"

"Anton told me. He helped me, too, a long time ago."

"Oh. You were the success story," I mumble under my breath.

"It's generational, I think. My pain, my suffering, my anger, passed on to you. And then when that accident happened, and you and that poor Khamari being ripped from each other. Well… all those things just made you ripe for the pickin'."

"You still remember Khamari?"

She snorts. "Yeah. Poor baby tried to pull out my memories, and I let 'em think that way. But the boy was grieving. Had tears in his eyes when he did it. Said he was doing it to protect me."

Another memory appears—this one of us dancing on her porch during a rainstorm.

"Whatever. He's a liar."

"He did the best he could, given his situation."

"Are you defending what he did? He…he basically—"

"Calm down, gal. I'm just givin' you some perspective."

I rub my stomach. That's where it feels like that dark energy is located. Lying dormant, waiting for the next tragedy to trigger it. "How do I get rid of it?"

"You don't. You live with *it*, you manage *it*. You use *it*. Turn that pain into power. And then when The Architect gives you them walking papers, you let 'em give you beauty for ashes."

I pinch the bridge of my nose. "I don't even know what that means."

"You will. Studying is gonna be a part of your training, too."

I hold in my exhale. I don't want to test the strength of Grandma Lou's backhand.

She squeezes my hand again. "Go on and get some rest."

I try to keep my eyes open, make sure Grandma Lou doesn't disappear, but my eyes are heavy.

A few hours later, I wake up and decide to visit my new commander. I rush through the door. "What's the plan for—"

Charlotte breaks away from Rich.

Gross.

He's looking younger, at least.

"Did Robert reverse his aging?" I ask Charlotte, completely ignoring Rich. I'm still mad at him for holding pertinent information hostage.

"We've slowed it down. Robert wants to see if he can work with you—or, rather, the power of the stone—to reverse it."

"Oh. Is that right?" In true dramatic fashion, I slowly turn my body and attention toward Old Man Richmond.

"I don't know." I tilt my head, tapping my chin. "I kinda like his get-off-my-lawn chic look."

"It's up to you how you want to navigate it, Texas." Charlotte ignores my joke. "But he could be a great mentor to you and—"

"Girl, be for real." I roll my eyes. He isn't mentor material, but I'll help for the sake of Charlotte. She's already lost too many people she loves. "I'll talk to Robert later."

"Thank you, Texas." Rich stands from his seat. He's steadier on his feet, and even his heart sounds stronger. His power level is so weak, I can barely detect it.

Charlotte grabs his arm to support him. "I'll be right back."

I wait. Seeing as Charlotte is the new commander and all.

When Charlotte returns, she gives me a hug. "I know we have much more important matters to attend to, but I thank you for your kindness in helping Richmond."

I step back from her hug and shoot her a look. "You need to make better choices in men."

Charlotte lifts an eyebrow. "Pot, meet kettle."

"Touché," I mutter. As much as I want to tease her, I want to kill Alexander more. And Dakota. I quickly bring her up to speed about Grandma Lou's theory about the tablet.

Charlotte shakes her head. "I figured Alexander would try to find the Emerald Tablet. Paris was one step ahead of me and left me instructions."

"Do you want me to find the tablet?"

"Soon, yes. I need to get our research team to triangulate a few locations and monitor the Ankh clan's whereabouts. For now, you can focus on Dakota and bring her to me. We need to cut off Alexander's source of insider knowledge."

I place a fist over my heart and bow. "Yes, Commander Charlotte."

Pride shines in her eyes. "You're going to be a great Maximus, Texas. I can feel it."

"You're not so bad yourself. Already making boss moves and running around with your boy toy."

"He's… It's complicated."

"Oh, I bet." I turn to leave. "Mind if I play around on Dakota's computer to see what I find?" I jerk my thumb toward the door.

"You do what you need to do."

Speaking of doing what I need to do…

"When's the next meeting?"

"What meeting?"

"The group therapy stuff."

Charlotte's eyes widen, a look of stun and awe transforming her features. Tears well, but she quickly squeezes her eyes shut.

"Wednesday. But you'll be gone."

"Oh," I sigh.

"You can call in. Sometimes our slayers in the field will do a video chat."

I nod. "If I'm in a secure location, I'll log in."

"I'll send you the details. You can pop in anytime," she says in a hoarse voice.

After I leave her office, I search Dakota's work desk, but there's nothing. Dakota kept her records tight. There's no slip in information, and her side of the room has been cleaned out.

I return to my room and pack a bag. Instead of staying in my room, remembering all the fake bonding moments I had with Dakota, I grab a notebook and slink through hidden passages and back hallways that descend to the underground chambers.

I pass a few slayers on the way down. One of them offers congratulations.

I give her my thanks and jog down the steps. I don't know the extent of my powers, but it feels like I'm plugged into a city's power source. I can hear better, see better; my pace, my steps are faster. I feel like I can rip through an army of Royals in a matter of seconds. I can't wait to test it out.

The King Arthur–style table is empty. As I sit in the chair at the head, memories flash of Paris barking directives at Maestros while Charlotte smooths over the commander's roughness with constructive feedback. Dakota scribbles notes at lightning speed.

I open the notebook, flipping through the sturdy, lined pages. The pen point hovers just above the paper. I just want to write. I'm not sure what to say, but I know something has to give.

Maybe words can make the nightmares disappear? Maybe words can chase the hurt I felt from Dakota and Khamari's betrayal. But words aren't wands, and my issues are legion.

Still, I write for hours, until my hand cramps. Until the ghosts in my head cease to whisper. Until sunrise.

I flex my hands and read my first sentence out loud. It is my mantra. My affirmation and mission for my existence. There is no running anymore—from my problems, from my destiny.

"I am the Maximus, the most powerful being on Earth. I will

defeat Alexander." I scratch out "defeat" and, in all caps, write *SLAY*.

I close my journal and walk upstairs with my bag slung over my shoulders. It's time to roam, just as Rich did for six hundred years. First stop: Dakota.

Waiting in the entryway are Anton and Grandma Lou. Anton holds two bags in his hands.

"Heard we're going on an adventure." Grandma Lou nods at my backpack.

"I'm going by myself. I've got a mole to quash."

"Three heads are better than one." Grandma pats my shoulder and then walks toward the door.

"But—"

"But nothing, gal. We've got to get those powers under control. Anton and I will help you."

"When you're not hunting, you're training." Anton walks at pace behind us.

I sigh. "Geez."

"What have I told you about back talk?"

"But I'm the Maximus, Grandma Lou. I don't need your help."

"I don't care if you're the Queen of England. We're coming with you, and that's that." She adds a little harrumph at the end.

So much for being the most powerful being in the world.

Acknowledgments

Thanks so much to my critique partners: Constance Gillam, Pamela Varnado, Mary Marvella, and Ison Hill. You've read a dozen versions of this book, and I appreciate you having just as much passion as I have for this story.

Special thanks to Amanda Leuck and Tara Gelsomino. You've both worked with me and *Sign of the Slayer* in different parts of this publishing journey, and I appreciate you both for pushing this book forward!

To my mentor, Vanessa Riley—thanks for encouraging me to keep the faith. To my Destin Divas: I appreciate your love and sisterhood.

To my besties, Ashley C., Ashley N., Jannae, and Jasmine: thank you for the encouragement. I love y'all to the moon and back.

And finally, to my husband, Jason. You were here at the beginning when I wanted to write a book about a Black vampire slayer ten years ago. You've supported me by reenacting fight scenes, critiquing my world-building, and giving me the space to write. I love you.

Sign of the Slayer is a snarky paranormal romance full of thrills and adventure, with a happy ending. However, the story includes elements that might not be suitable for all readers. Violence, blood, death, injuries/wounds, and alcohol use are shown in the novel. Readers who may be sensitive to these elements, please take note.

Let's be friends!

 @EntangledTeen

 @EntangledTeen

 @EntangledTeen

 @EntangledTeen

 bit.ly/TeenNewsletter

entangled teen

an imprint of Entangled Publishing LLC